D0528725

Gillian White is a former journalist who comes from Liverpool. She now lives in Totnes, Devon, with her journalist husband. *The Sleeper*, *Unhallowed Ground*, *Veil of Darkness* and *The Witch's Cradle* are all available in Corgi paperback. *The Sleeper* has recently been a major drama serial on BBC1, and three of her previous novels, *Rich Deceiver*, *The Beggar Bride* and *Mothertime*, have also been successfully adapted for television.

'Gillian White is a skilled manipulator of the normal and ordinary into a chilling, nightmarish experience. Knowing that, it's clear that the heroine of *Unhallowed Ground* is not going to find an idyllic escape from her problems in her newly-inherited cottage in the depths of Dartmoor. The gradual increase in tension is cleverly handled, leading to an atmosphere of real menace and a shocking climax'
Sunday Telegraph

Veil of Darkness

'Compelling novel of suspense'
Good Housekeeping

'Simply spine-tingling'
Woman & Home

The Witch's Cradle

'Ten out of ten for topicality . . . strong narrative keeps the pages turning to the end where the reader is left guiltily wondering about TV intrusion and the viewer's complicity in it'
Home and Country

'This fast-paced tale explores the lengths to which people go to be loved, as well as the ruthlessness of the media when transforming real life into drama'
Good Housekeeping

'A gripping read which will make you think twice about the influence and motives of TV media'
Shine

Also by Gillian White

THE PLAGUE STONE

THE CROW BIDDY

NASTY HABITS

RICH DECEIVER

MOTHERTIME

GRANDFATHER'S FOOTSTEPS

DOGBOY

THE BEGGAR BRIDE

CHAIN REACTION

THE SLEEPER

UNHALLOWED GROUND

VEIL OF DARKNESS

THE WITCH'S CRADLE

NIGHT VISITOR

Gillian White

CORGI BOOKS

NIGHT VISITOR
A CORGI BOOK : 0 552 14766 4

Originally published in Great Britain by Bantam Press,
a division of Transworld Publishers

PRINTING HISTORY
Bantam Press edition published 2001
Corgi edition published 2002

3 5 7 9 10 8 6 4

Set in 11/12 pt Times by
Hewer Text Ltd, Edinburgh.

Corgi Books are published by Transworld Publishers,
61–63 Uxbridge Road, London W5 5SA,
a division of The Random House Group Ltd,
in Australia by Random House Australia (Pty) Ltd,
20 Alfred Street, Milsons Point, Sydney, NSW 2061, Australia,
in New Zealand by Random House New Zealand Ltd,
18 Poland Road, Glenfield, Auckland 10, New Zealand
and in South Africa by Random House (Pty) Ltd,
Endulini, 5a Jubilee Road, Parktown 2193, South Africa.

Printed and bound in Great Britain by
Cox & Wyman Ltd, Reading, Berkshire.

For Rosie.
Go carefully, angel. I miss you. You were lovely.

ACKNOWLEDGEMENTS

I owe many thanks for the help and valuable time given to me by Hugh Peplow MA, Vet MB, MRCVS and Dr Michael Loverock MBBS, MRCGP, DCH, DRCOG, MRCS, LRCP, and I beg their forgiveness for straying – only slightly – from the true pathway on the occasions when their expert advice did not quite suit my plot.

ONE

'Oh no! Oh no! It's OK, baby, it's OK. I'm here, I'm here.'

The primitive sound came stealthily onto the silent fabric of night, a tug at the black material.

Glaring wakefulness.

Sick trepidation.

The Aura Epileptica.

Rose could recognize it now almost before it happened. The magnificent otterhound stirred on his bed in the corner of the room and Rose, so in tune, had already turned on the bedside light before the dog's limbs started their rictus dance, began their hellish tango with madness as his gentle brown eyes rolled back and spume flecked his hairy lips.

'Hang on, baby, hang on.'

These dire fits of Baggins' were mostly nocturnal, at four in the morning, the death hour, around the full moon, as if the tide filling the river, silvered by the lunar presence, were calling to the oldest souls. And this hound was an older soul, a wonderfully, marvellously older soul who knew his way well round this tiny earth. His illness seemed, to his loving owner, to be as awesome as it was horrible.

'It's all going to be OK. OK, baby, OK. I won't leave you.'

But by now the fits were as much of a ritual as rising at night to feed Rose's babies had been, the difference being that years ago she had woken to lime juice and Cadburys chocolate, whereas now, at nearly fifty, she preferred a snack of milk and cashew nuts. And now all that was required of her, instead of changing nappies and waiting for dawn with her boobs hanging out, was that she kneel on the floor beside her dog, whispering re-assurances, stroking the gasping sides of the animal, waiting until the convulsions subsided and then helping Baggins downstairs to the kitchen to cope with the manic aftermath.

From there he could roam and pace for an hour, from backdoor to garden shed and back along a pitifully well-worn path, bumping, shivering and cowering, until his normal faculties returned.

Agonizingly slowly.

But those faculties, once so keen – sight and smell and speed would gallop him over the hills and fields quite impervious to the human voice – were gradually being eroded by the ferocity of the fits.

Each time he recovered with a fraction missing. Homoeopathic cures wouldn't touch him.

By the time Baggins was five he could no longer find his way home and had to be rescued from sanctuaries and pounds. The local dog warden knew his name.

Once he turned up in a stranger's bedroom, covered in mud and doing an enviable Pavarotti. So Baggins was forced to stay on the lead and lost that precious, snuffling freedom.

His vision dimmed. He could no longer see to recover his sticks from muddy rivers and water-holes. Huge and heavy, he banged into lampposts and parked cars, denting bumpers.

And worst of all the drugs turned him old. They knocked him out. He hardly woke to go on his walks and collapsed straight to sleep on his return. He slept twenty hours out of twenty-four, but what was there left to dream about? He grew confused, dizzy, wobbly, and lay and snored and farted and twitched, and the fits increased and intensified because the drugs were making him weaker, so Rose decided to lay off the barbiturates and let nature take its course.

She did this gradually.

But then came the fatal night when Rose, an ordinary, decent woman with no stain on her character, committed the only crime she had ever knowingly carried out in her life. It was not premeditated, but it was serious. And, maybe because of her impeccable character, she got away with it scot-free.

The vet arrived in the early evening, after Baggins had suffered a cluster of fits lasting more than six hours.

He had had enough. He was exhausted.

The vet, a kindly, sexy man, went straight out to his Renault estate and, lifting the boot, rooted around for an ampoule of the dangerous drug Pentobarbitone. Rose and Michael watched in relief as the foaming Baggins with the crucified eyes suddenly slipped into perfect peace, as near to death as was possible.

'Thirty-six hours of perfect peace,' said the vet

happily, viewing Baggins with pride before disappearing into the kitchen. 'His brain is now completely closed off and can no longer function normally, or abnormally as in poor Baggins' case.'

A sharp parp from the drive informed Rose of her mother's arrival. Dinah would be annoyed to find her habitual parking space blocked. Almost unable to reverse, but refusing to admit it, she displayed enormous resentment towards anyone who had the gall to take her precious position alongside the house.

Terrified of a scene with the vet, Rose shot out to inform her mother of the emergency situation. Dinah was Baggins' biggest fan and would be first to give way to anyone who was there on the dear dog's behalf.

Outside, in the drive, Rose caught sight of the boxes, some neatly stashed, some higgledy piggledy, and implements in the back of the Renault. The vet had already announced he had several calls to make, some out on the moor. It would take him hours; he probably wouldn't get home till ten. He had already phoned his wife.

With the relief of Baggins fresh in her mind, exhausted by the afternoon's hell, watching him suffer so cruelly, something must have snapped; she could explain her appalling behaviour in no other way.

She snatched a small box, already opened, with the brand name Pentobarbitone on the side. This would mean that Baggins' relief would, in future, lie in her hands. If she had the cure safe in the house she'd have no need to watch him writhe in agony while she waited for the vet to arrive. She was

14

spurred on by the knowledge that in the boot of that car lay the answer to so much suffering.

She could stop Baggins' regular pills, which were turning him into a zombie, if she could find a way of administering just a few milligrams of this magic potion every time his fits merged together into a devastating cluster.

After a quick explanation to Dinah, Rose slipped back inside like the thief she was and dropped the box in the black bear umbrella stand. Immediately she'd done it she panicked. There would be an inquiry. The vet would surely remember how he had left his car outside her house, and he would recall the fact that she had left the room when she'd heard her mother arrive.

But equally well, her bad side whispered that if she denied any knowledge of the crime, how could they prove she was the culprit? He had other calls to make. Some in the dark. Might he not, unwittingly, nudge the box onto the road? Another client might nick it, or some passer-by, some addict . . . her brain went round and round trying to get herself out of what might be a serious dilemma.

Scandal. Court proceedings. Accountant's wife and mother of two. Suspicion of drug addiction. But it was too late to go back.

She had committed a serious crime and she would have to live with it.

Later she hid the disgraceful box with the rest of Baggins' pills, which were now unnecessary.

It was, after all, an act of mercy.

Inside the box were five smaller boxes all crammed full of ampoules.

She didn't share her secret with Michael, nor did she discuss her decision to withdraw the tablets, because he was more disturbed by the fits than Rose had ever been. He preferred Baggins dozy and old – anything to avoid the horror of those hellish nightly contortions – which he mostly missed as he slept so soundly on his back with his mouth wide open. He loved his dog as much as his wife did, but felt the pills were essential. He was an obedient patient and did exactly what the good doctor ordered. He was meticulously punctual with his own medication; it rattled him if he was an hour late.

Rose continued to order and pay for the high doses of Phenobarb, which she hid. She bought a box of disposable syringes, the vet bills continued to arrive, Baggins had the occasional fit, but there were no more of those hideous clusters. If he started, she could stop him.

The first time Rose administered the drug she thought her heart would crash through her ribs, and her hands vibrated so they seemed to hum, as if there was a battery inside them.

The needle had to go intravenously. First, the vet had shaved a small patch on Baggins' foot, but Rose, undercover, couldn't afford to do that, nor could she squeamishly close her eyes or look away at the moment of entry.

This was Baggins' third fit of the day and, in the end, compassion drove her to ram the needle into his foot – he was completely unaware – and draw back the plastic tube. After the deed it slipped from her hand; her whole body was running with sweat.

Peace, perfect peace for Baggins. Enormous relief, and some pride, for Rose.

It was only a small deception. But for her to deceive Michael over anything at all was such an extraordinary event that, over time, the magnitude of the deed began to eat away at her. She never could keep her mouth shut. When Michael was fifty the girls threw a party; it was so secretive she was sworn to silence.

If she blabbed she would ruin everything.

She told him.

She just couldn't not.

If she sided against him in anything, no matter how small, that amounted to betrayal in her eyes. Apart from her secret smoking. So naturally the thought of either of them deceiving each other in anything so large as an extra-marital affair was so enormous she had never considered it.

Anyway.

Enough canine capers.

The first box of ampoules was a quarter empty, she daren't stop ordering the pills for fear of discovery – the vet had not only rung them up, but had come round the next morning to scour their garden – and over the next two years Rose's supply of barbiturates grew into a sizeable pharmacy of little black bottles, which she zipped away in a shroud of plastic in the oblong box under the bed where her wedding dress had been stashed for thirty years. Never touched, save by her. Never moved, save for hoovering.

Somehow she couldn't be sensible and allow the box to join the family relics in the attic. The cobwebbed attic with its fibreglass lining spelled the end of life for everything that went up there, like a hangman's hatch but the other way round. Seldom did anything consigned there see the light of day again. No, Rose liked the idea of keeping her wedding dress and all that it stood for living and breathing and near her, directly under her while she slept.

When Baggins died peacefully at the good age of eight, Rose and Michael were inconsolable. They would never forget him.

Oh yes, of course; she should have thrown the medicines away, but being so aware of their lethal effects she feared a child might find them. And if she'd flushed them down the loo some might float back, little white clues to her tiny treachery, and Michael would catch her out.

Eventually she forgot they were there.

A loyal, gentle, loving dog, how could they replace him? And to be fair, they were getting on, and another puppy might be too much to handle. Now was the time when Rose could sensibly confess her deception to Michael, but what was the point, and she soon forgot the little boxes of lethal liquid and stock of barbiturates scattering the white wedding veil; life goes on as it must. In time the memories faded of the hairy shape by the fire, the smell of river mud in the bedroom, the sandy leavings that stuck to the skirting boards, the wet nose marks on the window, the wicked wolfing of food off plates.

Sometimes some sense of Baggins would return, and then they would look sad and stare, and even call out loud when nobody else could hear, by the river, in moonlight, in new grass or in rain, 'Go carefully, angel.'

At that time she had no reason to suspect she would ever need those drugs again. But loss has to be coped with, and loss of a pet is no real comparison to loss of life's human soul mate. Swans have been known to die of grief.

Thank God she and Michael were both fit. With luck they had years ahead of them and Rose hoped she would die first.

He would probably let her.

Michael was such a decent, dependable man, happiest with a regular routine. He ate the same meals over and over, wore the same clothes till they wore out, paid his bills on the third of each month; he wasn't unpredictable. That's why his business had done so well. He was unlikely to be so reckless as to drop down dead with no advance warning.

He had been quite a catch at the time, but dangerous. For a start he was dreamy to look at and therefore a target for unscrupulous women. Tall, slender, cool, with a collarful of curling black hair. He was twenty-eight, well-off, ambitious and clever, with a dry wit that was often shocking.

'Michael is not a comfortable man,' Dinah had told her with caution. 'Rather too thrusting for my liking. Not like your father.'

Thrusting?

Yes, there was a danger around him.

'This passion for self-destruction,' said Dinah. 'Where the hell does it come from?'

And in one sense her mother was right. Rose did have a destructive urge; it had been with her since early childhood. At five years old her terror of blindness forced her to take up the challenge, and for days she went round tapping with a stick and

19

trying not to cheat by looking out from under her blindfold, practising just in case the worst happened. Perhaps she thought that facing the monster would take the terror away. It never worked, it made things worse.

Then it was death, and every night she shut herself in her toy cupboard, where the darkness was total and she could hear no sound save for her own frightened wimpers. But then came a loudness she hadn't expected as the air tore round her ears. All red-faced and furious she wet her knickers to prove to herself she was warm and alive. Words like 'grave' and 'coffin' filled her with a trembling horror. When the awful realization dawned that one day Mummy and Daddy would die, she refused to speak to them or acknowledge their presence in order to defend herself and show she could do without them.

Many times Rose was tempted to fling herself from great heights to put a stop to her vertigo. Maybe that's why she was drawn to Michael: she sensed some terrible drop.

But any fears about Michael had quickly been dispelled. He was faithful.

The thirty years they had been together meant that Rose could read Michael's mind; there was sometimes no need for talking. She knew his views about most things, politics and personalities, holidays and home furnishings. Her friends with more difficult men sometimes said they envied her, and she didn't deny it; she just nodded and said, 'I know, I've been lucky.'

'He listens to you,' they said, 'and that's unusual, a man who listens.'

And her house, mortgage paid, was warm and friendly; sunlight drifting off freshly washed drapes, sunbeds on the lawn, the kitchen with its Aga and smell of home baking, the bathroom with its fleecy towels and, up until quite recently, the sound of children's laughter.

Rose felt proud that her marriage had worked while so many around her had failed. This success was deeply fulfilling; her primitive warding off of danger, division, disruption and chaos. Her judgement had been sound. She had chosen her partner well, the best sort of father for her children, which, after all, is the point of it all. Daisy and Jessie both adored Michael. A hands-on father before they got stylish, he knew *The Three Little Pigs* by heart, he helped with the demands and the mess and let Rose sleep in on a Saturday.

But best of all Michael made her laugh, sometimes till she felt sick, her sides ached and her jaw felt bruised. He was the best of company, an easy man to love and to like, and so they shared a large circle of friends. People were attracted to Michael. Rose, she supposed, rather trailed in his wake. That was the way it had always been, and she saw no real harm in it.

'But you have no life of your own,' said Kate, married to a man who was never home, too involved in his work and his golf. In Rose's eyes their marriage was a sham; they passed like ships in the night on their way to their various activities, preferring the company of others. 'What if anything happened to Michael?' Kate asked in her sickly-sweet voice. 'What on earth would you do with yourself?'

21

Jealous?

No wonder.

Rose sometimes sensed other friends thought her a woman of narrow vision. That she should be a working wife. They said her degree had been wasted. She braced herself for the right defence.

'It doesn't worry me actually. I'm perfectly happy at home.' She felt she needed to expand as the look on Kate's face was unconvinced. 'Michael and I play tennis, go off for weekends, the theatre, and we enjoy being at home together, reading, sometimes gardening, listening to music, drinking, eating. Anyway, what's wrong with that?'

'But now the children have left home, what will you do with yourself all day?'

Kate talked as if time was a drag, something to be endured, and that to stop for *The Archers* or sit in the sun or go round the shops or have lunch with a friend were all props to drag yourself from one night to another. These days, if you weren't constantly rushing from one place to another, busy, busy, busy, coping with work and home, you were sad. Well, Rose would have none of that. She even enjoyed sitting and thinking. Just staring at nothing, sniffing fresh coffee and dunking the odd digestive. But how could you confess to that?

Later Kate proved Rose right. She moaned, 'I honestly don't know what I'll do when Derek retires. Having him hanging round the house under my feet all day. We'll drive each other mad.'

Oh dear, how sad and predictable.

Rose realized and appreciated how privileged her life was.

She still had her children.

Their youngest daughter, Jessie, nineteen, left home just a year ago, but she lived in at St Marks teacher training college, only half an hour's journey away. No point in her living in really, she could travel from home each day, but she wanted her independence. At least she hadn't gone off to London as she'd first threatened to do; Rose had Michael to thank for that. He'd talked her out of it.

And Daisy, three years older, worked at the local library, sharing a flat with a press reporter who came and went as the mood took him.

Yes, Rose was blessed.

This might be a reason to feel some shame, and to compensate she did good works – read newspapers for the blind, drove patients to the doctors, picked up their prescriptions and took turns to man the local museum.

She enjoyed being *nice* to people.

Fate had been *nice* to Rose. Not for her the ceaseless round of shopping on the cheap, poking around charity shops, waiting for buses to carry her and her pram and bundles to some soulless housing estate.

She saw these people through the windows of her Saab. Coping with some violent man and a bunch of snot-nosed kids. Endless telly. Endless mess. Ugh!

Hers had been a minuscule rebellion. Back then she'd worn white leather – boots, skirt, jerkin. Even her looks had been better than most. Not beautiful, but striking, with thick black hair that curled towards her face and never needed much attention, and eyes to match, with long dark lashes.

But out of leather and thirty years later Rose wasn't wearing well.

Now into cashmere with scarves and bracelets, ever a cheerful motherly soul, despite spending time on her looks and experimenting with make-up and hairstyles, wanting to look good for Michael and needing him to feel proud of her, nothing seemed to make much difference.

Even with Mexican yams.

The lines increased.

The body sagged.

The hair grew more brittle and more grey.

She never neglected her underwear, never wore curlers at night or dressing gowns with stains. Michael, so natural, so unselfconscious, even of his middle-aged pot belly, age turning him more distinguished, preferred to sleep in the nude, but Rose, even at her best, had never managed to overcome that last vestige of shyness, especially now when her breasts started drooping sideways on in the mirror.

But in Michael's eyes she was beautiful, as lovely as she had ever been, and he often told her so.

Sometimes her life sounded just a little too glib. Too lightweight a life. Tempting fate. So that when she stumbled upon Michael's adultery she went straight into a state of shock.

Worse than death. Far worse.

Michael was loving somebody else, not safe in his grave, secure under soil, for ever her partner until death claimed her, too.

They would never share a memorial stone.

She would never be the 'beloved wife'.

Their ashes would be separately scattered; his on the moor, hers by the river.

Shock was followed by total denial.

She had jumped to the wrong conclusion. She must have. Just because she'd driven to the office to collect Michael's watchstrap which needed mending, just because she pulled up by the foyer in time to see him returning from lunch with a young, glamorous companion with his arm familiarly under hers, so deep in discussion he failed to see her, just because the girl's bulging eyes never left his, why should Rose imagine such a horrifying scenario?

No.

Through her fingers she watched them go through the doors together. Mesmerized, like a praying mantis, her eyes achingly out on stalks; limbs, knobby, bat-like and thin, poised to spring to her own defence.

Automatic doors.

Typically, Michael let the woman go first.

There was freedom in her stare, in her hair, in her dress. There was freedom and daring in her smile. The girl was smart in a dark-grey suit, high heels, hair shaped, shaggy, boyish and aggressive.

Immediately Rose was the outsider she had always felt herself to be.

She scrambled about in the glove compartment and found a packet of stale cigarettes.

Chain-smoking all afternoon Rose thrashed around in a knot of tangled emotions. She squeezed her eyes tightly closed, willing it, willing it, willing it not to be, and begging over and over, 'Please, please, please . . .'

Pain fugged the car. It misted up the windscreen. She drove dangerously – so unlike her – down this street and that one, then turned into a cul-de-sac.

She struggled with a three-point turn and went twice round a roundabout.

I am going mad.

I am losing my mind.

Some children in a garden shouted something at her. It was a damply hot day in late September. An ice-cream van played 'Just One Cornetto' and jangled her nerves like a dentist's drill. She clenched her fists round the steering wheel.

Sweat beads stood out on her forehead.

It was possible to smell her own pain.

Oh God. Oh somebody help me.

In her misery and hopelessness she knew she dare not ask him outright. He would be so hurt. Her dark suspicions would spoil a relationship which had never been tainted by anything so vile. But how could she possibly greet him this evening without giving her terror away?

Pour him a drink?

Kiss him?

Show him the new book she'd picked up in Smiths?

Start discussing the inconsequentials that cemented their contentment?

If she put her hand on his sleeve would he pull away?

She envied an old man walking a poodle, he looked so completely untroubled. She was forced to stop at a level crossing when the barrier came down, after the lights had stopped flashing. When she heard the roar of the train she was almost tempted to barge straight through in order to end the agony of doubt which shrieked through her brain, a ceaseless screaming.

What a farce.

They were going to Venice next week, a winter break, his suggestion. She had always wanted to go there, and the thought of her packing, half finished, laid out on the bed in Jessie's room, brought on such a bout of self-pity that she mounted the pavement, blinded by tears. She reversed and the windscreen wipers came on. *Damn them. Damn them.*

But would Michael have booked a week's holiday while deeply involved with somebody else? Wouldn't it be far more likely that he'd lie about some business trip and take his lover with him instead? Or was his way of deceiving Rose to make out all was well? Or even a guilt thing? Who knows?

Safe back on the road again Rose racked her brains. Had he been gentler recently? More considerate? More tender? Had sex been better? More frequent? Or less enthusiastic? Should she have noticed some obvious signs? And what were the signs?

Dammit, dammit, dammit. She couldn't even remember what they were supposed to be. She couldn't answer her own stupid questions.

She couldn't go on driving this way. She was likely to kill someone, if not herself. Her own death wouldn't bother her, but the thought of killing somebody else jolted her back to a kind of sanity.

She pulled in at a layby to try and stop the trembling and sickness. She struggled to empty the blasted ashtray. Michael would be really pissed off to find that she'd been smoking.

Calm down, calm down.

Just one little episode and what had she done?

27

Built it up out of all proportion. She forced a brittle, inhuman laugh.

Ash spilled out all over the floor, covering her hands with stinking grey dust. She thought of urns full of human ashes. Her terror had invented a monster, a self-devouring, rampaging fiend that existed in her own sick head.

What the hell was the matter with her? *Think about it. Think.* Rose's breath halted and quickened. She lit the last cigarette. After all, it was equally likely that Michael, returning to the office, had met some new girl from the typing pool and was merely trying to be kind. Rose's bizarre reaction suggested that Michael habitually bed-hopped – a rake; an old lecher; a fornicating, wenching wanker probably flashing in the park while he's at it.

God. Oh God.

At last Rose made herself laugh properly. Comical, that's what it was. The tears turned into pent-up hysteria. Her face in the mirror was horribly distorted, twisted with grief and hilarity, raw and half insane.

These descriptions were so wrong for Michael. Laughable, ridiculous. He would be utterly astonished if she told him about the madness that had seized her back there. She had never realized such fear was inside her, crouched, curiously energized for such instant release, like a wild creature chained in a zoo. She had never needed to be jealous of Michael. Maybe it was her age that caused it, that ridiculous, dreadful assumption that leaped at her out of nowhere, ripping into thirty safe years.

*   *   *

That night, while the dishwasher was finishing and Michael was upstairs having a shower, she pressed the redial button. She did it for her own reassurance.

'Belinda can't come to the phone right now, but please leave a message after the tone.'

Rose gasped and pulled back as if burned.

Belinda?

And that rolling accent; it must be Welsh.

A client surely? Rose would know nothing about it; Michael rarely brought his work home. Michael had spent half an hour making phone calls in his study before she'd called him for his supper.

Perhaps this was no special affair. Maybe Belinda was Michael's mistress. Her imagination slipped into overdrive. It was even remotely possible that he spent his life with a series of mistresses. How would Rose ever know?

Rose sat alone in soft lamplight, surveying the lovely room she'd created. Furniture of soft white leather, Persian rugs on a polished floor. She sat perfectly still, her hands on her knees, her teeth digging into her lip. Just another perverse coincidence on a day when she'd had her sanity shaken.

She was very tired and morose. She had drunk too much wine with her supper to help move conversation along, talk which seemed false and stilted for the first time in thirty years. Had Michael noticed her nervousness? It would seem not. He'd acted the same as he always did, amusing, lively, keen to discuss the holiday and laughing about a threatened strike by the air-traffic controllers. His appetite was as hearty as ever.

But now . . . Belinda?

To Rose the name suggested some floozy with sharp earrings and golden hair. Belinda. Belinda. The name was sharp; it cut like a dagger. The girl outside the foyer at lunchtime?

What was she supposed to do next? Search his pockets for clues? Sniff his underpants? Check his diary? Time his comings and goings?

She didn't want to discuss this with anyone. To talk about it would make it real, apart from the fact that she couldn't bear to see the pity in some friend's eyes or hear their sympathy over the phone.

And the shock. The shock of it.

She thought about Lady Moon who had distributed her husband's collection of wines among the villagers along with the milk. She thought about other acts of revenge she had read about or seen in TV dramas. But Rose didn't want to reach that stage. Rose didn't want Michael to leave her, however many women he might be bonking.

Would he leave her?

How would he tell her?

Gently, or by phone?

Robin Cook's wife had been dumped at the airport.

All these things flashed through her mind until she felt they were driving her crazy. Because the point was that she didn't *want* to know, didn't want to have to tell the girls that her thirty-year-old happy marriage was over – her friends, her mother, the neighbours. She didn't want to be left alone in this big house in their double bed. Didn't want to sit her armchair next to the empty one beside it, cook for one person, stop sorting socks, take taxis home, unfold one sunbed, arrange to play tennis with Di or Sue. She didn't want to watch TV and not be able to comment, 'Look at him,' and, 'This is silly,' and, 'Shall we record that?' and, 'We've seen this stupid film before.' All the pointless remarks that broke such a comfortable, easy silence.

And going upstairs alone.

And waking up cold and unable to cuddle.

And what about Christmas?

And what about holidays?

And no-one to kiss her or touch her again.

Rose wrapped herself in her arms and rocked like a lost, frightened child.

'Oh no, baby. Oh no.'

TWO

Sometimes Daisy found it amazing that her mother could be so unaffected by what she called 'life's ups and downs', while Granny had turned so bitter.

To anyone else the death of a twin would have caused major trauma, and the disappearance of a father somewhere in the Bay of Biscay at the impressionable age of fourteen could, in anyone else, have caused severe mental problems.

But no. If Rose referred to those most tragic events – and she wasn't even disturbed enough to find the subject taboo – she compensated by emphasizing the closeness and happiness of her little family, and after her father's disappearance she had grown very close to her mother.

'Everyone has suffered,' she used to say. 'It's trendy to suffer in childhood these days, an excuse for failure in later life. I wasn't abused. I wasn't deserted. And I know you think I sound trite, but good has been known to come out of heartbreak. After Jamie died, that shattering disaster, we certainly learned about perspective. Little things ceased to matter. I can see by your face you think

I'm preaching, but you do, you know, Daisy. You learn how to cope.'

You either cope or go under. And Mum wasn't the type to go under.

Brave.

A brick.

Mum's quiet stoicism was either appealing or galling, depending on how you were feeling. Dad still felt he had to act the great protector after 'everything she's been through'. But Dad protected everyone, he felt that was his role. That was the way he had been brought up: to be a strong, responsible man. And that might well be why it was proving so hard for Daisy to find a comparable man for herself.

Mum had been lucky to find someone like Dad. But she was owed a little good luck after the losses of her childhood.

As far as Daisy and Jessie could tell, their parents' marriage was a perfect blueprint. Neither girl could ever remember hearing voices raised in serious anger. If there were disagreements, they were dealt with using reasoned discussion, and Dad was the one most likely to back down, but stalemates like that were rare and seldom over important issues. Dad was good looking, for a man of his age. He was romantic, too, coming home from work with flowers, chocolates, or a new dress. He knew Mum's size and taste. He could have dressed her perfectly from head to toe; he could choose her a picture, a book or a colour scheme and know that he would get it right first time.

It was uncanny the way Mum and Dad each knew how the other was feeling.

Family was important to Mum, sometimes it felt like an obsession, but this was understandable when you remembered the early devastation of her own family. Both girls bore this in mind during their troublesome adolescent years, when Mum was being overprotective, interfering and trying to run their lives, as they felt she often did.

Dad was quick to remind them of what had happened to her if they ever came near to forgetting. But inside Daisy stirred a quiet, secret anger, and she knew that Jessie felt it, too.

She would have liked to take a year out between school and university. Her friend Charlotte had invited her to backpack through South America. Charlotte went in the end, but with Jennie. Daisy had wanted to go up to Edinburgh University, but Dad took Mum's side and persuaded her to stay closer to home. Exeter was only a short train ride away.

She felt Dad had betrayed her. This was Daisy's life and future, and instead of supporting his daughter Dad had succumbed to pressure from Mum. But surely that was Daisy's fault? Surely she should have been more assertive.

'Listen, darling, there's time for all that.' Dad poured her a drink, a tactic he used when he wanted to show she was his equal, not just his child. 'Your mother is going through a difficult patch. And it's times like these, when you're low, that unpleasant memories tend to come back. Those old insecurities you've been coping with rise to the surface again and you need all the support you can get. Rose needs all our support. If you left home now it would make her very sad. And you know that as well as I do.'

'But Dad, she's got Jessie. Jessie comes home every day.'

Both girls went to private schools. But they were day girls, not boarders, which sidelined them from the main life of the school, the social life, the part that mattered, and that was Mum's fault, too.

'We're not talking about Jessie here, we're talking about you.'

'Well I can't think of any kid my age who would have to work round their mother's menopause.'

'That's unkind,' said Dad. 'That's not fair.'

Maybe when Jessie came to make her plans Mum would be on the mend. But no, her younger sister fought the same battles and ended up training at St Marks without a gap year either.

And now Mum and Dad were going to Venice. Daisy felt one small achievement – at least she hadn't been invited. Holidays had been bones of contention over which the two girls had fought together, starting when Daisy was sixteen and they'd sunbathed beside the pool of a villa in the Dordogne. They had both been bored out of their minds and Dad had accused them of being spoilt.

'We're not spoilt, just bored,' Jessie argued, adjusting her absurd bikini which had nothing realistic to cover. Flat on her back she looked like a toast rack. 'Look, Dad. What is there for us to do here? We're miles from the nearest town or beach; there's not a shop within walking distance, let alone a bar.'

'Would you prefer it if we'd gone to Benidorm? Is that it?'

'Of course not. You know what I mean. Why can't Daisy and I have some say in where we go?

Why not a hotel with a disco and stuff for us to do at night?'

'This is Mum's holiday, and mine, not just yours.'

'Well, we know that,' said Jessie peevishly. 'But wouldn't we all enjoy a hotel? And anyway, Daisy and I have been talking, next year we'd like to go on holiday on our own.'

'Jessie, you're thirteen.'

'Yes, and next year I'll be fourteen. Rachel Caldwell's going on holiday with a group of friends this year. Her parents don't mind.'

Daisy joined in, but knew the battle was lost. Jessie was younger but more successful when it came to aggression, which she thought of as persuasion. 'I feel silly coming on holiday with you and Mum all the time. Nobody else does it, so why should we?'

Then they were given the old lecture again: 'You both know how important it is for Mum to have her family around her . . .'

Dad was on her side again.

Yes, they knew. And how.

They'd been through it with her so many times they felt they'd lived the tragedies themselves. And Granny's descriptions were vivid. 'That poor little Nicky Wainwright, a waif of a child. He came running, covered in mud and howling, still in his Indian headdress. It took us ages to hear what he said.' At this stage Granny's face would tighten and her eyes would shine with a brilliant pain. 'Jamie had gone over the edge of the cliff. They'd been riding right to the edge on their bikes, daring each other.' Granny would pause and lower her head, as if to fend off a blow. 'He looked as if he'd been strawberry picking. It was down his chin. Round his mouth.' She fiddled with her fingers. It would have been useless to ask her to stop. You felt she wanted to say it again . . . and again . . . and again. 'His face was white as chalk. He was tangled up in his bicycle, a bit like those puzzles. You know, those metal shapes you have to separate. And his poor head was at such a terrible angle. A pedal had almost severed one leg. My poor little boy. My poor baby . . .' And she would dab her mouth with a hanky. Never her eyes, always her mouth.

Granny still lived in the same house as she had on the day her son was killed, sitting on the same wrought-iron chairs, sheltered by the same privet hedge with the same pattern of daisies growing round it.

The cliff was at the end of the garden, on the edge of the river at Bantham. A wide expanse of lawn ran to the edge of it, bordered by hydrangeas, rhododendrons and gorse. The river was eroding the clay at the bottom, and Grandpa had built a stout wall in order to contain it. Jamie had virtually flown like a bird on his brand-new ten-year-old birthday bike, from the top, right over the cliff and, thud, onto the wall below.

He'd died instantly of a broken neck.

His back was broken, too.

'It was just luck that Rose wasn't with them,' Granny used to say. 'She was in bed with flu, thank God. If she had been it would have been her. She was the hothead of the two. They might have been twins, but they were as different as chalk and cheese.'

To lose a child must be unendurable.

37

To lose a twin must come pretty close.

'Who was Nicky Wainwright?'

'Jamie's best friend.'

Mum and Granny dealt with it differently.

Granny, unable to let it go, had been affected all her life, while Mum, though sad, was more resigned, probably because at the age of ten you're more resilient.

Dad used to say, 'It's easy for us to assume that Mum took Jamie's death in her stride, but remember, in those days there was no help for people who suffered from mindblowing traumas. How can we know what Mum went through inside? She might have buried her feelings because of Granny and Grandpa.'

And if that wasn't bad enough, if that wasn't sufficient agony to endure in one lifetime, when Grandpa disappeared after a holiday touring Portugal, Granny suffered a breakdown and Mum, aged fourteen, somehow had to cope with all that.

Granny's eyes watered when she remembered that hideous night, but she still needed to tell the story again and again.

Grandpa Tate did a Maxwell.

Granny told the terrible tale in a faraway kind of voice, like a gnarled old seadog sharing storm-blasted legends.

'We shared a cabin, Rose, me and John. We'd had a meal in the restaurant. We'd just got to sleep. John must have woken up, I suspect it was indigestion, he suffered terribly from indigestion and I suggested we have a snack, but John insisted on a proper dinner. It was the last night of our holiday and he thought we ought to celebrate with a meal and some wine.

'And the awful thing was that it wasn't till morning that anybody missed him. By then it was too late for any effective search, although they did try. Nobody knows exactly what happened, but he must have fallen overboard.'

Granny went back one year later to throw white lilies onto the water. 'I threw one every half hour,' she said, 'because I didn't know the exact spot.'

It was essential, Mum warned them, that they never mention suicide to Granny.

This suggestion, put at the time, upset her more than John's death itself. Granny knew her husband was happy and wasn't the type to do such a thing. 'He loved us,' she used to say. 'Especially Rose. He adored her. What with Jamie and everything. He gave her a double dose of love and would never have deliberately left her.'

Because Grandpa Tate was an accountant all his affairs were in good order and the provision for his depleted family was more than sufficient to keep them in the manner to which they were accustomed. So Rose, without a loving father, suffered no material deprivation.

'Don't you think', said Dad encouragingly, 'that those sorts of experiences might leave someone a little bit possessive?'

Daisy and Jessie found this hard to answer.

Was Mum as possessive with him?

It was true that while Mum and Dad had plenty of friends Dad never went off and played golf or squash on his own like some men did. He wasn't the type to go off to the pub in the evening. Mum and Dad's leisure time was spent together, and if one couldn't go nor did the other, but neither appeared to resent this. It was just how it had always been.

Occasionally Dad went on business trips, but he would ring Mum every night, and she knew exactly where he was staying and when he would be back. Dad made it plain that these trips were a bore, and if he could take Mum with him he would. He used to come home laden with presents.

All Mum's activities took place during the working day; they never encroached on her evenings and neither did her female friends. Mum even left the phone unanswered if one of her friends rang up for a chat after six. Six o'clock was her watershed. Dad's time and nobody else's.

Daisy found it odd the way Mum preferred Dad's company in everything. After all, there were times when it was far more fun to go places with female friends, and how can you suddenly cut off all interest after a certain time of day to renew it at your own convenience?

You would think they'd get bored of each other.

Daisy's own experiences were nothing at all like her parents'. At university she shared her activities with a host of different people, nobody seemed to feel the need to settle down with one partner, although Daisy tried. She kept on trying. All her men would be far more likely to jump out of her bed without question to go to the aid of a friend in need halfway across the country if necessary. No one person in this world seemed able to give her the range of responses she required.

Unfortunately William, her present partner, did not feel the same as her. The son of divorced parents he had grown up in a family of stepchildren and had come out of it perfectly normal, although he maintained that he envied her the blissful family background.

'No, you don't see the drawbacks. You're romanticizing it because you never had it,' Daisy argued. 'It would be perfect apart from one thing: Mum's awful possessiveness.'

'You don't know how lucky you are,' was William's short reply.

'It can be stifling. You must see that.' Most of the time William was with her when Mum phoned with her unwanted invitations. He even helped Daisy invent excuses. He could see how trying it could be.

'How many times does my mum ring me up?' he asked.

Daisy agreed it was hardly ever.

'Yes, and that's because she's much happier with me out of the way. Without me there to argue with Graham. Without the tension there used to be between his kids and me.'

But to Daisy something about this felt healthier. William was outgoing, independent and more honest about his feelings. William had travelled. He'd been to drama school, he'd worked in a shipyard, he'd driven a taxi, he had even been out on a boat for Greenpeace. And now he worked for the *Western Morning News* as their chief reporter. 'It's a mother, daughter thing,' he said. 'She doesn't want to lose you. You're a friend, or she thinks you are. She doesn't know what you say about her.'

'You think I'm disloyal to her, don't you?'

He paused for a few moments. 'I think you

41

underestimate the benefits of being brought up loved.'

Daisy's eyes turned hard. 'But I don't see it as love. I see it as imprisonment.'

They were on their way to have lunch at home.

They'd invented excuses for the last three weeks, and together with Jessie, Daisy had agreed that if they went this Sunday they wouldn't have to go again before Venice.

'And Granny'll be there, no doubt.' With two hands she pulled back her hair, long, straight and black, sleek as water.

'Good,' said William. 'Granny's a star.'

'She's an obnoxious old bag.'

'Yes. Sometimes. But she makes me laugh.'

'In small doses.'

William hummed as he drove along in his ancient green MG. His brown leather jacket squeaked against the seat. He reminded Daisy of Snoopy. 'Well, I wouldn't want to live with her.'

'It's not the same at home without Baggins.' Daisy looked out of the window as they turned off the main road and onto the familiar lanes where, years ago, she had walked the family pet. She'd found it hard to get over Baggins' death. Mum had decided to have him put down. He was eight. She said he was tired, he had had enough. But how did Mum know that?

She was a little surprised that another dog hadn't materialized by now. After all, a pet gives complete control to its owner, and now that her daughters had both left home, Mum, a mega-control freak, might find that some compensation.

'What I think is strange', mused William, 'is how you always blame your mother. Why do all women do that? It's a betrayal of your sex. You do it. Your own daughter will do it, and as far as I can see poor Rose is utterly blameless.' He threw his cigarette out of the window after taking a long, farewell puff. The Redferns didn't know that he smoked, so these visits were mega stressful. He wished that Rose, a closet smoker, would declare herself and come out. Everyone knew she did secretly, but they all pretended she'd given up.

'It's not a question of blame,' Daisy said, defensive now, as they drove through the familiar gates and crunched along the drive. She shrugged. 'I love her. She's great and I owe her, but Mum's a control freak and Dad makes it worse by playing along with her all the time. Jessie and I, we never knew freedom, not like you. If we had done we'd be different people, much more independent and confident. It worked for you. Mum stopped us from growing and sometimes I hate her for that.'

'My heart belongs to Daddy,' trilled William, turning the engine off. They looked at each other. He said, 'You're jealous of him aren't you?'

Daisy scoffed. 'What of?'

'The way he loves her. And he fusses over Jessie.'

'Get lost. Jerk.'

Jessie was already here.

Her filthy red Mini had been abandoned with the door left open and litter trailing out of it – a twist of cellophane, an empty bag of Walkers salt and vinegar crisps and a browning apple core.

Granny's awful Nissan, a sickly hearing-aid beige

43

colour, was more carefully parked in her special place against the wall.

Mum, who must have been watching out for them, hurrying between the kitchen and the porch, came out in her apron, shaking her head in an elderly way. Surely it hadn't been that long since Daisy had last seen her, but Mum looked washed out, her cheeks were drawn and the skin slung brownishly under her eyes.

Older.

Worn.

In this family there were topics it was best not to mention, the menopause being one, Dad's fraudulent uncle another, along with Jessie's shoplifting stage and Great Granny's incarceration for ten years in a mental asylum. It must be the change that was dragging Mum down. Some days were better than others. But she sounded the same, just as perky. 'Daisy! Thank goodness. Go and get Michael from the garden and tell him to put that machine away. He's been determined to give the grass one last cut before we go away; he's thrashing about with the strimmer now and I'm worried about his blood pressure.'

'Why? Has he said something?' Daisy was confused. She had never worried about Dad's health, in spite of the mild stroke that had so shocked them all last year. He was taking his medication regularly, 75mgs of Clopidogrel daily. The doctor said he should live life as normal. She didn't think of her father as old, as someone who ought to slow down.

'No. But . . .'

'Doesn't he feel well?'

'Well, he hasn't said so exactly . . .'

44

'But Dad's had high blood pressure for years. Why are you so worried now?'

'He's been looking tired lately, that's all,' said Mum, giving her daughter a welcoming kiss and patting William's hot leather back.

You'd think that Mum was an Eastern guru the way she prescribed her alternative drugs, forever dabbling in her magic book to find the right kind of relief, and yet, so far, she had discovered no working formula for strokes. She couldn't bear to watch suffering. She had attempted to cure Baggins' epilepsy with homoeopathic powders, sadly without success. But give her her due, the herbs she'd unearthed for Daisy's painful period pains had worked. To live on the fringe of Totnes, the country's alternative capital, home to the spiritually enlightened, was a temptation to anyone remotely interested in cranky, curious cures. A poster outside the health shop pushing colon hydrotherapy declared the United Kingdom to be the most constipated nation on earth.

All around their little town lay the heart of the English countryside, hilly lanes and hedgerows that still grow flowers in springtime. Cottages in hollows and farms on knolls. A luxurious spread of green, now turning to the coffee, chocolate and malt of winter, and wrapping-paper skies of pale blue and gold.

The succulent smell of roast beef wafted through the house from the Aga, the sort of monster joint families don't buy any more. Mum and Dad had a joint, even if they were on their own, as part of a thirty-year Sunday ritual. Beef for everybody else except Jessie; a nut loaf would be cooking for her, although Mum had failed to get to grips with serious vegetarian cooking. She bought veggie stuff ready made.

From the sitting room the tinkle of ice in glasses sounded tempting. Granny was at the bottle already. Daisy saw her shoot a look towards Mum; the same look she'd seen before many times, a questioning look. There was fear in it, but then she was back to the matter of the moment, swilling the ice in her over-large gin.

Rose smiled reassuringly. 'Tell your father to come in now dear,' she said. 'I want him well for Venice.'

THREE

That morning Rose applied too much blusher. She came straight from the bathroom and the face in the mirror had shocked her. Michael used to hold this face in his hands, his dark eyes full of love, and then he would circle her lips and her eyes with a finger that tickled so much she would laugh. Her mouth was firm then, her eyes unlined, and her cheeks had their own natural blush.

Does Belinda wax her legs? In summer only or in winter, too?

Were Belinda's breasts larger than hers? What did her nipples look like? Inverted? Brown or pink? Rose had watched a programme recently and been shocked by the variations in shape and form of women's breasts.

She swallowed and swallowed again. How to dislodge this thick wedge of misery? She felt like death and looked like a corpse. Mummified. The boulder that weighed down her heart was taking its toll on her physical appearance, and that wouldn't do. Nobody must guess how she was feeling.

If only she had a friend she could trust. She remembered how, when she was little, she used to run outside with hope in her heart, looking for someone to play with, but it's not so easy to run and call out when you're grown-up, verging on elderly.

It took all she had to prepare the dinner and greet the girls and her truculent mother. The magazines would call it 'some inner strength', which women are supposedly blessed with when faced with any ordeal in their lives.

Well Rose could do with some inner strength now.

'Thank you, dear,' said Dinah, her faced twisted, not with pain, but a shrewd sort of satisfaction as she shamelessly exaggerated the effect of the latest treatment on her arthritic knee. 'Yes, please. Gin and tonic. Delicious.'

Rose felt her false smile flutter away as she watched how fondly Michael kissed his petulant mother-in-law and the trouble he took to make her comfortable. 'To the right a bit? Does it feel better like that?' There was something sinful about Rose's mother and the malice that flowed between them.

Rose wished her mother was kinder, someone to talk to about pleasant things, with something else to swap other than endless grievances. This familiar type of conversation, which was so much a part of her now, was exhausting and set the pace for the day, so that come evening, when Dinah had gone, Rose found herself mixing the custard as if it were a cauldron of bubbling wrath.

In the room beside Rose stood a wickedly sharp Yucca plant. Whenever she passed it Rose breathed in to avoid its cutting edges. Rose had never liked it, but she watered it responsibly and gave it an occasional feed, moved it from direct sunlight in summer

48

and wiped its leaves with a damp J Cloth. Why did she bother if she disliked it so much? And why did she bother with Dinah when she felt she'd rather not?

Couldn't she change her mother?

Influence her for the better?

Couldn't Rose throw out the Yucca and put a soft, gentle plant in its place? No, like Dinah they were related, merely by the fact that it had lived for years in her house. The Yucca was dependent on her.

She tried a Busy Lizzie once; it was a mass of bright red flowers when she bought it, but it failed to thrive. It just went brown at the edges and grew all messy and tangled, dropping its leaves all over the floor so that she had to clean up after it.

The Yucca never dropped its leaves. It wasn't a messy plant; she only had to wipe it. Maybe that's why she put up with Dinah. In a false terracotta pot that wouldn't break her heart if it broke.

Dinah could be a pain, but to Michael, gallant to the last, she was special. Dinah had called Michael 'too thrusting', but her opinion had changed over the years and now the two were close. He had the patience Rose often lacked these days when it came to her mother. He liked to believe that the losses they shared during Rose's childhood had created a special relationship between them, but this was romantic fantasy from a man whose own family had split, both his parents dead and his sisters living in California.

'I'd lay it on if I was in pain. I'd demand as much sympathy as I could damn well get.'

But no. No he wouldn't. Nor would he suffer with that beautiful dignity that makes everyone lesser feel mean. Michael would scorn martyrdom.

49

He would compensate by being extra cheerful and using a skilful self-mockery which would make everyone feel that their sympathy would be wasted. His performance would be so convincing that Rose would nearly be taken in.

But not quite.

She knew him too well.

The last few days she'd spent looking for clues to confirm her worst suspicions: she watched his appetite; timed his movements; went through the pockets of his suits; checked old bank statements to see if there was anything odd, any purchase he might have made that would give his infidelity away.

Flowers.

Chocolates.

Jewellery.

A sensual silken negligee.

But if he was cheating on her like this Michael would surely use a card. Still torturing herself, Rose rifled through his desk, checking on the Access statements, the Visa, Diners and American Express. The mental stress of this wore her out, but on Saturday morning, after a ritual pampered lie-in reading the papers and drinking tea, she'd come downstairs and checked Michael's jacket pockets, only to draw out a folded envelope written in bold, childlike writing.

Rose winced.

She held the envelope between finger and thumb as if it might carry some infection. Why wasn't this with the rest of the mail, placed in the letter rack on the table?

These things didn't really happen to people like

her and Michael. These sordid aberrations hit flippant couples who got married in Tobago, selfish and superficial folk, all sex and image and white leather bibles.

And she knew these were his feelings, too.

Rose glanced out through the kitchen window. Michael was busy in the shed, dressed in his old gardening cords. She locked herself in the downstairs loo and sat there shaking as she pulled out the folded notelet that was to change her life.

A notelet with ducks on the front.

How tasteless.

There was no address. No date. Just a firm, round hand. Very bold. Very clear.

Don't do this to me, please don't do this. When are you going to reply to my letters? You said not to write but I had to. You know how I feel, I've told you often enough and I know you feel the same. The only thing that keeps me going is the knowledge that we will be together. It might take time, but it will happen. The kind of love we have can never die or fade, and to deny it is to deny life itself. I love you, Michael, and I always will. Please, please ring me soon.

And it was signed with a bold blue, 'Belinda'.

Rose dropped to the floor and curled up on the lavatory mat. No, no, no, no. She dug her teeth into her lip so it bled. She rocked herself backwards and forwards. She hugged the lavatory bowl and leaned over the pan, as if she was vomiting into it. There was nothing there, though, nothing but misery.

No need to play the sleuth any more. The confirmation was in her hand.

How curious that Rose felt it was she who was in the wrong. She was a schoolgirl again, cribbing during an exam and in fear of the teacher catching her and declaring her a cheat, the worst crime of all. She pulled herself upright, breathed in deeply and, face puce with embarrassment and shame, scuttled out to the hall and replaced the notelet where she had found it. By then she'd learned the words off by heart. They panned through her brain remorselessly whatever task she was doing.

Michael came in from the garden. 'You're up then?' He removed his boots and looked at his watch. 'I thought I'd take you for lunch as you'll be cooking for six tomorrow.'

So thoughtful.

So decent.

She didn't dare turn round from the sink lest he see the fear in her face. A kitchen which smelled of lemon and a wife who smelled of tears. Automatically she stacked the dishwasher. 'That would be nice.' Were those her words? Was that her voice? How utterly unbelievable that she could utter such commonplace remarks while inside her everything churned and shredded like peelings in the waste disposal.

'Where would you like to go?'

'No, you choose.'

That inane conversation came back to Rose as she poured a drink and, for a moment, she and Dinah were alone because Michael had gone off to put the red wine on the table.

Many women, in Rose's circumstances, would confide their fears to their mothers. Would be reassured and comforted. Would be cuddled and stroked better. But between Rose and Dinah those days were over. The tables had turned long ago. Since her seventieth birthday Dinah had demanded the childhood role and Rose accepted that of protector. Rose knew that instead of offering her sensible advice, Dinah would lap up the scandal, relishing and embellishing it, and only exacerbating the situation.

An outspoken woman all her life, any sensitivity Dinah had once had seemed to be leaving her. Instead of softening in her old age, Dinah was hardening, along with her arteries, and this embarrassing behaviour became most apparent in her dealings with those she considered to be her inferiors: traffic wardens, waiters, shop assistants, council workers, mechanics and anyone else in overalls who crossed her.

Michael defended her. 'She's getting on. She can't help it.'

Rose was more realistic. 'Huh. So how come she chooses who to insult? I just wish she'd make the effort to try and be a bit nicer, that's all.'

Her mother's small personality traits had sharpened with age, like the bones in her face, so that little envies and grievances were magnified and distorted. A few awful months after her father's drowning Rose had watched her mother's bravery disintegrate into a nervous breakdown. She had eventually recovered from that, but now it was the unfairness of life that seemed to cause Dinah most anguish, and this new bitterness was manifesting itself in an open dislike of other people.

Daisy and Jessie had noticed it first. It was their jokes and clever mimicry that brought this trait to Rose's attention – Dinah's fascination with gossip and scandal, with the downfall of strangers and the besmirching of personalities. What used to be amusing now felt unpleasant. What used to be witty was vitriolic.

Dinah wasn't the sweet old lady she used to say she would like to be and it was sad to watch it happening. She wasn't someone Rose could confide in, even if she felt able.

'The only thing that keeps me going is the knowledge that we will be together . . .' Belinda's words went round and round in her head, like a mantra.

Obviously Michael hadn't replied and Belinda was upset.

Was he trying to end the relationship?

Belinda obviously believed it would go on. He had tried to phone her from home in the week, Rose had proof of that. All day at the office and Michael was free to do exactly as he liked. There was nobody to check on him there; nobody to care who he telephoned or how long he was on the line.

Just before lunch Jessie arrived, as shambolic as ever in ragged jeans and a shrunken old jersey, or had she actually bought it like that?

She should have told Rose she was bringing a friend. Rose was in no mood for strangers. Some psychopath had cut Jessie's hair, chopping it with a blunt-edged axe so it tufted out all over the place, and the green streaks didn't help her complexion. The friend, of masculine build and wearing a tracksuit and trainers, had a feminine name, Jasmine, and her face was open and friendly.

'I knew you wouldn't mind, Mum, there's always too much anyway, and poor Jasmine is starving to death.'

'Of course I don't mind.' Rose smiled. 'It's good to have you, Jasmine.' She purposely did not shake hands because she knew it would irritate Jessie, as all good manners appeared to. 'Is Jasmine vegetarian, too?'

Jessie threw her coat on the sofa and Rose picked it up and smoothed it. 'Jasmine is a disgusting slut. She's a carnivore of the worst kind. She even likes liver and black pudding.'

'Jessie's anorexic,' said Dinah annoyingly, through her gin.

Yes. Jessie was disturbingly thin. But how many times must Rose warn her mother that these days this might be true, and to refer to the problem so casually was not the best idea.

But Rose had more on her mind. And five minutes later Daisy arrived with William in tow. Michael was needed to sort out the drinks. Where was he anyway? Not still thrashing around with the strimmer? She sent Daisy to find her father, and only then thought of his mobile phone. Was it on the hall table, where he usually left it to charge?

Rose hurried through to turn on the vegetables. One glance told her he must have it with him. Had he phoned Belinda from the safety of the shed?

Rose picked at her food. The conversation felt like listening in on a crossed line. She hardly knew the people, she heard what they said but she wasn't one of them. And then Michael made the extraordinary announcement that some colleagues at the office were planning a flying weekend in November and that he would rather like to go with them. Would Rose like to come, too? Of course she wouldn't want to learn, he said, but she could join in with the social life afterwards.

Since when had Michael been interested in flying? Of course she would not want to join in an all male adventure at some seedy flying club headquarters. No other wives would be there.

'That sounds like real fun,' said Jessie, eyeing the dried-out nut roast. She scratched at it like a scrawny old hen turning over pieces of grain.

'You'd hate it, Michael,' Rose heard herself say.

'You don't know that,' said Jessie, maddeningly. 'How d'you know that? Dad's never tried flying before. I'd love it. I'd love to go.'

'What on earth will you do in the evenings?' Rose asked, unable to stop herself.

'Oh, I dunno. I suppose they'll want a few drinks. Maybe a game of darts.'

Rose couldn't believe this was Michael speaking.

'It'll be good for Dad,' said Jessie, all innocence, piling on the roast potatoes. How could a girl stay so thin and yet eat so much? But Rose used to be like that. It was only lately that she'd become 'dumpy' as Michael liked to put it. 'All the more for me to get hold of.' He thought that was a compliment, but it set Rose's teeth on edge.

'Good for him?'

'Yes. To get away on his own for a while.'

Rose put down her knife and fork and turned to challenge Daisy. 'What do you mean by that? He could always go away on his own, but until now he's never suggested it.'

Daisy looked startled. There was some hysteria in Rose's tone. 'It's no big deal, Mum. Leave it out.'

'It's not important anyway,' said Michael. 'I haven't told them I'd go.'

'Dad,' now Jessie interfered. 'It *is* important. Of course it is. You go. Mum'll be OK. Won't you, Mum?'

'Well, of course I will,' said Rose.

'You don't sound very enthusiastic.'

William and Jasmine were embarrassed. The undertones were becoming uncomfortable. It felt like an attack on Rose and yet she had done nothing to deserve it. And the terrible knowledge came to her that if Michael did leave her and go off with his floozy her daughters would blame her for being too possessive. The injustice of that almost caused her to slap both their faces. Neither Daisy nor Jessie would see her as the wronged wife, thrown aside for a younger model after thirty years of happiness.

Was Michael's announcement deliberate, knowing what her reaction would be and preparing the ground for his departure?

Surely he didn't have that sort of cunning?

Surely he didn't hate her that much? She would know if he did, wouldn't she?

She could read Michael like a book.

Rose's brain scrolled up the divorces of friends and acquaintances. Even if they started off determined to avoid confrontation, in every case she'd heard of they ended up as enemies.

*　　*　　*

Daisy came out between courses to give Rose a hand in the kitchen. Rose burned her hand on the apple-pie dish, but her cry wasn't one of physical pain. Daisy forced her blistered hand under the cold water tap. 'Hold it there while I get you a plaster,' she said.

'What was all that about?' demanded Rose.

'What?' Daisy had already forgotten.

'Suggesting I was trying to stop your father going on a flying weekend.'

'Did we suggest that?' Daisy dried her mother's hand on the nearest tea towel. Rose wished she would leave it alone and concentrate on the subject.

'Yes. Yes, you both did.'

'You're taking it too seriously, Mum. Dad won't go anyway. You know he never does things like that.' And she wrapped the plaster round Rose's finger. 'Chill out, Mum. You're all tense, I can feel it. I thought you were acting funny when we first arrived. I thought it was Jessie's girlfriend.'

'Sorry?'

'Jasmine. She's sweet. I like her.'

Rose hadn't given Jasmine a thought. Why would she?

She watched Daisy stirring the custard. Some mothers would confide in their daughters, and she was close to both of hers, or thought she was. She asked, 'Daisy, did you mean it when you said your father needed a break?'

'It was you who seemed to be worried about him when we arrived. Remember? It was you who suggested he'd been overdoing it.' Daisy poured the thickened custard into the waiting jug. 'You look tired, too, Mum. Maybe this holiday is just what you need. Both of you. A good rest.'

58

Rose had never been so tempted to fling herself on her daughter's shoulder and beg for some kind of help. But she didn't want to swap relationships. She was Daisy's mother. She'd seen what had happened between her and Dinah, that reversal of roles, and she wasn't ready for that. If Michael's philandering turned into merely one moment of madness it would be a mistake to involve the girls and spoil what had once been so perfect.

When they returned to the dining room Michael was engrossed in conversation with William about flying. It seemed as if he'd read up on it; it was something he'd always been interested in learning, and this weekend idea was no sudden impulse he had thrown into the conversation. And when William asked, Michael went into his study and came out with a glossy brochure. The two pored over it together, like lifelong enthusiasts.

So why had he failed to mention it; he hadn't uttered one word on the subject to Rose? Why hadn't he shown her the brochure?

So this was to be his dirty weekend. November the twenty-second. Was it his first or just one of many over all the years when Rose didn't question his business trips, the one-nighters he spent in London hotels when Rose couldn't go with him, yet ringing her up unfailingly to ask if all was well. Was that why he had conjured up the whole flying idea? Knowing that Rose would refuse?

The apple pie tasted of cardboard. Rose went to make the coffee.

* * *

'Are you cold, dear?' Rose asked Jessie, who was cuddled up on the two-seater sofa with her large new friend. 'Shall we light the fire?' It was that time of year. Not quite cold enough for the central heating to be turned on.

'No, Mum, just sleepy after all that food and booze.'

It was a relief to see Jessie contented, although she was still far too thin. Perhaps this new friend, a boisterous girl with a raucous voice, would be good for Jessie and help bring her out. Of Rose's two daughters Jessie had been the most troublesome. As a baby she started off colicky, but having said that, on the scale of difficult children Jessie would hardly register. She couldn't decide what she wanted to do when she left school with three good A' levels. It was left to Rose and Michael to push her into teaching. 'You've got to do something. You're not just slouching about round here,' Michael told her.

'I want to go abroad, you know that. I want time to think. I want to find out what I'm good at,' she huffed. 'Nobody else I know is going straight to college. Hell, I want some experience of life.'

Michael, in his sensible way, sorted her out and calmed her down. And after a difficult first year at St Marks, she now seemed to be settling, although who would employ her as a teacher with her crazy hair-style and her shabby clothes was anybody's guess.

Rose shivered. Because it would be in that same calming, comfortable way that Michael would explain to his daughters why he was leaving their mother. And in the same loving, admiring manner they always had for him, they would accept it.

She would be left out in the cold.

FOUR

Pretty Belinda.

Belinda McNab.

Petite, cute and bubbly, with eyes of such a disturbing blue that people asked if she wore contact lenses. She dressed in a most individual style – a curtain would look like a caftan, a fluffy scarf would make a bolero. Belinda flowed rather than walked, even in clumpy rainbow DMs. She expressed herself with her childlike hands, every finger sparkling with rings, and she sang rather than spoke.

She'd started at St Marks at the same time as Jessie. She wanted to teach infants. She sang pretty nursery rhymes so sweetly – Little Miss Muffet personified.

It was Daisy who went to Michael about her.

It was Jessie who went to Daisy for help. Jessie, who had struggled for months and could no longer cope with the girl on her own.

Nobody could.

She was barmy.

Belinda's obsession with Jessie had begun on the first day of college, but it wasn't until two months later that Jessie came crying to Daisy for help.

'She'll be out there now,' hissed Jessie, rushing in through the front door, across the sitting room to flip back the curtain and search through the rain-swept darkness. She looked very young and vulnerable standing there with her wild hair and dripping jacket. 'She'll have followed me here. I know it.'

'You're paranoid,' Daisy said, shocked by the agitated state of her sister and the thought of some demented woman lurking outside in the shadows. 'Look at the state of it out there. Anyone would have to be mad . . .'

William had been despatched to the bedroom. He'd been quite happy to go after one look at Jessie's face.

'She is mad,' Jessie whispered quietly, as if she might be overheard.

Daisy struggled with a cork. The sooner she opened the wine the better, for her sake if not her sister's. 'But she's not . . . violent . . . You don't think she'd hurt you?'

Jessie shook her wet head. The water scattered off a spiral perm that had never worked, reminding Daisy of spaniels' ears. 'She threatens. She threatens all kinds of things, but so far she hasn't done anything like that.'

That first term at St Marks Belinda and Jessie paired up straight away. 'We got on so well. It was so good to find a friend on day one. You know what it's like. I knew nobody. I didn't want to be there and nor did Belinda, so we grumbled around together and laughed at everyone else. Oh God.' Jessie dropped her head in her hands.

'Here,' Daisy pushed a large glass of Chardonnay towards her. She pulled the chair closer so she was sitting directly in front. Drops of water dripped off Jessie onto the table between them. At last she shrugged off her shiny black jacket and threw it carelessly onto the floor.

'We even asked if she could move rooms so we could be together.' Jessie sighed, then shuddered as she remembered. Daisy wanted to fetch a rug and wrap her sister in it, but she knew that Jessie would be annoyed by any break in her concentration now she'd come this far. 'Thank God they didn't agree to that. But she was on the same landing as me. She was in most of my classes, too, and we stuck together, you know how you do. We excluded everyone else. Oh God. We thought they were all pathetic. So serious; real nerds. We went off together during break. We made it clear we didn't want anyone else to share our table, and in the evenings we didn't join in with any of their boring, childish activities. Or social ones. We started going to a pub further out so we wouldn't meet up with the others.'

Typical, Jessie in trouble again. The adored black sheep of the family.

This state of affairs carried on for weeks before the physical stuff began. Holding hands seemed so innocent, and Belinda's first kisses were platonic. When, very gradually, her behaviour grew more intense, at first Jessie laughed it off.

She was lonely.

She had no other friends.

She missed school.

She missed home.

63

The others had long ago taken the hint and left the couple alone. The excluders became the excluded, although, now that she knew them better, there were several students Jessie liked and wished she'd met first.

'Belinda was a manic depressive,' Jessie explained to Daisy. 'We used to sit in her room because her room mate was a film buff and mostly out until late. There were no lights on, just a candle and music and cushions on the floor.' Jessie fiddled with her fingers, then pushed them away as though irritated by their interference. 'I've always liked having my feet stroked, and so she used to do that and I let her. It seemed normal at the time. Oh God . . . even quite nice.'

Jessie stopped and shook her head, got up, took her wine to the window and pulled the curtain back again.

Daisy watched her. 'She can't get in, Jessie, even if she is out there. The door's locked. Come back. Sit down. Relax. Go on.'

Jessie put down her wine and began to massage her neck. 'I don't know if I can.' She looked at her sister, then averted her eyes. 'I don't know how to tell you.'

Daisy sat forward. 'It's me, Jessie, remember. It's me you're talking to. And I don't give a damn what happened. All I care about is you.'

But Jessie sat silent for a long moment, breathing in and out deeply. 'The trouble is . . . it's such a mess. It went on from there. The touching became more intimate. It was never me, always her, but I allowed it to happen, and Daisy, I enjoyed it.'

'It's OK. It's OK.' Daisy, ever the serious one, held her sister's hands.

But Jessie pulled away and angrily wiped her eyes. 'Shut up. Shut up. Belinda began to tell me she loved me, and I responded, I suppose. It's easier to respond, hard to stay silent in that situation. And I can't explain, but she is . . . kind of compelling. It was exciting, breaking the rules. She's got this hypnotic quality. I dunno. By then, I suppose, you could say we were . . . intimate? Her' – Jessie paused to search for the word – 'her passion was overwhelming. I know now that I should have realized there was something obsessive about it, something daunting. I hate the word unhealthy, but that's how it seemed to be getting. Belinda was so irrational and jealous, and I began to feel devoured by her.'

Apparently even a smile became a betrayal in Belinda's eyes and she rarely left Jessie's side. She left notes in her bag, under her pillow, between the pages of books. These notes, pathetically childlike, told Jessie how much she loved her and how she would die if she lost her. Belinda began to discuss a future in which she and Jessie were together for ever. She said she had never loved anyone else and never would now that she'd met Jessie.

'She stopped being discreet. It was awful, Daisy. Everyone knew we were an item. Queers. Lezzies. They used to make jokes about it. She tried to kiss me in public places, she *wanted* other people to see. She sent me poems, she bought me presents. Look,' and she held up her arm, 'this watch. And Belinda couldn't afford it; she was as strapped for cash as I was.'

As the weeks went by and the Christmas holidays approached, Jessie prayed the intense relationship would cool down, but Belinda's behaviour became even more bizarre. 'It was to do with power, not love.' Jessie tried to reason with her. One day she told Belinda that the relationship was unequal and that she couldn't respond with the same intense fervour; she worried that Belinda was going to get hurt.

'I don't think she even heard me. I'd ceased to be a person in my own right,' moaned Jessie, crushed. 'Belinda seemed to assume we would be spending Christmas together, me at her house or her at mine. But I was longing for the break. She was really beginning to frighten me and I wanted out.'

Daisy shrugged, impressed. 'Last Christmas? You never said anything. Nobody would ever have guessed.'

'No. I suppose not.' Jessie's hands were still shaking. 'But I spent a lot of time in my room, on the phone, reassuring Belinda. Trying to stop her carrying out her threat and turning up out of the blue. She started threatening to top herself. She said she'd write to Mum and Dad, that I ought to tell them about us and come out of the closet, reveal my true self. I handled it badly, I know that. I made out all was well, so when this term started I was no nearer to ending the whole manic mess.'

'Oh God, you poor thing.' How useless – that remark. But what else could poor Daisy say?

Then, over the first weeks of the new term, Belinda's infatuation intensified. The threats began in earnest. Initially they were threats directed to-wards herself: self-mutilation if Jessie didn't respond as she wanted; suicide; self-destruction, but then the threats turned on Jessie. If Belinda couldn't have her, nobody would – all the same old clichés.

Belinda would kill Jessie, then herself. She would hurt her so that Jessie knew the kind of pain Belinda was suffering. She would cut her. She would burn her. Whatever she did she would never escape from Belinda's all-encompassing love.

The soft-hearted Jessie felt sorry for her. Her life had been unbelievably sad, her childhood so unhappy. She'd spent her earliest years in hospital. She had never bonded with her mother, and her father and two brothers had abused her. She'd been lonely all her life. She poured all this out to Jessie, who wished she could do more to help her.

But there was nobody for Jessie to talk to.

She had brought this on herself. She couldn't confess to a lesbian affair. She didn't even know if she was one. She had had relationships with boys before, she wasn't a virgin by the time she went to college.

Hell.

Perhaps she was bisexual. What did Daisy think?

'I don't think you can use any label in the state you're in,' Daisy said. 'And anyway, what does it matter? It's what you're going to do next that counts. Belinda is obviously off her head. She's stalking you. She's making your life sheer misery. You've got to tell somebody, Jessie. Somebody must be able to help.'

'How can I? Think about it. Who could help me? And why should they? I feel so ashamed. And I got myself into this. I should leave St Marks. I should go away.'

'That's silly. Would it help if I talked to Belinda? If I tried to explain how—'

'No. No. She'd just drag you into it. She's manipulative, and she's clever.'

'How about Dad?'

'You're joking? *Never!*'

But Jessie ought to have realized, Daddy could make anything right.

That night Jessie slept at Daisy's flat. By morning they were no nearer a solution. Jessie went back to college the same emotional wreck she'd arrived but cheered by the thought that Belinda must have suffered a cold, wet night waiting for her to come out and harangue her.

It was Daisy who approached her father. The beloved, the all-powerful one.

Some daughters would be appalled at the thought, but oddly neither Jessie nor Daisy saw Michael as off-limits when it came to confidences, in spite of their ages.

He was ultra-dependable, super-reasonable. He was no ordinary dad. He was a kind of English Atticus out of *To Kill a Mockingbird*. For a start he was unshockable, and he had no firm feelings about homosexuality. He would sort out the problem sensitively, with as much concern for Belinda's welfare as that of his own daughter. His firm acted as accountants to St Marks Teacher Training College. He knew his way round there; he had contacts. And he was used to handling people and problems. He was an expert at that.

Daisy started describing the nightmare as if a friend of hers was involved. It was Michael who interrupted. 'Let's get one thing clear, this is Jessie we're talking about, isn't it?'

Daisy was gobsmacked. 'But . . . ?'

'Never mind. Get on with it.'

She told him the whole motley story.

The subject was not referred to again. Daisy and Jessie often wondered what he'd done, how he'd achieved it. But it was understood that a tricky subject had been dealt with discreetly and that Dad would rather leave it at that.

Had he met with Belinda? What stories had she told about Jessie? She had a wild imagination. Had a solution been arrived at amicably or were there bitter tears and resentments?

Before Belinda left St Marks she hid a last note under Jessie's pillow. There was no reference to Michael or his management of the situation. 'Dear Jessie. No matter what happens to me now I will always love you. You are my world.' And she wrote these three old chestnutty lines of Yeats':

'But I, being poor, have only my dreams;
I have spread my dreams under your feet;
Tread softly because you tread on my dreams.'

Jessie hadn't heard from her since, so at last she was starting to relax.

Daisy doubted very much that Dad had told Mum about any of this. He was so bloody protective of her. Oh yes, they shared most things, but Dad knew how she worried over Jessie and, as the problem was somehow solved, there would be no need to make her more anxious.

But was Jessie still confused about her sexuality? Hence her new friend, Jasmine, who she'd taken for lunch last Sunday? Dad obviously didn't mind and Mum didn't seem to notice. Now that Daisy thought about it, Mum had seemed abnormally distracted throughout the whole day.

At one point, in the kitchen, Mum had seemed over-prickly, and Daisy wondered if it was Jessie and Jasmine who had upset her. Dad already knew about Jessie's particular leanings, but for Mum it would come as a shock. It was hard to tell how she felt about queers, but Dad's attitude was OK – he used to joke about them, but who doesn't – so hers was likely to be the same. But no, it wasn't Jessie and her friend that had upset Mum, it was the idea of Dad going away and the fact that they had supported him.

The change of life was affecting Mum; they really must remember to be more sensitive towards her in future. Family meant so much to her; it must be especially hard on her now that both her children had gone. She would be expecting grandchildren soon, and Daisy wasn't averse to the idea if she could get William to propose.

Her children would be doubly blessed to have such loving grandparents.

Daisy smiled.

Dad would be so foolishly proud. She wanted so much to please him.

Daisy sometimes wondered if Mum was at all resentful about her life closeted at home. Although she had a degree in history, she'd never bothered with a career. What was the point of her education?

In a way she led the life of a parasite, feeding off

the experiences of others. They flew home, Dad, Daisy and Jessie, with their various bits of life, like seagulls feeding their waiting chick, and Mum picked at the second-hand pieces. From them, from books, from the telly and Radio 4.

In two years' time Mum would be fifty. They'd been married nearly thirty years. *Awesome*.

Mum was married at twenty-one and Daisy was born when she was twenty-three. In those days being a housewife and mother was normal. Did she think of her life as a sacrifice? Had she had aspirations before she got married? If so she'd never discussed them; she seemed content with her good works, which kept her in touch with other people. But only at arm's length. Never absorbed. Always apart from the seething masses, who she visited was strictly on her own terms. She chose the old and the blind to support. She didn't delve deeply into life's pot of depravity, deprivation and dirt.

What would Mum really feel if she knew about Jessie's sexual inclinations? How would she honestly react if either of them came home with a Rastafarian? Or if Dad turned into an alcoholic? Or she found out William was beating her daughter? Or if one of her family had Aids?

Yet Daisy and Jessie owed so much to Mum. For their happy, secure childhood; for always being there, waiting at home when they returned from school; for the bowls of yummy cake mix; for beds always made, dolls clothes; for all the laughs and adventures. Yuk, it sounds so sickly sweet when you put it like that; it sounded as if they'd been so spoilt. They were the envy of most of their friends, who usually chose to play at their house.

71

Mum was wholesome, fragrant. Even the books Rose read were mostly historicals with happy endings. The blackest she got was *Flowers in the Attic*, and that upset her and kept her awake at night. But she wasn't fazed by her daughters' choices, not even when Jessie went through a horror phase and brought home *American Psycho* and Daisy bought books with black jackets off the top shelf just to find out what they were like.

So was there no dark side to Rose? Rose and her sheltered, privileged life.

To Daisy it would seem not. Rose was almost too good to be true.

FIVE

They say that real love means letting go.

Well bugger that for a start.

Still unable or unwilling to accept that Michael was getting his kicks elsewhere, Rose continued packing for Venice and cleaning the house from top to bottom, as if, once she'd gone, she'd never be coming back. This entailed moving furniture, emptying the freezer and hoovering under the beds.

In the back of her mind Rose imagined being burgled while they were gone, and CID coming into her house and digging around in the grubby bits. What if they were killed in a crash and the house-clearance people moved the sofa?

Sometimes her irrational thoughts broke through the routine and drove her, like when she telephoned Michael's office and asked to speak to Belinda. She'd rehearsed the conversation aloud while cleaning the bath. Because the receptionists knew her voice she had to change it slightly, so she pinched her nose and tried to sound nasal.

My God. If anyone could have seen her standing by the phone with her legs crossed. She felt such a bloody fool. She was asked, 'Belinda who?' and put the phone down in a hurry, ashamed of herself.

Could there be more than one? It wasn't such a common name, surely?

She was determined to deal with this, an aberration, some paranoid part of her mind that had never surfaced before. It must be her age and the books she read. The stuff you watch on TV where nobody stays loyal to anyone any more. She considered her reactions to the notelet unhealthy; she was acting like some character in a soap. She should have come out and asked Michael straight, but on the Monday, when she'd rechecked his jacket the fatal envelope was gone, so he'd obviously been worried enough to move it.

No matter how hard she tried Rose couldn't remember if the love note had been addressed specifically to Michael. She'd read it so fast that she'd skipped the first bit, and yet she remembered the rest word for word. He could have picked it up in the drive to dispose of. Michael detested litter.

'Do we know anyone called Belinda?' she asked her friend, Jane, when next they spoke, the possibility being that the name might have slipped her mind. The girls were constantly joking that she was going senile since the time she absent-mindedly posted the letters in the litter bin down the road.

'No?' said Jane. 'Why? Should we?'

'No reason.' And Rose changed the subject.

She would be out shopping, her mind on her list, when the nagging doubt would come back to obsess her:

The message on that answerphone.

74

Michael had dialled that number.

There was no way Rose could dismiss that.

'You'd never leave me, would you?'

Michael turned over and switched off his light. Her remark was part of an ancient ritual. She'd made it so often over the years that it was meaningless now, which is why she could use it.

'You know I'd never leave you,' he sighed.

'Would you marry me now, if we'd just met?'

'Like a shot.'

'Love you,' said Rose.

'Love you,' said Michael.

She listened for some defensive tone, but there was none she could detect, just his breathing turning heavy and regular as he innocently slipped into sleep. Rose lay awake beside him and ached with the pain of deprivation.

Was it her over-possessiveness that was driving Michael away? She wasn't so distanced from her psyche that she didn't recognize her own failings, and over the years, as you do, she and Michael had talked and concluded that they could deal with anything.

Humour had helped, and the kids, of course. You can't get away with much with children. When they were small Rose had sometimes wondered who Daisy and Jessie would have chosen to go with if she and Michael had split up.

She was kidding herself. She knew the answer.

Michael was always the favourite, the calm and logical one, whereas she could be moody and over-emotional, blowing hot and cold. When she'd taken him up on that, he'd laughed and told her not to be silly. Her daughters adored her, and they did, she just used to wonder why she, as their mother, never came first with them.

She went to buy a new outfit for Venice. Strange, she chose black, a colour she'd never favoured before – a black skirt and jacket, cool and well cut. In the shop she looked good, in their special mirrors designed to make you look slim and healthy, but when she came home and stood in her bedroom her confidence slipped away.

Belinda. Belinda.

Who are you?

She went to have her highlights touched up.

'Going somewhere nice tonight, then?' asked Sonia, massaging Rose's head at the basin. Rose wished she'd stop; her neck ached.

But for once she could give a positive answer. 'Venice. Tomorrow. Can't wait.'

'You lucky thing,' said the toneless Sonia.

Rose gazed up at the girl's flawless face, so untouched by time and fags, at her thick hair, cut wildly like Jessie's, and the childish figure, all youth and energy underneath the overalls. You could hardly blame men for desiring this when you think they are programmed to scatter their seed on the most fertile ground available. Survival, that's what it's about after all.

If Michael left her would he have more children?

When she reached home Mrs H was just about finished in the kitchen.

'All ready for the holiday now, I expect?' she said,

hanging the J Cloth over the sink. 'Your hair looks nice. They do it well there. I must book myself in at Audrey's for a perm before Christmas.'

To Mrs H, who was in her mid-fifties, Rose's hair probably did look good. Unlike the cleaner's it was still shiny and had a recognizable style. Mrs H had gone down the road of pubic curls; hers was a short, permed scramble of brown, which signified that she had ceased to care. Rose would have liked to sit her down and ask at what point that had happened.

Had it been a deliberate decision or had Mrs H never bothered overmuch?

Mr Hargreaves, who often picked up his wife in his van, didn't seem to care either, and the thought that either of them would stray from the path of devoted matrimony would be unlikely to cross anyone's mind.

So where had Rose gone wrong?

She was putting the final touches to their suitcase – they had agreed to take only one, and already it was a bit of a squeeze; it would need all Michael's strength to close it – when the phone rang beside her.

'Hello?' Rose puffed.

'Is that Mrs Redfern?'

The tone was so direct it was shocking.

Rose answered cautiously, 'Yes, who is that?'

'You don't know me, Mrs Redfern, but my name is Belinda and I'd like to talk.'

Rose dropped stiffly to the bed. What was this? She couldn't believe it.

'What d'you mean? I don't know what you're—'

'Mrs Redfern, please believe me, I don't want to

77

be difficult or to cause you more pain, but I do think you need to know, and I'd like to help you understand. It's just that Michael and I are . . .'

How she despised that lilting accent. Rose gasped. 'I'm sorry, but I'm just not prepared—'

'Please, Mrs Redfern, just a moment of your time. Michael and I are seeing each other. We've got plans. We're in love. He'd have left you by now, but he's too caring. He's fond of you and that will never change, but some decisions have to be made; we can't all keep pretending nothing's changed. We've all got our futures to consider; we've all got things we'd like to say. Nobody wants this to happen with too much hurt for anyone involved . . .'

The next bit was lost to Rose through disbelief.

She wanted to bang down the phone, but couldn't. She wanted to find out more and yet she couldn't bear to listen. She suddenly remembered to breathe.

'I do hope you don't mind me ringing, but I feel we must talk, you and I. After all, we both love Michael and want the very best for him, and you have to understand that there are no victims here, no winners or losers, just human beings with feelings.'

Once again Rose lost the drift. With her free hand she smoothed out the duvet, trying to make it tidy and nice, the feel of the cotton was cool on her fingers.

'And your children, of course. They're in trouble, I know, both needy, both mixed up and very unhappy just now.'

Rose banged down the telephone.

If she wasn't sitting down she knew she'd have

fallen, twisted and flattened onto the floor. The dizziness overpowered her, and she let her head drop into her hands. This wasn't how she'd imagined things, not this sick concern pretended by this predatory stranger. And the nerve of it, to mention the kids; the things Michael must have confided to this sad drama queen.

There were no tears. In fact her eyes were quite dry. So dry they felt like grit in her head. She opened them wider and spotted a button that Mrs H must have missed when she'd hoovered in there that afternoon.

Rose reached out gratefully towards something normal. On all fours she crawled towards it over the carpet, like an aching old dog. She had no strength to go further, she just sat staring blankly into space.

What sort of woman would ring her like that? And now she'd phoned once, would she keep on ringing? Did Michael know that his Belinda had planned to do that? Would he come home as normal tonight?

And how about Rose? What should she do now?

Could she pretend that nothing had happened? Or would she have to confront her husband? She would do that if she thought she could bear the idea of him admitting his adultery and saying he wanted to leave her. Even if it meant living a lie, Rose just couldn't face that. Not yet.

She ought to get up, draw the curtains and make sure the doors were locked, but all her strength had been knocked out of her, and all she could do was sit and shiver as she'd done after Jessie's birth, her teeth chattering, limbs jerking. 'Shock, dear,' the midwife had said. 'Quite common.'

79

The bundle under the bed made her jump until her mind identified it. Calm down, calm down; it's just the wedding-dress bag, it's not going to hurt you. There's nothing in this house that's going to hurt you. Everything is familiar and safe. The voice on the phone was only a voice, and the rest was in Rose's head.

But the voice; it was as horrible as the sentiments – thick, guttural, breathy.

There was dust all over the wedding-dress bag. When was the last time she'd moved it? Rose dragged the bundle towards her. It was surprisingly light for such a large parcel and she trailed her fingers through the white dust, making hopeless patterns. She supposed she ought to have had the dress cleaned, but she hadn't bothered at the time, thinking she might do it one day. It must have her wedding smell on it, the perfume she'd worn, the flowers she'd carried, the musky memory of the day's heat, the champagne, the laughter, the sunshine.

'Please, please.' Now she needed to hold it close.

Slowly she unzipped the dress from its shroud-like casing. The effort involved in freeing the yards and yards of foaming material weakened her so that she could hardly go on, but she persevered and wasn't disappointed. In a rush the memories came back to her in a cloud of perfect white.

Music.

Kisses.

Smiles.

All wrapped in a gold marquee.

The little black bottles and ampoules were scattered around like beetles, with their claws sunk deep in the silky material. They were embedded in the veil and crawling over the stiffened petticoats; they were spattered on the spangled bodice and hidden in the voluminous sleeves. They spilled out all over the bedroom carpet and settled like hard growths of mould in the tufts.

Bottles and bottles of phenobarb. Three boxes of ampoules. And syringes.

Baggins.

If only he was here with her now. Oh how she missed him.

Finally the tears came, washing her eyes and freeing her terror.

She wished now that she'd held on to the phone and asked the questions she needed to have answered. How long had Michael been seeing Belinda? Where did they meet and when? Had they made plans about living together and when was he likely to leave? Would he go at once, or would they spend one last, miserable, edgy year trying not to say the wrong thing, missing all the connections?

The need to know focused her and her hand was steady when she redialled, only to get an answer-phone and that same guttural tone, made sweeter for strangers.

But the question she really wanted answered would have to be directed at Michael. Why do you suddenly hate me so?

Rose sank onto the carpet once again, with her hand clutched round a bottle of tablets. How many would she need to take before life slipped away and freed her from this hell? They were strong, she knew that; she had spent years watching their effect on her beloved Baggins, until she changed the treatment and gave him the knock-out jabs instead. Baggins, being a large heavy dog, needed high doses of the stuff, and yet there was plenty left.

Plenty for what?

She felt she was hanging on for dear life.

Rose couldn't bear the thought of living if she had to survive without Michael. Not knowing that he was alive and well and enjoying himself with somebody else, looking after somebody else, making love to somebody else, laughing and eating with somebody else.

Murder came to mind as she sat there, distraught, on the floor. Murder of Belinda, not him, and she knew she could do it, right now, if she could, using any weapon available, no matter how bloody or painful. She'd never get away with it, other people besides herself must know about Michael's carryings-on, and she would be the first person they'd look for.

Who else knew?

Oh the ache of it all. The telling her friends, she thought wearily. Their sympathy. What they'd say behind her back. The way they would separate into factions. She'd be the one left behind without a partner. Who would want her, alone and miserable, at their houses? She had seen this happen so many times to older, abandoned women.

She grasped the bottle of tablets more tightly and played with a wrapped syringe. If she attempted suicide surely he wouldn't leave her? Michael was too kind to do anything so cruel. How often she had been exasperated by Michael's too-soft heart.

But was it?

The very fact that he had been seeing Belinda

made him a man she no longer knew, and Rose could no longer predict his reactions.

But she loved him so. How she ached.

She skidded around, slipping on mangled thoughts. She imagined how reasonable he would try to be in the face of her desperation. She would lament and rage and look ugly, snot down her face, swollen-eyed, while he sat quietly beside her, probably holding her, whispering words of encouragement and sorrow.

Merciless and passive.

'It just happened,' he'd say, and then give a lengthy explanation. She could hear him now. 'I never wanted to hurt you.' All those old meaningless platitudes you're left with when there's no more truths.

And the world would expect her to be reasonable, after a given amount of time, to discuss the situation like an adult, to pull herself together, to get on with her life, even to enjoy her new-found freedom and find a new role for herself. How Rose had always sneered at the women who said that in magazines. 'I'm a new person now, with lots of friends and a brand-new career in front of me. He did me a favour by leaving. I found myself at last.'

Well bollocks and good luck to them. Rose wasn't like that.

She was struck by a sudden thought, which broke through the tears and left her sniffing. She slowly opened her hand, finger by finger, every one wet from her crying. She unscrewed the top of the bottle and the white pills made a pile on the carpet.

A little pyramid of death.

Or helplessness.

Or sleep.

Why her? Why not Michael?

She thought about Baggins' last month, spent in a semi-conscious state, only able to amble round with his sight half gone and his sense of smell departed. He ate OK and he walked, but only slowly. He was alive, but similar to an old dog one of the neighbours had, who'd suffered from a stroke. Michael told the neighbour, 'You should put him down; it's not fair.'

How would the drug work on a human?

And how could she give a jab? In the hand?

She'd had ways and means of tempting Baggins with the pills. Baggins could never refuse a chunk of cheese, no matter how bad he was feeling. And when she gave him his shots he was always too far gone to care. One thing Rose was sure of, after the first dose, if she got it right, the second would prove no problem. After the first dose the victim, dog or man, would be powerless.

She even managed a smile and caught sight of herself in the long mirror. She sat up straighter and stared. Her shoes had fallen off, her newly done streaky blond hair was roughed up and tossed, her mascara ran like sloppy graffiti and her lipstick was smeared down her chin. She sagged and her body looked huge. Her own startled eyes frightened her.

So bright.

So angry.

She looked like a mad woman, and maybe she was; driven to lunacy after thirty years by the man who had promised to love and protect her.

SIX

Why here?

Why now?

Why must life be so cruelly perverse?

She wanted him to say, 'Listen, Rose . . .'

She wanted him to explain.

This was a masquerade.

From the moment they stepped on the water taxi off a landing stage at the airport Rose felt masked, cloaked and feathered, outrageous, like a carnival queen, devious, cruel and cold. Venice itself opened its heart as it rose from a sun-washed mist, promising more than she'd ever hoped for. The city of lovers sucked them in with its façades of pastels and golds, and she stared hard at the winged lion that marked the famous square, a symbol of oppression that had been allowed to continue to stand by virtue of its magnificence.

It seemed to confirm her belief that destruction of something that had been wonderful was no real salvation. Far better to accommodate the good, to see and admire it, but most of all to keep it intact, in full view. Which is what she intended to do with her husband.

They slid narrowly towards their hotel, the silver canal water lapping beside them, under bridges, past elegant cafés with flowers tumbling down the steep walls while an orchestra disturbed the air somewhere in the distance.

One glance at Michael's disbelieving face told her he was as dazzled as she was.

She felt steeped in intrigue, like a wicked queen, when the concierge came to greet her as she stepped up to the landing stage leading straight into the foyer of their hotel. How delighted Rose would have been if the last week of her life hadn't existed. It would have been perfection for them, and she went along with his delight as they threw themselves down on their canopied bed, laughing in excitement, like two big kids. From the small canal below their window, through the heavy closed shutters, along with the sweetish scent of sewage came the song of a passing gondolier, 'O Solo Mio'.

'I can't believe we're here,' said Michael, relishing the whole experience.

'Neither can I. It's a miracle.' And she hit him playfully with a pillow.

A miracle, oh yes.

And as far as Rose was concerned, it was. She had managed to keep up this happy pretence since Michael had come home last night. Such enormous deception. How she did it she would never know, and she had to assume that Belinda hadn't mentioned her vicious phone call to him.

All the time she was expecting him to turn on his serious face and tell her he couldn't come with her to Venice, something else had cropped up, or maybe he would bring her a drink and try, gently, to tell her the truth. She watched him like a hawk for clues, but his behaviour seemed absolutely normal. He was more devious than she had ever imagined, so callous, so deceitful.

Quickly, so as to waste no time, they unpacked into the sparse three drawers and one small hanging chest. Rose struggled to keep her mind on the job and away from the awful plan that was forming in her head, a plan she considered so bizarre she believed it to be a fantasy. It fitted well into this fairytale place.

She used it as a defence against pain, that's why it must have surfaced.

Pentobarbitone.

But not yet. Oh no.

She pretended to be brave and strong, as she had all of her life. This time she had the strangest feeling she was turning into somebody else as they set off together, arm in arm, jubilant and full of energy. It seemed as if they walked for miles, and every step brought them closer, infected by the beauty around them and the atmosphere of romance.

But for Rose every step made her feel worse: this was not a city to visit without a lover.

She imagined herself, in the future, returning here with a couple of girlfriends, pointing out the places she and Michael had visited. She wished they had come here on their honeymoon and not gone to Bermuda, which had been cold, with a sea full of Portuguese men of war, so they hadn't been able to swim.

Michael bought her a blue rose from a man with an armful in every colour. She wondered why he had chosen blue, the saddest colour in the world. Was there a message behind his choice?

This searching for signs was wearing her out.

Jessie had rung that morning, just before they were due to leave.

'Look after each other,' she said. Had she guessed?

'We will, don't worry,' Rose had assured her. Jessie, her youngest, her pride and joy. What would Jessie's reaction be if she knew what her mother was thinking? She had tried to be brave and strong for her children but it's hard when you love them so desperately. She wanted to give them the perfect childhood; she wanted lambs in the fields for them always.

'So why did you never tell me', she asked him, 'that you harboured this yearning to fly?'

Michael laughed dismissively. 'It was never a yearning, more of a small desire.'

Michael was surprised when Rose insisted he buy her a mask from one of the many elaborate shops that fashioned them on the premises. She would have liked to go the whole hog and demand a cloak and hood, a feathered headdress and the golden dress to match.

'But you'll never wear it. It's a waste of money. I thought you were after a handbag.'

'I might wear it,' said Rose demurely, holding it up to her eyes. 'If we get asked to a fancy-dress party.' The devil disguise with the skeletal head would have suited Michael perfectly, but she bit her lip and kept silent. 'And I've got a whole week to find a good handbag.'

Inside Rose felt manic, determined to drain the last drop of romance from this, their last holiday together.

That night they dined beside the canal, under the Rialto bridge. They shared Antipasto di Frutti di Mare, drank wine and held hands, with the blue rose lying between them on the table. When Rose had to blink away the tears she didn't need to provide a reason. Michael thought he understood. The setting alone would make anyone weep.

She soon put paid to his miserly habits which, although dulled over the years, still surfaced at motorway cafés, hotel bars and smart boutiques. 'But this is ridiculous,' he would say, glaring at the price but knowing the reasons as well as she did. She no longer bothered to argue that the prices reflected the ambience, the chandeliers and the service. She merely smiled and said, 'Don't start, of course the prices are outrageous. You knew that before you came.'

They ordered liqueurs with their coffee in the Piazza San Marco, and when he frowned at the bill she ignored him and told him she fancied another. Gradually Michael began to relax and throw his money around as recklessly as the next man. They sat until after midnight listening to the orchestra, with the stars above their heads silver in the black square of sky.

She held the blue rose in her hand and squeezed the stem till the thorns dug in.

On their stroll home they stopped to smooch in the centre of the piazza, just one of dozens of couples of all ages and races, moved by the magic of the music.

Gradually the pretence became easier.

That night they made love – of course they did – and when he turned over and dropped off to sleep, the thought of being here without a man left Rose wakeful, cold and frightened. OK, this wasn't a feminist attitude, she knew she ought to be able to rally and enjoy life just as well on her own – maybe more, as the magazines told her. Try as she might Rose couldn't believe it. She was a weak and feeble woman; it wasn't any man she needed, it was someone familiar, who knew her like Michael.

Gothic, Byzantine, Renaissance, Baroque, bold ornamentation, garlands, swags and cherubs and grotesque masks, buildings and paintings. They saw them all and they still had the islands to visit. She was sure they had crossed all 400 bridges. Day three, and Michael was after more culture. Awed, she had stood beside him in the Basilica di San Marco until her neck felt twisted by all that staring at ceilings. She had spent three hours in the Doge's Palace, oddly attracted by the prisons and especially the *Pozzi*, the dark dank dungeons with their rusting black bars and freezing atmosphere of terror. The old graffiti was still there. She followed the writing with her finger and shivered. Man's cruelty to man and animal had always appalled Rose, but this time she could see some point in keeping someone securely confined, for his own good, if necessary.

The sad side of life.

She began to look for it.

She noticed early the barred windows and closed shutters in the houses at night, so many of them empty, weekend homes for rich men and the death of real life. She was unreasonably upset by the sight of the lagoon lapping its way into vaulted doorways at high tides, the black, rotten damage of damp and decay and the beggars in the streets. But at the same time she felt resigned to it all.

She'd told him to pack his most comfortable shoes, but Michael moaned about his blisters. Normally Rose would have sympathized; she would have worried about him, genuinely concerned and sad to think of him in any kind of pain. But now things were different. She almost hated him. No, that's not true, she really did hate him at times. Rose was shocked to experience a stab of glad satisfaction when she saw his mouth twist in pain and his left foot hobbling slightly.

What was she turning into?

And so quickly?

She left him at a waterbus stop. He headed back towards the hotel and a *farmacia* along the route. He asked for the phrase book. 'Just show them your foot,' she told him. 'Anyway, they all speak English.' She might need the phrase book herself.

He said, 'Don't worry. I'll be fine when I've got a plaster on.'

She was going to look for a handbag, and they'd agreed to meet for a lobster lunch at La Caravella.

Rose had spotted the Ospedale Civile on one of their many waterbus rides. A fifty-two would take her straight there. She headed there now and disembarked. She was awed by the grandeur of the place, its mighty arcades, its marble panels, and the two lions of St Mark guarding its massive doorway. The façade rang a bell, and she suddenly remembered watching the news when Michael Heseltine was brought out of here after his heart attack. The elegant entrance hall was crowded with people; there were queues in the emergency department, mostly fussing relatives and children running, chewing slabs of pizza. It was even more disorganized and chaotic than the National Health, and this boded well for Rose.

She hung around the reception area, so cool after the heat outside, glancing earnestly at her watch in the way she imagined it ought to be done, trying to be anonymous. And when she snatched the form off the pile her heart was banging out of control, but nobody took the slightest notice. She saw a boxful of envelopes, half open; it took all her courage to casually remove one and walk towards the huge double doors.

It wouldn't take her long, with the help of Michael's computer, to turn the form into a credible headed page, and the envelope, blank but so obviously foreign and thin, would add the finishing touch she needed.

On her way to meet Michael, her plunder safely in her bag, she sat watching Venice go by in a turmoil of emotion. A French family riding beside her chatted together in ceaseless excitement, nudging her with their camera each time they tried to take a picture.

It wasn't a hot day but her hands were sweating. She lit up a fag and puffed at it desperately. Never before had she stolen from anyone. She pulled herself up; oh yes, once she'd stolen drugs from a vet.

She was acting out phase one of her fantasy like somebody with personality problems who needed urgent treatment. Maybe, she thought, she had needed to do this as a vehicle for ridding herself of her rage. Control was what she must aim for now, but Venice wasn't proving to be a great reminder of stark reality. Here, in this wonderland, everything felt unreal.

'Did you find one?'

He got up to help her to her chair, something he'd always done for her and which these days made him seem special. He looked so good in his new black shirt, which he'd laughed at when she showed him. Trying to make him look Italian, more like the Mafiosa, he'd said, donning his sunglasses and posing.

'Did I find what?'

'Your handbag.'

'They were all too expensive.'

She ought to have known this didn't make sense. She had promised herself a splendid new handbag from the moment he'd told her they were going.

'Too up-market,' Rose tried to backtrack. 'Too formal, all hard with gold clips. You know I like a baggy one.'

The hospital form hidden in her purse felt as if it was burning through the leather.

She stared at him as he poured her wine and she couldn't believe what she'd just done. How often her fingers had stroked that so familiar, friendly face; she knew all the moods of those soft brown eyes; even his toughening eyebrows – one of his tricks which amused the girls, was to pull one hair down to his mouth like Denis Healey. Disgusting they said, laughing, grimacing.

'How's the blister?' she asked, trying to sound as if she cared.

'Fine,' said Michael, believing her. 'I've got to slow down a bit. I'm trying to do it all in one go.'

She got out her cards and began to write them while they waited for the meal to be served. It was easier than sitting there and trying to make small talk with him. She had bought cards for friends; he had none, but then he'd never bothered with cards, even for his sisters in the US. She was the one who kept in contact, never forgetting them at birthdays or Christmas. She made him write a few words to the girls, and he wrote Dinah's; she'd like that.

'I can't say wish you were here,' he said about her mother. 'When you think she can hardly walk. Venice isn't a good place for the infirm; most of the bridges have steps.'

'Sad,' Rose mused, 'to think this is somewhere Mum will never see. But then, she'd only moan. She'd hate the food and the crowds.'

'Seeing all this, she might change,' said Michael hopefully. 'She'd enjoy the decadence.'

'You need to be here with a man,' said Rose.

'I'm glad I'm here with you.'

'Are you?' Rose looked up and waited, giving him an opening.

'Of course,' said Michael, rubbing his hands when he saw the arriving lobster. 'Who else would I want to be with but you?' He beckoned to a passing rose seller, but she said, 'No, it's a waste.' Back at the hotel the blue one lay already half dead in the sink.

So that was the end of that conversation. Rose was no further forward.

That night they took a gondola ride, choosing to go silent rather than have an accompanying accordion player/singer. They heard enough of them at nights, the singing went on into early morning. As they reclined on the red velvet seats Michael held her hand. Other pairs of lovers floated by, the water hardly moving, so skilled were the gondoliers. If only she could lie there and ask him by making her questions part of the scene.

'Who is Belinda?' That's all she need say to end this torture one way or another, like leaping from a cliff, but those three dreadful words wouldn't come.

She might as well say, 'Kill me now.'

Rose dare not let them pass her lips. She feared his lies and his awful confusion. Denial would be impossible after that phone call, after the notelet and after she'd redialled his last call.

So she lay back beside him in the dark, with just the tiny red light to illuminate their pathway under the bridges of the lagoon. Was she the first victim to pass underneath that notorious Bridge of Sighs to a fate she considered much worse than death? The story goes that Casanova escaped through a hole in the roof. Maybe Rose could do that, too?

She made the same excuse to go off on her own the next day. She still needed that special handbag, and he had to visit another palazzo which a colleague from work had recommended.

'Do you mind?' she asked him.

'Not at all.'

She mingled with the pigeons, in every way as grey as they were.

She bought an ice cream and watched the crowds.

A party of Italian students sat on the steps to sketch the Campanile, a tall brick tower which Rose thought hideous. She brought out the Filofax Michael had bought her three years ago. She never used the calendar bits – her life wasn't that busy and the dates soon ran out – instead she used those pages for notes.

She sat beside a black-eyed boy who must have been about eighteen years old. He didn't seem to mind when she looked over his shoulder at his sketch. She nodded and smiled, then lit a cigarette and handed him one from the packet.

He smiled back. 'English?'

They all recognized the English. They saw them coming from a distance; she and Michael were always greeted by a clear 'good evening' at every restaurant. It was shameful how everyone here seemed to speak some English – the Germans, Dutch, French and, of course, the Venetians themselves.

'Yes,' and Rose lied. 'I'm an author and I wondered if you would do me a favour?'

As she suspected, he understood.

'What sort of books do you write?' His English was sure and precise.

'Romances,' she said. 'Mostly medical.'

He laughed and said something in his own language.

'I want to write a letter in Italian,' she started to explain, watching to make sure he understood. 'It's a letter to a doctor about a patient he's recently seen.'

The dark-haired boy nodded.

'If I read it out in English, could you translate it into Italian for me, do you think?'

She hung on his answer.

'*Prego*. No problem.' She should have expected that phrase. It must be one of the most used in Venice.

Rose couldn't get over her luck at having such success first time. She had been prepared to spend most of the day in the square if necessary, until she found someone who would oblige her.

She passed him her pen, the silver one Michael had given her. The letter was short and to the point, and it took no longer than ten minutes.

The boy seemed happy to help, perhaps her desperation was showing and he was afraid of a scene. He asked no questions, only her name, the name she used to write under. She gave him her own and he said he would look out for her books. She commented that she doubted very much that they were translated into Italian.

She left him to his sandwiches and to complete his picture. When she looked back he was flapping off pigeons, who had got wind of his bread and cheese. She wondered which must be most annoying, the birds or the flocks of tourists.

Rose sat down at a café on her own to try and gather her wits. Angrily she stubbed out her sixth cigarette of the day. She ordered a large Martini with ice. She had three more days. Three more days to accomplish the rest of her plan and then there would be no going back.

Still she couldn't recognize this other, alien self

which had, over the last few days, taken her over and controlled her thoughts and actions. In her heart of hearts she felt safe, believing she was incapable; she hadn't the stamina or harshness to carry through such a monstrous idea.

She swirled the hard ice round in her glass, saw it tumble against the sides, so hopeless, swimming for its life. Already it was half gone, had disappeared into the clear liquid, leaving no trace.

Something mutant was lurking inside her, something she must overcome to avoid what she saw starkly as a creeping madness.

Rose swigged down the rest of her drink, then got up carefully, making sure her legs would support her before heading back towards the hotel.

SEVEN

All the rain and wind you could wish for on a typical English October day drenched and blew Daisy as she hurried from her car.

Although the house wasn't isolated, there were neighbours within a few hundred yards on either side, the tall wooden fence which surrounded it was rotten and broken down in places by fully grown trees, elms, ash and chestnut, which overhung the garden borders.

Seymour House, a white square of Thirties' architecture, must once have been the latest word, with its stark angles, flat roofs and metal French windows which led from the upstairs bedrooms onto a wrought-iron balcony. Daisy eyed the windows; they were a bone of contention between Mum and Dad, as he had a horror of double glazing and refused to install up-to-date replacements. Mum said they leaked and were an open invitation to thieves. Daisy switched on alternative lights, as if any burglar worth his salt would be fooled by such a ploy.

Seymour House was large and homely inside, welcoming with its wide open spaces on three levels, stripped floors and colourful rugs. It was here that Daisy and Jessie had enjoyed a blissful childhood. For Daisy it would have been more blissful if naughty Jessie had never arrived.

Daisy paused, tempted for just a moment to get out one of the old home videos and watch her favourite days, her baby days – sunshine and paddling pools, prams and windmills, when Daddy would throw her up in the air; she loved to see the look on his face. She hurried on, there was no time for this.

The garden was a child's paradise. An old treehouse, built by Michael, still housed the tiny handpainted cups and saucers Daisy and Jessie had used as children until Jessie broke off most of the handles in a tantrum. There were deep dens in the rhododendrons, a pond which they used as a newt farm, a rusting swing and a sandpit covered with a piece of broken fencing. There were still vast holes once dug by Baggins, and Baggins' grave lay in one shady corner still, with its jam jar of coloured leaves and a tattered union jack.

Baggins' funeral was beautifully childish because it was the end of an era, and to make things all the more poignant the moon had been full that night.

Daisy had promised to check on the house a couple of times while her parents were in Venice. Her room, and Jessie's, were still untouched, as if the ether were wordlessly waiting for the spirit of the wallpaper to come back.

The neighbours weren't the prying kind. They were middle-aged professional people with old-fashioned family values who kept themselves to themselves, except for once a year, at Christmas, when the Flocktons invited their neighbours for pre-luncheon drinks. Most of them had lived in the road for over twenty years and had seen their children grow up and leave. Of the ten smart houses in the road, two of the owners were now retired, three had teenage children at home and five were lived in by couples whose children had flown the nest.

They weren't the type to leave their homes and move to something smaller; they could pay for cleaners and gardeners. Most of their offspring had good careers and didn't need their help, save for cars on twenty-first birthdays, the odd contribution towards a deposit and trusts for emerging grandchildren.

Most voted Conservative, had Range-Rovers parked on their drives and were contented with their lots.

Daisy warmed herself up against the old Aga, in which so many family meals had been cooked. Nothing enterprising or experimental, because Rose swore that Michael preferred his meat and two veg, just as she bought him traditional clothes, mostly from Marks & Spencer.

Michael seemed to approve. He never complained and he praised every dish Rose brought to the table.

Why couldn't Daisy find someone like that?

When Jessie had telephoned the day before, Daisy had picked it up without thinking.

She'd laughed, 'It's such a relief with Mum away. I don't have to wait for the answerphone and I don't have to get into long conversations and make excuses for not going over.'

'Mum rang me last night,' said Jessie.

'Oh? Whatever for?'

'Oh, the usual how are you and is the house OK and we're having a wonderful time. Well, it was Dad who rang, did the dialling and got through, Mum couldn't deal with the system. But Mum soon took over.'

'She does.'

'But she really rang to remind me we've got to see Granny before they get back. We promised we'd go over. So when would be the best time for you?'

'Oh damn. Do we have to?' For Daisy it was a busy week.

Jessie sighed. 'For God's sake, let's keep the peace.'

'It would be easier to go over to her house.'

'I'll ring her,' said Jessie. 'How about Friday night? We could pop in before supper and then it would be done.'

Daisy said, 'Are you OK? You sound very flustered.'

There was a pause before Jessie replied in a hushed voice, 'Belinda's back.'

Daisy gasped. 'Oh God, no.'

'She didn't see me,' Jessie explained. 'But I was sure it was her. Outside Boots on her own, wearing that same old gold velvet curtain.'

Daisy asked, 'But she's not back at college?'

'Oh no. She wouldn't come back. But what's she doing back in this area?'

'God knows.'

The strain in Jessie's voice was obvious. 'Where is

she staying? As far as I knew she didn't know anyone from round here. She lives in Cardiff. That's where she comes from.'

'How long is it now?'

'About six months since I last saw her.'

'Look,' said Daisy, sounding confident. 'You mustn't worry, Jessie. She's not likely to come on to you again. I thought she'd had treatment.'

'That was the rumour.'

'It must have given you one hell of a shock.'

Jessie paused again. 'Honestly, I nearly collapsed, seeing her suddenly like that. I've started locking my bedroom door. And I look around before I get into the car. Stupid, but when you think of some of the things she said.'

'Yep. She was profoundly weird.' Daisy had to ask, 'Does Jasmine know?' She would have liked to go on and enquire as to the nature of this new relationship, but of course you don't. Jessie had been incredibly embarrassed when the story first came out – all that sexual stuff – she'd hate her older sister to raise the subject again.

Maybe Jessie was queer. William said he thought it unlikely. He said it was a phase. But the large and bouncy Jasmine Smith, in maroon tracksuit and trainers, would certainly fit the bill.

'No,' Jessie said quickly. 'And I don't want her to know. I don't even want to remember it myself, let alone pass it on.'

On Friday night Daisy collected Jessie from college and they drove over to Blue Waters.

Not that Granny needed a visit, she coped perfectly well on her own, but ever since the midge bite

103

that went unreported and caused a small infection, Mum was fanatical, never letting more than a week go by without checking on her.

Granny, in her high-backed chair, was watching *Watchdog* when they arrived and refused to turn it off.

'Are you staying for supper?'

She knew they weren't and it was her way of rubbing it in.

'Well pop my lasagne in the oven so it's ready when this is finished.'

Jessie took the postcard off the mantelpiece and read it. 'They're having a brilliant time.'

Granny, irritated by the disturbance, stared at the telly and refused to answer.

Since Grandpa's death on the way back from Portugal all those years ago, Granny had not been on holiday, although she'd often been invited to go with Rose and Michael. 'Holidays just aren't my scene. They never really were. I only went because I felt I ought to. From the moment we left these shores, me and John, we argued, and Portugal was the worst. All the way back from Guarda to Santander, all that long drive across the hot Spanish plains, was all done in total silence. Rose hated it the silly thing. She got ludicrously upset if we argued, which we only did when we went away. We'd only just started speaking again when John died.'

Now Dinah went on daytrips instead with her spry old friend Sarah.

Daisy shivered. She'd been feeling out of sorts for days. She sneezed and said, 'I think I've got flu.'

If she wanted sympathy she was disappointed.

Watchdog was over and Granny clicked off the TV and readjusted her leg on the stool. 'That's what everyone says these days. They call it flu when it's just a cold. Real flu, now that's quite rare. In all my life I don't know anyone who's had real flu but me. When you've got real flu you can't move.'

Daisy didn't bother to remind her that Rose had had flu the day Jamie died.

'What I need is a holiday,' said Daisy, gazing absently at the gondola postcard.

'They didn't ring *me*,' Granny said accusingly when Jessie told her about the call, unable to see that the very last person anybody would want to contact when they were off having fun was Granny. She'd bring anyone down with her gruff remarks. Joy was something she had forgotten.

Dad used pain as her excuse. How frustrating it must be, he said, to have arthritis and sleepless nights and corns. But Dad made excuses for everyone; he looked for the good and ignored the bad. Look at the way he favoured Jessie.

Why hadn't Granny moved house after her only son was killed at the end of her riverside garden? You'd think it would be unendurable, looking out at the gruesome spot where her little boy had gone to his death and where curlews rustled and remonstrated from their nests in the brambles. From the sitting-room window and the tall chair Dinah sat in, you could see the garden drop away at the end, the space filled in places with the high tips of broken pines.

A wooden seat was positioned in an arbour of hydrangeas overlooking the very spot where Jamie's bike had flown. Granny said they used to sit there, she and John, for hours in silence, listening to the waves lapping in, toppling and tumbling over and over as the tide came in and the river bed gurgled, mourning their child.

Mum said she didn't remember that. Was that denial or the truth?

And sometimes now, on summer evenings, Rose would go with Granny and two large glasses of sherry and sit on that seat beside her. Swapping memories? Or listening, so silent they heard the fishes breathe and the little crabs scuttle.

Daisy didn't know how she did it. She couldn't have borne to go with them; the whole thing was too tragic.

Framed photographs of her twins still haunted Granny's house. Had neither of them ever been photographed alone? It would seem not. From baby to toddler to school-age child, their identical faces appeared together, and after Jamie's death, at ten, they seemed to have stopped having portraits done, because there were none of Rose on her own. Not until she got married, and then, of course, she was paired off again, or joined by her two daughters.

'And where is sweet William tonight?'

'Working.'

'That boy is a workaholic. No future for you there.'

Daisy sighed. Granny would be the first to moan if William was constantly hanging around; if he was jobless she'd go spare. Either she liked to insinuate that Daisy was being used, or she did it purely to annoy. Either way she made sly enquiries about who paid for what, suggesting that William was 'on to a good thing' and 'knew which side his bread was buttered'. There was no point in trying to explain that they shared the bills equally, that money was no big issue between them and that it was none of her business anyway.

If Granny found out about Jessie and Belinda she'd be in her element.

Mum swore that Granny's sourness had developed over the last few years. She had been a devoted mother, determined to rise above life's torments for the sake of her precious daughter, and that was the reason Rose was so patient with her nowadays. Objectionable, Granny might be, but Rose played the selfless daughter and made sure her children followed her example. Otherwise why would they be there now?

There was no pleasure in her company nowadays.

Granny insisted on moving to the table to eat her lasagne, even though she said her knee still hurt after having had the bits of gristle flushed out. She had to lean on Daisy and Jessie to get there, thus ensuring they would have to stay with her until she'd finished.

The table had to be laid precisely to her satisfaction, and the food had to be nicely presented – no dishing it up in the kitchen.

Jessie and Daisy caught each other's eyes. She was artful. If they weren't there they knew very well she would have managed to bring the food through and sit quite happily in her chair, eating from the adjustable table.

They watched her munching deliberately slowly. From the beginning she must have sensed their urgency to be off: Jessie had an essay to do and Daisy was decorating her flat.

'There's plenty left if you'd like some,' said Granny.

Daisy left the room. She hated her, really hated her; she just couldn't stand Granny any longer.

Granny didn't hide her annoyance when Jessie's mobile rang. Her eyebrows came together and her mouth almost reached her chin. Jessie started to leave the room while wrestling the gadget from her back pocket, but Granny stopped her by saying, 'What's the matter? Got something to hide?'

How ridiculously infantile, but Jessie resolutely sat back in her chair. She reddened, half got up and sat down again. Just the reactions that Granny enjoyed.

Her voice was low, but not low enough. 'Oh no, that's awful.'

Then a silence as Jessie made folds in the table-cloth.

'I can't. You know I can't.'

She tried a weak smile. No name was mentioned. Granny, eavesdropping with no sense of shame, left her fork on her plate and waited.

'Tomorrow, or as soon as I can.'

Jessie grew more uncomfortable. Where had Daisy gone? She could have started some conversation, provided a little cover.

'Well, I'm so, so sorry this has happened. I'll speak to you later,' said Jessie at last and turned off her mobile.

'Trouble?' asked Granny, dabbing her chin.

'No more than normal.'

'Some boy, no doubt?'

Jessie smiled weakly. ' 'Fraid so.'

'Well, you should have taken it out of the room if it was so private. Huh. Embarrassing everybody like that.'

Jessie fumed in the car. 'Bloody hell she's a witch. I hate the hold she's got on us. I hate the way we have to kowtow just for Mum's sake – that's why we do it.'

'Chill out,' Daisy smiled. 'You made her day.'

'Well that's great then. I've done my duty.'

'Who was it anyway? On the phone?'

'It was Jasmine Smith. Booming. I'm surprised you didn't hear her.'

Daisy fixed her eyes on the road. 'Oh no, Jessie, don't tell me.'

'No!' protested Jessie. 'It's far from what you're thinking. Jasmine's straight; she's good fun, but she's just had a freaky phone call. Belinda. Can you believe it?'

'Why would Belinda . . . ?'

'You tell me. Oh God. And she sounds just as screwed up as ever . . .'

'I can't believe . . .'

'Nor can I. But it's true. She's been warning Jasmine about me. Slagging me off, saying I'm sick, that I ruined her life, that I'm an oversexed psycho luring Jasmine into my bed in the same way I lured her.'

Jessie stopped, too choked up to go on, and Daisy was out of answers.

Jessie stammered on through her tears. 'Well, she's back all right, and what else will she do?

Who else will she tell to get her revenge? Just when I thought it was all over.'

'Surely you can talk to Jasmine.'

Jessie, exasperated, shouted, 'I know! I know that! Jasmine'll be OK when I explain what happened. I hope. It's what happens next that puts the shit up me. I've only just got rid of the labels, I'm only just being accepted again by the rest of the group. The jokes, you know, the innuendoes. And now . . . God knows what that sick cow is planning to do. I mean, how did she know I was friends with Jasmine?'

'Don't be thick. She'll have seen you around.'

'What? You think she's been watching me? Without me knowing? *Again*? And that she dug around – nothing better to do – until she found where Jasmine hung out, and then made it her business to dial her number?'

Daisy scanned her brain to think of something useful to say. 'The more effect she has on you, the more delighted Belinda will be. You mustn't over-react. I'm trying to remember the things we've read or seen on TV about stalkers. They seem to follow a similar pattern. God, sometimes they go on for years. The police can't do much about them despite the new laws to protect their victims. Some are so sick they kill.'

'Great. Thanks Daisy. I love the way you're so reassuring. But is Belinda a stalker or just a sad woman after revenge? "Hell hath no fury like a woman scorned."'

No greater fury, or no greater love?

There must be a psychological difference, but where did the boundaries lie?

110

Maybe the police should be told?

No, said Jessie; she would never agree. The only sensible solution was that Jessie should seek out Belinda and try to reason with her again. Exactly what was Belinda after? It was the powerlessness of the thing that felt so defeating.

'Swear to me you won't tell a soul?'

'Of course not. You don't need to ask me.' Daisy tried to sound encouraging. 'Jessie, come round to the flat for a drink. Stay the night. It's Saturday tomorrow.'

'Just take me back.'

'I don't like to leave you.'

'I'm OK.' Jessie gave a weak smile, but under the streetlight her face was ashen; her eyes stared from it darkly. Daisy waited until she went through the door of the college's student quarters.

Her younger sister looked frail and helpless – that made a change.

It was obvious what Jessie was thinking: either this was Belinda's last desperate fling or the start of something which could get very nasty.

EIGHT

If she did this thing, if Rose actually did this diabolical, monstrous thing, what the hell would that turn her into? Every thought and action now seemed to be infected by the spreading spoors of this festering plot.

No sane woman in the world would have the slightest sympathy with Rose's outrageous intentions. The fact that she was weak and afraid, that she loved her intended victim, that she was already sweating and terrified of inflicting any kind of permanent injury on him, would not enter into the equation.

She could imagine the judge's words should the matter come to trial. 'Rosalind Allison Tate' – the use of Rose's maiden name seemed more apt; something to do with school – 'rarely in all my years of experience have I witnessed such calculated, selfish cruelty. And all towards a man whose decency, love and kindness has been testified to so many times before me in this court today. You are a wicked, predatory woman and a danger to society. I intend to show you no mercy, just as you showed none to your husband. Take her down.'

She would have to plead insanity.

And yet Rose was quite surprised that more women hadn't tried it before. She'd certainly never heard of any.

If she had been a battered wife, women's groups would come out in her support. The press would be sympathetic and her friends would testify to her good character.

But the fact was that, in Rose's eyes, abandonment felt worse than battering, the results far more long lasting and painful than a few broken ribs and black eyes. All that fear in the night those poor women must experience, but the tears and loneliness that would haunt Rose for the rest of her days as a result of Michael's betrayal must be equal to that in every way.

After thirty years.

A lifetime.

And yet she couldn't stop loving him, although she could never forgive him.

She pressed Michael to phone home from Venice so that she could see how the system worked. Yes, she was that unworldly.

'We're only here for three more days. What's the point?' he grumbled.

'I know I'm being silly, but I need to feel reassured. Pander to me, please, just this once. Use Jessie's answerphone. Then we'll know we'll get an answer.'

She watched carefully, sitting beside him on the bed as he dialled what seemed like hundreds of numbers. She would need to do this herself before long and she'd have to get it right. She even copied down the numbers.

'Just in case,' she told him.

He smiled, loving her for her motherly concern.

Of course there was no reason to phone them and Jessie sounded vaguely surprised. Michael soon ran out of chat, so Rose took over convincingly, full of the holiday, full of interest – had Jessie checked the house? Had they been to see Dinah yet? Don't forget what happened last time we left Granny for a fortnight. The insect bite . . .

'I know, Mum. I know.'

'She's not as confident as you think.'

'Who is?' groaned Jessie.

'We've walked for miles. We feel quite achey,' Rose remembered to add. 'We've taken some brilliant photographs.'

'Spare us those, please, Mum,' said Jessie.

There was a horrible, morbid list of things Rose had to do if she was prepared to go through with her scheme. And all with Michael so close beside her.

The lists she was more used to were those for Christmas presents, shopping at Safeway, letters to write and bills to pay. She ticked off each stage in her head while the sane side of her brain assured her that this was only a game she was playing and that it could easily remain a game. She had no need to make it real. The only pressure was of her own making.

She calculated the dosages over and over in her head. It was essential she got this right. Baggins had weighed 100 pounds and needed 120mgs of pills twice a day to keep the fits at bay.

They failed.

She'd started giving him jabs, not as a preventative but as a cure. She worked out that a fifteen-stone man would need 22mgs for thirty-six hours' effect.

At fifteen stones – more than double Baggins' weight – she would need to give Michael 400mgs of Phenobarb by mouth each day to render him helpless. As the tablets were 60mgs each, she would need to force down four each morning and four each night. Too much. She would have to use the jabs and tablets for top-up purposes.

She'd rather be left with a cabbage than nothing at all.

The hospital form was safe in her handbag, the Italian letter folded beside it.

But she never seriously intended to carry out this crazy farce.

Did she?

Well, for goodness' sake. She was a forty-eight-year-old mother of two, a woman who did good works, a loyal and caring wife, a supportive and dutiful daughter.

Nothing she'd done before was irreversible; she had to remember that. All she was doing was defending herself in the best way she knew how against the very worst scenario Rose could possibly imagine: Michael leaving her for another woman.

The thought of that wrung out her guts.

It racked her.

It serrated her, and she simply couldn't accept it.

She certainly wasn't closed minded about it. She'd given Michael every opportunity to bring up the subject. How much simpler it would have been if he had come out and confessed to his infidelity. Rose could have wept and pleaded, using all the wiles she had accumulated over thirty years to influence him. She knew what behaviour affected him most and what turned him off. They could have talked things through. She wanted a chance to understand, then she could have forgiven him.

She could change if he wanted her to. She could have a facelift, liposuction. She could get her body in shape at a gym if she knew it upset him. She could start to wear a wig.

And what about the possessive behaviour that everyone seemed to insist was her fault? If he'd wanted more freedom he should have told her. She just assumed he was contented to spend most of his free time with her, at home, being companionable. She would tell him he could go out every night, he could go flying every weekend if only he would come out and discuss it.

Sex?

Well, Rose had naively imagined their love life to be perfectly normal. But maybe he wanted to experiment – at his age men can go funny. Maybe he wanted her to suck him, like all the magazines told her she should. Perhaps he wanted to be tied up, or whipped, or put in nappies like a baby? OK, OK. Rose was game for that if it would keep him by her side.

That night, tentatively, she tested the theory.

'What are you doing?' asked Michael as she slid down the bed.

Saying nothing, she caressed him gently until he squirmed and grew hard, stroking her hair with his hand. She took his penis into her mouth and nearly gagged at the size of it and the way it threatened to choke her, but she drove herself on with her eyes closed and her fists clenched tight in determination.

When he came she couldn't help it, she gagged but muffled it with a cough.

'What was that all about?' he asked her when she came up again, puffing and gasping for air.

'I just thought you'd like it,' said Rose. 'Did you?'

'Is it my turn now?' he asked her smiling.

Rose had never been able to bear the thought of somebody's mouth down there. When they were first together he used to do it to her fairly often, but her embarrassment finally stopped it. Men's genitals were bad enough, but she couldn't imagine anything worse than licking out a woman's fanny, all slimy and slippery and smelly. Michael said he enjoyed it. But Rose didn't like having it done, so she'd stopped it.

'No, I'm OK,' said Rose demurely, stroking his forehead where the hair was receding. 'But would you like me to do this more often?'

'Why do you ask?' His smile was puzzled.

'I just wondered.'

'Rose, we're doing just fine as we are. I'm absolutely happy with our sex life, and you don't have to do what you don't want to.'

'But I do want to,' she said. '*I do.*'

But the look on his face said he didn't believe her.

Belinda was probably better at it. It was an age thing, Rose was certain, unless you came from bohemian stock. Even in the fabulous Sixties oral sex was a secretive thing, whereas now it had become the norm, like anal sex and vibrators.

Rose shuddered. She thought of Belinda's juices on Michael's lips when he came home and kissed her. She thought of what might be on Michael's penis if they did enjoy anal sex together.

But when he told her he was contented he sounded absolutely sincere.

It was the same when she brought up independence.

'If you need more freedom, or space as they call it, I wouldn't mind at all,' said Michael. 'Although, to be honest, I'd miss you.' He stared at her, holding her eyes. 'I like having you around. Are you sure everything's OK, Rose?'

'Why wouldn't it be?'

'I just wondered, that's all.'

'It must be Venice,' said Rose.

This would be the defining moment after which there'd be no turning back.

Rose sat on the bed, the phone beside her. Her hands were shaking and her mouth was dry – too dry to speak?

Michael had gone out to look for a set of lace place mats for Dinah; Rose had seen them earlier, but when she'd gone back the shop had been closed. She'd described the shop and given him directions. She'd told him her feet were just too sore to do any more walking that day.

She had the number of Jessie's mobile and all the relevant dialling codes spread out on her knee. A throbbing ache spread through her bones as the awful urge began to possess her. Some devious, cunning puppetmaster had got hold of her strings and was pulling them for his own dread purpose. The woman on the bed was no longer the Rosalind Allison Redfern she knew and understood so well.

This was a stranger with stranger's hands, long, veined and bony.

She held her breath and hung on for dear life.

'Jessie? Jessie, is that you?'

'Mum? What's the matter? What's happened?'

The connection was so clear her daughter might be in the next door room.

'It's awful, awful,' wept Rose, gradually coming to believe that what she was telling her daughter was true, convinced by her own expert acting. She'd rehearsed the scene so many times that now it felt more true than real life. 'Dad collapsed this afternoon and he's in hospital. They say it was a stroke.'

'Oh no, Mum! Oh no! I can't believe it! How is he?'

'He's stable, thank God. I've only just left him, but he still doesn't know who I am. They came for him in a water ambulance. There were tourists all around, staring; I'm sure someone ghastly took a photo. It was dreadful. Of course I went with him.'

'I'll come as quickly as I can.'

'No! No, Jessie, please don't. Please listen, darling. It's going to mean we don't get home until a few days later than planned. Not tomorrow after all. But you know Dad, he won't want a fuss. It's important we play this down, for his sake, we don't want him thinking he's worse than he is.'

'But I want to be with you, Mum. So will Daisy.'

'I know you do. Of course you do.' The perspiration rolled down Rose's back. 'But he's in safe hands. The doctors have been very good, and the nurses. It's not as if we're in Zimbabwe; this is a civilized place with state-of-the-art facilities.'

Jessie was still in deep shock. 'How did it happen, Mum? What happened?'

119

Rose let herself sob, it felt natural. 'We were sitting out in one of the cafés having our afternoon tea. He'd been complaining about his legs, but we both thought it was because we'd done so much walking.'

'I remember you saying . . .'

'It never occurred to either of us that it might be something worse. And now, of course, I'm blaming myself.'

'Come on, Mum. Come on. You know how silly that is.'

'I know, Jessie, but I just can't help it. And now I feel so helpless.'

'Where are you, Mum?'

'I'm at the hotel.' She wiped one palm nervously down her side. 'But I only came here to phone you. I'm going back to the hospital in a minute to be with Michael. So please don't phone me here or start leaving messages. That will just worry me more. I'll let you know if there's any change and I'll phone you again sometime tomorrow but I can't say when.'

'Don't you worry about us, just concentrate on Dad. Phone us when you get the chance, but don't worry if you can't. We'll understand. Just as long as you're sure you don't want us to come and be with you.'

'No, Jessie. No. That wouldn't be a good idea.'

'Can we phone the hospital to ask about his progress? Hang on. What's the name of the place?'

Rose heard Jessie scrabbling around for a pen. 'They don't speak English, Jessie. It would all be hopelessly complicated. Much better to wait for me—'

'OK, Mum. OK. If that's what you want. But what about Dad? Can he walk? Can he talk?'

Rose paused dramatically. 'N–not at the moment, I'm afraid. It's something to do with a weakness in the blood vessels of the brain.'

'And he was struck down, just like that?'

Rose imagined it all in her mind. She saw Michael fall, the tea spill over, the waiters in their white uniforms hurrying over to help and the fascinated faces of passers-by.

'I'm told that's how it happens.'

'But was he in terrible pain?'

'He lost consciousness, Jessie.' Rose's voice broke; she could see Michael's red apoplectic face against the marble floor, his strenuous breathing, the way his eyes failed to contract against the medic's light.

'Mum, I'm sorry. It's just that I feel so far away. I just want to know. But he's going to be OK, isn't he? Dad's going to be OK?'

'I'm sure he will be,' said Rose. 'I'm sure. You'll pass the news on to Daisy, dear?'

'How about Granny?'

'There's no need to tell Granny yet. We'll wait until we get home.'

'Have they said when that will be?'

'I don't think it will be long,' sniffed Rose. 'But of course I'll let you know.'

No going back now.

Far below, outside the window, a gondola floated past.

Shaking, Rose lit a cigarette and hung over the canal to smoke it. Either the sweet smell of sewage had gone or she had become accustomed to it.

What an awful shock for poor Jessie. Rose regretted the necessity of that, but in the end this way would be kinder than for the girls to have to go through their parents' divorce and face their father's treachery. Hell, Belinda must be around their ages.

Not only was Rose protecting the girls, but one day Michael might thank her, too. How his colleagues would sneer behind his back at the thought that their boss had allowed himself to be seduced by a little floozy half his age. His reputation would end up in tatters. Only the nudge-nudge, wink-wink brigade would view him as a rutting old stud who'd done well to get his leg over. Everyone else, including most of their friends, would sigh sadly over the loss of a man who had once been honourable and respected.

Belinda herself sounded so coarse and hard that Rose felt she had saved him from her. Their love, their lust, would never have lasted. He'd have ended up a broken man, a bloody fool in the eyes of the world.

As this was their last night in Venice, Michael suggested returning to their favourite restaurant beneath the Rialto Bridge.

He was at his most romantic, holding her hand, full of compliments, ordering champagne. He looked good, too; a successful, confident escort.

Cool.

Sophisticated.

A man of the world.

If he'd only known that his behaviour was hardening Rose's heart, because the thought of losing all of this was more than she could stand.

'I rang home', she confessed, 'while you were out. Just to tell them what time we'd be back.'

She had to tell him, after all. The phone call would be on the hotel bill.

'But how did you know what time we'd arrive?' Michael asked. 'I've got the tickets.'

'I thought it would be around about lunchtime.'

'But you're wrong, we won't get home until dark.'

'Oh well,' said Rose. 'It doesn't really matter. It's not as if they're coming to meet us. We'll see them when we see them.'

'Why don't we forget about them for now and concentrate on us, you and me.'

He held his glass to hers.

His dark brown eyes were deeply sincere.

'To us,' said Michael softly, giving her one sickening stab of doubt. 'And to our future together.'

Rose smiled.

NINE

Jessie sat sobbing and snuffling on a bench in Rumours winebar, with Jasmine's stout freckled arm around her shoulders.

'I know how you feel. I know, I know. But strokes are quite common in men of his age,' said Jasmine knowledgeably, in her white Aertex T-shirt, tracksuit bottoms and trainers. 'Especially when he's already had a warning and was on Clopidogrel. Most recover, even from an acute stroke, which it sounds like this one was, with the right kind of therapy, massage and rest. It's rest your dad's going to need now. There's no other treatment apart from that, I'm afraid.'

'He'll hate that. Poor Dad.' Jessie ripped another tissue from the wet, torn packet. 'Poor Mum, too. How is she going to cope with all this? I feel we ought to get over there no matter what she says.'

'Why do you always reckon your mother won't be able to cope when, from the little I've seen of her, she's a very capable woman?'

'It's the crap she's already been through,' wept Jessie. 'Her twin died when she was ten and her dad was drowned when she was fourteen. Then her own mum had a breakdown. You'd think that would be enough? God lives. How I hate him!'

'I know this might sound clichéd, but that suffering will probably stand your mother in good stead now. She'll have reserves to fall back on, reserves she's had to draw on before.'

'Bollocks,' said Jessie, eyeing Jasmine's crucifix. 'The only defence Mum had was to cut herself off from life and surround herself with her family. But now Dad . . .'

'Jessie, stop it! You're talking as if he's dead.'

Jessie raised her tear-stained face to Jasmine's much larger one. 'What if he does die?'

'He won't.'

Jasmine sounded so certain. So sweet. So kind. Jasmine was turning out to be what Granny would call a rock or a safe port in a storm.

Jessie had first met her when she went to take part in an observation day in a local special school with a group from St Marks. She went to Kingsmead, a school for kids with mild handicaps, where Jasmine worked as assistant matron to children aged between five and eleven. Despite her size and clumsy gait it was surprising how bustling and light-footed she could be among the kids.

Much against her will, Jessie was cajoled into taking part in a game of rounders with a class of giggling eight-year-olds. Their handicaps were almost unnoticeable. Any difficulties with hearing or sight were lost in the thrill of the game. Breathless and excited, she found herself laughing until she cried. She'd forgotten how good it felt. And afterwards, in the dining room – no common canteen at

Kingsmead – she and Jasmine swigged down three bottles of Evian between them.

After Belinda, Jessie was wary of forming another close friendship, especially, to be honest, with someone as formidably masculine as Jasmine, whose hair was no more than half an inch long, like some army cadet, who never bothered about underarm hair and whose wardrobe consisted of navy, maroon and black tracksuits and trainers.

Jessie, while loathing herself for being image conscious, was worried about her reputation. It had suffered a knock in the first year at college and she was only just getting over the label of dyke. It wouldn't have worried her if she was one, but hell, she needed time to find out.

But Jasmine, apart from her obsession with cricket, and women's cricket at that, was genuine and fun. A Jesus freak into the bargain, she might be hearty, loud and give out the wrong impression, but Jasmine had proved herself to be trustworthy.

Jasmine was three years older than Jessie, the same age as Daisy although she seemed far younger, and she owned her own flat in town.

A spartan, unfeminine place, it consisted mainly of stacks of decks, computer gear, canvas chairs and one uncomfortable put-you-up. It was to this flat that Belinda had traced poor Jasmine and taken the trouble to phone her up and warn her about her new friend's motives. Jessie was a psychopath, a roaring, manipulative lesbian, a destroyer of lives, a freak of nature. And Michael Redfern was the devil himself.

Jasmine, though shocked, had stayed calm and telephoned Jessie on her mobile at her granny's –

not the best place for such a call, with Dinah's ears flapping as her slimy lasagne went cold on the plate.

The following day Jessie was forced to tell Jasmine the whole sordid story, but all Jasmine was concerned about was Belinda's effect on Jessie, who had already begun to jump at shadows and imagine footsteps following her. She'd started locking her door again, just as she'd begun to feel safe. They spent one long evening discussing the way this new attack should be handled, and they both agreed, as Daisy had, that to respond would be playing right into Belinda's hand.

As long as Belinda stayed focused on Jessie herself, and maybe Jasmine, they reckoned they could cope with anything. Jessie gave Jasmine a careful description in case she was approached in the street. Belinda was tiny, dark and thin. She was cute and pretty, with long, curly hair and blazing blue eyes. The last time she'd seen her, her hair had been red, a kind of harsh carrot, 'but she changes the colour every two weeks. It's been purple, black and streaked with pink.' Jessie thought hard and shuddered. Belinda wore blankets, shawls and fringes, lots of scarves, jewellery and DMs. 'Oh, and she's Welsh.'

'But she's never shown any violence before?' Jasmine asked.

'No,' Jessie told Jasmine. 'Only threatened it. If she had been violent Dad would have gone straight to the law. Maybe they could have done something about it.'

If Belinda, in her obsession, had hoped her malicious phone call would break up the friendship she would be disappointed. During that week they drew even closer, both targets now, both deeply involved.

And then came this appalling call from Venice. Jessie couldn't have wished for a more sturdy shoulder to cry on than Jasmine's.

'And how am I going to tell Daisy?' cried Jessie. 'She's going to flip; she's mad about Dad.'

'Best to get it over with now,' said Jasmine sensibly, guiding Jessie towards the door of the darkened, smoke-filled student haunt. With Jasmine's arm still round her shoulder, Jessie, stooped, returned to her digs.

Jessie sat down hard on the old springless sofa in her room, crouched over her mobile. How she was dreading this.

It was William who answered the phone, and Jessie was relieved to hear his voice. Let him break the news to Daisy . . . and thank God he was there to keep her calm.

After her brief announcement, Jessie heard William explaining softly. Daisy came straight to the phone, voice high pitched, close to hysteria.

'We've got to get over there now.'

'Daisy! Mum said no. She was adamant.'

'We can't stay here just waiting for news.'

'It won't be for long. Just a couple of days.'

'How the hell does Mum know that?'

'Somebody must have told her. I'm assuming they've dealt with strokes before in this hospital.'

Daisy scrambled about for words. 'But Dad wasn't ill. We saw him last Sunday. He was fine. Christ, he was cutting the lawn.'

Jessie trembled, fighting back tears. 'I can't answer your questions.'

'I just can't believe it, Jess, that's all. I want to be

with him. I want to see him! I need to speak to Mum. Is there no way we can get in touch?'

Jessie repeated Rose's instructions. Behind her Jasmine ripped open a can of lager and offered her a swig. Jessie declined.

'But how are they getting back? Can't we call the travel agent? I mean, will he be able to walk? Will they have to use a stretcher?'

Into Jessie's muddled mind came the image of Princess Di's final return, carried by a bevy of soldiers across the grey tarmac with a flag laid over the coffin.

'Listen, Daisy,' she said, inadequate in this rare role as comforter, 'if we were needed to do anything Mum would have said. You know Dad, they'll be well insured, and if they need any special travel arrangements the people in charge over there will see to it. We are talking about Venice. They are civilized over there.'

Daisy's hysteria was quite natural. The difference between her and her sister was that Jessie had had time to digest it, and Jasmine's sensible support.

'Who do we know who we could phone to find out more about strokes?' cried Daisy.

'Here,' said Jessie, 'talk to Jasmine, she knows more than I do. She's a trained nurse.'

'You probably know more than I do,' said Jasmine, 'your dad's had a stroke before.'

'Nothing so serious,' Jessie put in. 'Just little ones.'

The next few minutes were spent listening to a bald description, all that Jasmine could remember but, as she admitted, she hadn't had much to do with the nursing of middle-aged men. As a psychiatric nurse you didn't. A stroke is a cerebral hae-morrhage, she said, and it sometimes starts with a blurring of vision or a headache.

'Or aching legs?' Daisy must have asked.

'Aching legs, I suppose, yes.'

It was vaguely encouraging to hear about the number of strokes some people suffered without it having much effect on their lives. But they could experience, Jasmine warned, difficulty in speaking, finding the right words, paralysis down one side of face and limbs, and there could be an impairment of their mental powers, but this rarely lasted. 'As far as I can remember the recovery time can vary from six months to a year.'

'My God. *My God*,' Jessie cringed.

'It all depends how severe it is,' Jasmine tried to console her and Daisy.

'But I wish we knew,' said Jessie, taking over the phone again and hearing her sister's laboured breathing.

'Didn't Mum give any clues?'

Jessie searched for the answer. 'No. No she didn't. And I was so shocked I didn't think to ask.'

'We could phone Neil, I suppose.' Neil Jarvis, the family GP, and Rose were well known to each other because of Rose's voluntary work with the surgery, running backwards and forwards with prescriptions, ferrying patients who didn't have transport. 'He wouldn't mind, would he?'

But there wouldn't be much point in that, they agreed. How could Neil give a prognosis when he hadn't seen the patient and could only guess at his condition? They would just have to wait until Dad came home and Neil had examined him. Reluctantly, they decided to do nothing except contact each other instantly either one heard any news.

Poor Dad.

Poor Mum.

Poor us.

'I'll be here to help you, whatever happens, you know that,' said Jasmine comfortably, leaving a ring from the base of her can on the smeared glass of the coffee table.

It was only then, with the world slightly calmer, and Jessie slumped down on her messy sofa with her hands over her eyes, that Jasmine sniffed and said, 'What's that?'

Jessie wrinkled her nose. 'It's shit! You must have brought some in on your shoe.'

Jasmine checked. 'No,' she said. 'And you've got yours on the sofa.'

'Oh no.' Gingerly Jessie sat up and checked both soles.

'Where the hell is it coming from?'

Jessie, exhausted, sat watching her friend as she went sniffing around the room like a child playing a foul version of hunt the thimble. 'It's somewhere here in this corner.'

'It can't be shit.'

'What else smells like that?'

'Rotten carrots?'

Jasmine tutted, then stared, then stiffened. She bent down, and then turned towards Jessie with a horrified look.

'What is it?' asked Jessie, startled by Jasmine's expression.

'Jesus Christ. You'd better come and see.'

What they were staring at was sheer mania. It was like a grotesque hot dog. The turd was wrapped in a used sanitary towel and laid out on a piece of lavatory paper, like you'd lay out a table arrangement if you were trying to impress – a log, a robin, a sprig of holly – centring and admiring it.

After standing still for ten endless seconds Jessie went limp and started to cry.

Jasmine couldn't move. She closed her eyes and stammered, 'I–is there anyone else . . . ?'

'No,' sobbed Jessie, 'only Belinda. She must still have a key.'

'Did she try anything like this before?'

Jessie could only shake her head. Her stomach was churning.

'This is serious, Jessie,' said Jasmine. 'Not just some nutter with one screw loose.' She started searching around for a bag. 'You must have one somewhere. Anything. We've got to get this odious obscenity out of here.' She held her hand to her mouth, almost retching.

Jessie pulled open an overstuffed drawer, chucked out a muddle of tights and handed it over.

'I just can't touch it,' said Jasmine, blanching.

So Jessie bent down beside her in the corner of the room by the window and, using a couple of biros as chopsticks, picked up the gross offering. She dropped it into the bag, together with the biros, and wordlessly Jasmine took it out, along the corridor to the communal dustbin.

Jessie smoothed back her chopped tufts of hair.

That was it. There was no choice. She would have to go and talk to Belinda.

Going to see the college authorities would be a total waste of time. After all, they had dealt with her once, expelling her, and so they were no longer responsible. The police wouldn't take it seriously and anyway, Jessie, embarrassed, didn't feel like disclosing her past to them. There might well come a time when she had to, but she didn't feel it had come yet. No. This was a private matter and Jessie must work it out for herself.

What about Belinda's parents? They lived in Cardiff, and they must be on the phone. There couldn't be that many McNabs in that part of the world. If Jessie rang she could ask if they knew where their daughter was and what sort of frame of mind she was in. Had she received any treatment? Did they know where she was living?

Jessie needed to know exactly what she was dealing with. Belinda's state of mind, never predictable, had obviously deteriorated to a profoundly low point, and if she could resort to this, what else would she be capable of?

To think that Belinda had been in her flat and might have gone through her things, might have hidden something else . . . With Jasmine's help Jessie cleared the room, hoovering and dusting for the first time in a month.

She emptied the bins and the washing basket, turned over the mattress and stripped the bed and inspected every corner with careful trepidation. She ran over the surfaces with disinfectant from an unopened bottle Mum had brought with her last time she'd visited in the hopes that Jessie would clean up a bit.

There would never have been a good time to

133

experience such a despicable invasion, but on top of the news from Venice it drove Jessie to utter despair.

Thoughts of her father's helplessness – no longer could they turn to him as a last desperate measure if all else failed as they had before – towered over everything else. OK, perhaps it was wrong; they were both grown up now, no longer Daddy's little princesses, but they had depended on him. He'd always been there, a safety net in life's menacing sea. Would he get better? Dear God! Or remain an invalid for ever?

And with Dad dependent Mum would have more on her mind than her daughters' problems. Jessie viewed the bottle of disinfectant with new, approving eyes. There'd be no more fussing from Mum now that Dad was more needy than her daughters. And she had Granny, who grew more and more difficult to cope with as time went by.

Although it was illogical, Jessie felt suddenly abandoned and helpless. Life was so unfair.

Of course she'd known, and accepted, the fact that one day in the far distant future Mum and Dad would die and she would be left alone in the world, but hopefully, by then, she would have a family of her own. Why did this have to happen now, when Jessie felt so threatened? But then came a flood of guilt at how selfish she was, how self-centred and uncaring when all her thoughts should be with her parents, going through hell in a foreign land.

She was tired and desperate for sleep. She wished that Jasmine would go, but was fearful of upsetting her. She needed someone like Jasmine now. Jasmine the dependable had moved the objectionable object, disposed of it in the bin, helped clean the room, comforted and reassured her and seen her through a telephone call that would have been much more traumatic without her sensible input.

But Jasmine, in charge, was not finished yet. Capable and organizing, she was sorting out some clean pyjamas for Jessie, running a bath and fussing about the drooping curtain.

She sounded like she had on the playing fields that day when they'd played rounders at Kingsmead. All she needed was a whistle round her neck.

It was so suddenly, so blindingly obvious, as obvious as the crucifix she wore at all times. When would Jessie learn to be a better judge of character?

Jasmine, so genuinely kind and helpful, loved to be needed. She rose to such occasions, like a leaf expanding to catch summer rain. Other people's pain brought out the best in Jasmine.

She refused to leave until Jessie had bathed, eaten and drunk half a mugful of Horlicks, and when she finally went she made sure to programme her number into Jessie's mobile.

God bless you my child.

All the wretched Jessie could do was say thank you, thank you, thank you for being so terribly kind.

TEN

Oh dear Jesus she's killed him.

Rose's calculations were wrong.

Michael lies beside her, back in their comfortable king-size bed in their homely house at the end of the road, his skin tight, white and glazed, his pupils distended, deathly still, not breathing.

Exhausted after her harrowing night, Rose darts to the bathroom, teeth grinding, wets a flannel, pulls back the duvet and scrubs it roughly over his naked body like she's seen farmers do with limp little lambs to give them a chance of life.

She slaps his cheeks and shrieks his name.

Breath bursting from her own body, she straddles him and presses his heart, counting between the pressure, and sobbing, 'Jesus. Oh please, Jesus.'

It had been dark when they'd arrived home last night, and when she'd seen the house in darkness Rose felt a five-pound weight leave her heart. She had been dreading the possibility that the girls might, in their panic, have moved in to be near the phone and to prepare the house for their father's homecoming.

So far so good.

From the airport they had used a taxi for the last hour of their journey. The flight was short and on time. Customs proved no problem, and if Michael had sensed Rose's mounting fear he made no comment about it. She was usually excited to be coming home. They both were; they were home-loving folk.

Once through the front door she'd instantly leaped to turn off the answerphone. If Daisy and Jessie had spread the word, friends and colleagues would have left messages. And what if Belinda had rung again?

'Damn! Look what I did,' she told Michael, bending to pull the connection out from the skirting board; he was following behind with the case and bag. 'I left the answerphone off.'

'I don't expect there were many calls,' he said.

She would listen to the messages later.

She went directly to the bathroom and searched the cupboard shakily for Dinah's spare supply of the sleeping pill, Zopiclone.

'Drink?'

Michael shook his head. He looked tired. 'I had enough on the plane.'

'Oh come on, I am. We're still on holiday after all. Until tomorrow we're allowed to be irresponsible.'

Not wanting to play the killjoy, Michael agreed.

Rose put the pills in her mouth, ground them between her teeth and hooked the whole mess out with her tongue, wincing at their bitterness. She spat it out into his drink and mixed it with three large chunks of ice. She hung a lemon slice over the side and peered into the swirling mixture. The slight silt on the bottom could well be the grit the dishwasher left behind when it wasn't performing perfectly.

She held her breath till it hurt.

'When d'you want to phone the girls?'

'Not tonight,' she said, passing him the overlarge gin, unable to look at him directly. She edged quickly back to her chair and her voice sounded lighter than normal. 'I did speak to Jessie yesterday.'

'How about Dinah?'

'I can't face her now. Let's just pretend we're on our own in the world for a change.'

They went through the mail, which was mostly for him. No premium bonds, just lumps of cellophaned Christmas catalogues, which Rose would normally have enjoyed over endless cups of coffee and one or two secret cigarettes. Giving presents was, for her, a big delight in life. She was lucky she had the money to be able to chose what she liked. The children had been spoilt when they were small. She knew it but couldn't help doing it, and in spite of parsimonious warnings, particularly from Dinah, they had turned out none the worse for it.

'I didn't spoil you when you were a child,' Dinah would say, forgetting. Rose had been given most things she'd wanted, being an only child. The survivor.

Now she was performing like a robot, obliterating her feelings completely. A tin woman with no heart. All feeling had flown, apart from the abject terror of living her life without Michael.

Rose insisted on cooking a meal to celebrate the last real night of their holiday. Michael was due back to work the next day. It felt satisfying to be back in her own kitchen again, using the familiar Aga and preparing good homely food.

But tonight she'd be slightly more enterprising. She took haddock from the freezer and prepared it in a rich wine sauce. This time she chewed two Zopiclone and removed them from her teeth with her finger before mixing them into half of the sauce with a wooden spoon. She hoped the dilution of spittle would not weaken the potency of the tablets. Carefully she arranged the fish in individual serving dishes, adding the drugged sauce to Michael's dish, and piping hot mashed potato round them before slipping them back into the Aga to brown.

She chose frozen broad beans as a vegetable – bitter, like Michael's medicine.

Her face was flushed by the time she had finished, the rosy-faced housewife fresh from the oven. Mrs Apple in a frilly pinny. Mrs Be-Done-by-As-You-Did.

She set the coffee maker. Espresso was Michael's first choice, thick, black and sickly sweet. Another pill would go into his cup, ground up with the dark brown sugar.

'It's no good, I can't stay awake any longer.'

No wonder. He had drunk two mammoth gins and swallowed five Zopiclone. Michael's eyes were closing.

She got up and switched off the news.

Upstairs, she couldn't be still.

'Don't do that now,' he moaned, watching her scuttle round the bedroom, busy unpacking. 'You're tiring me out. We only need the washbags now.'

139

He was naked under the duvet. He wandered round the room naked, brushing his teeth with nothing on. After his shower he habitually rubbed himself dry in the bedroom; he was so confident in his body. Rose watched him out of the sides of her eyes while she automatically filled the wash basket. Michael, at fifty-two, wouldn't think twice before stripping off in front of a lover, whereas Rose felt certain that one look at her would turn lust, at best, into laughter, at worst into disgust.

Not that she'd had any offers lately, but then, if you're not looking you just don't see.

Michael must have been on the lookout for Belinda to attract his eye.

She felt a sharp stab of rage as she unpacked his shirts, washed by her, ironed by her, mended and chosen by her.

Before she got into bed beside him he was snoring and, characteristically, lying on his back with his mouth wide open. In her long frilly nightie she sat beside him and tried to read in the dimness of her bedside light.

Rose could no more have followed a sentence of her latest book than fly, but she still turned the pages, applied her nightcream and filed her nails. She remembered the afternoon of the phone call, when Belinda's words had her on the floor on all fours, like a beaten old dog, shivering and half dead with pain.

'*We can't keep pretending that nothing's wrong . . .*'

Too damn right. I can't and I won't.

Finally she turned out the light and forced herself to lie still for an hour. She burned and sweated till the fresh white cotton clung to her body.

140

She could still pull back if she was willing to confess to a mental delusion so sudden and urgent that it forced her to terrify her own daughters . . .

That was no longer an option.

The burning question was, would this work?

Her eyes had long since adjusted to the dark in the room by the time she got up carefully and tiptoed to the door with the drugs and a needle, retrieved from the bedside drawer, in her hand. Michael hadn't moved, apart from the occasional grunt and the odd, heavy sigh. He was as deeply asleep as he'd ever been.

In the kitchen, she made tea, sitting at the table and drinking it. The central heating was off, but still Rose burned as if she had a fever.

She went to the cupboard over the sink where she kept odds and sods which she hardly used. Many times Michael had asked her why the hell she didn't clear it out. When would she ever find a use for old Christmas doilies, half-burned birthday candles, cake frills with icing stuck to the edges, toothpicks, an icing bag with a tear in the side and out-of-date hundreds and thousands? Somewhere amongst all this was poor Baggins' dispenser.

The vet had given her this useless tool when Baggins' epilepsy was first diagnosed, along with his first bottle of pills. Unexpected tears sprang to Rose's eyes. She wiped them away angrily.

The wretched thing must be five years old. It was a kind of syringe with a tube on the end for administering tablets to reluctant pets. But Baggins' greed had rendered it redundant. A piece of ham or a chunk of cheese and Baggins would gobble down anything.

If Baggins was here now things might be different. Baggins' presence was a grounding one. His dirt and mud kept things in perspective. He expected so little from life, just a full stomach and a warm bed and walks in filthy places. In exchange for that he gave all his love, disloyalty was unthinkable. Yes, he might approach strangers, roll over and frolic and make out they were friends. He might attempt a quick hump at a passing leg. But his heart belonged to Rose and Michael. One look from his bold eye told anyone that.

If Baggins was here he would share her pain gladly, as so often she had shared his. He would sit up with her all night if need be.

But Baggins was gone and the mania was hers. The *Aura Epileptica*. The sound that made no sound. That defining moment of no return – she looked at the kitchen clock; it said four – when nothing could stop the hellish approach of what was fated to be.

She tipped the tablets onto the table and fetched the garlic crusher.

She pounded each pill with all her might until it turned into grains of salt, bitter on the end of her fingers. She filtered the little pile of danger into the wide end of the syringe and pressed home the plastic lid, then she pushed the plunger and watched as a spurt of white powder came out of the tube.

Waste not want not.

Carefully she replaced it.

Then, into the other syringe, she sucked the mixture from the ampoule in her dressing-gown

142

pocket. She held it up to the light and depressed any air, which might be so dangerous. She caught sight of herself in the kitchen mirror. Lady Macbeth, but with something white and dry on her hands. Her expression was gauntly resolute, her face shiny with Oil of Olay and her lips quite bloodless.

Quietly she climbed the stairs and got into bed beside her husband, just as she had done for thirty years. She placed the tablet mixture in the drawer for back-up. She was going to rely on the needle . . .

In this same bed the children were born.

In this bed Rose had hoped she would die surrounded by people who loved her.

But this time Rose did not lie down; she squatted with her knees to her mouth, as she used to sit as a small child, licking the salt or the itching scab. Sucking her hair and thinking.

She had liked to sit quietly alone like this, especially after Jamie's death, when she could hear her father crying downstairs. A man's sobs, racked and raw, as if his whole body were under torture, quite unlike her mother's soft grief, which flowed more naturally, like blood, like water.

But Dinah cried more like a man when she had her breakdown. Ugly sounds. Nothing gentle. Bestial. Jurassic.

She sat and stared at Michael, so confident, even in sleep. How did he know that some fat brown spider wouldn't climb down the light cord and make a home between his teeth? He slept on his back, always, while Rose curled up in a ball, protectively, like a foetus.

On her haunches, propped up on the pillow, Rose held up the syringe and tapped it. A spurting droplet told her all was well.

She knelt down beside Michael and helped one hand droop outside the bed. She wanted an easy vein. She wanted his hand to be as numb as she could get it. At best this was going to hurt, and at worst . . . ?

What if some atmospheric movement near his sleeping face disturbed him? What if, right now, he opened his eyes and saw his wife poised to administer the drug? What if the needle refused to go in? What if he woke in the middle of the job? What if he leapt up demanding answers?

Confidence was the answer. This time her hands were perfectly steady, so intent was she on the work in hand. His breath smelled of peppermint toothpaste. She guided the needle to the spot, and with the other hand she gently pinched the vein till it was raised, blue, almost black amidst the hairs on the back of his hand, his loving hand, his sweet hand. She longed to hold it up to her face but . . .

The needle was sharp. Rose was swift. The action itself took milliseconds.

Screwing up her eyes, steadying one hand with the other, she quickly depressed the syringe and withdrew.

Her heart started up again when Michael spluttered and sat bolt upright. Coughing and cursing roundly, he shook his hand while fumbling for the light switch.

'God! God! What the shit . . . ?'

'Michael? Michael, what's happening?'

He sat on the edge of the bed and peered at his hand. 'Shit. Some blasted mosquito. Jesus that stings.'

'I can't see anything.'

'Why aren't you in bed?' His voice was still woozy. Dinah's pills were designed to work at a quarter the level she'd dosed him with.

'I was going to the loo,' said Rose. He gulped half the glass of water she brought him. He panted, 'I just can't imagine what that could have been.' He slurped down some more water and shook his hand. 'It could even have been a wasp, the bastard.'

'One of those biting flies?' said Rose.

'At this time of year?' He inspected the place, holding it directly under the light.

She shrugged.

He wasn't convinced. 'Could be that, I suppose.'

All he wanted was to go back to sleep. Rose passed him a cough sweet. 'Chew that.'

She could hear it banging around in his mouth as he sucked. She could smell the sweet cherry flavour. Then, with one more 'shit' he sank back onto his pillows and Rose turned out the light.

'Stand by your man.'

All night, like a sentinel, she kept watch over him.

And when dawn came, gradually brushing the room with grey, she leaned over gently and stroked his forehead. 'I love you, Michael. I love you.' He was still on his back, but his eyes were wide open and his skin felt as cold as the marble floor in their Venice bedroom.

Michael is dead and she has killed him.

In manic desperation she rubs him roughly with a flannel.

With all her might Rose tries and tries to pump him alive, as if he's a kid's inflatable pool dolphin,

145

punctured beyond repair but just floating.

A soft groan is her first reward and her cries turn from rage to relief. 'Michael, can you hear me? Michael! Wake up. Wake up.'

What had she expected? Well, nothing as comatose as this.

The Aga kettle is hot. She fills three hot-water bottles and packs them around him, pleading like a chattering monkey.

Moving as timidly as the dawn his colour begins to return. Not the colour of a healthy man, but yellowed by poison, sickly with barbiturates. The texture of his skin is that of a chicken that's almost thawed. There are no questions in his eyes, nothing that Rose must immediately answer.

She grasps one of his hands, which is quite limp. It falls back onto the mattress as soon as she lets go.

Now his nakedness feels intolerable, too childlike and vulnerable to endure. She finds a pair of pyjamas, still new, never unwrapped, and tears them out of the packaging. How heavy and ungiving he is. Panting, she manages to get them on as she whispers, 'Michael, Michael. Everything will be OK. I'm not going to leave you. I'm here. We can get through this together.'

The same words she had whispered to Baggins what feels like a lifetime ago.

What must he be thinking? This carcass with flesh still on it, lying there paralysed. Can he see her? Can he hear?

Are questions forming behind those eyes? Or has his brain ceased to function? Turned black, turned into a rain-spoiled fungus.

Impossible to answer such hideous questions in

these first five minutes. Time will tell. But that's no good. Rose doesn't have time. Either later today, or tomorrow, she's going to have to make contact and bring in the outside world. She has no longer than that. One sight of Michael in this cataleptic state would sound alarm bells in the stupidest person. No right-minded professional would have let him come home, let alone travel hundreds of miles.

Can he swallow? Can he blink? Has she done irreparable damage by getting the dose wrong?

She will make him some sweet, weak tea. She'll try to spoon feed him and see what happens. There is certainly no need for any back-up pills yet.

On her way to the kitchen Rose pauses by the phone. She doesn't reconnect it, not yet, but she presses the replay button.

'Rose,' goes the worried voice of her friend Jilly, 'I've just seen Daisy in the library and she told me the terrible news. I know you might not be back yet, but I wanted to leave a message to tell you that anything you need, any help at all, and I'm right here, waiting for your call. I've heard that the float tank can work miracles in these awful circs; it works on many levels, physical, emotional and intellectual. Ring me.'

Rose clicks it off in despair.

God help me. Dear God help me.

The whole world is out there waiting.

147

ELEVEN

The scent of sex . . . no Persil, freshly ironed laundry, underwear and pillows.

Michael Hudson Redfern exists in the lost world of Atlantis, deep, deep beneath the sea.

'Michael row the boat ashore . . .'

And then, touching a place more profound in his soul, a Rachmaninov piano concerto and stars shining softly in a midnight sky and a sense of wonder – there is an afterlife, there is a heaven. This shocking surprise rouses him an inch or more from his bed in the mud of his mentally churning washing machine.

To think – about anything – requires all the mental stamina that would be required to run a mile. But the underlying terror of opting out of the challenge, and the dread of the hell he would find himself in, makes cowardice impossible.

The voices floating around him sound like those in a speeding car, toneless bursts between the wind. Likewise the moving shadows, hidden behind storm-tossed branches. In spite of colossal concentration he is unable to move a limb, let alone a finger. Michael wouldn't begin to know how to start the process off.

The something soft and gentle running across his forehead is powered by a shrieking jet engine of feeling. Sickness comes and goes in waves, he needs to heave to empty himself, but his body hasn't the power. Sleep beckons with its cool oblivion, but the sheer terror of disappearance forces his eyes to stay open.

'Onward Christian Soldiers . . .'

The snatches of song which take over his mind with monotonous regularity cause such intense irritation that he would cry out if only he could. But let them keep coming, let these attacks continue; the more fury he feels the more alive he knows he is.

The idea that he might have fallen ill takes so long to form that Michael is weary by the time it dawns and can follow the thought no further.

It is only in semi-consciousness that he finds his daughters, Daisy and Jessie, frolicking under the garden hose on a hot sunny day, while Rose, his wife, swings in the hammock and he throws balls for Baggins.

But there is an undercurrent of concern; all is not as it seems. He and Rose have disagreed about allowing Daisy to go on the school trip to France for a week.

Daisy desperately wanted to go. Why should she be the only one in the class to miss out on such a great experience? It wasn't fair. Mummy was foul and she hated Daddy for taking her side.

Rose held firm in her belief that Daisy would be homesick before she crossed the Channel, that she would hate staying in a house of strangers who spoke little English, and that, anyway, it would be fun to have her and Jessie home for a week to enjoy this unusual weather for early June.

'But even if Daisy does hate it, won't it be a learning experience?' Michael observed calmly. 'She'll be all the more appreciative when she gets back, and we don't want her to be singled out as a sissy.'

'My instinct tells me I'm right about this,' Rose insisted. 'We don't have to go along with everything the school suggests just because it's in vogue at the time. They might be the professionals, Michael, but I know my daughter better than they do.'

In their bringing up of the children Rose and Michael stuck together and refused to break ranks over major decisions. If one disagreed, they would shut up and support the other till later. And this worked. Wheedling or theatening was a waste of time.

But on this occasion, behind Rose's arguments lay her horror of a family split. OK, it was just for a week, but Daisy was only twelve and, crazy though it was, Rose lived in terror of losing her. When faced with this it was hard to argue, knowing where Rose was coming from. Michael's childhood had been contented, with no great loss or trauma, and being a sensitive man he could sympathize with Rose's dilemma.

He backed down, as he so often did when faced with this particular argument. But Daisy had never forgiven him, and referred to that lost holiday to this day – jokingly.

It seemed ironic, but Jessie, the more difficult

child, was easier in many ways. She was never afraid to show her feelings, while Daisy's thoughts ran quiet and deep.

Through the swirling foetal waters which seem to surround him, Michael hears a new, deeper tone, and intense thought, verging on the painful, tells him that this is the voice of a man. Subconsciously he knows that he ought to be responding. The varied inflections in the tone tell him questions are being put to him. With all his might he attempts to speak, but the growl in his ears vibrates with such aching force that he stops.

The man is touching his body. Once more the feeling comes across as the ear-piercing shriek of an aeroplane, or an engine leaving a station.

The man is tapping his knees, stroking the sole of his foot. Thank God he has all the right sensations. He might not be able to identify the various parts of his body correctly enough to move them, but he can feel another's touch. There is contact, on some basic level, with this other, unfamiliar world, of which he now knows he was once a part.

In spite of his mighty efforts, sleep claims him.

Early on, Michael believed that Rose's psychotic obsession with family would be overcome not just by him but by her daily experiences.

Here they are now, without the girls, at Oliver Slattery's New Year's Eve party, one of the few they've ever attended because parties aren't their style. This must be ten years ago. Rose looks good at thirty-eight, the laughter lines round her eyes are attractive, her slinky green dress shows a sexy figure, her smiling lips shine temptingly and her voice, unlike some women's, is level and low. She appears to be enjoying herself, with a drink in her hand and the gossip flowing.

Pressured into it by Michael and the girls, she gave up smoking six weeks earlier and appears to be keeping her promise.

Flora, Oliver's wife, is well gone. Although her walk is steady enough, her firm eye control gives her away as she approaches Michael with a pout and a punch. 'I haven't seen you dancing, darling.'

Michael smiles wryly. Flora will feel such a prat when she remembers all this in the morning. And he knows, from experience, that it's hard to stay sober when the party is yours. For a start you begin to booze too early, and fear of failure leads to the bottle.

Flora takes him by the hand and pulls him away from his circle of friends in the dimly lit conservatory. 'Hold that,' he laughs, raising his eyebrows and handing his splashing drink to Robin. He is dragged like a doll through the sitting room behind her and into the near-darkened dining room, which has been cleared for dancing.

'Lady in Red'.

Her head rests against him.

She is little and firm.

All efforts to dance come to naught. Poor Flora is beyond them, and anyway, there's no room. Instead, like idiots, they sway to the music, and Flora's drunken arm flops up and her hand plays with his hair. She is pressing so hard against him he can feel the firmness of her breasts and the softness of the tops of her legs, her stomach, her urgency.

When she tries to give him a slobbery kiss Michael laughs – she's going to be mortified about this – and moves his face so she can't quite reach.

'You're so sweet,' she whispers, and she's crying to the music.

Rose is silent coming home in the car. Hell. He knows very well what she's thinking. Half of him wants to punish her for deliberately altering the truth to suit her own paranoia. She knows damn well what happened, just as everyone else does. To refuse to dance with poor Flora would have been a cruel snub and unnecessarily priggish. But the other half of Michael, understanding where Rose's insecurities come from, is prepared to reassure her as usual.

'Come on then, Rose, what's going on?'

Still she refuses to speak.

'I know you're upset, but you're being very silly.'

She tenses up and says nothing.

'If I was aiming to make love to a friend's wife I wouldn't chose his dining room in front of an audience of forty people.'

Michael is losing patience. He is tired, he wants to get home and the heavy rain makes the driving hellish.

'What I want to know is why she chose you?' Rose mutters under her breath.

'Because I was there. I was available, dammit.'

'You needn't have gone that far.'

'Rose, I just stood there, like a dummy. You saw me.'

'You bet I saw you. *You loved it*,' she hisses.

'Well, if that's what you want to believe there's nothing I can say to change your mind. I've never looked at anyone else. You sound like you think I'm some sex-crazed loon lurking about in a brown mackintosh.'

'I'd kill you, you know,' she promises.

'Fair enough.'

'I warn you, Michael, I just couldn't stand it.'

'Rose, neither could I,' he says sincerely.

And it's Rose, that Rose, who is beside him now, holding something to his mouth and Michael knows he should open it.

He feels her fingers; they sound like chainsaws, fumbling with his lips, and then the shock of warmth on his tongue and wetness in his throat. With one enormous effort he swallows, a cavernous, echoing sound, and he feels a pressure, as if his lower body is trying to escape through his mouth.

While any sense of time or place is beyond him, Michael knows this is lukewarm tea. Rose, his wife, is spoon-feeding him tea with a bitter taste and his head is somehow propped up on a pillow of Persil white, Persil bright. All his concentration must go into swallowing correctly. The prospect of his air-way being blocked and of the gigantic effort it would take to clear it concentrates his shattered mind.

He cannot decipher her words, but the inflection is encouraging and kind, just as the male voice had sounded earlier.

How much earlier? Months? Weeks? Or just a few minutes?

It seems only a moment ago that he walked down the aisle with Rose at his side, still ignorant enough of her past not to know what losses had befallen her. It was up to Dinah to tell him, but not until they returned from their honeymoon, when still no mention was made of the violent death of Rose's twin and the drowning of her father, John.

'But why should I have made a big deal out of it?' she'd asked when he told her he knew. 'Michael, it was all a long time ago. There must be events in your life which you haven't revealed to me yet, things that don't really matter much any more.'

Not matter? Her reaction had seemed odd at the time. Especially as he came to realize the lasting damage that it had caused.

Dinah briefed her son-in-law while Rose was out buying fish and chips one evening soon after the wedding. They hadn't much time, but the subject came up and so it had to be dealt with. 'Rose has never dealt with Jamie's death, not even to this day, and all that grief has been left lost inside her. Of course John and I tried our best, but when you lose a child you're so engrossed in your own pain it's hard to empathize with anyone else. In those days it was thought you just had to try and get over it.' Michael listened hard. 'Rose doesn't deal well with loss, or even the threat of loss. She has found friendships tricky. You know what school is like, best friends come and go, intense friendships break down overnight, someone you thought was on your side turns out to be whispering behind your back.'

'It's no wonder,' Michael sympathized. 'It sounds like a natural reaction to me.' But there was one thing he found hard to accept. 'Why didn't she tell me before? Why did she leave it for you to explain?'

'Because Rose is determined that she's left these

hurts behind her, that they play no great part in her life. She doesn't see them as relevant now.'

'She never actually lied,' mused Michael, 'and if I'd asked her outright I'm sure she would have told me. Whenever I asked her about Jamie she said he wasn't around any more. She didn't enlarge on that, so I just guessed they'd fallen out and she'd rather I didn't push it.'

Although Michael knew that Rose's father had died when she was fourteen, he'd assumed it was cancer and Rose had never put him right. The discovery that her father had disappeared into the sea and that his body had never been found, and all when Rose was at such an impressionable age, made sense of her possessive behaviour.

'Oh, of course,' said Dinah, 'you'll have fallen foul of that already.'

'She's jealous for no reason,' he said. 'At first it was quite flattering. Then I felt sorry for her; she was going through all kinds of agonies.'

'She believes you're going to be taken from her, just like her brother was, and her father. Loss, that's Rose's room 101.'

'I can see that now,' said Michael. 'And it adds up; it makes sense.'

Dinah's advice was, 'Talk to Rose. Reassure her. Be understanding.'

And he did. Of course. He tried his best. But she looked at him with such surprise, so curious did she find his concern that she almost laughed it off. She was perfectly happy to talk about Jamie; she was sad but resigned, and it seemed she had accepted it. It was the same with her father. Of course she missed him, but life goes on; it was her

156

mother's loneliness that seemed to upset her the most.

To anyone who knew no better, Rose appeared to have coped most admirably.

Is Michael's imagination beginning to play cruel tricks, or does he feel he is rising up through the thousands of fathoms of heavy water?

He knows he is moving his little finger.

'One finger, one thumb, keep moving. One finger, one thumb, keep moving . . .'

Dammit. Dammit.

His mouth is parched.

He begins to sense his face, not as a thick mask of plaster, but as a tangible part of himself, over which he has some small control. His eyes still stare out vacantly, but the walls of the room are definable and he can identify the ceiling lampshade as salmon pink. Fat ladies' knickers on seaside postcards. He's never really liked the colour scheme in here, but, as in all matters inside the house, he defers to Rose's judgement.

He imagines the bee-stinging tingling in his arms and hands to feel like the effects of an amputated limb; they say the itching is worse than the pain. He can't feel his legs at all. Maybe they really are missing.

For Christ's sake what has happened to him? Was he in an accident? Has he spent months drip-fed in a coma? Will this be a permanent state? Almost total paralysis with no method of communication? For the rest of his life? Till the day he dies. Kept alive by drugs, bed-bathed by a series of nurses?

BURIED ALIVE.

Oh God, no. He starts to hyperventilate, and every gasping breath is his last.

The scream starts in the pit of his stomach and rises, searing each nerve in his body as the awful reality strikes home. But no sound comes.

To Michael this is the worst scenario, and Rose has always known this. Years ago they made a pact: no tubes, no drips, no resuscitation if either of them was ever reduced to a vegetative state. A quick pillow held to the face or a plastic bag over the head is the final mercy they promised each other.

So where is she and why has she failed him? Oh God help me. How can he make her understand?

He feels pressure on the edge of the bed and knows that someone is sitting beside him. He tries to speak Rose's name, but against his massive, aching head the word bangs hollow and senseless.

Once again loud fingers prise open his mouth, and Michael tenses nervously for more of the drowning tea. But this time it is far, far worse. The bitter mixture is thick and cloying and clamps at his throat. He feels his eyes wrenching wide open as he tries to convey his agitation. Rose becomes clearer in his sights, but the violent panic inside him passes messages to a helpless brain.

She looms large beside him; he is an infant, dependent for life on this gross lump of mother. Her fingers begin to massage his throat and at last he feels the knot dispersing; little whiffs of breath can again squeeze through. She is saying something, but the roar is too loud for Michael to decipher.

There is something familiar about the lingering taste, but Michael is in no state to place it. This is the sick man's medication. This vile poison is being used to keep him alive against his will. How many times must he endure this? Once, twice, three times a day? He must have been given it before, but his memory has only just returned, along with his sense of being. Perhaps he's getting better! Yes, of course. How sluggish his brain is. If this state was a permanent one Rose would refuse to keep him alive.

He trusts her implicitly. Therefore there must be hope after all, and it's up to Michael to play his part. He was doing well until a moment ago, but now he feels he is losing it, sinking back into the mire from which there might well be no return.

'Oh land of my fathers . . .'

The light in the room goes dim. The lampshade turns a liquid brown and then disappears.

All Michael has is a pinpoint of light, which he tries with all his might to cling to before it finally goes out.

And the dummy returns to the dark.

TWELVE

Nobody knows they are home yet.

She has to search for the goodness in her, so for one quiet hour Rose gets out the Christmas CDs and plays childish carols: 'Silent Night', 'Little Town of Bethlehem'. If she was a more cultured person she would probably turn to some great piece of music, but for Rose the carols release that silver-tinsel innocence buried in baby memory.

She was committing a fiendish act, but something good was still there, deep inside, she knew it. She cried with relief when she found her goodness, tiny and safe as a foetus, curled deep inside her, living and breathing, although out of sight, and the tears rolled down her face.

But now Rose has twenty-four hours to get this right, and one thing in her favour is her nodding acquaintance with medical matters, her handling of prescriptions, her work with meals on wheels and the fact that she transports patients to the surgery and has done for the past two years.

A do-gooder. A brick.

Many, many times Rose has visited the homes of patients suffering from strokes, arthritis, MS, heart

160

attacks and dementia etc. Maybe, as in childhood when she pretended to be dead or blind, this was her way of confronting the unendurable.

She has dealt with their prescriptions. She has comforted their families.

In the amateur hospital letter that Rose had translated in the glorious atmosphere of the Piazza San Marco, she knew enough to state that on arrival at the hospital Michael had a CT scan which had proved beyond any doubt that he had suffered a stroke. That would remove any initial doubts as to the diagnosis.

Ospedale Civile.
Castello.

Re: Michael Redfern.

Dear Dr Jarvis,
    Your patient above presented with unconsciousness on Thursday. His wife gave me a past history of hypertension, type two diabetes and one previous small vascular accident. He currently takes medication – Atenolol 50mgs daily, Metformin 500mgs and 75mgs Clopidogrel daily.
On presentation the patient did not respond to stimuli.
Total muscular weakness.
Reflexes were poor.
BP 160/100.
A CAT scan confirmed the diagnosis of a serious cerebral vascular accident. The patient was discharged by his wife expressly against

my professional advice. Private arrangements were made with the airline to transport the patient home. In my opinion his condition is serious, but there is no recommended treatment.

Yours sincerely,

And it was signed, Giovanni Franceschi.

But worryingly, as far as Rose could see, his present symptoms – the lolling head, the drooling, the unfocused eyes and the heavy sleeping – looked more like dementia.

Was it possible that a massive stroke could trigger such a condition? Or was it possible that Michael, unknowingly, suffered from several tiny strokes which he used to call indigestion? Or how about those agonizing attacks of sciatica . . . ? Sometimes he almost passed out with the pain. Multi-infarct dementia?

Yes, of course it was. She thought about Elizabeth Stokes – so sad, a retired head teacher, only sixty-five, who suffered a series of minor strokes over a two-year period. Now she is in a nursing home, helpless and behaving exactly like Michael.

Neil Jarvis, GP, who knows Rose well and trusts her, is unlikely to question her too intensively over Michael's treatment in Venice, especially after he reads the letter.

And all the time she is plotting and planning and reassuring Michael, the telephone goes almost constantly with messages of support and good will. Rose didn't know they had so many friends. The moment she announces their presence the house will turn into Piccadilly Circus.

162

All through that long day she spends hours sitting silently beside Michael's bed, staring at his waxen face, praying he will survive this. He doesn't appear to know who she is.

There is no way he can hear her. But after twelve hours of the drug being administered she did notice a steady improvement, a distinct bubbling, a rising to the surface of a bottle held under water. She watched and waited, needing to see how long it would take before his faculties became too sharp for comfort.

Then, unable to risk it but wishing she could, she drugged him again with the back-up pills.

And then, out of the blue, the phone rang.

'Michael, you know who this is. Where are you? Ring me.'

The unmistakable voice of Belinda.

A quiet but seething rage replaces Rose's gnawing anxiety.

Jesus.

Here she is, so concerned for his welfare, so careful not to hurt him, and here is that brazen slut trying to arrange a sleazy assignation, no doubt at some disreputable hotel.

How is it possible to mix love and hate together so fiercely?

Angry and more sure of her motives than ever, Rose sits in Michael's study and turns on the PC and the scanner. She knows enough to make good copies; she uses it herself when she prints out posters and flyers for her various charitable works. She slips in the hospital form and copies just the heading. Ospedale Civile. Castello. The name of the doctor,

Giovanni Franceschi, is the name of the student. Usefully, the artistic young man in the square had signed his work.

She works on the finished effect until she feels she has it right, or as right as it can ever be. Nobody's going to be looking for tricks. Daisy can take it to the library and have it translated there, although, by then, the doctor will have examined Michael and formed his own opinion.

Although Michael is right here beside her, Rose has never felt so alone.

What she wouldn't give for somebody to confide in, somebody who would understand what was driving her to such awful extremes, somebody who would assure her that her actions were for the best. For Michael's own good as well as that of the family.

In happier circumstances that person would have been Michael; they loved each other so deeply she had thought they were inseparable.

She takes a freshly made cup of tea and goes to sit beside him again. After a moment she fetches an ashtray and the cigarettes she keeps in the bread bin and lights up in front of him for the first time for ten years.

'What's worrying me most is the future,' she says, drawing comforting nicotine deep into her lungs. She steels herself to be natural. They might be discussing the weather forecast. 'This can't go on indefinitely. Sometime, and I don't know when, we will have to communicate. You'll have to tell me what has been going on between you and Belinda. And somehow I will have to believe it when you say it is finished.'

164

Michael breathes in and out deeply, with his eyes firmly closed. She kisses his cheek. It feels cold to her lips.

They used to know what each other was thinking without the use of words. Is there any way now, deep in his subconscious, that he understands what she is saying and why she has to do this to him?

'It could be a matter of weeks,' Rose thinks out loud. 'It could be that the telephone messages gradually peter out when Belinda grasps the fact that you are just not interested.'

She gets up, and with the cigarette firmly between her lips, she makes sure he is tucked in warmly.

'It could be that we start communicating with you pressing my hand. One squeeze for yes, two for no. That might be the answer. Once the first hurdle is over why don't we experiment with that? Once I've got the dosage right and you're up and moving around. I'm not going to hurt you, Michael. You know I would never hurt you. I love you far too much to do that.'

No response whatsoever. Well, Rose hadn't expected one. It just felt good to confide like this and have him listen to her problems.

But there is blame in his continuing silence. Rose's voice rises. 'You might have done the same if you'd caught me being so deceitful. Don't go all Godlike on me, you know how I hate that. Bloody holier-than-thou.'

She looks at him crossly. On a body unused to the drug, the dose she had given him last night would have knocked him down like a slaughterer's bullet. But from her long experience with Baggins she knows that dosages have to increase as the body

165

becomes attuned to the drug. She is going to have to watch him closely.

She pleaded pathetically. She wanted to know, 'What sort of person is your Belinda? Is she kind? Does she love you? Does she make you laugh? Oh, Michael.'

It's good that no-one can see her or hear her, sobbing beside a carcass, but venting her feelings gives such sweet release, like a chain round her head being loosened at last.

And then comes the anger; it comes with such force it's frightening. 'How many times did you fuck her, Michael? And was she good? I bet she was. Did she do things I wouldn't do? Did you talk dirty? Did you dress up, play doctors and nurses? Well, look, you dog, I can play that game, too.'

Never in her life has Rose spoken like that. And to Michael. It's extraordinary. Funny, she knows how to do it. All that after-the-watershed TV, she supposes.

All these questions. She so badly wants answers, but the man on the bed can give her nothing. 'How were you going to tell me, you bastard? But then, you have so many secrets, don't you? Dear God, how could you Michael? How could you be so cruel?'

She stubs out the cigarette angrily, hoping the smoke nearly chokes him. She'll light another one in a minute. 'I'd like to stub it out on your face,' and she'll blow the smoke straight up his nostrils. That ought to reach him, wherever he's hiding.

'Come out, come out, wherever you are.'

Rose wakes up to total darkness.

The rigid body beside her sleeps on.

She switches on the light and takes a quick look at the time. Eight thirty. Normally they would be sitting together, enjoying some wildlife documentary or a drama – Ruth Rendell, or *The Bill*, Rose likes that. Rose doesn't mind Michael watching football, it's cricket she really can't stand. Or maybe he'd start the crossword and read out the clues when he needed help. She'd get out the dictionary and check his spellings. They might play a CD, open a bottle of wine, and she might read while he dozed in the chair alongside her.

Those lost days will come again. In her pain Rose really believes that. It's only a matter of time and patience. At least he's still here where he belongs. At least she can take care of him.

As Rose takes the opportunity for a soak in the bath, she wonders at the way life's lesser problems depart once you've got real grief on your hands. Daisy's erratic lifestyle, which once used to drive her to tears, now leaves Rose cold. The fact that William isn't the sort who is likely to settle down, and the sad knowledge that misguided Daisy expects him to, is nothing to do with Rose any more. That silly child is searching for someone who probably doesn't exist. Someone like Michael.

Michael's type aren't around any more. They are dinosaurs, a lost species. How many times has Daisy come crying over some shattered affair, and on every occasion, according to her, she has been let down, betrayed. It's never her fault, always his.

'You expect too much,' Rose used to tell her.

And here she goes again with William, who's pleasant enough, well-mannered and friendly, but far too excited with life to want to settle down. He has always made his ambition quite clear: he wants to travel the world. And while Daisy might imagine that she'd like to go with him, Rose knows how wrong this silly fantasy is. Daisy would change her mind before she'd even crossed the Channel.

Daisy enjoys her comforts while William would rather go hirsute in sandals and an old sunhat.

Rose sighs deeply and submerges her body beneath the bubbles. She needn't worry about the lights or anyone coming to her door. Some had been left on in their absence, and Daisy would have alternated them from hall to landing to bedroom during one of her check-up visits. The cars are still in the garage and, to keep the chill away, the heating was never switched off.

Luckily Rose, as usual, had cancelled the milk and the papers till after the weekend. It was less confusing for Mr Gant, who wasn't an organized man, to start up again on a Monday.

So unless someone has a key and walks in, nobody will know they are home.

And Jessie, what about her? Jessie is normal for her age and pretty as a picture, in spite of her coarsely cut hair and appalling taste in clothes. OK, she's had her problems, but at last she's beginning to settle down, and one day she will make an excellent teacher.

No, Rose has more on her plate than the fate of her two beloved daughters. They will work things out for themselves, given time, without her interference. Michael spoils them, that's the nub of it. Not so much in a material way – it is she who tends to do that – but by treating them still as his little princesses. Nineteen and twenty-three and still emotionally dependent on him. It's about time they stood up for themselves and stopped needing his constant support.

This illness of his might give them the strength they never imagined they had. They love him too much, that's their trouble.

Rose had to learn to do without Daddy, and it never did her any lasting harm. It's time they started to appreciate their mother, as the teenage Rose had been forced to do. She had been her father's darling, the light of his life. And then, one night, he was gone. And she was left with a mother demented with grief.

Rose has been sliced open, and the stone inside her hacked in half.

One half of the peach is a stranger, a wild, maddened, rotten creature, prepared to do murder in order to keep her man. But the other half, the sweeter half, is still recognizable; the half that must deal with the damage, smooth over the cracks and perform. Whatever the spoiled half does, the good half must try to make good.

She must keep a careful eye on Michael. She cannot allow speech, but she needs more movement, particularly an improvement in his ability to swallow, and she'd prefer his eyes to stay open, too.

Poor, dear Michael. How wretched he must be feeling and how relieved he will be to know that one day, when Rose is convinced of his loyalty, he will be back to his old self again.

This time she allows him two more hours before she gives him his treatment, after all, there's no danger of this husk of a man overpowering her. Warily she watches his minuscule progress, the way his eyes begin to focus and take on that look of utter surprise; how his fingers begin to flex, as if of their own accord; how a pulse above his eye begins to beat like a quickening heart, and finally how his tongue begins to moisten his dry, cracked lips.

It's still far from certain if he recognizes her or not.

If she could keep this balance Rose feels she might succeed.

'Feeling better?'

He cannot reply.

There is no other way. She must harden her heart. 'Well, I'm sorry. If you only knew how hard it is for me to do this to you, but I'm going to have to give you some more. I know this is unpleasant, but for everyone's sake it has to be done.'

This procedure is so distressing. Rose looks away when the needle pierces the skin. She gets his poor hand in the best position; she has to make sure her own are steady and she stares him straight in the eye.

With this hand, his right hand, did he make love to Belinda? Did he stroke her breasts? Did he trace her eyes? Did he moisten her vagina, ready for entry?

A lower dose this evening. She's going to risk 20mgs.

He ought to be grateful she cares so deeply. This is his fault, not hers.

After depressing the syringe she massages the skin to make sure there's no bruising. Still his eyes stare straight into hers with a look of bewildered puzzlement.

170

'You might well ask. You might well wonder,' Rose mutters to herself. But then, 'Please don't hate me. Please love me.' And then, 'Belinda, *Belinda*,' she hisses through her teeth. 'You wouldn't want him now.' His penis looks childlike and helpless, as does he.

'We'll start you on some soup tomorrow,' she says, puffing after her efforts, tucking him in once again. Poor Michael must be made comfortable.

'Chicken or mushroom? I'd let you choose but you can't.' And her laugh sounds like somebody crying.

Rose herself needs a good night's sleep.

Tomorrow's tensions will be exhausting, and somehow she's got to be able to cope. She would rather sleep in the spare room tonight. Having Michael's body beside her disturbs her, his unnatural stillness and silence is far, far worse than the loudest of snores or the wildest gnashing of teeth. But she daren't leave him untended.

Rose, to whom religion means little, feels impelled to kneel by the bed and chant a familiar childhood prayer. She says it on Michael's behalf; she doesn't want him to die.

She chants it as she did then, so that it had no meaning.

Jesus tender shepherd hear me bless thy little lamb tonight
Through the darkness be thou near me keep me safe till morning light.

THIRTEEN

Daisy had begged William to come with her on this first, terrifying visit.

Mum had rung the library at ten that morning to announce their arrival home. She was full of grim warnings: prepare yourself for a shock; don't break down in front of him; he looks very poorly; he's confined to his bed; he can't move; he's not the dad you knew.

Alarmed but determined to be grown-up and supportive, Daisy rang William. He'd had a job last night so she knew he would be at home.

His reaction was not what she wanted. 'Don't you think it might be better, for your mum most of all, if you and Jessie went on your own?'

'What d'you mean?'

'Daisy, think about it. She's going to be very upset. You all are. And at times like these you don't really want a stranger hanging around.'

'But you're not a stranger.'

'You know what I mean. This is a time for family.'

'But William, *I need you to be there*.'

But he wouldn't be persuaded.

Obviously Jasmine had no such qualms. From the moment she and Jessie walked in Jasmine took quiet command, making tea; collecting the washing, which she insisted on doing herself – 'That's the last thing your mum wants to think about' – drawing back overlooked curtains; clearing and cleaning the kitchen; stacking the dishwasher and turning it on.

So sweet, so kind. And all done discreetly, without aggravation, so that Daisy and Jessie could concentrate on the matter in hand.

No-one could prepare them for the sight of Dad so ill. Hardly living.

When Daisy held his hand she almost flinched and pulled away, so shocking was its fishlike limpness.

She tried talking to him, they both did, while Mum stood and watched, biting her lip, arms tightly folded.

'Hi, Dad, it's me, Daisy. How you doing?' Her voice broke and Mum frowned. Before she could stop herself she said, 'But there's nothing there. He's just a dummy . . .'

Jessie took over, hysterically bright. 'What have you gone and done now, Dad?' As if he were a naughty child who'd fallen off the slide and needed a plaster.

'Can he hear us?' Daisy turned and asked Mum.

'We must just assume he can,' she said, 'and go on chatting normally.'

It was a relief when the doctor arrived and someone experienced took charge.

He spent ten minutes talking to Mum, listening to how it had happened and the anguish she had been through in these last few days. He sounded impressed by the efficiency of the Venetian medical services. They had rushed their patient to the hospital within half an hour of his stroke, and on arrival he was taken for tests, which included the CT scan.

'There was no doubt about the diagnosis,' said Mum. 'They sounded absolutely certain.'

Then, hands trembling, she produced a letter. 'From the doctor in charge,' she told Neil. 'It's all in there. I'm afraid it's in Italian, but maybe Daisy could get it translated?'

The chance of being able to do something practical was such a relief, like a fountain of light. 'No problem, Mum. Whenever you like.'

'Well,' sighed Neil Jarvis. 'Not that that's going to make much difference, whatever it says.'

They stood around Dad's bedside like students round a gurney, hanging on to every pronouncement the eminent doctor made. They all watched solemnly while the doctor sounded Dad's chest, professionally displaying no reaction when he took Dad's blood pressure – twice – and tested Dad's reflexes with a miniature metal hammer. 'There's a good chance of partial recovery, a small chance of a complete one. Rose, it's a matter of time.'

The doctor tested him over and over, until Daisy felt like shouting, 'Leave him alone for God's sake.' Both his legs gave half-hearted kicks – proof that he was alive.

It was awful. Mum kept stepping forward to wipe the drool from Dad's mouth. Her expression was a picture of agony. You could see how hard she was hoping the doctor would tell her it would be all right, that this was nothing serious, he'd be up and about in a couple of days, just give him a couple of aspirin to take his temperature down. No such luck.

Neither Daisy nor Jessie had seen a seriously ill person before. Why did it have to be him? When there's so many bastards around. Muggers, paedophiles, rapists, torturers. Life is so unfair.

'To be honest, what really beats me', said Neil Jarvis, GP, 'is why the hell they allowed someone in Michael's condition to leave the hospital, let alone travel.'

Mum, pale-faced and drawn, confessed. 'That was me, Neil. My fault. I insisted. I went against all their warnings. You see,' she wrung her hands in the tea towel, 'I knew that's what Michael would want. He'd be desperate to come home, scared to death in a strange country, with nobody speaking a word of English, except for this one nurse.'

'But the journey, Rose. It could well have been fatal.'

Daisy could hardly watch, the sight of her father was so pathetic. If Dad had done bad things in his life he was certainly suffering for them now.

'I know that now. And I'm so sorry. But the airline were very good. He was on a stretcher all the way, with a doctor in attendance, and an ambulance with paramedics was waiting at Exeter to bring him home and help me get him into bed.'

'I'm glad you brought him home, Mum,' said Jessie in a supportive rush. 'He'll get better far more quickly here with us around him.'

'I just hope you're right, Jessie,' said Neil, a very serious look on his face. 'Michael is not a well man. He's going to need a great deal of care, and I'd be happier if he went to hospital so we can do a few more tests—'

'Neil,' said Rose, 'please listen to what I am saying. Michael has a horror of hospitals. If he could speak he'd tell you that he would far rather—'

'Please let's go along with Mum,' said Daisy, quite distraught. 'Please, Neil, let's give it a chance. Can't you just leave him here for a while?'

Jessie said, 'Mum knows what's best for Dad. Let's give loving care a chance before we start all this hands-on stuff, which might well do more harm than good.'

The doctor accepted a drink. Unsurprisingly Mum swigged hers as if she were dependent on it. 'I know this is no real consolation right now,' Neil said to Mum, who was weeping on and off, 'but of all the people I know, you, Rose, will be able to cope with this. You are solid, sensible and capable, your daughters are a credit to you, and you and Michael have hundreds of friends. Now is the time to let them prove themselves. Don't try to manage alone. Accept all the help that's offered. Michael's recovery is going to take time. Don't stick at home, get out and about, get busy. Whatever happens, don't allow yourself to get sucked under by this.'

Mum nodded. 'I'll try, Neil.'

She sounded so young, so impressionable.

'I know you will.'

Picking his coat off the sitting-room chair, the doctor left. The nurse would come and see Michael later that afternoon and do whatever needed to be done. 'But in these cases,' said Neil on the doorstep, 'apart from keeping a check on his blood pressure, it's time that's going to do the healing.'

'You've all got to eat,' says the stalwart Jasmine, having warmed up some frozen shepherd's pies. 'Especially you, Mrs Redfern.'

'Call me Rose,' says Mum. 'Please, dear.'

'You know I don't eat meat,' starts Jessie, just as unhungry as Daisy feels.

'Don't worry, I found a veggie one for you.'

'I always keep a stock in the freezer,' says Rose. 'I'm not too hot at vegetarian . . .' Her voice runs out, unable to concentrate on such trivia. She lights a cigarette automatically, as if she's been smoking for years.

'Oh no, don't say . . . Mum, you shouldn't.'

'Leave her to do what she needs to do,' says Jasmine calmly. 'She stopped once, she can stop again.'

But William will be pleased to hear that Mum has come out of the closet.

And anyway, how come Jasmine could take time off on a sudden whim like that?

'A free morning,' she explains, 'luckily. When Jessie called she was so distressed I felt I had to come. If anyone feels uneasy about me being here, you would say, wouldn't you?'

Nobody minds. Jasmine's a good sort, and plucky. The sort of best friend everyone dreams of having. Are they involved in a biblical way? Jessie denies it and there's no way of telling. The two are obviously fond of each other, but then girls do kiss and hug a lot.

*   *   *

177

Whatever problems are besetting Jessie, Dad is no longer around to help. And that applies to Daisy, too, and the dawning realization of that fact comes as one hell of a shock.

It's the little things just as much as the big ones.

William is totally helpless under car bonnets or basins; he wouldn't know how to handle a saw, or paper a room, or lay a carpet. And what's worse, he doesn't appear to care. He doesn't see DIY as a necessary manly function. He can sit quite happily watching while Dad adjusts the ballcock or tightens the washers. He will just about agree to help clear a room for decorating, but when he's expected to go up a ladder he holds his hands up and admits defeat.

Daisy can't help being intensely irritated by this. 'Didn't your dad do things like this?' she has enquired in the past.

'No, never. It was always Mum. Dad was mostly out working.'

It's amazing. Every family is so different.

But who's going to do those little jobs now? Daisy is revolted that she should be asking such a selfish question.

Poor, poor Mum. It must be like living with a corpse. What about keeping him clean? Does Dad mess the bed? Does she keep him in nappies? Does Daisy really want to know?

This is her father, the adored, all-wise one.

'I'm going to have to, probably,' Mum answers Daisy's hesitant question. 'So far he's just wet himself. I've got a rubber sheet on the bed, nothing else, but then he's eaten nothing. They had him on a drip in Venice, he was hitched up to one on the flight, but I'm going to try him on soup tonight.'

178

'Complan,' says Jasmine.

'Probably,' Mum agrees.

They toy with their pies automatically.

Jasmine clears the plates away and makes a welcome pot of tea.

Dr Jarvis might be a colleague of Mum's, but he doesn't know her as well as he thinks if he expects her to get out and about.

Six o'clock is her curfew, and then she fusses if she's not indoors preparing for another homely evening. Neither of them ever seemed to need any-one else. The idea that she'd go out without Dad is hard to get to grips with. And Mum's not a natural mixer; she wouldn't go out for a drink and a gossip. She used to rely on Dad; he led when it came to social interaction.

As the telephone messages keep coming through – some she answers, some she doesn't – it's interesting to speculate on which of Mum's friends she might call on in this time of trouble.

All offer sympathy, most throw help in, too. 'Anything I can do, Rose?' is the oft repeated question.

Di Fellows is more specific. 'Shopping? I do a good casserole and my sponges mostly rise.'

Like Mum, Di also reads for the blind, and that's where they met. She organizes a weekly newsletter; she cries and laughs too easily. The last of the Sixties hippies, she wears velveteen smocks and hand-made boots from a local women's co-operative. Divorced twice, and now with a troublesome partner, she has problems with her relationships and Daisy knows why. Di is too benevolent for her own good, too

179

sickly sweet and helpful. You will never catch Di Fellows without a goodwill smile on her face, and even Daisy, who hardly knows her, has felt the urge to smack it off.

Di would drive Mum mad if she pushed herself too far in.

And then there's Jilly Essery, JP, a horsy, healthy lady with a mass of broken veins from the weather and whose idea of fun is a twenty-mile walk. Sometimes they go shopping together or meet up for coffee. Jilly's involved with meals on wheels, mainly the raising of extra funds through fêtes and coffee mornings, and although they might speak on the phone, having lengthy discussions about Jilly's wayward son, there are no real depths to that relationship, either.

So that disposes of Mum's closest friends. The others are spare; they sit on life's margins.

One call Mum has to answer is Jack Bennet's from the office.

Daisy wants to cover her ears; she doesn't want to hear it all over again. The picture is now vivid enough, it doesn't need any more colour.

'He's a sweet man,' says Mum when she's finished. 'So concerned and eager to help. I mustn't worry about anything. It's all under control. Michael's work will be shared out with absolutely no difficulty. Isn't it incredible, Daisy, how kind people are?'

It is incredible, Daisy has to agree, when even strangers like Jasmine are determined to do their bit.

'Any evening you want to go out,' she tells Rose, her large face beaming with kindness, 'I can come round and take over. Because I live on my own it makes no difference to me where I watch the TV. In fact, it makes a nice change for me to go out somewhere different.'

Is Jessie wishing, like Daisy, that she had suggested this first?

But she has to admit it would be easier for Jasmine than it would be for her. If William isn't prepared to spend evenings round at Seymour House, either babysitting for Dad or keeping Mum company, what is poor Daisy expected to do? William prefers to go out when he has a free evening, to the Blue Angel Club, or to meet his mates at Alfie's Bar, or to a concert if he's got the funds. And Daisy feels she needs to be with him. Anyone could snap him up. He's so laid back he wouldn't notice.

God. William would be bored stiff if he had to spend many evenings in watching telly with Daisy and Mum.

But Jessie is free, she ought to offer. OK, she has piles of work to get through, but there's nothing to stop her bringing it here; it's not as if Dad needs constant attention. If only. Oh, if only he did.

'And I can do any weekend,' is Jessie's contribution.

'You know where I am if you ever need me,' is what Daisy is finally forced to say.

Tonight she will have it out with William. Damn it, it's time he told her. Is he prepared to support her or not?

Daisy would pull out every stop if he needed her help. Daisy desperately wants to look after Dad; she needs him and loves him madly, and the sight of him so weak and sick is the worst experience of her life, almost more than she can stand. He has no right to be ill like this, as if he's ignoring all their needs. Daisy remembers feeling this way when she was little, when Jessie pushed in and Dad seemed to forget all interest in her, his firstborn.

Granny is her usual disparaging self. 'Oh no, Rose, not a stroke! But I suppose we should have expected it.'

But Mum is as patient as ever. Her wry smile is a small one. 'People have been known to recover.'

'I know, dear, but at what cost?'

It's not worth answering such a daft question.

'Dr Jarvis says time will tell.'

Granny sniffs. 'Oh, him.'

Granny is worried about losing out now there's someone more needy than she, but unlike Daisy and Jessie she is brazen enough to come out with it. 'I suppose I'll have to manage on my own.'

Mum's hand tenses. 'Oh don't start that, Mother.'

'Well, what else can I expect now Michael's a virtual cripple?'

'He didn't do it deliberately, you know.'

'Huh.' She is actually making out that he did!

'You'll just have to spend more time over here,' Mum explains to her gently. 'After all, you can still drive.'

'Ah, but for how long?'

Isn't she going to ask about Dad, the son-in-law who has been so good to her? Apparently not.

Daisy hates her. She hopes she's in terrible pain. How can Mum stay on the phone and listen to such

182

garbage? Granny is an evil old cow and somebody ought to tell her so.

'Typical reaction,' says Mum eventually, sitting down, exhausted. 'Never expected anything else. But at least she knows now. I'm glad to get that phone call over.'

Leaving Mum on her own with Dad is a painful experience, no matter how many pledges are made about coming round tomorrow, ringing tonight, getting the letter translated, taking it round to the surgery etc.

Mum keeps saying, 'Don't worry, I'll manage. The nurse is coming this afternoon and Neil's calling in again tomorrow.' But she sounds so brave and pathetic.

'Promise me one thing,' Mum tells them both, 'don't just call. Always warn me if you're coming, because I don't want to be caught cleaning Michael up or changing the sheets or giving him a bed bath.' She looks away. 'I don't think he'd like it.'

Both the girls and Jasmine promise. They wouldn't have dreamed of doing such a thing. They always ring before they visit to make sure there's somebody home.

But now it's different: there will always be somebody home in this house. Maybe there should be a mark on the door, daubed in red paint, the colour of pain.

FOURTEEN

The fear of the unendurable layers his body in sheets of sweat. Rose, are you out there? For Christ's sake help me!

He pushes back thoughts that, apart from the pain, the pea soup of consciousness might be clearing, unwilling to tempt the fates that have cursed him. Between his doses of medication, which Michael is beginning to recognize as such, his mind is less befuddled, recent memories are becoming clearer. He can now, sometimes, remember Venice, and the journey home, the pleasant evening he and Rose spent together before he was brought to this. What sort of vicious attack could produce such mind-blowing results? A heart attack maybe? A stroke? A virus?

But if he's so terribly ill, why is he home and not in hospital? This last thought gives him hope. Whatever he's suffering from can't be that serious if he's at home. There must be a good chance of complete recovery; he'd go raving mad if he thought otherwise. For Michael, so vulnerable and paralysed, negative thoughts are not an option.

One more hopeful sign is the way he is managing to move his head, in a series of uncomfortable jerks which must look obscene to any observer. Not only his head, but with the grimmest concentration he can just about raise his arm up off the bed and slightly bend his elbow.

The bovine grunts he thinks he is making drive him into a hopeless fury. Hour after hour he practises, because communication is his only way out. The sound, if you can call it that, sends no message and makes no sense, not even to himself.

How is Rose coping with this? Poor dear Rose. Even if she is trying to reach him, he can hear nothing but muffled echoes.

His wretched suffering and appalling self-pity can be no worse than hers. And what sort of emotions must she be feeling? What sort of rejection? Realizing that her own husband can't see her, doesn't even know her.

If he gets out of this – when he gets out of this – he will make things up to her a hundredfold.

Daisy and Jessie, if they can see him, will be so frightened by the sight of their father, such a healthy, fun-loving man, splayed out on this stinking bed. But if this affliction had to happen to someone, Michael is glad it has happened to him. A hundred times in the lives of his daughters – toothaches, broken wrists, fevers and all the normal pains and heartbreaks which afflict all human beings – on every single occasion they suffered, Michael wished it could have been him. And even if the ultimate nightmare, this vegetative state for the rest of his life, is to be the final conclusion, thank God it is him and not one of his children.

Rose has often accused him of being far too indulgent, even of halting their adult development because of his willingness – no, pleasure – to help. But Rose doesn't know all of it.

Several times he has helped them out recently, and not only financially, but has considered it more circumspect to keep the issues to himself. Particularly the last mess Jessie got herself into.

Rose, though firmly on Jessie's side, would have found the whole business too distressing. She might have suggested therapy for Jessie, or insisted she leave St Marks. She might have confronted Belinda's parents in a not particularly sensitive manner.

There was no doubt that it was an iffy situation, and one to be handled with the greatest of care. Clearly Belinda needed help. She wasn't a happy girl and her background wasn't the most stable. Luckily, through work, Michael knew Sheila Gordon, the head of St Marks, and he spoke to her in confidence, knowing her to be a wise woman.

From what Jessie eventually told him after Daisy's approach, Michael could see how easily the situation had developed. Jessie had not behaved well; she had used her loneliness and sense of frustration – she had never wanted to go to St Marks, she'd always made that perfectly clear – to encourage a friendship which was doomed from the start. The two girls had nothing in common, and despite Jessie's denials, there must have been early, tell-tale signs that Belinda was disturbed, not one of the group, the odd man out, a mischief maker, a whisperer. And together, each for their own motives, they had built a defensive fortress against the world, separating themselves, becoming exclusive, apart from the rest. That way lies psychosis.

Jessie, not a stupid girl, should have got wise to

186

what was happening when Belinda made her first physical approaches; she ought to have picked up the warning signals and not just gone along for the ride. But because she was bored and stubborn and had backed herself into a social corner, she closed her eyes to the obvious.

For someone as well-adjusted as Jessie this was unforgivable, and Michael told her so.

'You used her,' he said to his daughter. 'And Belinda wasn't able to cope.'

Jessie put on her flabbergasted air. 'Dad, you're taking her side! It wasn't like that. Belinda is manipulative; she's evil, a freak. Just wait till you meet her.'

'Belinda is mentally ill,' Michael stated flatly. 'And you know I'm not talking about sexual leanings, so don't start accusing me of being prejudiced. Whatever you did together is your affair, that's not why I'm here. It's Belinda's worrying behaviour ever since that tells me the girl needs help. It can't go on. Not only is she ruining your chances, Jessie, she's throwing away her own life, too.'

'She stalks me, Dad.'

'I know.'

'I've shown you the letters.'

'Yes.'

'She keeps cutting her arms and threatening to top herself or hurt me so nobody else can have me.'

'Yes, I understand that.'

'I keep finding things missing and I know she's been in my room and taken them. She won't take no for an answer. She's always embarrassing me in class, coming to sit beside me and holding my hand, whispering things.'

187

'And it's time something was done to stop it,' Michael said, 'before it goes any further.'

Sheila Gordon agreed that she and Michael should have Belinda into her office and talk to her together.

He had built up an image in his mind of the disturbed child who was hassling his daughter, but Belinda put paid to that. She was elfin and dark and extraordinarily pretty, except for the purple streaks in her hair. Her blue eyes had a hypnotic quality that drew you deeply into them. Draped in colourful shawls, she wore clumping DM boots. For some reason Michael had expected acne, a sallow complexion and poor communication skills.

Belinda suffered from none of these. She was open and friendly, and her lilting Welsh accent was attractive. She listened to what he and the principal had both decided to say, and betrayed little emotion other than a casual interest.

'It's all lies,' she said easily when they paused. 'Your daughter is a liar.'

'So none of these odd things actually happened?' Sheila Gordon asked her.

'No. It's all in Jessie's imagination. She's sick, didn't you know that?'

'Well why don't you tell us your side of the story,' said Michael patiently.

Belinda turned everything on its head. The sexual approaches were made by Jessie. Belinda felt sorry for her. She spent hours talking to her, trying to help her, but Jessie was so obsessed she couldn't, or wouldn't, listen. Belinda herself had been wondering what to do about the situation which, she agreed, was getting out of hand.

'She comes into my room at night and just stands, looking, by my bed. I have to pretend to be asleep. But I'm frightened about what she might do. Once she had a knife in her hand.'

Michael laid out the pile of letters Belinda had written to Jessie.

'That's not my writing,' Belinda insisted.

At this point Sheila Gordon took over. 'Oh, but it is, Belinda,' she said, producing a written essay and making a simple comparison. 'And earlier this morning I took the liberty of going into your room, and I found several items of Jessie's which she claims have disappeared over the weeks.'

Like a conjurer producing doves from a hat, Sheila produced a Mason & Pearson hairbrush, a sling-back shoe, a worn and elderly Uncle Bulgaria, a half-empty bottle of CK One scent and one grubby pillowcase. 'She planted them there,' said Belinda, her eyes suddenly ice bright, on the defensive, her voice a near shriek. 'She's sick. I told you, she's a bitch. She needs locking up in a bloody asylum.'

All this hard thinking wears Michael out, but he feels he can't let go, his thoughts are becoming so lucid. He has learned already that this means it's time for his medication.

'Let's be realistic about this,' advised Sheila Gordon sensibly. 'And let's not lose our cool.'

'*Fuck you, you cunts*,' yelled Belinda, and Sheila and Michael were startled by the sudden infusion of blood to her face, which turned in seconds from pretty to odd to downright ugly.

In one urgent fist Belinda McNab scooped up a glass paperweight and smashed it down on Sheila's desk. What once had been a splendid eagle broke into chunks, like slippery ice, and the shards were as sharp as Belinda's fury.

While Sheila cowered from the violence, Michael stepped forward and slapped the girl's face. His hand left a white impression on her cheek and caused her to gasp, pop-eyed, before breaking down into clumsy tears.

'Nobody ever believes me,' she gulped and Michael looked away. Her nose was running into her mouth and her voice was thick with catarrh. He thought this would be a good moment to exit and leave the rest to Sheila's more experienced ministrations. He raised a questioning eyebrow and Sheila nodded – not too confidently he noted. Poor child.

Michael waited outside the door until he felt quite certain the situation was under control.

Later he learned that the governors had decided that Belinda McNab should be excluded from college on a permanent basis. Sheila interviewed the girl's parents, who expressed the expected natural concern.

Apparently, as Michael had suspected, the sad tale Belinda told Jessie about being unloved and abused was no more than an unhappy fantasy. An only child, she had always been difficult. At school, because of her violent behaviour, she had been referred to a child psychiatrist, the very worst scenario for any youngster in Michael's book. She had a long record of truancy, a history of petty thieving and a reputation for bullying. In spite of this her IQ was high and she had sailed through her exams.

Her distraught parents were at their wits' end. Four weeks later they wrote to Sheila, thanking her for her help and concern, with the information that Belinda had been admitted to Bullwood, a hospital specializing in serious behavioural disorders.

'We're hoping and praying', wrote Belinda's mother, 'that at last Belinda will receive the help she undoubtedly needs.'

Michael, discreet as ever, kept the details to himself. All Jessie needed to know was that the problem, as far as she was concerned, appeared to have been solved. No more was said and the subject was closed.

He was glad to have been able to help, but best that Rose didn't know.

It feels like the evening is drawing in.

He hopes there will be more improvements tomorrow. He almost managed to stand today; tomorrow he might be walking.

Michael accepts the soup he is fed, although hunger is a forgotten need. He knows he must eat to gain strength. Gentle hands feed him slowly. Tomato. And was it yesterday he was pleased to note that his sense of smell was returning?

Maybe he is learning to fight the terror.

Jesus, Jesus, help me.

A moaning in the ether turns out not to be him after all, but somebody out there speaking. Who? And how many are there? Frantically Michael attempts to bend his right arm once again, to give

191

some signal of his distress – don't let them go and leave him like this – but the drugs make this feeble gesture impossible.

Once again the dummy feels nailed to the bed, heavy and monstrously huge. The trick he has learned with his head won't work, and even his eyes refuse to stay open.

Now there's a different weight on the bed. More meaningless words move the atmosphere. They go on and on like a chanting, like plainsong or nursery rhymes. Someone is trying their damnedest to reach him. Oh, dear Jesus. Don't they know he would respond if he could?

He hears the sliding of what might be a drawer, and hope makes his slumbering heart beat faster.

He can feel his heavy lids being forced open and his blurred eyes see shadows moving, while at the same time he smells acetone. Rose's nail polish remover?

And then the blinding white fire. His tortured eyes are held wide open.

My, what big eyes you have.

All the better to see you with.

The ultimate torment – drip, drip, drip – like eyedrops made of cyanide. A bath of pure acid.

But who? Who?

His wounded brain writhes away from this anguish. No conscious man could take any more, and Michael escapes to the depths of the pit, leaving the savagery briefly behind him.

FIFTEEN

You're going to have to make the effort. Effort? Effort? Rose is sick of hearing about effort.

'The effort' encompasses many options: to rest, to watch her health, to stop smoking before she gets hooked, to mix with her friends, to keep her sense of humour and to get away from the house.

If only these well-meaning people knew. Rose's life is one long effort of deceit and finding the will-power to carry on.

Since their homecoming was announced Seymour House has been, as she dreaded, as open and beckoning as a whorehouse in a red-light district. People bearing grapes and flowers expect to be welcomed in, and once inside, with a cup of coffee, they feel it their duty to express, in detail, whatever opinions they might hold about the role of the carer.

Those banners – 'PARTY HERE TONIGHT' – she could design one: 'ROLL UP, ROLL UP. TEN MINUTES TO FREAK SHOW.'

All my own work.

She wheels them in for their view of Michael, and their voices turn hushed in 'the presence', as if they were in church.

The crucified.

The sacrificed.

He exceeds all their expectations. A pitiful husk of the man he once was, in spite of the lighter dosages, he sits in his chair beside the fire, unaware of his scandalized audience.

Mrs H's attitude had surprised her. That doughty woman waging war upon germs, with her insistence on Dettox for all surface wipes, came to Rose on the first day back, wearing her Elvis Presley apron, and said, 'I'm sorry, Mrs Redfern, but I just can't do his room.'

'His room?'

Mrs H sucked at her teeth, one of her many nervous habits, which included going round the house slamming down lavatory seats for fear of snakes coming up. 'Well your room, then. Mr Redfern's room,' she explained. 'Not with him in there like that.'

'It upsets you too much, Mrs H?' Of course. Rose should have been more considerate.

'I wouldn't mind if the poor man could speak,' Mrs H went on. 'It's his silence, that's what gets to me. That room has a pink glow all around it. Puts me in mind of a chapel of rest and I just can't handle it.'

Since then, thank goodness, he has learned to walk, if you can call that slow shuffle walking, and Mrs H habitually brings curious infusions of herbs: hawthorn berries, lime blossom and, the latest, yarrow to one part mistletoe, to be taken three times a day.

Rose finally bowed to the pressure to 'make the effort and get out'.

The invitation was there, the babysitters were

willing, and she really ought to go and discuss her financial situation. She couldn't find fault with her hosts, Jack and Barbara Bennet, nor could she moan about the venue – Arden Hall, an excellent country house restaurant only five miles from home. They're a sensitive couple, 'in case you need to get back in a hurry'.

Jack, Michael's fellow senior partner at Redfern and Bennet, chartered accountants, decided that an exclusive setting would be more beneficial to Rose than an evening round at their house. 'Bring you out of yourself a bit,' he said gamely.

How could she go and leave Michael? Anything could happen.

It was only four days since the first of the drugs had started running through his bloodstream and Rose was still experimenting with varying doses. She appeared to be succeeding because, according to Neil Jarvis, Michael's symptoms were those of a patient suffering from dementia after what could have been several small unreported strokes, followed by an acute attack. The fact that Michael could swallow his food and get himself around, albeit in a drooling, zombielike fashion, seemed to suggest he was making progress.

'How is our patient today?' nurse Susan trills breezily at the start of every visit. 'Shipshape and Bristol fashion?'

Rose makes perfectly sure there is little for her to do. She has changed him, bathed him, brushed his hair and cleaned his teeth by the time the young woman arrives. All that's left for the nurse to do is an injection for his blood pressure.

'We'll start on some physio soon,' she said over tea, 'when he's a little stronger. Just you make sure he keeps moving around and gets plenty of stimulus.'

'I'm lucky I've got so many kind volunteers,' Rose told her confidently.

'You're right, they can be tricky', said the nurse, 'when they're as wobbly as that.'

Explaining to her many supporters that it would not be wise to leave Michael at this early stage did no good. She tried her best.

'He can only communicate with me,' she lied glibly. 'We've always had that knack, and now it's essential that he knows he can reach me.'

The answers to that were simple. She would only be gone for three hours. Michael would be asleep for most, if not all, of that time. Jessie and Jasmine would phone her the minute there was any change, which everyone knew was unlikely. But most powerful of all was the message that Rose could not remain closeted away in the house day in, day out without some relief from the pressure.

'You'll go mad,' said Dinah, who knew all about madness, on her first visit to view the patient and contribute to the pool of expertise.

'If I'm not mad already,' said Rose.

Dinah was hanging over the bed like a carrion crow observing fresh offal.

'It doesn't look too good, does it?' she observed.

'No, Mother, it doesn't.'

'That man should be in a home.'

'There'd be no point in him going into a home,' said Rose, quoting the doctor's opinion. 'If he needed to be there he would be.'

196

'But maybe Michael would feel more comfortable being looked after by experts.'

'Michael is better off where he is.'

'How could you possibly know that?'

'We have our ways of communicating.'

'But the man can hardly move,' said Dinah.

'He's not always as bad as this,' Rose explained. 'He uses his good hand, his right hand, which is getting stronger all the time. But apart from that we've been together for almost thirty years; there are ways of knowing these things, feelings come into it. It's hard to explain, but I do know what I'm talking about.'

'I'm glad to hear that,' said Dinah. 'But I still think that man should be getting more expert care or some other recognized treatment. Craniosacreal therapy looked likely until I read that the client's intelligence system dictates the pace of the work, so not too apt, I'm afraid.'

Back in the sitting room, with Dinah propped up carefully in her favourite chair, Rose scattered the pamphlets and printouts before her on the coffee table. 'I've got so much information on taking care of a stroke victim it's coming out of my ears. The doctor is on the end of the phone and calls daily, the nurse comes every afternoon. I've read two self-help books on the subject and heaps of leaflets from the spiritually enlightened – Love yourself, heal your life. I've got all the support I need. What possible benefit would there be in carting poor Michael off and sticking him in an uncomfortable bed, with germs and contaminated water supplies, to be cared for by underpaid strangers?'

'You know best,' said Dinah.

But she was firmer when it came to Rose's unwanted night out.

'You're looking washed out and old,' she told her daughter. 'How's Michael going to feel if he does eventually get better and finds that he has turned his wife into a dowdy old hag?'

Not without cunning, Dinah knew she had hit a sore spot.

'Go on, make an effort,' she said. 'Doll yourself up, have a few drinks, try a few smiles. There is life out there, you know, everything doesn't begin and end in this house.'

When Jasmine volunteered her babysitting services Jessie jumped in and said she'd come too.

'You don't have to,' said Jasmine, so pushy and bold. 'I can cope, and you've got piles of work.'

But Jessie couldn't be outdone. 'This is far more important,' she said. 'I'll bring my essay and you can help me with it.'

And so it was decided that Rose should go out for dinner with Jack and Barbara Bennet and leave Michael behind with his loving carers.

It was over the main course that Rose heard the good news that she mustn't worry about her finances. Typically, Michael was well insured for a rainy day and Jack was dealing with that side of things. No need for Rose to concern herself.

Apart from that it had been agreed that Michael's full salary should be paid into the foreseeable future. 'Whatever happens you'll be looked after,' Jack assured her. 'And I'm here twenty-four hours a day if you should run into any problems. Anything at all, Rose,' he said with warmth.

Rose agreed with Barbara when she said how much worse things must seem because their marriage had been such a close one. 'So many people were envious of you,' Barbara told her, while Jack poured more red wine into her glass. 'Your marriage is one in a million.'

'We were just lucky,' said Rose, sipping thoughtfully. 'We happened to find each other without really trying. So many don't.'

She was beginning to feel that making an effort had been a good idea after all. Senses she'd thought were dead started to return – the floral decorations were beautiful; she was surprised at how hungry she was and how she enjoyed the decor here; how easy she felt in the Bennets' company – he was charming and witty, she was attractive and interesting – chatting on about the apartment they had just bought in the Algarve, and how much lighter of heart dressing up and doing her hair made her feel. Her image in the ornate mirrors, coming down the chandeliered staircase, had pleased her, too.

How would the Bennets have behaved if Michael had upped and left her? Not like this, that much was certain. Naturally they would have sided with Michael; Jack was his colleague after all, and Barbara was no particular friend of hers. And all this support and sympathy, there would have been none of that, more likely pity and the observation that it takes two to make a marriage and two to break it. There would have been speculation as to what sort of wife Rose had been to make Michael stray in the first place. She'd probably denied him sex, or nagged, or spent all his money, or grown too old.

When Barbara left the table to go to the loo, Rose

was surprised to feel Jack's hand on hers. She looked up and their eyes met. His were saying unexpected things; Rose blushed but kept on staring.

'You need never be lonely, Rose,' said Jack.

She felt a giggle arrive in her throat and fought it back determinedly.

'You know, I expect, that Barbara and I lead independent lives?'

'Well, no, Jack, Michael never told me.'

'Oh, Michael,' Jack shrugged, 'he didn't know. And I realize this might be the worst time to bring up such a subject, but you, Rose, are a lovely lady.' His eyes left hers to roam over her body before fixing back on her own again. 'But much more than that, there's some part of you that shines, and I've always admired that. You've always attracted me, Rose. I think you and I have a lot in common.'

Rose struggled for composure. She'd never viewed Jack in any other way than her husband's partner. But then, she supposed, she hadn't felt the need to be on the lookout for anyone else. Affairs were not her scene, and she had believed that Michael felt the same.

She studied Jack's face, the mellow blue eyes, the greying streaks in his overlong hair, which she thought might be coloured, the lips, with their slight, expectant smile, and she thought, ugh.

She couldn't.

She wouldn't.

This man was nothing compared with Michael, a shallow sham, a false charmer with an arrogance and self-confidence that made her want to wince.

Sometimes she and Michael had played the game

of who do you fancy? Of everyone here in this room, they would jest, who would you chose to screw if you had to? The task had been so impossible that in the end they would burst out laughing and wonder how that woman in the corner had actually chosen that awful man. They hadn't meant to be unkind, it was just a way of telling each other how satisfied and pleased they were with the choices they had made.

What would Jack look like with nothing on? Would he have sex slowly and feelingly? Or would he go at it hammer and tongs?

'I'm flattered. Of course I am,' she told Jack in as convincing a voice as she could muster. 'But you're right, this is a bad time for me.' Carefully she moved her hand back across the tablecloth. 'I haven't got any feelings to spare. I'm sorry if you and Barbara have problems, nobody would ever guess.'

No, they wouldn't, thought Rose, because his excuses simply weren't true. This became obvious when Barbara came back and Jack's expression changed so quickly and he fawned all over her, pulling out her chair.

'OK, darling? More wine? A liqueur? How about one for you, Rose?'

The perfect husband. Oh yes, Rose knew a fair bit about those.

'It's been like a public park in here,' said Jessie when the Bennets dropped Rose off, declining, thank God, to come in for a coffee.

'Daisy and William called for a drink, June Drummond brought you a Madeira cake and Monica came with this acupuncture brochure.'

'How's Michael?'

'Not a murmur.'

'You checked him?'

Jessie laughed. 'Did we? Ask Jasmine. She must have been in and out every ten minutes. Was it good? Did you enjoy it?'

'Yes, I did.' Rose took off her coat. 'Although I didn't expect to.'

'Well,' said Jasmine, 'now you've done it once you know you're safe to go out whenever you feel the need.'

What a strange girl Jasmine is. Why does she insist on wearing those dreadful, shapeless track-suits? But she's so friendly and good-hearted, so eager to help. A real pleasure to have around. She seems to be having a good influence on Jessie, too, who seems calmer, happier within herself, in spite of all the trauma of Michael.

When she goes into the bedroom Rose senses a restlessness in Michael which she hasn't noticed before.

She feels his forehead and checks his pulse.

His breathing is irregular – he must be dreaming – and there's a certain tension about him, although his features register nothing.

Are his eyelids swollen or is it her imagination? And what's that smell? Some kind of solvent? Probably her hairspray still lingering in the air.

She'll check him over tomorrow before the doctor's visit. She wants Michael to be at his best; she wants to help him downstairs again and maybe he can have a short spell in the garden. She missed his company badly tonight; it was the first time she had ever dined in a classy restaurant without him.

In time, if this charade continues and she gets his dosage right, she imagines taking him to the theatre; there are special places for the disabled. She could certainly help him out for short walks and take him to exhibitions and galleries once he gets more compos mentis; he would enjoy doing that.

She could take his medical feeding cup and a bib to put round his neck. She could use nurse Susan's incontinence pads to make sure he stayed acceptable.

They might even attempt a holiday, somewhere warm where the sunshine would put a glow back into his cheeks. They could sunbathe beside the pool together under raffia umbrellas; one might even slide him into the water with proper safety floats. Airlines cater for people like him; there's probably a special group they could join, with all the appropriate aids and facilities.

But hold on. Hold on. What's this long-term view Rose is taking?

Michael's helpless dependence was planned as a temporary measure until such time as he could convince her that his dalliance with Belinda was over. Is she now seriously considering that, if she can get away with it, she'd prefer her beloved husband to exist as a necessary accessory, to be loaded in with the luggage? No! What diabolical nonsense.

The children are wrong when they accuse Rose of demanding too much control. It's because she cares; it's because she loves them that she needs to feel in charge. And no wonder, when you remember the tragedies of her childhood, those circumstances over which she was powerless but which so influenced the rest of her life, that ache of absolute helplessness to prevent the agonies of loss.

Total control over Michael so that he will never stray again?

Just as, in those dark days, she had yearned for control over Jamie, so she longed for more power over her father, so she could stop the quarrels and atmospheres and make life sunny and bright, as it should be? So she could make them love her best.

Is this the way her thoughts are turning? Is that really what she wants? Is it what she has always wanted? Was that dark desire the true inspiration for Rose's deed? No, no, no. Rose pushes back these uninvited thoughts firmly. The sooner the Michael she knows and loves is back on his feet by her side the better.

But wait, when and if that moment arrives, Michael will have his own opinions, won't he? He will have to know what Rose has done and her earlier belief that he would feel such shame and guilt that he would sympathize with her position, maybe even be grateful to her for saving him from scandal, is now riddled with questions.

Once Rose thought she knew the answers, now she's not quite so sure.

Rose has a restless night full of dreams.

She wakes early and, after making tea, goes to pick up the post. On the kind of plain postcard she once used to go in for competitions – address on the front, fifteen clever words on the back – she has read it before she recognizes the writing.

But instead of the fifteen-word witty slogan describing why the product is best, there are only two, in large, childish print:
'I know. B.'

SIXTEEN

Jessie Redfern, pale and twitchy, walks on rusty leaves down the broad residential avenue towards her sister's flat. She feels the world's invasion pressing against her head like a hard rubber swimming cap. Nearly at the railings, beside the road where staked and spindly sycamores replace the long-dead elms, she hears a scuffling in the bushes – a dog, perhaps, or a fox? At the crossing is the usual six-o'clock traffic jam, and Jessie hates to walk along beside the cars because how can you tell who is inside or what they are saying?

Other, ordinary people are making their way home from work with briefcases and umbrellas; their expressions range from bored to urgent, but none of them show fear on their face, unlike hers. She normally uses her Mini, of course, but two tyres were flat when she went to retrieve it from the student car park that evening, and Jasmine the capable mannishly jacked up the car, removed the two offending tyres and has pledged to collect two new ones and put them on in the morning.

Why they suddenly went flat like that Jessie

doesn't know. The garage will tell Jasmine when she takes them in.

Once, when Jessie was visiting here, Belinda lurked outside in the bushes.

This evening, summoned by a phone call from her sister – an urgent call demanding her presence and refusing to expand any further – Jessie leaps at every sound and her eyes are permanently on the swivel for any sudden attack.

She keeps her mobile phone switched on and pretends to be deep in conversation.

Daisy's spacious flat, consisting of half the top floor of the house, is basically two large rooms divided by an arch – off the bedroom is the bathroom and off the sitting room is the kitchen. Comfortably furnished, with large, shabby sofas and chairs, rugs that fall on top of each other and floor-to-ceiling bookshelves, the lamps normally give the high-ceilinged rooms a cosy warmth. But when Jessie walks in this evening the tension cuts her like an arctic draught before she's even sat down.

William is standing by the window, as stiff as a guardsman on parade. He and Daisy have been having words. Daisy says nothing, but she seems to have rehearsed this well because the coat she holds up has the kind of dramatic effect she must have planned.

'I'd only worn it twice,' she says, the cold words jolting the silence. 'It was an early Christmas present for myself. William was going to give me half the money nearer the time.'

The full-length blue-grey coat with fur round the

207

collar and cuffs must have cost Daisy a bomb. It's wonderful, a once-in-a-lifetime coat, until, years later, you find another. The ugly rents from hem to waist, the mindless slashes that trail on the floor like dead men's fingers, are an abomination on something so beautiful.

Jessie starts out of shocked disbelief. 'And you think this was . . . ?'

'It was hanging in the staff cloakroom,' Daisy goes on, her voice expressionless. 'The staff cloakroom at the library is supposed to be kept locked.' She shrugs. 'But of course it isn't. It's a drag to have to keep finding the key when you're in a hurry, and up until now there's been no problem. Sod's law, this morning it was unlocked. At lunchtime I went to get it and found this.' She shakes the coat, as if trying to punish it for allowing its own destruction.

'You've got to go to the law,' interjects William in a clipped, cold voice.

At this Daisy breaks down. 'How can I go to the law and tell them all about Belinda when Mum's in the state she's in and Dad can't help, either? Imagine what effect knowing there's a lunatic at large would have on Mum at the moment.'

'It doesn't matter,' says William, impassive. 'Look at that coat. Think of the mind behind that. You have no alternative. This nutter is deranged.'

'Could Belinda do something like this?' Daisy asks her sister, dropping the coat across her lap, suggesting this is Jessie's fault.

Jessie shakes her head. 'Honestly, I don't know. I suppose she could. She's back, we know that. She must have found out where you worked.'

'Aha. A bit of cunning detective work there.'

208

'William, stop it. There's no need for sarcasm,' snaps Daisy sharply.

Jessie fingers the rent shards of material. Some large, sharp cutting instrument must have been used to make these slashes so precise. Sheers? Dressmaking scissors?

'And nobody saw anything?' she asks Daisy mournfully.

'No,' says Daisy. 'And I don't mind admitting that I'm sodding-well frightened. I've got to go back there tomorrow. What else has this lunatic got up her sleeve?'

William isn't responding in the way Daisy would like him to. She wants to be hugged and comforted, but instead he's quietly angry. In his opinion there is no other answer but to go straight to the police. 'What's this blind insistence from everyone in your bloody family that your mother should be protected from real life?'

'Well if you can't see it, it's no good anyone trying to explain,' says Daisy shortly.

William, still at the window, barks, 'Someone is going to get hurt. And what's Rose going to do then? Thank you for protecting her? So what if she thinks Jessie's a dyke, she's facing life with an imbecile, permanently crippled, by the look of him.'

'Why don't you shut up, William.'

But he ignores the loud interruption. 'The knowledge of her youngest daughter's sexual leanings is hardly going to faze Rose now. For Christ's sake, give the lady the benefit of the doubt and tell her before it's too late.'

'Too late?'

'Bloody hell, yes! Belinda could start on her next, for all we know.'

Daisy lowers her head. 'You think we need police protection, but you're not even prepared to walk me to work or collect me afterwards.'

'Too right I'm not. Not while you go on treating this like some smutty schoolgirl adventure. Jesus Christ, you're playing right into Belinda's hands.'

'It seems to me that you're shitting yourself in case she starts on you.'

'Oh grow up, do,' says William strutting crossly away from the window and pulling on his coat. 'I'm off.'

Daisy's neediness sounds pathetic, and it is. 'Where to?'

He winds a scarf round his neck. 'Anywhere away from here.' But at least he throws an 'I'll see you later' into the room behind him.

'Oh God, I wish Dad was OK.' Daisy weeps.

When Jasmine arrives with a Chinese takeaway she brings with her, as always, a sense of proportion.

Daisy seems more cut up about what she calls William's lack of support than the attack. But she's frightened and she shows it, so Jasmine volunteers to pick her up from the library at night and run her to work each morning.

'You leave your car here. We'll take mine. Just until you feel better.'

This seems rather overzealous, even for such a Christian soul, a fanatical believer in the Lord, who taps along to godly guitars, with her large feet in white Nikes. Alleluia. Happy-clappy, happy-clappy, and kiss the neighbour on your right. Country

210

dancing and do-se-doing. Recently she has taken to exhorting Jessie to accompany her to church. Jasmine's got her own life to lead — a full-time job, cricket practice, babysitting for Rose, on top of her many church activities. I mean, Jessie, Daisy's own sister, didn't even consider the idea of escorting her backwards and forwards from work. And anyway, isn't Jessie supposed to be the prime target in all of this?

But Jasmine has answers for everything. 'You only have to cross the courtyard to get to your classes, and you can surround yourself with other people. And you should. There's no car-parking space at the library; Daisy has to use the public car park two blocks away.'

'Maybe William's right,' moans Daisy. 'Perhaps we ought to tell the police.'

But William's a bum — fun, but a bum — marginally more interesting than some of the other guys Daisy has hitched up with. Daisy's heart has been broken more times than Jessie can count. William doesn't want commitment, and if Daisy continues to demand it he's just going to walk straight out of her life. He's only been to see Dad once, and then he couldn't handle it. He hurried out to the shed to roll himself a fag. William is great-looking, charming and laid-back, but the dimmest girl in the world would know he's not up for anything permanent. Except Daisy, of course.

And look, all she wants to do now is deny her own instincts and follow his.

'Before you do anything official,' says Jasmine, spooning out the fried rice into three portions, 'I think you should try to find Belinda yourselves.'

211

Jessie was thinking of doing this before Dad had had his stroke. Since then the effort has seemed too great; all her concentration has been directed on her mum and dad.

'Could you ask the college for Belinda's address? They must still have it on file somewhere.'

Jessie argues, 'But she's not at her address, is she? She's somewhere here, around Plymouth. We know that.'

'Talking to her mum and dad would be a start,' says Jasmine, busy with the prawn balls. 'They might well know where she's living.'

Daisy agrees with Jasmine that this would be a more sensible step than rushing to the law. 'And then we could all go and see her, or ask the police to have a quiet word rather than some big drama which Mum could get to know about.'

'But is William right?' asks Jessie, worried sick. Her romance with Belinda was a passionate one, far more passionate than she has ever been able to honestly admit, even to Daisy. At the time, for a while, she believed it was love. 'Are we being over-protective? Shouldn't Mum know what's going on? Surely the fact that I had a fling would seem quite small beer to her now. She'd take it in her stride, wouldn't she?'

But Jessie seems to have forgotten what the results of going public might be. Jasmine is quick to remind her: 'If there's any proof that Belinda sent that letter to me, deposited that turd in your room, attacked Daisy's coat and pierced your tyres, they might be worried enough to charge her. The whole débâcle might be taken out of our hands. Court, witnesses, evidence, the lot. All that old stuff would

212

come up. And then you'd have the papers digging around and telling the whole grubby story. Would you be OK with that, Jessie? Do you think you could handle it?'

Jessie, imagining it, covers her face with her hands. 'Oh God, no. Not if there's any other way.'

Apprehensively the following morning, Jessie makes her way towards the college admin block. She believed she had put that part of her life behind her. So far she's had no worrying urges, which might suggest she doesn't fancy women after all, although, at the time, Belinda's caresses had turned her on in a way she finds hard to admit, especially to herself. In many ways she'd encouraged Belinda, before she realized how obsessional and strange she was becoming. Jessie can almost sympathize with Belinda's vindictive behaviour now, after someone who once promised to care so suddenly turned against her.

Dad had been right to blame her.

She can feel her face redden as she asks a secretary for the information she is seeking. Will the woman remember some odd correspondence earlier that year? With Belinda's parents, perhaps? Or with Dad? Or some sensitive meeting about an unmentionable subject in which she knows Jessie to be involved?

'I'm a friend,' she feels it essential to explain, 'and I've lost her address, that's all.'

'Hang on.' The secretary departs into a backroom full of computers.

Jessie waits a good ten minutes. She watches the clock above the door, which goes more slowly as time passes. She's missing her first lecture. She will have to borrow somebody's notes unless there are enough handouts.

The woman comes back wearing a frown behind her smart bi-focals. 'This is odd,' she says, as if Jessie has the answers. 'I've checked and double-checked, but strangely there's no file for any Belinda McNab. Are you sure you've got the name right?'

'Absolutely.'

'And she was in your year?'

'Until last spring, yes.'

'Why did she leave? Do you know?'

Jessie thinks quickly. 'She was ill.'

'Well, I still don't understand', says the woman, looking blanker than ever, 'why that file would have been removed. I shall have to investigate further.'

Jessie can't stay there any longer. She rubs her sweaty wet hands together. 'It doesn't matter, it's not that important. I can probably get it from somewhere else.' And she picks up her holdall and makes to leave.

'That's not the point,' says the secretary, pushing back her specs with one worried finger. 'The point is that her file has gone.'

Maybe it would have been better if Jessie had gone straight to the principal.

'There are six McNabs in Cardiff, so that's not too daunting,' Daisy tells her later that day, home from the library where she'd gone through the directories.

'How's William?'

'Still sulking.'

'And how are you?'

214

'Still nervous. I hate the way this poisonous cow is selecting her targets.'

'You'd rather she concentrated on me?'

'That's not what I mean.'

No, but it's what you meant, thinks Jessie.

This news might make Daisy feel better. 'Both my tyres were write-offs. The garage told Jasmine there were six-inch nails right through them. Identical nails. It was deliberate.'

Daisy pauses for a few seconds. 'But you can't be absolutely certain that Belinda is guilty of that sabotage, or mine. We can't be certain of anything. Maybe these events are just random and we're jumping to conclusions.'

'Don't kid yourself,' sneers Jessie. 'What about that repulsive hot dog she left? The shit in my room?'

'It was just a thought,' says Daisy.

Jasmine comes to hold Jessie's hand when she takes the plunge that evening, with the six names and numbers on a scrap of paper before her.

They share the saggy bed in her room while Jessie gingerly handles her phone. 'There's no point in telling me God's rooting for me, that's not going to help us now,' she snaps at her stalwart friend and then feels guilty. She's often mean to poor Jasmine, but Jasmine has the ability to shrug off insults as if she hasn't heard them, and her unswerving good-ness is really quite aggravating.

Virgin, like a graveyard angel, she calls for des-ecration.

Sometimes the need to shake her out of it, to triumphantly bring out a string of obscenities, like bunting, to get her to admit to being pissed off or to confess to some shameful perversion, is almost too strong to resist.

Now Jasmine sits beside Jessie and eats her egg-and-cress roll. Cress tumbles down her white Aertex shirt and a can of lager rests on the table.

'I'm sorry to disturb you,' says Jessie politely, 'but I'm looking for an old friend of mine, Belinda McNab. Do I have the right number?'

No.

No.

No.

But the fourth phone call brings some reward. Jessie tenses and nods to Jasmine. She can recognize the accent. In a nervous voice she asks her question, but the pause on the end of the line sounds ominous.

'Who is this?'

'I'm an old friend of Belinda's.'

'And what did you say your name was?'

'I didn't. But it's Jessie Redfern. She was at St Marks with me . . .'

Her name is repeated by a snapping voice thick with aggression.

'Is that Mrs McNab?' asks Jessie.

'I don't know how you've got the nerve.'

'*Sorry?*' Jessie's mouth drops open as Jasmine munches happily beside her.

'Ringing here, of all places, asking that kind of innocent question after everything you've done, you and your bloody father. Ruined all our lives, playing games with other people—'

'Look,' says Jessie weakly. 'I'm really, really sorry you're taking this attitude—'

216

'Don't talk to me about attitudes, young woman. *Don't you dare.*'

'But I only wanted to know where she was. I didn't mean to—'

'You know what you are, don't you?'

Jessie shakes her head and closes her eyes against the blow.

'You're evil, that's what you are, pure, unadult-erated evil, and God will never forgive you for the wickedness you have done.'

'But what have I done?' She begs. She has never before met such savagery. Jasmine looks across in alarm.

'You and your devilish father. If you so much as dare to contact me or my husband again, I warn you, Jessie Redfern, your life won't be worth living.'

Jessie's fingers are stuck to the phone after the line goes dead and her body is too numb to react.

SEVENTEEN

'I know. B.'

This morning, after the postcard had arrived, Rose dragged herself into the kitchen, cut it into bits like an old credit card, lest anyone else might use it, and threw the devilish thing in the bin.

What did it mean? Dear God, what did Belinda know?

Rose only has one secret, a secret so nauseatingly evil it would destroy everybody she loved if it ever came out.

She calmed herself by using deep breathing and forced herself to sit down and stop pacing. She lit her first cigarette with difficulty in her jerking hands; the wretched lighter kept missing the tip. She told herself that the distraught Belinda had used this undermining ploy with no idea of the real threat she posed. Anyone, even a saint, would be disturbed by such an ambiguous statement.

Black magic. The power of suggestion. The victim had only to believe in the spell to make her own downfall come true.

Well, Rose was not such a simple target. It was absolutely impossible for anyone to guess what she'd done. Not only had she fooled her own family, but the professionals as well. Michael could have contacted no-one. He was the last person on earth to possess the kind of reasoning power necessary to work things out, so Belinda couldn't possibly know.

Could she be referring to something else? Something Rose had overlooked? If so, how pitiful. How frustrated Belinda must feel with her inability to influence Michael.

Perhaps, in her desperation, she would visit the house and demand entry. The woman was blatant and coarse enough, confident enough by the sound of the tramp. And then what would Rose do? The answer was easy, there were no dilemmas, Rose would take her straight to her lover and give her a nappy to change. If she loved him let her prove it.

No. Lovelorn Belinda was trying it on. But how long would she persevere? Had she heard about Michael's illness? If she worked at Redfern and Bennet she'd have heard on the grapevine only too quickly, but Rose wasn't sure she did work there. Michael could have picked her up anywhere, off the street most likely.

Was Belinda dirty? Was she diseased?

But why would Michael go for that type? For him that would be way out of character. But then, men of a certain age develop these masochistic tendencies, look at the MPs and judges who get a thrill from picking up whores. The fear of being caught played a part, Rose supposed. The risk, like a gambler, of putting everything of worth on the table: wife, family, career and reputation.

On top of all this that dratted nurse noticed some problem with Michael's eyes.

During today's visit she called Rose over. 'Look. His lids are terribly swollen, and if you widen them like this you can see how red and sore they are. The poor man must be in awful pain. Can you think how this must have happened?'

Rose had no idea.

'Doctor will have to look at this,' said nurse Susan worriedly, efficiently washing out Michael's eyes with a pad of lint in a kidney dish. 'I can't understand what can have happened. You don't touch his eyes at all, do you, Rose? You're not giving him any kind of drops?'

Rose shook her head, as bemused as the nurse.

Before she left, the two women dressed Michael and helped him totter down the stairs. And then there were the steps between the various room levels but once down, the floors were all wooden and the rooms were spacious. Rose could place him so he could watch whatever she was doing. He must be so bored stuck in one place all day long.

She propped her husband upright. There. He might be slumped like a sack of potatoes, but he looked so much more familiar like that.

Late as usual, inundated by work and rushed, Neil Jarvis examined Michael's eyes. 'Has he ever been allergic to any household products? Room spray? Hair laquer? Have you shampooed his hair lately with an unfamiliar brand? Or taken to using different soap?'

No, but there could well be a severe reaction to 22mgs of Pentobarbitone administered twice a day.

'I suppose, being such an amateur, I could have accidentally got soap in his eyes. And maybe the fact that his tear glands aren't working made the reaction worse?'

Neil Jarvis frowned. Was the frown one of disagreement? Or of annoyance that a lay person should have the nerve to put forward a medical theory?

'Anyway, Rose,' he said, standing and clicking the silver torch back into its case. 'Apart from this little snag you can congratulate yourself on the progress Michael is making. His blood pressure is normal and his heart rate is satisfactory. Any improvement in his mental impairment will take longer, as I've already explained.'

'How long?' asked Rose innocently.

'It's difficult to predict precisely how long it will take.' The doctor glanced at his watch. He was running forty minutes behind schedule. 'I'll leave Michael in your capable hands,' he said, to her enormous relief, picking up his coat. 'I must say, it's good to see him up and moving about, although I can't say how aware he is of his surroundings.' He wrote out a prescription for eyedrops to be administered three times a day. 'And let's hope that inflammation clears up. Johnsons is the answer. Use baby products whenever you can. Nothing with a scent, and mind you avoid his eyes.'

'What a blessed relief,' said Mrs H, leaping backwards when Rose came in. She must have had her ear pressed hard against the kitchen door. 'That poor Mr Redfern can stay at home and get better. I would insist. I know what goes on in those hospitals

221

and homes' – Mrs H's daughter worked as an auxiliary nurse and was always coming home with gruesome, hair-raising tales – 'and they're no places to be if there's anything wrong with you. He'd likely come out with a broken hip on top of everything else.'

Mrs H, into spiritualism in a big way – she regularly attended seances at her friend Rita's house, and had seen with her own eyes several uncanny manifestations – had no trouble understanding Rose's ability to transfer her thoughts to Michael. 'If they can manage to speak to the dead then you're already halfway there with him,' she said in her excited state, still flustered after being caught eavesdropping. 'These hoity-toity doctors and such expect us to kneel down and worship them. Well, I've never been one to do that. If you want to speed things up try homoeopathy. If it's good enough for the royals then it's good enough for us, is what I say. And I dare say spiritual healing has its place as well. Have you asked the vicar?'

With all Mrs H's jabbering Rose forgot to remind her to check the French windows. Greatly opposed to double glazing, Michael had turned down all suggestions that these ancient, ill-fitting metal doors should be replaced by sliding patio ones. 'They have character,' he insisted. Every bedroom had one, giving access to the balcony, which circled the house like a concrete ribbon. The one in Jessie's room had been left open last night and the fault could be nobody else's. Who else would have gone upstairs?

It was Mrs H's habit to go out onto the balcony to shake out her mops and dusters, but she really must learn to lock the doors behind her. As Rose used to argue, it couldn't be simpler for any burglar to shin up the fire escape and straight into the house with his swag bag. Rose would have removed the keys from the locks except for fear of fire.

Having Michael sitting beside her, with a tartan rug over his knees and a bib round his neck to catch the saliva, is Rose's great achievement.

OK, he doesn't contribute, save for the odd twitch, snort or groan, but it's companionable just to have him there. It makes it worthwhile to light the fire, draw the curtains and make it cosy. Jasmine has promised to pop over this evening to help Rose get him back into bed and clear up. If this was going to be permanent Rose would need to install a chairlift.

Rose chats on, like she used to chat to poor Baggins when there was nobody else in the house except him.

'Shall we stay up late and watch *Crimewatch*?'

But no, that all depends on Jasmine and what time she arrives to help.

'I'll put another log on, I think. There's plenty left in the shed.'

Rose's attention is suddenly caught by Michael's contorted facial expressions. Don't say he's trying to speak? She checks her watch. It's been over twelve hours since his last dose of barbiturates. What should she do?

Ideally she needs him flat on his back to be sure of getting the needle in, upright like this it could be tricky. Jasmine, casual as ever, hadn't given an exact time. She said she'd come when the church meeting was over, and how could Rose argue with that? Jasmine is so overwhelmingly kind, so determined to help. But if anyone could be accused of batting for the other side, Jasmine and her love of cricket would certainly be a prime suspect. Could she and Jessie . . . ? The thought is too awful, and Rose is ashamed of herself for thinking it.

As a child Jessie was ultra-feminine. She loved her dolls and fluffy toys, preferring pretty dresses to jeans, adoring ballet dancing and playing princesses. She might look slightly macho now, with that hair and those shapeless clothes, but most girls her age go through a similar phase.

Jessie and Daisy had been so close as children, and still are, and this knowledge gives Rose such pleasure. They will never be left alone in this world while they have each other. Rose happily reminisces as she stares into the fire.

Would she and Jamie have stayed so close had her brother lived? She and Jamie had been inseparable, and Dinah and John had been sympathetic, insisting they share a classroom when they first went off to the local school. They shared a bedroom till the day he died, although, at ten, it was thought improper. They even had a language of their own, invented in infancy and expanded upon as they grew older.

Rose was happy to play the Indian to Jamie's cowboy in their games. They went through measles and mumps together, refused to eat sprouts, but permitted carrots and peas. When Jamie cried, Rose cried, and vice versa. When Jamie took off his bike stabilizers, Rose disposed of hers. He could do wheelies and so could she. She even insisted on the same haircut as his – straight, in a pageboy, too long for a lad, Father said. Their clothes were sexless, jeans and T-shirts. Some people said they couldn't tell which one was Rose and which was Jamie.

Whenever Rose looks back like this all she can see is fields, sea and sunshine.

And then along came Nicky Wainwright. Jamie taught him their special language, and Nicky now played the Indian chief, while Rose was relegated to the role of squaw. His bike had a crossbar, like Jamie's; hers had a girly basket on the front. She felt like Ann in the Famous Five.

She would arrive on the shore to find their rowing boat gone, and Jamie and Nicky waving and laughing as the waves splashed the prow and they rowed away round the point without her. She would visit one of their secret dens deep in the roots of the rhododendrons and find Nicky's initials carved on the seat. She would slink into the greenhouse to find that those delicious, tiny, warm tomatoes had already been picked. None left for her.

Sometimes that summer Jamie would disappear in the morning and spend the whole day at Nicky's house, making dens, having picnics and playing with Meccano.

Rose stayed at home and read in her room. *The Secret Seven. The Mountain of Adventure* and *Five Go to Smuggler's Top*.

'You like Nicky Wainwright better than me.'

'He's a boy, you're a girl,' Jamie would murmur from his bed.

'You hid from me this afternoon. I saw you. You can't deny it.'

225

'Nicky made me. He thinks you're weedy.'

'Why am I weedy?'

'Oh, you just are.'

'I hate you, Jamie Tate.'

'Go to sleep, Rose. Leave me alone.'

Mum took them to the travelling fair, one of the great treats of the year, and Jamie and Nicky shared a bumper car and pushed Rose off the track.

'*I know. B.*'

What does Belinda know?

It's gone half-past ten. When is Jasmine going to turn up?

Should Rose give Michael his jab or should she wait until he's in bed?

'What d'you think?' she asks him, sure in the knowledge that he will not reply.

Her attention is caught by his change of colour, an apoplectic purple, as if every vein in his face is pulsing with extra blood. The effort he makes is enormous.

Rose jumps up. Not a heart attack!

Oh no, not now. Don't leave me, not after all this.

But his strenuous struggle continues; it's exhausting to watch his pitiful efforts.

'It's OK, Michael, I'm here, I'm with you. What is the matter? Are you in pain?'

Michael bares his teeth. His mouth twists into distorted shapes. His good hand appears to be in spasm where it lies on top of the tartan rug.

'D–d–d'

Babbling, like a baby. Like a deaf child learning to speak.

'D–d–d'

226

In his eyes is the dawning of recognition, for the first time since his sickness began.

Rose draws back, afraid of her own reflection.

She used to finish his sentences for him, a habit she tried to break because it irritated him so. But she can't help him now. If Michael is really trying to speak he will have to manage on his own.

Where is the wretched Jasmine? Rose daren't wait much longer. This dependence on others is taking its toll. She would prefer to be in total control of every minute of Michael's care.

His eyes, still swollen, strain in his head as Michael's mouth forms an imperfect O. In spite of not wanting to hear, Rose leans forward, at the same time listening sharply for the sound of a car in the drive.

'Do . . . do . . . don't.'

The effort has left her patient exhausted. He shrivels back into his sack while Rose's heart misses so many beats the blood seems to stop its race round her body.

If she could doubt her interpretation of the grunting sound, which could be a word, she would do her damnedest to ignore it. But this word, which Michael must have chosen with such care, had been as worked on and laboured over as carefully as would any great poet.

'*Don't.*'

Don't what? He must have imagined that Rose would understand the meaning. He wouldn't have wanted to waste all that effort over something which could be misconstrued.

She looks at him hard. The dummy, he could be asleep, sitting there so limp and innocent.

And how many other words of condemnation will he learn to utter in the next few days? He could, of course, be referring to the unpleasant taste of the back-up barbiturates. It might even be that, in his confusion, he doesn't want more logs on the fire. It could be something as petty as that.

Who knows?

Belinda knows.

But does Michael?

EIGHTEEN

DON'T
LEAVE ME
ALONE
But powerless to utter anything more than the first word, Michael failed in his attempt to warn Rose there was something wrong.

One week later and his mind is beginning to heal. It is vastly preferable to be propped upright, to have something to watch, even though he can still only see the flicker of shadows and vague outlines. He fears that his sight will never be right again after that searing attack of pain. His general condition must be improving, and that is why his mind can function on another level beside his own suffering.

Apart from Michael's continuing and infuriatingly erratic mobility, his sight and hearing worry him the most. He knows when the TV is on; he senses the fire when he's near it; he can hear when people are talking, and even recognize the sex, but he can't decipher what the sounds mean or untangle himself from this stifling cloud of cotton wool that lies between him and real improvement. One moment he feels the world taking shape, and the next he is back in the land of the zombie.

His main aim, and he practises constantly, is to be able to press Rose's hand. But since that searing, unforgettable incident with his eyes, his mind has been taking him on a disturbing journey. It might be that his illness is causing delusions, that the lack of stimulation is affecting his once-active brain, and he has heard of the paranoid side-effects some strong medications can cause. But try as he might, he cannot dismiss the terrible suspicion that one night somebody sat on the side of his bed and deliberately filled his eyes with acid.

Apart from Rose, who is in this house with her? Who is helping her to care for him? She can't be coping all on her own. Somebody helps her bring him downstairs and gets him back into bed every night.

Is she employing some agency nurse – certainly his insurance would cover her for that sort of help if she required it. Maybe she uses a team of nurses, and is it too far-fetched to suggest that one of them is a headcase? It has been known. Look at Beverly Hallitt, the nurse with Munchausen's syndrome. Good. His brain must be clearing rapidly if he can remember details like that.

But while he can't see or hear or give Rose any warning, how can he avoid something equally terrible, or worse, happening to him again? He just can't take that; he knows he can't.

And what if it's not some dastardly nurse? What if it's someone who knows him? Daily and nightly Michael racks his beleaguered brain to try and work out who the hell he has upset in his life to make them hate him with such unholy venom.

Clients? If there are any he has long forgotten them. Former girlfriends? That's laughable. How far back would he have to go? Employees he might have upset? Anyone he sacked who might bear a grudge? There's only one he can think of, that lazy swine Hobbs, who had to go because he refused to pull his weight. And Hobbs was so completely lethargic the thought of him finding the energy to carry out revenge attacks ten years after the event is so unlikely it's not worth considering.

These musings are broken by long periods of sleep, which he cannot resist. One minute Michael is deep in thought, another he is oblivious. It is always a fight to find his way back to the place he was when he lost it. He struggles for continuity. He must learn to control the stagnancy of his fluttering brain.

But to what purpose? If, by some miracle, he could make sense of that attack on his eyes, how is he going to defend himself?

His efforts to stay alert and wakeful for as long as he can are useless. A deep, drugged slumber inevitably claims him. If only Rose would decide to sleep beside him in their bed, he could relax and concentrate on his recovery. There are other reasons for wishing that his wife would share his bed. The sense of her perfumed softness, the reassuring, gentle sleeping movements she makes, the light going on in the night when she can't sleep and reads for a while, the awareness that he is not alone in this cavernous void of nothing.

But no wonder Rose needs rest and peace away from him and his constant demands. How ironic. Michael's aim was always to shield her from life's worst troubles, if he could. But now look, because

231

of him she must be enduring hell on earth, probably with a smile and even a kind of pitiful pleasure that she is here to take care of him. But how long for?

Michael doesn't doubt her love. But if he doesn't improve will they decide to cart him away? Has he got six months, a year before they persuade poor Rose that she can no longer cope with him, that he ought to be put in a home? And in all honesty, could he blame her for wanting a life away from the sick room, free of an aching back, sleepless nights, bed baths and incontinence pads?

And yes, he would want that if he could have a say in the matter. Rose deserves more from life than caring for a vegetable, no matter how devotedly. But images of those grim places take over his head: himself in a corner cot stinking of excreta, despised by the staff, the despair of the doctors, teeth rotted away from slops and sticky medication, and the screams of his fellow imbeciles as they cry out to God in the night.

Jesus! Help me, Rose. Help me! You promised. Remember?

Has Michael had any dealings, knowingly or otherwise, with the criminally insane? Insane, he supposes, is too strong a word for poor Belinda McNab. But there was some strange behaviour following that incident when she was forced to leave St Marks.

According to her letters and the manic phone calls she made to the office, all the passion and obsession she had felt for his youngest daughter had been transferred to him. Transference, that's what they call it officially.

It sometimes happens between client and counsellor. Weak people turn to the strong and woo

232

them with pledges of love and devotion, turning themselves into sacrifices in exchange for care and protection.

Something pretty much like that must have happened. It had been disconcerting at the time, and he hadn't been sure how to deal with it. All those phone calls, those desperate pursuits of the unworthy. All that looking inward, eternally searching for herself.

He would like to have told Rose about Belinda, but that would have involved Jessie, and he decided that wasn't the answer.

His conscience was clear. He had done nothing to encourage the girl. The only time he'd met her was during that first confrontation in Sheila Gordon's study.

Her parents took her back to Cardiff and she started ringing him at work. Because of his involvement he felt obliged to give her some of his time but, with her mental problems, she must have misconstrued his interest. The phone calls rarely took less than an hour and they grew in frequency to five a day. Work became impossible, but she grew so distressed when he tried to end their conversations that he felt responsible for her state of mind.

Gradually Belinda became more personal. She would end her calls with, 'I love you Michael.' She often suggested that he take her away, just the two of them, so she could feel safe.

Uncomfortable though this made him, Michael could not be bluntly cruel to a young woman so in despair. Just as she had threatened suicide during her infatuation with Jessie, so she began to blackmail him: 'But why don't you love me, Michael? What do I have to do?'

What sort of hospital was she in, where they would allow such endless phone calls? All that monotonous self-exploration, all those protestations of devotion. Was there nobody there to help her or pay attention to what she was doing? He would have loved to be passed over to somebody in authority so he could relieve himself of this intolerable burden.

It turned out she used a mobile phone, and she told the staff she was ringing her family.

He wondered if he should contact her parents. They were reasonable people, according to Sheila. But would Belinda feel he had let her down, in line with her pessimistic view of the world? Would she think him a traitor who'd been 'leading me on like all the other wankers'?

The letters were just as long and hysterical as the phone calls had become. Poor Jessie. What she must have gone through.

Michael grew increasingly uneasy over Belinda's suggestions that their relationship was a two-way thing. Just before he and Rose left for Venice he'd found an old letter from her, which he had left carelessly in his jacket pocket. The girl lived in a fantasy world. She was highly manipulative and her pursuit was relentless.

What a fool he was. He realized, too late, that he should never have encouraged any contact at all, believing he might be able to help. He had no experience of anything like this. He ought to have put the phone down the first time she rang him. Jesus Christ. All those hours he'd spent reassuring her till his eyes swivelled round in his head and his work mounted up behind him.

Finally he had made the reluctant decision to go and see Sheila Gordon again and ask for her advice. They saw each other quite often, he in his role as college accountant. He had to admit that part of his reasoning was to cover himself should matters deteriorate. Belinda, intentionally or not, had set him up as a perfect target for accusations of taking advantage – the sex aspect of this raised its ugly head – and the prospect of such an action was hideous. Innocent though he was, shit sticks – there's no smoke without fire – his reputation would be tarnished and that he could not risk.

But to Michael's enormous relief, before he could act, both phone calls and letters suddenly stopped. Perhaps some other poor sod had taken his place in Belinda's sick head.

Michael had had it up to here, and he didn't much care what the reasons were, certainly not enough to investigate. He was more than happy to leave well alone.

Can it be remotely possible that Belinda, free once more, having somehow discovered his condition, has taken it into her head to come to his home by night and wreak whatever revenge she might believe she owes him?

If Michael could, he would laugh his head off. His paranoia is awesome; it knows no bounds.

He knows when he is alone, and back in his bed once again, dosed up, he is not alone now.

Someone is speaking in his ear; he can feel their hot breath, so close, too close? Is it Rose come to reassure herself that Michael is all right?

Today's wild thoughts have made him nervous,

235

like reading a Stephen King novel too close to bedtime. Michael can't even be certain if he's asleep or awake.

He can't recognize faces or voices, so how the hell can he recognize stealth?

One side of his bed goes down, the springs on his own side taking half the strain. Alarm jangles his nerves like a bell, but he can make no defensive movement.

Not his eyes again. Dear God, not his eyes.

There's the acrid smell of a cigarette lit by a match, not a lighter. Maybe it is Rose; he knows she smokes, but understanding how nauseous it makes him why would she light up in here?

Five minutes go by – no movement, nothing, but Michael knows there is somebody here. If only the mental tension would transfer itself to his body, he'd be out of bed and away, running blindly from this unknown thing.

But Michael can't. He lies helpless, waiting, praying that this is merely a dream.

My, what big ears you have.

All the better to hear you with.

When the burn of the tender flesh inside his ear reaches the highest pinnacle, when he can smell his own charring skin, still his prayers go unanswered. Still his consciousness won't go away.

The pressure being applied to the wound is such that he fears perforation by fire. Someone is pressing so hard that the red-hot end of the cigarette must soon go out.

But this is no cigarette.

Now the stench of gas mingles with the odious scorching deep inside his head – France, that old range, the lighter with the direct flame, so essential when you need something powerful to light hot plates or reluctant fires. Theirs was a red one, it matched the fly swat. Dear God, dear God.

Dawn and no doubts any longer. Not paranoid, just unable to stand the pain. Unable to raise a hand and cradle the wounded place.

This concentration on his eyes and ears, is it to stop him from seeing or hearing the person who comes into his room with such sinister motives? Is the burn so deliberately centred deep inside his inner ear that Rose won't see it tomorrow? Somebody noticed his eyes, he remembers, because somebody soothed them with balm, and now he feels the coldness of drops being applied at regular intervals. Although they still pain him, Michael's eyes fade into insignificance compared to this red-hot electric bar which some fiend has planted inside his head.

His earlier efforts at detection seem so ludicrous now. He knows of nobody on this earth who could carry out such gross acts of cruelty. His first assumptions were right. This has to be the work of a stranger, a psychopath who comes to this house disguised as a pair of helping hands, but with no other motive than to torture the helpless.

How many other homes does he or she visit to satisfy his warped needs? How many other innocent victims are suffering from these grotesque attacks?

Michael no longer attempts to rein in these morbid ideas. This is happening. This is real. This is no product of his own sick imagination, and unless he can find a way to prevent it, this is going to happen again.

'D–d–don't.'

'D–d–don't.'

'le–le–lee–lee.'

A splash of fat, just the touch of an iron or to accidentally clutch a hot pan, these are the kinds of tiny burns Michael has known in the past. And what a fuss he used to make. They used to agree, him and Rose, how excruciating it must be to suffer from really serious burns. Witches, traitors, young fanatics with political messages, evil racists who think it funny to set a black man alight. All those people engulfed by flame. All those poor, poor souls.

Why can't they see it? Can't they feel the heat? Are there no tell-tale marks on the pillow?

Michael is drugged, washed, changed, fed and makes his wobbly way downstairs. Leaving that torture chamber behind, with its clinging stink of blackening flesh, is relief enough for the moment. So long as he is downstairs with Rose his crazed assailant can't reach him.

'D–d–d–d.'

Somebody wipes his mouth with a cloth.

Dear God, he must be dribbling.

Witless, dummy, feeble-minded, imbecile, and all those other descriptions which are now so politically incorrect. But how seriously would anyone take the babblings of one of these dolts if he should manage to form them?

Are they listening? Or would they prefer, like most sensitive folk, to look away and ignore him? Maybe he ought to try the word 'Help.' But surely they are doing that already?

NINETEEN

The bare trees are mauve with winter. A luminous empty sky heralds a bleak November, and the river at the end of the garden at Bantham is churning brown with mud. The flower beds are tatty with sprawling dead stems, and old leaves make the grass slippery to walk on when you're trying to hobble about with a knee that jibs every time you use it. She must have a word with Dick the gardener; the man is starting to slack again, spending most of the hours she is paying him skulking about in the shed, drinking tea with condensed milk.

How John used to love his garden. The hours he used to spend out there, the sweet-smelling fires he used to have round about this time of year.

But inside, in the warm, Dinah Tate totters quite capably around her overlarge house.

She won't have a cleaner – they are untrustworthy; give 'em an inch and they take a mile; they get too chummy, look at Mrs H – so she uses a firm called Mrs Mops and gets them in for a whole day once a week. They come in twos and start at the top and work down. They're efficient and quick and they bring their own elevenses and eat in the van outside.

Her hair is well done, her face powdered, and a gold chain hangs round her heavy bosom. There's a large leopard brooch on the collar of her blouse, which is very white and prettily embroidered. She congratulates herself on her accurate assessment of Daisy's latest 'bloke' – how she loathes that common expression. A ne'er-do-well, she knew it. Not that Daisy will ever admit it; she will cling to him until it's too late, until she drives him off, as is her habit.

Daisy really should give more of her time to her poor, stressed mother, rather than making excuses and leaving it to that sweet but ungainly friend of Jessie's. Now is not the time for the girls to be moaning about Rose's desire to keep her family tight around her. Now is the time to rally and forget about all that.

It must have been difficult, for all of them at times. Rose was blessed when she married Michael, a man so sensitive and understanding that he contained her worst excesses and managed his daughters into acceptance.

Dinah has to laugh. It's the genes; it must be.

While Daisy and Jessie staunchly maintain that no relationship of theirs will be as restrictive as that of their parents, while they insist on independence from their various partners, poor Daisy is silently crying out for William to give up all his activities and become a fatherly pillar of support.

Well, he won't. He's nothing like Michael. And the more Daisy nags him and drags him round to babysit, the more he'll resent it.

*   *   *

Last Sunday, when Dinah went round to see how Michael was faring, young William was positively sullen, although he managed to demolish most of the lunchtime joint. These days Daisy looks unhappy, and it's not just because of her father's stroke; her relationship was doomed from the start.

As for Jasmine, what a brick. And what a miraculous find for Rose at such a stressful time. Nothing, it seems, is too much for her, and because of her odd working hours she can be round at Seymour House during the day. She'll even pop round to help Rose when she's got a free lunch hour. She can't have much of a life of her own, but then, girls like her don't attract men and often turn to charitable work to work off some of their energy. In the summer it would probably be cricket. And she's deeply involved in the church, of course. She's probably just very lonely.

Dinah could do with someone like that, someone at her beck and call, only too pleased to be of service to help her with awkward little tasks, but she doesn't like to ask while Rose's needs are so great.

How well Rose is coping. How patient she is with Michael. Michael doesn't look good – poor pallor, virtually paraplegic – Rose swears he is improving, but Dinah's not convinced, and that doctor of Rose's is not the best.

Jessie and Daisy have stoutly defended their mother's misguided decision to keep him at home and not stick him in a nursing home to relieve herself of the work, taking advantage of the professional care offered and paid for by Michael's insurance scheme. If you pay to go private for all those years, what a waste not to take advantage.

Dinah tried her best to convince her daughter while waiting for the gravy to heat. William had poured most of it onto his plate like a sea. 'I think you're being very silly, Rose.'

'I knew that's what you'd say, Mother.'

'That's because you know I'm right.'

Rose tried to ignore her. 'Pass the horseradish, please, darling.'

'There's some lovely nursing homes in the area.'

'Home is always best,' Jessie interrupted.

'It's not just for Michael's sake,' said Dinah, 'Rose could do with a rest as well.'

'Nonsense, Mother,' said Rose.

'Give everyone a break,' said Dinah.

'For goodness' sake, Granny, nobody wants a break,' Daisy insisted, and William gave her a look.

'And has anyone thought,' Dinah pressed on deliberately, inspecting her knife and fork for specks, 'of what will happen if he doesn't get better? Are you all prepared to carry on like this for the rest of your lives?'

'Oh, Mother, please stop this,' pleaded Rose. 'Of course we haven't. We wouldn't consider it. Michael is going to get well, and he's going to do it here, at home, surrounded by the people who love him.'

'Prayer has been known to help, Mrs Tate,' Jasmine put in disconcertingly.

'I'm a non-believer,' said Dinah sharply. But she did admire the girl's pluck, bringing up God at the table like that. Might as well discuss blow jobs. 'God didn't do much for my damn health, did he? He didn't protect my loved ones, either.'

Nobody wanted to go into that and so the subject was finally dropped.

Home again, and in the gathering dusk Dinah sits in her high-backed chair and stares out over her garden.

Jamie and Rose, being twins, had enjoyed an extraordinary closeness; it had bordered on telepathy and was uncanny to watch. Sometimes it appeared to Dinah that they only existed through each other.

When Nicky Wainright came onto the scene Rose had no special friends of her own. Before Nicky, neither twin had bothered; they'd found all they wanted in each other.

It was painful to watch Rose's daily heartbreak as Jamie's friend took her place by his side. Dinah had tried to explain to her son the consequences of his behaviour. 'I know you want to be with Nicky, but please try not to leave Rose out. Imagine how she must be feeling, and don't deliberately run away or hide things from her. That's cruel and unnecessary and not like you at all, Jamie.'

'It's Nicky; he makes me,' was his excuse.

Dinah was disappointed in him. 'Well, I'm sure you're big and old enough to deal with that sort of childish attitude.'

'I need Nicky to like me, at school. I don't want to be with the girls, and Rose can't run.'

Rose did not have flu on the day of Jamie's accident. The truth was that Dinah couldn't find her, and when she did she was hiding under the hammock cover, face filthy, eyes wide and frightened.

243

Not knowing how much the child knew, Dinah quickly comforted her and put her to bed, safely out of the way, before the shaking sobs took over again and she went to confront the horror downstairs.

By now the police had arrived and Jamie had been taken away, prised out of the mass of twisted bicycle parts. They had already interviewed Nicky at his house, but the boy was in shock and remembered little.

Dinah suddenly started to wonder if the accident was the awful result of some childish prank, if Rose might have been involved, might be interviewed and pressurized into saying things she didn't mean or couldn't understand.

Her motherly need to defend came to the fore with an animal cunning. Without a second thought she happened to mention in passing that Rose was ill in bed with flu, knew nothing of the incident and ought to be left to sleep. John, immediately understanding, quickly supported her story.

And it wasn't until some time afterwards that Dinah was anywhere near fit enough to turn her thoughts back to that afternoon and the sight of Rose hiding timidly under the hammock, as if she knew she had done something terribly wrong.

Rose had been there earlier that day, on the edge of the cliff with her bicycle, Dinah's memories told her that much. It would have taken only a push, or a take-off from the wrong angle – a new, more daring track set by somebody – for Jamie to have crashed to his death.

But why Jamie? Why not Nicky?

Because Jamie was abandoning Rose.

Luckily for them all, perhaps, Nicky's memory remained confused.

If John harboured the same dreadful doubts, he never spoke of them to Dinah. And she kept this sorrowful secret very close to her heart.

As if some part of Rose felt deformed and shameful without Jamie, for the rest of her childhood she refused point-blank to be photographed. 'Not without him. I can't. I can't.'

Maybe Rose believed that old native story that, by allowing your picture to be taken, you give away some part of your soul. Maybe Rose felt too much of it was already missing.

For nearly forty years Dinah has lived with the dire suspicion that Rose, her own daughter, killed her ten-year-old twin brother. And for thirty of those years the dreadful question – and what about John? – has haunted her night and day.

After John drowned the burning doubts drove her mental. She couldn't bear Rose to be in her sight. She refused to speak to her or take her to school. To cook her meals or do her washing.

The doctors tried every cure they could – ECT, drugs, therapy – but how could Dinah ever give voice to such abominable thoughts? They would take Rose away if they found any proof, and then what would she be left with? Scandal, loneliness and a bitter old age.

If Dinah had known for certain, if this were more than a dark suspicion, then she would have denounced her daughter. But she didn't know; she doesn't know the truth even to this day.

She kept her suspicions even from Rose, stuffing them to the back of her throat; she'd rather be dumb

245

than speak them. But Rose, poor child, must have guessed. Abandoned at the age of fourteen by a mother who couldn't stand her, Rose nevertheless hung on in there, dutiful and conscientious, putting up with the mood swings, coming home from school, cooking her tea and shutting herself away in her bedroom. They both lived alone in that house, each guarding their secrets until Dinah finally grew to accept that her deadly suspicions might be unfounded and could be a symptom of the kind of grief that had no other exit save madness.

This took time; it took months. But Rose was her daughter, her only child now, and she must give her the benefit of the doubt or else stay in this bottomless pit for ever.

She compensated; she had to. If her crazed suspicions were unfounded, what lasting damage had she done to Rose? She, too, at a tender age, had suffered two tragic bereavements.

It was August, on a hot sticky night, when the second tragedy happened.

The four-bunk cabin was stuffy; it felt much better to be out on deck, and they didn't get to bed until late.

They'd had a full meal, a few drinks but not too much – John was nowhere near tipsy. After the long, silent journey of the day, it felt good to be returning to England. Dinah swore that never again would she take a holiday with John. It always ended the same way: they argued from the moment they left British shores. They just weren't holiday people.

Over the meal they'd made friends again, and Dinah felt happy, tired and relaxed. Rose was still pouting, angry over their display of coldness, and afraid, as usual, that the word 'divorce' would soon come into common use.

It didn't matter how many times they reassured her, she didn't seem to hear them; she was convinced that something awful would happen every time they disagreed. 'You need never worry about Daddy and me,' Dinah used to try to explain, 'our little sulks aren't serious. We always make friends again. You'll understand when you get older, most grown-ups have their ups and downs, and it doesn't mean what you seem to think it does. Now stop worrying, Rose. Stop being so silly.'

Dinah turned over in the night and was vaguely aware that Rose's bunk was empty. She must have gone to the loo. If she'd felt seasick she'd have woken them. Dinah drifted back off to sleep again, lulled by the thud of the engines.

In the morning, of course, John was missing. She hadn't panicked, at first, merely assumed that he had gone out on deck or decided on an early breakfast.

She woke Rose and they dressed and packed ready for the landing. They went on deck to find John, searched the lounges and dining rooms, the arcades, bars and shop, and still Dinah wasn't worried, merely annoyed that John had gone off without saying where they should meet. There'd be such a crush at the terminal, such a rush for the cars, and their overnight baggage didn't feel light when you were lugging it round on both arms.

Rose and Dinah found the car in the dark depths

247

of the ship. No sign of John. This was odd. Damn him. Where was he?

Dinah found her car keys. 'We'll have to drive off and wait in the car park. We can't stay here and hold up the queue.'

The worry began as an ant bite and grew into the grip of a python. It crushed, it mauled, it drove out the senses.

Rose wouldn't stop crying.

The ship's return journey was delayed as it was searched by experts from prow to stern.

Once again the police took control and arranged to return them safely home.

Utter despair.

Hopelessness.

Tearing, relentless grief day and night.

Dry-eyed after too many tears.

And then the thought, like a tickle in the throat that spluttered into a full-blown choking fit. Why had Rose got out of bed? Had John woken up and found her missing? Had he gone up on deck to find her, deciding not to disturb his wife? And had they been talking out there in the dark, hanging over the water, close and trusting, father and daughter?

Did Rose believe, in her misguided way, that John was determined to leave them after the arguments and the silences? Is that what she was expecting?

Yes, she was; she'd admitted it.

Better to do it yourself than have it done to you. And how much force would it have taken for an unsuspecting man playing games with his daughter, hanging over the railings, to be unbalanced and tipped over into the ferry's churning, moonlit wake?

All the misgivings Dinah experienced over Rose's involvement in Jamie's death rose to the surface and dragged her under like a great whale cruising the fathoms.

She hadn't, on sudden impulse, plunged her hand in a bag of ideas and pulled an unlikely one out. No, these thoughts were based on her knowledge of Rose, that intimacy between mother and child that starts before birth and buries itself in adolescence.

After John's death Dinah had neither the strength nor the will-power to overcome her enmity towards Rose. Maybe she conjured up this emotion, using anger to dull the pain. Fear was present in the bundle of agony, a very real fear of what might happen if she found she could no longer accept Rose and was forced to do her own abandoning.

How would Rose react to that? Would Dinah's car swerve off the road? Or would she fall out of a bedroom window?

Dear God, were these mad machinations the flounderings of a tortured soul? Or was there any truth behind them?

She lost herself in pain and confusion.

And what of her daughter? What happened to her?

In spite of gallant efforts by Michael, Rose has never managed to lose this illogical fear of abandonment. It showed from the moment she got engaged, and she still displays it now in her need to keep her family close around her.

Dinah's present beliefs might well be the result of the onset of dementia, but it seems to her that Rose is increasingly unsure of her mother.

249

Is she apprehensive that even now Dinah might air her suspicions? Might discuss the past with the children? Might run her ideas past Michael? Might even feel compelled to go to the law before it's too late?

No matter how objectionable Dinah's behaviour, on the whole Rose is tolerant and loving. Does she pity her mother? Or is this the result of a guilty conscience? Is it her way of making up? Or, after all these years, still a way of proving her innocence?

Dinah used to imagine, and hope, that her elderly self would be wise and caring. With age came the awareness that she could be none of these things, not with the questions that rankle, unsolved, and grow malignantly inside her head. When she's with Rose her behaviour deteriorates; she spars with her daughter and goads her shamelessly.

Maybe one day Rose will crack, infuriated beyond reason, and finally the fetid corpse of truth will come up from the darkness into the daylight.

Dinah Tate cannot know that the few hours she has left in this life are not long enough to unravel this horrible mystery.

TWENTY

Nine forty-five p.m. and Dinah turns off the telly and crabs towards the kitchen to make her nightly mug of Horlicks.

Nine fifty and the electric trips.

The lights go out.

The darkness is pitch.

Nine fifty plus five seconds and she curses, 'Bloody hell, not again!' This is one of the downsides of having a house in the country.

With her recently treated knee still giving her jip she heaves herself to the kitchen drawer where she keeps the torch. 'Dammit where are you? Come out, come out.' Wedging it under one arm, she makes for the understairs cupboard in the hall. She lifts the large oak latch and lets herself into the black cocoon of solid darkness. Puffing and blowing from all the effort and the irritation of this stupid trip switch going again when she's had men in time after time to sort the matter out, she directs the torch towards the maze of switches and dials just above eye level.

So inconvenient. Such an old-fashioned, unreliable layout.

A little surge of anger spits through her. It's Michael who is to blame for this. How many times has she asked him to sort out this archaic system? If a bloody bulb on the landing goes the whole damn house grinds to a standstill. If he wasn't a cabbage she'd ring him now and get him out to sort it out. Serve him right. Here she is, a helpless old lady, being forced to shuffle around in the dark playing electrician. She could trip, she could fall, anything could happen. Does anyone care? Do they hell.

Nine fifty-five and the cupboard door swings closed behind her, the oak latch catching firmly, and Granny Tate is a prisoner, seething now with anger.

No point in calling for help.

Ten o'clock and five candles are lit and placed strategically in the kitchen and down the hall, as if they have been used to light her progress.

Five past ten and the orange candle under the heavy hall curtains finds its way from its saucer onto the floor, directly below them, as if it has toppled of its own volition.

How silly these old folks can be. Why bother with candles when you've got a torch with a perfectly good battery inside it? But once you pass seventy who can fathom what goes through the minds of the daft and elderly?

By ten past ten the embroidered curtains, which have hung there since the Tates moved in over fifty years ago, are one flaring mass of flame. The hall-stand, with its pile of old newspapers, takes the strain before passing the scarlet licks across to the horsehair sofa and its burden of coats. The varnish on the banisters blisters before the wood catches light and carries the furnace, creeping through carpet and over old lino, upstairs to the bedrooms. The door to the cupboard under the stairs is consumed by billowing smoke and heat, the oak latch turns to charcoal, leaving no trace of itself behind.

By twenty past ten any life that might have been trapped in that tiny space has been reduced almost to carbon.

The windows in the house turn black before bursting out of their frames. The rafters hold out for a good half-hour before becoming engulfed.

Through a haze of helpless tears Daisy and Jessie Redfern watch their grandmother's house collapse under the extra burden of water directed at it from four fire engines.

No-one is able to go in yet. The whole structure is unsafe, and nobody knows for certain what caused the hellish inferno. A dozen sightseers from neighbouring cottages gather around the fiery furnace, faces tight from a mixture of cold and heat.

'How was the old lady when you last spoke to her?' asks the chief fire officer, who was the first to turn up in his van after the alarm was sounded.

Jessie can't take her eyes off the sight of Granny's beautiful house crackling towards broken ruination. 'Who? Granny? She was fine.'

'Same as ever,' says Daisy, shivering with shock.

'What are her chances?' asks Jessie. This can't be real. She has to be dreaming. That phone call from Mum never happened. 'I can't leave Michael. You go please, Jessie!'

But Mum hadn't understood the serious nature of the devastation. Nor had Jessie until she arrived and saw the skyline lit up like a sunrise.

The fire officer shakes his head. 'I don't want to give you any false hopes, not at this stage. We won't know for certain until we go in.'

'Could it have been a firework?' It is, after all, Guy Fawkes Night.

'Some firework,' says the officer.

William is at the rugby club, helping to organize their display, and can't be contacted, and because it's half-term at Kingsmead Jasmine has gone home for a week to see her parents at their farmhouse in Cheshire.

'If anything's happened to Granny,' starts Daisy.

'I don't think Mum will be able to take any more,' Jessie finishes the sentence for her.

'I believe the old lady was slow on her feet. Is that right?' asks the fireman.

'Yes, but she's pretty agile,' says Daisy. 'Especially when no-one else is about.'

Jesus Christ. Great beams of wood that have been supports for 200 years, bend, twist and then explode in sparks into the night. Tiny explosions pop and crackle as if someone with a family box of fireworks has crept in with some Golden Rains and a couple of Catherine Wheels. There are mind-blowing crashes as timbers fall, bringing down tons of bricks and mortar. Half the side of the house is gone, split open like a long-wrecked ship, with only its bony bare ribs to support it.

Nobody inside could survive.

Granny is dead.

Burned to a cinder.

And that's what they're going to have to tell Mum.

*　　*　　*

No time would be a good one for this kind of disaster to happen, but now, on top of everything else, it seems as if the fates are conspiring against them. What foolish mistake did Granny make to cause this extra tragedy? And why now? There are so many strong emotions, but one of the strongest is definitely anger. Does Daisy feel this, too?

Neither of them liked her. She was a difficult woman to like, and getting worse as the months went by. If it wasn't for Mum they wouldn't have gone near her, with her bitterness and caustic remarks. Even over Dad she couldn't prevent herself from uttering dire warnings and witchy predictions. But Jessie shouldn't be thinking like this. There had been happier times, though they were hard to remember; she'd always been an odd, demanding character, never like the kind of granny you read about in books.

All their lives Daisy and Jessie had been forced to make allowances for her because of the suffering she had endured. Dinah's own mother had been taken away in a straitjacket when she was only fifty.

'Jessie? Where are you going?'

'I can't stand here any longer. I'm going to the end of the garden for ten minutes to sit down.'

'God, it's freezing.' The flames are subsiding and Daisy's teeth chatter madly as she keeps her sister company.

On the seat set among the hydrangeas, facing the river, Daisy suggests the unthinkable, the one thought Jessie has fought from creeping into her head.

'You don't think Belinda . . . ?'

'No! No, I don't.'

'She could have found out where Granny lived.'

'But if Belinda wants to hurt me, why would she turn on Granny?'

'She must think you love her.'

'She knows me well enough to know that's a laugh.'

Daisy shivers and cuddles herself. 'Don't say that, Jessie. Not now.'

Jessie turns towards her sister. 'Are you going to miss her? Be honest.'

Daisy doesn't answer.

'Maybe it's better to die like this, suddenly, when you're old, with no warning, instead of rotting away in some gruesome home dribbling and pissing yourself.'

'Like Dad you mean?' asks Daisy quietly.

'You don't really think that will happen? Not to him?'

'I dunno any more, Jessie.' Daisy shrugs. 'I just dunno.'

Jessie stays the night – or what's left of it by the time they get there – with Rose at Seymour House, where she breaks the appalling news.

When the fire brigade bring out the body there are no means of identification, save forensic methods.

'What would your grandmother have been doing in the cupboard under the stairs?' asks the chief fire officer before bidding them a tired goodnight.

'The electricity must have tripped,' Jessie says immediately. 'Granny was always going on about it. Have you any idea yet what caused the fire?'

'We won't know that for some time, I'm afraid. The place is a terrible mess.'

256

'Did you see her?' sobs Mum, grasping Dad's lifeless hand.

'No, and I don't think they'd have let us,' Jessie explains as gently as she can.

'Why didn't they go in sooner?'

'You should have seen it, Mum. Nobody could have got near it.'

'And the house is gone? *All gone?*'

'You wouldn't recognize it.'

Mum desperately needs Dad's support, but there he sits beside her, drooling and nodding like an ancient man or the sort of patient you see in geriatric wards, yellowing away towards death, with shroudlike sheets pulled up around their necks to cover them.

Mum's head falls to her chest. 'Poor Mother. Poor, poor Mother. That she should go like this, after everything . . .'

'She wouldn't have known much about it,' says Jessie, in the way they talk about passengers in a plane crash to make the horror possible for relatives to bear. 'The smoke would have knocked her unconscious. Mum. Mum, don't cry. Granny probably just fell asleep.'

'I'd have been there if I could.'

'I know you would. But you couldn't leave Dad. You couldn't do anything. It was better that you stayed here.'

'I had no idea the fire was so bad.'

'When they rang you they didn't know either.'

Does Mum, in her heart of hearts, in spite of appearing so defeated and genuinely broken-hearted, feel no shocking stab of relief that her mother is no longer around, with her selfishness and her constant demands? Especially with Dad as he is now? One thing's for certain, Mum has no need to go through the guilt some daughters must feel for not doing their best. Perhaps this thought might bring her some comfort.

'Mum, you were lovely with Gran. So was Dad. You never lost your patience, no matter how foul she was; she only had to click her fingers and you were there to help her. She relied on you for so much, and she took you for granted, but you never grumbled. Not really. Granny was lucky to have you.'

'You think so, Jessie?'

'I know so,' says Jessie.

'Her life was so hard,' says Mum, sobbing again.

'And she made damn sure everyone knew it,' says Jessie before she can stop herself. 'Your life was equally hard, and look at you now, coping with Dad, but you never turned bitter.'

Jessie helps Rose get Michael upstairs, undress him, wash him and put him to bed. It is after five in the morning before Jessie and Rose get any sleep themselves.

'What do you mean, the last straw?' Daisy demands William's answer.

'I mean, and I'm not being unkind, don't take it that way, but I'm trying to say that it's like a net closing around us. All these calamities one after the other, and then there's this nutter lurking in the background, slashing coats and leaving turds on the floor.'

'You're talking about me and my family, William, and the closeness you once said you envied.'

258

Daisy's voice rises higher as she gets closer to snapping. 'How fond you were of Granny. "What a character," you used to say. And me, I was ungrateful, according to you, because I sometimes moaned about Mum. How lucky I was, you used to tell me, if I remember rightly, to have been loved as a child. Oh, poor you, your mum never rings. And your stepfather can't stand you. Well it's slightly different now that we're expected to give a little.'

'*Give a little!* My God!' And William slaps his forehead. 'It's claustrophobic. Your mum's certainly got you both now. Christ, Daisy, you're never here.'

'*You selfish bastard.* You haven't a clue what it means to put someone else first in your life. You can't even give up one of your precious evenings to come round and sit with Mum and Dad. And now you're saying you refuse to help me with the funeral arrangements. You think poor Dad should be shipped off to hospital.'

William, back from the rugby club, with beery breath shooting dragonlike and mud all over his boots, shouts back, 'I just don't believe you ought to be so totally immersed in it all. And now your granny gets fried in a fire. What is this going to mean?' He goes to the fridge and roots around for a beer. 'Will I be expected to scratch through the ruins, with you weeping beside me, looking for mementoes worth saving? Will I have to chauffeur your relatives backwards and forwards to this bloody funeral? Jesus fucking Christ? It's all so fucking HEAVY. What's happened to normal life? *Why am I always holding your hand?*'

'And I expected some sympathy from you. What

a laugh. What a fool I am. I've just returned from the kind of experience that would leave some people gibbering idiots. My granny has been burned alive and you joke—'

William snaps back the lid of the can. He deflates, letting all his breath go. On the surface, but only on the surface, his voice seems quiet and reasonable. 'I'm so sorry, Daisy. I really am. I can't imagine how dreadful this night must have been for you. And Jessie, and your mum. I want to hold you in my arms and kiss all the pain away, but I can't.' He flops down drunkenly on the sofa. 'I can't make any of these things better and I feel useless. Fucking useless. I'm just no good at this sort of thing. Maybe I can't deal with it, I'm not mature enough or something, but all I know is that all these disasters are tearing us apart. Your life is being taken over.'

'You disgust me,' Daisy says. 'People like you. Anyone would think this was all my fault. That I was enjoying it all.'

'I dunno. It's as if there's a curse on you and your family and you attract these disasters.'

'Infected, are we?'

'Yes, in a way.' William starts to roll a fag. He's so drunk he can hardly see it and there's tobacco dropping all over the floor.

'And you're afraid you might catch it?'

'I don't think you're dealing with it properly. None of you are, to be honest. You should tell the police about Belinda, your dad should be in hospital just as the doctor ordered and you never could stand your granny. I liked her better than you did, so why this awful hypocrisy?'

Daisy's voice is cold like stone. 'You don't think

we should be supporting Mum? You think we should let her get on with it?'

'No. I didn't say that. But you've got this idea that Rose can't cope. Your dad spent his life protecting her, but she can cope. She's a capable woman. All you and Jessie are doing is turning her into a martyr.'

All the disdain that Daisy can muster goes into her next remark. 'You really are an arsehole, aren't you?'

William is too far gone to be serious. 'If you say so.' He bows and almost falls off the sofa. 'You know best, m'lady.'

'Take, take, take. That's all you know. How sad.'

'Daisy,' William pleads with a burp, 'can we talk about this in the morning?'

'No, we can't. I'm going straight over to Mum's in the morning, and if you refuse to come with me you can go straight to hell for all I care.'

She loves him – oh, how Daisy loves him – but she's not letting that wanker into her bed tonight.

She slams the door behind her and locks it, then throws herself down on her bed and weeps for the granny she never loved and for a man she has somehow lost.

TWENTY-ONE

'I am the resurrection and the life, saith the Lord: he that believeth in me, though he were dead, yet shall he live.'

Here is a church and here is a steeple, fold back your hands and see all the people.

Here and there a fir stands dark amidst a crowd of yellowing trees, dark and heavy yet firm and constant, like death itself. The black asphalt path is bordered with leaves. The clergyman in his violet stole welcomes them at the vaulted door, with his surplice blowing in the wind like the wings of a welcoming angel.

Dinah goes in, head first, and the congregation follow, eyes down.

The church is cold and shoes ring on stone. They don't bother with heating or lighting for short funeral services. Can't afford it.

Does Michael feel uncomfortable, all dolled up in suit and tie? Even his shoes have been pushed back on for the first time since his illness. No. He sits in the pew, alongside Rose and their grieving family, and there must be truth in collective thought waves, how else can he sense, without any doubt, that this is a tragic occasion?

But he does, in spite of the fact that most of his concentration is directed on his blistering wounds. It burns as if that torturous flame had burst through his eardrum and pierced his throat. His swallowing, never good, is affected, and he regularly gags with the pain. The sensation at the back of his nose is that of melting sealing wax and the ear itself is still raw flame.

Every time they come near to touching it he tries to scream out his warnings.

But because of the potent power of the drugs Michael still can't communicate, and rubbing his ears seems to make them think the TV is on too loud.

He can't see Dinah Tate's coffin sitting there, so dignified and prettified by lilies, on the plinth that leads to the ovens. He doesn't know that his mother-in-law has been cremated already, turned into pieces of bony charcoal so that only the dental experts could confirm her identity.

'As soon as thou scatterest them they are even as asleep: and fade away suddenly like the grass.'

And because nothing at all remained of the heavy oak door to the understairs cupboard, let alone the latch itself, there was no suggestion that some unseen hand must have clicked the latch behind her.

All sorts of doubts had been expressed about the likelihood of her using candles, because the professionals had eventually surmised that a candle had been the cause of the fire and that the epicentre had been the hall curtains. Because of the blackened batteries and some tiny fragments of glass it was evident that Dinah had had a torch in her hand when she'd died. Maybe she'd lit the candles so that she could find her way to the torch. Maybe she kept the torch under the stairs. And the candles, Rose told them, were usually kept in the kitchen drawer.

'Mother was often confused,' Rose told the coroner. 'She was becoming quite difficult, but what with the pills she had to take and the constant pain she was in as a result of her arthritis, this was understandable. She wasn't a happy woman.'

So it seems to all gathered here today that Dinah Tate might well have lit a pathway of candles to light her last passage from kitchen drawer to hall cupboard. The really awful part of it all – the burning – is left to the imagination of the small congregation.

Was she unconscious before she burned? Did she attempt to beat her way out of the house? Did she cry out for help as the smoke swirled around her and she staggered in confusion? Did she know the horror of what was happening?

'*Man that is born of woman hath but a short time to live and is full of misery.*'

How true.

Rose looks down at Michael. Her face is drawn, her eyes quite dry. There are no tears left. She leans over to wipe the drool from his chin.

'*In the midst of life we are in death.*'

It would be kinder if the mourners were allowed to leave the church before the motor clicks into action. The curtains part with a worrying jerk and the coffin slides down that dreadful chute. The pall-bearers – a couple of old men in black suits – bow their heads in solemn respect, just as the Queen and her family did when Diana's coffin passed by at the gates of the palace.

They sing a flimsy hymn, led by a booming and confident verger, who sits behind as backstop.

Jasmine, in the second row, and back from her week in Cheshire, falls forward onto her knees whenever prayers are introduced. At other times she sits with her hands folded in her lap, staring at the altar with a beatific look on her face, ready and waiting for a message. Under her maroon anorak she wears a long black woollen dress. This is startling. Nobody has ever seen her in anything other than tracksuit bottoms.

Mrs H is there in her black funeral beret, with Mr H beside her in his best Sunday suit, while William, who has made an effort, his hair pressed tight to his head with gel, sits uneasily in a jacket and jeans beside them. He has refused to sit beside Daisy. He is not 'family' yet.

Jessie and Daisy, at their first funeral, are blinded by tears.

Lord, have mercy on us.
Christ, have mercy upon us.
Lord, have mercy upon us.

Home again and he flops into place beside Rose's chair.

There's motion. Sounds on differing levels, and people. Lots of people. They touch him, bringing their faces towards him like lazy, hazy suns, and yet strangely no-one can see the smoke which he feels must be billowing from his ear. He can smell smoked salmon, or is that prawns, and mayonnaise and cucumber and the tomatoes which he grew himself this last summer in his greenhouse.

They must be having a party, or maybe this is Christmas. How would Michael know? He would probably smell the Christmas tree, that evocative scent of childhood joy, that tinsel symbol of lost innocence, and there's no such tree in this room. The only certainty he has to cling to is that he must cut down on the medication Rose administers every night, doubtless under the impression that he needs it to recover.

Michael can't help suspecting that some of his wretched helplessness, combined with the comatose sleep these drugs induce, are actually causing most of his problems. Why else does he feel so much more alive by the time the next dose is due? He is more able to position his limbs correctly and even utter a few chosen sounds?

Rose, in her well-meaning innocence, is unaware of the enormity of the danger he is in. His priority must be to warn her and, God help him, if possible, fend off this lunatic.

Because of his exhaustive attempts to identify the kind of ghoul who would want to blind a man or set parts of him alight, Michael is almost certain that his assailant is a stranger, a blood-thirsty freak who, for some good reason, is being allowed into his house in disguise. He dreads their next encounter.

He curses his useless senses.

He tries to hear, he strains to see.

With all his might he resists the desire for that helplessly deep, dreamless sleep that renders him so vulnerable. One flashing moment of total clarity is all he needs to identify this fiend who is so intent on his torture. But the drugs are so powerful that resistance, so far, has proved hopeless. If Michael wants to continue to live he must not allow one drop to pass into his system tonight.

While there are people around him he's safe.

Funny, there is no music. If there was he would feel the beat. Must be a different kind of party. Let the party-goers rave on.

He wonders if Sheila the head of St Marks has been invited and then doubts it. Rose hardly knows her.

He had been forced to telephone Sheila officially again after Belinda contacted him out of the blue just a week or so before he and Rose went to Venice.

His heart sank. He felt real shock.

The last thing Michael needed was to find himself enmeshed again in the fantasies of this sick girl. The last time he had handled it badly, believing he could help her by giving friendly support and encouragement, like a mentor or a father. This response proved fatal, and the fact that the phone call was made to his home rather than his office was more alarming than before. Then he found an old notelet he had hidden in his jacket.

If Rose discovered it Jessie's secret would come out, and Rose would be mortified. She might even start to believe Belinda's ridiculous claims of love everlasting, and for the first time the fear of how this might affect his wife had crossed Michael's mind.

On several occasions he tried the number Belinda had left on the answerphone, to warn her off, but with no success, just the recorded message to call again later.

What the hell was she up to now?

* * *

Michael and Sheila, both busy people, had decided to meet for lunch. The pub was full, with no tables left, and so they went upstairs to the more discreet restaurant. Once again he was struck by her sensible approach to life and her wisdom. She wasn't bad to look at either; in her late thirties, he guessed, divorced, ambitious, worldly and elegant.

He explained to Sheila how enmeshed he had become last time Belinda had contacted him.

'You shouldn't have attempted to ring her back.' Sheila was shocked by his naivity. 'You should have come straight to me.'

'She would have accused me of betraying our friendship,' said Michael wryly. 'And I, like a fool, went along with it and played her game. Made things worse. I suppose, in some sad way, I was flattered. I'm not an expert, like you, at dealing with hormonally challenged teenagers. But I'm not getting embroiled this time. My fingers have been burned for the last time. Over to you, Ms Gordon.'

'Don't worry. I'll deal with it. But if she contacts you again, for God's sake don't respond. Get in touch with me immediately.'

The candle the waiter insisted on lighting brought out the green in Sheila's eyes. Her lashes were dark and long. Because of the wait for the food to arrive they polished off four martinis between them. 'And my advice', Sheila went on, childishly twisting one blond curl of hair, 'would be to confide in Rose. Just in case things get heavy. And yes, I do know how you feel about Jessie's dark secret, but really, these days that's nothing. Far better to bring this out in the open so there's no chance of a misunderstanding.'

It was three o'clock before either of them glanced at their watches. The waiters were standing around, eyeing them crossly. Lost in conversation, with so much in common, and charged up by each other's energy, time flew by until somehow they'd downed two bottles of wine.

Sheila, apparently, missed a meeting. She also mislaid a favourite bracelet, but they hadn't the time to stop and search. Michael was lucky, his diary was clear. But he spent the rest of the day muddle-headed.

He mulled over Sheila's advice. It was good and he would take it.

With Belinda back, he ought to tell Rose, and he would do so when they returned from Venice. Michael didn't want the holiday ruined by Rose's worries about Jessie's sexuality and whether it was something *she'd* done that had caused it? Wasn't it always the fault of the mother? Would the rest of poor Jessie's life be a struggle? And did this mean Jessie would never have children?

And no doubt, because of Rose's jealousy, they would labour their way through that hoary old chestnut of why Belinda chose Michael to obsess about, with Rose pouncing on the girl's name and tossing it in the air, before falling on it and tearing it apart. What encouragement had he given this girl? If any? Had he found her attractive?

Poor Rose would clutch and claw him with her fears, but he wanted this holiday to be special, not clouded by erroneous crap.

*   *   *

Another night on this carousel going round and round to nowhere.

Michael thinks, but is not certain, that it might be Jessie and Daisy who are helping Rose to get him upstairs.

He concentrates hard on putting one foot in front of the other. He tries for a grip on the banisters, but his hand feels withered, like a biblical beggar's. He'd be based at the foot of the temple steps with a wooden gourd and Gandhi sandals if he found himself in the Third World. God, how he hates them to see him like this.

He hopes they're not here when Rose undresses him. Surely she is sensitive enough not to put them through that. Even when the girls were small Rose, and particularly Michael, kept the bathroom door shut rather than let it all hang out.

He's drooling more today because his throat is so agonizingly sore that it turns swallowing into a fiery hell, white-hot volcano lava which bubbles all the way to his stomach.

Outside the house the last remnant of cloud allows the moon to sail clear, bright and full, and the light shines in through his bedroom window. If Baggins was still here this would signal another convulsion.

He will soon be in his pyjamas, wrapped in a talcum-powder aroma – Johnsons, for babies. A dull anguish washes over him. Michael lets his shoulders sag and gives a defeated sigh. Small muscles twitch at the sides of his mouth, the mouth he once used for smiling. He can smell his bathwater waiting for him, a hot mixture of lemon and steam. His skin is blotchy and his eyes stare warily, huge in his face. His helpers pause on the stairs, waiting for him to proceed.

After Rose has dosed him up tonight – it's the turn of the tablets – he's going to wait till she's gone and then let the mixture roll out down his chin and, hopefully, lose itself in the blinding whiteness of the sheets, like the dribble of a baby.

TWENTY-TWO

'With deepest sympathy.'

A cross against a stony background, a pagan symbol in this context, more in keeping with the Ku Klux Klan than anything remotely Christian. Rose shivers as she reads on:

'May God's promise of eternal life bring you faith and hope
And may your beloved rest gently in Jesus' arms for ever.'

Thinking of you, Belinda.

She throws the blighted thing on the fire and stands and watches it burn. So for some reason that whore must believe she'll get Michael back. Belinda is still involving herself in the trials of the Redfern family. How did she know about Dinah's death? It seemed funny that she hasn't tried to call. On the phone she had sounded brazen enough to relish any kind of conflict.

Rose goes across to the phone and dials Belinda's number. She knows it better than she knows her own, she has telephoned so many times only to get the same frustrating message.

272

She needs to confront Belinda; she needs to arrange a meeting. There are so many unanswered questions that stab at her brain like a poker stirring up a dead fire.

She'd had trouble with Michael last night. Exhausted after the funeral and the family arguments which took place after the guests had gone, all Rose had wanted was her bed, that safe place in the spare room, left blank and impersonal for visitors, devoid of reminders and everyday clutter, ugly deeds and poisonous thoughts.

What prompted her to go back to his room once he was tucked up for the night she still can't remember. But something was niggling, so after her bath she slipped back and turned on the light, only to find the barbiturate mixture foaming round his lips and beginning to trickle down his chin.

She slapped him; she couldn't help herself. Didn't he know the stress she was under? Didn't he understand that she was doing this inhuman thing for his sake?

His world might have collapsed around him, he might be frightened and in pain, but how the hell did he think Rose was feeling, what with him in this state, her mother burned to a bloody crisp, one daughter pale and lovesick and constant haranguing by those who thought they knew best how she should care for her husband?

Jesus Christ, he had a nerve!

She slapped him hard and he didn't flinch. She wondered if he could feel it, or did pain mean nothing to him now?

Sobbing and at her wits' end she mixed him

another dose and made sure the fluid slipped down his throat. Seriously frightened by this lack of control and the overwhelming urge to hurt him, she fled the bedroom in tears, tore downstairs and wrenched the top off an unopened bottle of Gordons. Like a hard-drinking sot she poured the gin neat into a tumbler, lit a cigarette and sat flopped over the kitchen table, trying to get a grip on her anger.

The conversation they'd had yesterday while clearing up after the wake had undermined her confidence.

Those two outsiders, Jasmine and William, seemingly unmoved by the fact that she had just endured the ordeal of her own mother's funeral, got on to the subject of Michael and the sensible option, according to them, of employing a full-time nurse.

It always seemed to be her doing it wrong, never him.

Taking sides against her.

She attempted to make her point calmly, while inside the tension tautened.

'I'm happy to look after him myself,' she said, 'and he would hate being messed around by some stranger.'

'But you look so worn out,' said William, halfway through yet another lager from her fridge. 'Are you sure it's not guilt that's forcing you to drive yourself so hard?'

Guilt? 'What guilt?'

'The guilt we all feel when we can't do enough for someone we love.'

'Look, all of you,' said Rose looking round. 'If anyone feels I'm forcing them to help me more than is comfortable for them, they must say so. If necessary I can cope on my own.'

'Don't get so defensive, Mum,' Daisy chipped in insensitively, 'it's not like that at all.'

Jasmine stuck her oar in. 'A nurse would mean more rest for all of you, and less of this heavy responsibility.'

'I'm sure she would,' said Rose with her back to the wall. 'Or even a team of nurses, a different one every day. But I'm not willing to see the man I love in the hands of some fleet of hard-hearted experts. Michael's improving all the time, even the doctor agrees.'

'But it's you that we're worried about,' put in Jessie.

'I think you're finding it uncomfortable to deal with your dad so helpless – and it is ugly; it's very distressing, a good deal more distressing for me, who happens to be his wife – better to get the obnoxious object cared for by somebody else, or better still, out of sight out of mind in some cosy nursing home, then you'd feel better, wouldn't you, William? Well it might work like that in your cool, clinical world, but not in mine, it doesn't.'

'*Mum*,' wailed Daisy, 'there's no need to go on like that. William's only trying to help. He hates to see us all so miserable.'

'Well it's not us that I'm worried about actually, Daisy, it's Michael,' said Rose trying to calm herself. 'And I really do feel that this is a matter between Michael and me. I'm tired and upset and I wish this argument hadn't started. I've had a terrible, terrible day.' And tears came to Rose's rescue.

*　　*　　*

The morning after the argument Rose has only just finished dealing with Michael, Mrs H gamely helping Rose direct him into the chair downstairs, when the doorbell rings; Rose silently curses.

Belinda's callous sympathy card has unnerved her enough for one day. People can be so thoughtless; it's not ten o'clock yet. They should understand that in the household of an invalid time takes on a different dimension. Ten o'clock and everyone's ready for a rest after the morning's labours.

'Rose? I do hope I'm not being too inconvenient. I realize it's early, but I wanted to call in to see Michael and offer you any help I can give.'

It takes a while for Rose to recognize this elegant figure on her doorstep, with a gorgeous bunch of flowers – she suspects M&S – in her arms. Sheila Gordon from St Marks College is neat, scarved and cultured in a beige suit with a black velvet coat swinging round her shoulders. Rose is painfully aware of her own unkempt hair, her morning face, overall and moth-eaten bedroom slippers.

Rose flusters, 'Oh no, not at all. It's good to see you, Sheila. Come on in, but we're in rather a state, I'm afraid.'

'Shall I make coffee now, Mrs Redfern?'

'Yes, if you don't mind, Mrs H. You will have a cup of coffee with us, Sheila?'

'That would be nice. Black, no sugar.'

'It's instant, I'm afraid,' says Rose, showing her visitor through to the living room.

'What an enchanting room,' says Sheila, heading straight for Michael. 'And the view.'

Rose, who has never lost her terror of teachers,

276

feels intimidated by this woman's presence and her natural air of authority.

'Hello, Michael, how are you?' Sheila bends to Michael's level and addresses him most politely.

'He can't hear you, I'm afraid,' Rose says.

'But do we know that?' asks Sheila smiling. 'Do we know that for sure?'

Rose feels irritated. Of course she bloody knows. She's been with him like this for a month, day and night, for God's sake. So-called liberal intellectuals like Sheila are so careful to be correct, so overly aware of the does-he-take-sugar syndrome that they have to insist they know best.

Sheila makes small adjustments so that her armchair is closer to Michael, so he can watch her face, if that's possible, which it isn't. This morning her husband seems to prefer staring abjectly out of the window.

'I wanted to get here much earlier,' Sheila makes her apologies, 'and I feel very guilty for leaving it so long. It was partly work and partly the knowledge that you would be so inundated with visitors during the first couple of weeks after Michael's stroke.'

She hands Rose the flowers. Rose says, 'They're beautiful. Look, Michael. Sheila has brought you some lovely flowers. I'll just go and pop them in water and leave you to chat to Michael for a minute.'

When Rose returns she finds that Sheila is holding Michael's hand and speaking intently to him, giving the patient the benefit of the doubt.

'You must have had more to do with Michael since his firm took over the college accounts?' Rose enquires politely. She's only met Sheila twice before, once when they toured the college with Jessie, and the second time at an official opening of the library extension.

'Michael is one in a million,' says Sheila disconcertingly. 'But then, you're his wife. You know that.'

Rose nods. 'We're very close.'

'Are you getting all the help you need?'

'Everyone is so kind.'

Sheila talks directly to Michael. She might as well speak to a dummy. 'I think we're all very keen to see you back on your feet again.'

Is she expecting some response? Some sudden, miraculous recovery that her sincerity might inspire? She's going to be disappointed. Michael stares on into the distance. But Rose knows that if she answers for him Sheila will disapprove.

The silence hangs in the air until, eventually, Sheila has to turn back to Rose. 'For this to happen to someone like Michael seems so terribly unfair. He's had one hell of a year, one way and another. I expect he told you about that unfortunate affair with Belinda.'

What? Rose catches her breath. She gasps. Jesus Christ she must handle this right. 'Yes. Yes he did actually.'

'Good. He was afraid of upsetting you, but I'm glad he followed my advice. These things are always better brought out into the open and dealt with. And let's face it, these days they're considered par for the course. And thank goodness; a person's sexuality is their own affair. At long last the English have grown up about sex. The sad part about the Belinda business was that she was young and so manipulative. It's no wonder Michael fell for it.'

'Yes, no wonder.'

'And now this double tragedy.'

What? 'Yes, indeed. I know.'

'How kind,' says Sheila Gordon, accepting her coffee from Mrs H's tray, the one with the bluebirds on it, happily unaware of the impact she is having on her hostess this morning.

'Is Michael joining us?'

'He has his drinks at regular intervals. He has a special cup.'

Sheila looks away, horrified. 'Ah yes. Yes, of course.'

Rose is mightily tempted to demonstrate to this fragrant being, who hasn't the vaguest idea of the mess and degradation involved in Michael's feeding, how unpleasant this can be. But she resists the temptation, far keener to get her visitor back on to the subject of Belinda.

How is it that this woman, almost a stranger to Rose, knows so much? Why should Michael use her as his confidante when his own wife was waiting at home? Did they meet often? She obviously has a high opinion of him, and he of her presumably.

'Jessie is doing very well,' says Sheila to Michael, cutting out Rose. 'We're very pleased with her, especially after that shaky start. And your work has been taken over very efficiently by a colleague, so no worries on that score. I got my bracelet back by the way. I went back to Boaters and they'd kept it for me – a piece of unexpected luck.'

Boaters? When had these two dined there?

'That's a nice restaurant,' Rose interrupts, digging for clues, any clues.

'It's not if you're in a hurry,' says Sheila, giving

nothing away. But would she be as flagrant as this if there was anything to hide? 'We'd had rather a lot to drink, I'm afraid, hadn't we, Michael? And on a working day, too.'

Michael stares on into space. Gaga.

'Well, time and tide,' says Sheila rising, offering a jewelled hand to Rose, who rises with her and holds it limply, fearing that she is blinking hard but quite unable to stop herself. 'I expect I am late already, I usually am these days. Racing around. Quite mad. It's been so good to see you again, Rose. And you, Michael. Get better soon. We all love you. We all want you back.'

Even her voice is sophisticated, slow, measured and velvety. Sheila Gordon oozes charm. If Rose were a man, Sheila would be the kind of woman she would probably fall for, and Rose and Michael feel the same over most things, especially when it comes to individual taste.

'Bit hoity toity if you ask me,' Mrs H says when Sheila has gone.

Rose remains beside Michael, seething inside.

Oh, Michael. How could you? You bastard.

Very young was she, your Belinda? And yet she could manipulate you, a man with daughters of his own, probably around the same age.

Michael, I thought I knew you. I would have trusted you with my life.

Sitting there like bloody Noddy – enjoyed your time in Toyland, did you?

No wonder you didn't come clean with me, in spite of the chances I gave you. You'd rather confide over bottles of wine to the glamorous Sheila in

280

Boaters. Did talking about it give you a hard-on? Yes we might as well resort to that kind of language now, you and I. You ignored her advice and no wonder. She told you I would understand, but how wrong she was. Jesus Christ.

Mrs H hovers around her. 'Are you OK, Mrs Redfern?'

'Yes, fine.' Rose sighs, easing herself off her chair, but her legs are still shaking with shock.

'Only I wanted to clean in here.'

'Sorry. Oh yes, you carry on.'

'So long as I'm not disturbing you.'

The sordid picture of Michael's sexual exploits begins to take a firmer shape. If Belinda is as young as Sheila Gordon implies, no wonder she's finding it hard to relinquish the hold she had on Michael. Daisy's young and she always acts on impulse, without an older woman's discretion. Young, single and lusty – girls these days don't spare a thought about wrecking somebody's marriage.

Michael never mentioned lunching with Sheila Gordon. Was it a regular arrangement they had?

Rose screams inside while the black wings of fear bat about her. What was it Sheila had said? – 'At long last the English have grown up about sex.' Her attitude suggested there was nothing wrong with sleeping around. No harm done. Everyone's sexual behaviour is their own affair.

Bullshit.

Who else has Michael had it away with? Belinda, Sheila and half of South Hams, for all Rose knows. Well, he's got his just come-uppance now.

This sick feeling, this plummeting of the heart, this terror. Even if she does get him back, sane and sensible again, does a womanizer like him ever change? And the thought of her daughters' reactions if they should ever discover her treatment of Michael leaves Rose in a freezing cold, private silence.

Knowing what he is, and what he's been up to, maybe Rose should be asking herself if she actually wants this man. This lecher. Does she really still love Michael after his enormous betrayal?

Better, perhaps, to throw him out and take him to the cleaners. A wife of thirty years' standing should be in line for some hefty payments. So what if she's lonely; she couldn't feel more alone than she does at this minute. So what if the girls turned against her, that would be their decision. So what if their friends sided with Michael, she never was the sociable type and she doesn't like them much anyhow.

She could start afresh. She could sell the house, get a penthouse in London, go on a cruise and start flirting with men. If a man like Jack Bennet fancies her, then surely all can't be lost. She could insist on making love with the light out.

And why the hell should she give a damn if Michael wears his balls off going round screwing his little nymphets? He's not the man she thought he was. In fact, he is now the kind of man Rose despises, but it's not as easy as that to stop loving someone.

She looks at him with agonized eyes and makes sure Mrs H is safely upstairs before letting the tears fall.

TWENTY-THREE

OK, OK. Although Daisy's relationship dramas come round with such boring repetition, this time, under the circumstances, Jessie feels she should offer support.

All this half of term Jasmine has been absorbed in her role as director of the annual nativity play put on by Kingsmead School. She even tried to drag Jessie into the fray. Would she help a group of autistic kids learn their lines? But, feeble and inadequate, Jessie admits she's not at her best around kids with special needs, while the godly Jasmine shines like a star. It's the mentally handicapped that Jessie finds awkward; they seem as needy and pathetic as Dad.

'Precisely,' said Jasmine. 'And that's exactly why you should help. It's only for an hour two evenings a week. It's only fear that defeats you, fear of the unknown.'

In spite of Jasmine's thespian interests she has no intention of abandoning Rose. Her hours might be more irregular, she might be more rushed and red-faced than normal, but she's still that old reliable brick who never lets Mum down.

Mum, always nosey when it comes to their friends, especially someone as odd as Jasmine, who seems to have sprung from nowhere, questions Jessie who knows no more than she does. 'You say she's gone to Cheshire for a week to stay with her family? What sort of people are they? Has Jasmine got brothers or sisters?'

'They farm,' Jessie told her. 'And she's got three brothers, but she doesn't talk much about herself.'

'I just wondered how long Jasmine had worked at the school?'

'God you're inquisitive,' said Jessie.

'No, I'm not,' said Mum, who's never got over her smothering ways of vetting Jessie's friends as if Jessie herself can't be trusted. 'Jasmine's a lovely girl, but you must admit, it's odd the way she's popped up out of the blue and adopted this family as her own. She just about lives here these days; she hardly uses her flat.'

'She doesn't keep much stuff there. It's spartan. Most of the time she sleeps at Kingsmead.'

'She's almost one of us,' said Mum, 'but I still know nothing about her.'

'Jasmine Smith is a child of Jesus,' said Jessie cynically, 'so she goes where she thinks she's needed.'

'Is that why she befriended you?'

Jessie laughed. 'Am I needy?'

'You tell me,' said Mum.

But Jessie didn't answer.

To Daisy's desolation William has moved out. She's an inconsolable wreck.

He is staying with a mate until tomorrow, when

284

he's off backpacking on his own, no-one knows where.

'We planned a week off together,' cried Daisy, 'so we could do some early Christmas shopping. And now look, he's sodded off. Why would he want to backpack in this weather? He's left his passport, so he can't be going abroad. I ring and he won't speak to me; he says he needs some space. Please, please talk to him, Jessie. Try and make him change his mind.'

In happier circumstances Mum and Dad would pick up the pieces, but this time even the heart-broken Daisy feels she can't put more burdens on Mum, whose initial amazing caring capabilities seem to be starting to crumble. She's looking more stressed every day, and although Jessie didn't add to the arguments ranged against her after the funeral – the pressure on Mum is great enough – maybe it is time they found full-time help.

Jasmine is right, Dad is making progress, even his constant shuffling around is better than sitting, vacant, in his chair. And now he can handle a spoon, with help, and Daisy said she'd once seen him smile.

Jessie tried, secretly, to communicate with Dad on the same mental wavelengths Mum seems to be using. She ended up feeling like a prat, sat there with her eyes screwed shut, sending messages through the ether, gripping Dad's hand as hard as she could, hoping for some sign.

Jessie had been shocked to notice Mum's hands trembling on her last visit home. She tried to tell herself Mum was tired and too much stress and overwork can make your hands shake. Hers were the same when she moved into her digs, lugging her cases up endless passages, shifting the shabby furniture around till she had it how she liked it. But that's not the only sign that Mum might be cracking. She's stopped caring about her looks: no make-up, wearing the same clothes for a whole week, and when she does bother to wash her hair she leaves it to dry on its own, so it ends up a witchy mess. There's this fraughtness about her which was never there before, but any suggestion of a live-in nurse only causes argument.

'I couldn't abide having some stranger in my house,' says Mum, 'so leave it! Forget it!'

Should she or Daisy volunteer to move back home?

Daisy says no. She worries, 'Look how hard it was for both of us to move out. I know this sounds awful, Jess, but imagine, if Dad didn't improve we could be stuck there for life.'

There's no two ways about it, Jessie would hate to move back home, out of the student building where there's usually some diversion and friends who bum round for a coffee, a spliff or a gossip. Being at home now is so depressing; there's only one subject and that's poor Dad. The whole routine revolves around him, and there's this underlying smell of sickness, or is it pee? She hates herself for thinking this way, but sometimes, when she leaves, she breathes in the outside air and just glories in life and the hope and freshness it offers.

Not so for Jasmine the good Samaritan. She holds the crazy belief that goodness can come out of pain and suffering. This idea is so abhorrent to Jessie that she can't discuss it rationally, or any

286

other aspect of her friend's priggish, tambourine religion.

If God is there he's a pervert.

Jessie, waiting at the beer-stained table, had been surprised when William had agreed to meet her.

'On your own,' was his only stipulation. 'Don't drag Jasmine along and don't sneak Daisy in, either.'

He's such a catch, she thinks as he slouches at the bar, ordering her a wine and a lager for himself. Daisy's definitely missed out here; he's sexy, clever and funny with it. Her own brief reaction to him ought to convince her that she is no dyke; she'd hop into bed with him tomorrow if he wasn't Daisy's lost property.

'I wanted to talk to you anyway,' he tells her, straddling a stool so his knees are disturbingly close to her own.

'You've left her,' says Jessie shortly, concentrating on the reason she's here.

William shakes his head. 'When every word you utter causes at best a sneer and at worst an outburst of loaded criticism, you're not going to hang around,' he says. 'But that's not the reason I wanted to talk.'

'Oh?' And Jessie waits.

He licks foam from his upper lip. 'This crap has got to stop.'

'What crap?'

'Do you really believe that fire was an accident?'

Shocked and unnerved, Jessie's hand stays fixed to her glass, sticky around it. She checks over her shoulder to see if anyone's listening, then lowers her voice so she sounds like a spy, 'Obviously you think not.'

He turns and puffs smoke over his shoulder, at least he's got consideration about that. 'Jessie, have you honestly never asked yourself if this wasn't more of Belinda's work?'

She had wondered, she can't deny it. But the very idea is so utterly monstrous that she has blocked it from her mind. 'Slashed tyres, yes. Turds in the bedroom, yes. Ripping a coat to pieces, yes. But Jesus, William, burning an old woman to death is something else.'

'I found this.'

He delves into his leather jacket and comes out with a blackened object that once could have been a cuddly toy. It reeks of smoke.

With some difficulty he balances the thing on the table. The remains of its rabbit ears flop repellently forward. 'Wait,' says William, with his finger digging out a half-buried chain from the tattered fur. The chain circles the animal's neck, and there's a silver disk threaded onto the chain and the letter embossed on the disk is an unmistakable B.

Jessie shivers. It's gone cold in here and every goose bump on her body has risen. 'How did you get that?'

'The day after the fire,' says William. 'If it had been anything to do with Belinda I guessed that she'd leave a sign.'

She stares him directly in the eyes. 'This is sensationalism at its worst. Tell me you're joking. This is some idiot trick.' But William's unblinking gaze is horribly sincere. 'But how could you have found it?

288

Surely the day after the fire the investigators must have been there?'

'Yes, they were. They were prodding about in the centre. But I had no need to go any futher than the scorched outer ring of grass.'

'How come they didn't find it?'

'Because they weren't looking at the bits of junk thrown out to the edges. They weren't after the sort of sign I was interested in.'

She still finds this hard to believe. 'Tell me the answer to this, then. If Belinda is so cunning it seems rather haphazard of her to leave this . . . thing on the grass in the hope that one day one of us might find it.'

William waves away her ignorance. 'Not at all. The investigators would have found it. It would have been added to the few other items which escaped total incineration. You would have been asked to identify it.'

The glassy eyes of the burned rabbit remind Jessie of Dad. She flinches away from the awful comparison. 'Has Daisy seen this?'

'No.'

'But she should.' Jessie stares but daren't touch. William's suspicions have made this thing evil. The toy makes her skin crawl.

'As she is now, Daisy would either go off her head or deny the connection completely.'

'Then why show me?'

William shrugs. 'Because this is your family, your problem, not mine. Although it seems to me that I'm the only stupid bastard who's refusing to hide my head in the sand. The rest of you seem either unwilling or sadly incapable of intelligent action.

289

Do you recognize this rabbit? Is it a favourite childhood toy? Did it once belong to your mum? Was there a particular reason why your granny would have kept it?'

Jessie, finding it loathsome, is forced to inspect it more carefully. Eventually she shakes her head wonderingly.

'No, I thought not,' says William. 'You've got to find this sick bitch Belinda. Jesus! You wouldn't listen. I told you. The police should have been called in from the start.'

'Back then it was different: the freak hadn't started a fire. And why the hell is she doing this? Is it revenge? Or to get me back?'

William slams his hand down on the table and the awful mascot slews onto its side. 'Don't play this game. It's gone way past reason. You've read about stalkers. You must know how these people work. The worst of them don't stop at sick tricks; they go on to kill. They're obsessives and they're dangerous. This woman, Belinda, is your business, Jessie. Your fault, if you like. And you're so damn terrified of your bloody mother finding out about your little lesbian liaison that you're willing to risk—'

'We have had other things on our minds.' Does he honestly need reminding?

William nods with exaggerated patience. 'I know, I know. And that's why I'm taking it on; doing something about it. I'm going to Belinda's home in Cardiff to make some enquiries with neighbours, friends, schools. Somebody's bound to know something.'

Ah, of course! Suddenly his attitude is making sense. Jessie sits back with a look of disdain. 'You're interested in a good story, that's what this is all about. Don't come the crusader with me, you tosser.'

'So what if I am? Do my motives matter?'

He always was ambitious. 'Let me come with you. As you said, it's my business, my fault.'

'I'm going alone, tomorrow. But thank you for your interest.'

'No need for sarcasm, William. If I'd had the slightest inkling that the fire was caused by Belinda I would have gone straight to the police, we all would, and I think we ought to do that now. Your private sleuthing might make matters worse, or even cause a fatal delay. Christ, if you're right, we can't afford that.'

'Do me one favour,' says William, nervously running his cigarette round and round in the ashtray until the wretched thing bends in half. 'Don't talk to anyone about this. Not till I'm back.'

'Don't be a prick, of couse I must. Daisy's got to be warned, and Mum and Jasmine. Any one of us could be her next victim. If she could target Granny she can pick on anyone. Anyway, why the secrecy? Afraid someone might sniff out your story and scoop you? Now who's playing dangerous games?'

William ignores her scathing remarks and goes to order a second round of drinks. There is nothing to focus upon save for the once-pink rabbit, with the smoky, venomous yellow eyes. A demonic effigy, infernal, hellish, the spirit of evil. It was impossible to imagine it being loved by a child, taken to bed and cuddled up to at night.

What William is suggesting is so outrageous, so utterly monstrous.

'*Listen to me, Jessie.*' He comes over deadly serious demanding her complete attention. 'I'm asking you for two days. By the time you've called in the police and they've taken statements, scanned their computers, begun their inquiries – and that's if they take you seriously, which they may well decide not to do; there's scant enough evidence to support my theory – I will have found what I'm looking for. If not, I'll give up and back you in whatever you decide.'

This is stupid. 'But what if Belinda decides to torch Mum's house, or strangle Daisy when she's walking home, or take a machete to Jasmine or Mum?'

'I don't think that will happen. Just give me two days,' William repeats. 'If anyone can get results, I will.'

'You won't get much out of Belinda's parents. They're hostile as hell and you're a cocky bastard.'

'No, I'm good at my job. And why don't you come clean and admit it? At least my way there's a chance that I'm talking out of my arse – a slim chance, but it's there – and that Belinda has nothing to do with this, in which case your mother might never have to hear about your unfortunate tendencies.'

'You sod.'

William smiles. 'Sticks and stones.' He picks up his glass and holds it to hers. 'Do you agree?'

But Jessie holds back. This secret, this terrible secret, is a massive burden to bear. 'I almost wish you hadn't told me. I'm still not sure why you did.'

'Maybe I trust you.'

'*Me?* Why? Not Daisy? Not Jasmine?' Jessie

frowns at her waiting glass. 'I still believe they ought to be warned.'

'Two days.'

Reluctantly Jessie picks up her glass and touches the rim of his. 'OK. But there's one condition, I want you to keep in touch. I want to know who you are seeing, where you are and what you find out. Belinda is here – I've seen her – she's hundreds of miles away from Cardiff. And if you discover anything relevant, if you get any idea where she's living, I want to be the first to know.'

William takes down her mobile number, that's the only guarantee he will give her.

'Well,' asks Daisy, falling on Jessie the moment she arrives at Mum's. 'What did he say? Is he coming back? Did you talk about me? Is it over?'

'He wants space,' says Jessie unhelpfully.

'Well, I know that,' Daisy cries in frustration. 'Where is he going? How long will he be? Is he coming back to the flat?'

Poor Daisy. She's in pieces. The least Jessie could have done was prise some reassuring words from her hour-long session with William. How can she tell her grieving sister that her name was hardly mentioned? Jessie has no idea what William's long-term intentions are. She's not even sure William's motives in tracking down Belinda have anything to do with his relationship with Daisy.

'Was he upset?' Daisy begs. 'Is he missing me?'

There's no point in causing unnecessary grief. 'Yes, he is missing you. But no, he didn't tell me what he was planning to do.'

'It's because of all this, isn't it?' Daisy pleads,

encompassing the room, the house and the whole hideous situation in one hopeless sweep of her arm. Mum is upstairs seeing to Dad. 'He can't take it.'

It's a valiant stab in the dark. 'Maybe William can't cope with seeing you so unhappy.'

'He's like a child,' Daisy moans. 'He needs my constant attention.'

'Does he?' This doesn't sound like William. This sounds more like the sort of man Daisy would like him to be. A home-loving, protective soulmate, absolutely contented with Daisy's company, and Daisy's company alone. Someone like Dad, who will tell her stories, someone past his sell-by date, a lost generation of men of slippers, hearth and home.

'He resents our family closeness,' Daisy sniffs miserably. 'He's never experienced anything like it, so how can he understand? He's no support. He does his own thing – like now – sodding off when I need him most.'

Jessie, guiltily, is relieved that Dad is upstairs and in bed and that consequently her help won't be needed. Jasmine, bless her, is upstairs with Mum now, sorting out sheets, bedpans and dirty laundry.

What would they do without her?

'Has anyone checked the French-window locks?' she jumps and asks suddenly, aware of her awesome responsibility since William shared his unlikely suspicions.

'Mum reminds Mrs H every day,' says Daisy, annoyed to be bothered by such trivia when her future hangs in the balance and Jessie is so oddly reluctant to give her the reassurance she yearns for. 'Is he really going away? Is he really going on his own or has he found someone else? You can tell me, Jessie. Don't keep it from me.'

'No, as far as I know William hasn't found anyone else, and yes, he is going away, but only for two days,' Jessie is happy to tell her sister. If only Daisy would leave it there and not keep up this relentless probing. She wishes she could confide in Daisy the enormity of the horrible truth. And Jasmine; her common-sense reaction would be more than welcome.

If only she hadn't promised William. If only she didn't have her own reasons for wanting William to succeed, rather than the more sensible option of calling in the police.

God help me. If anything does happen now, Jessie will be wholly to blame.

Belinda could be out there in the darkness, crouching in the flower beds, waiting for the moment to pounce, kill, burn, maim or destroy, while all Daisy is worried about is whether her man, her wonderful William, is getting his end away.

TWENTY-FOUR

Rose is his night tormentor. When this truth finally dawned on Michael he tried to scream. No sound came. He cried silently into the night and his eyes burned brilliantly in the darkness. Perhaps it was some self-protective denial that had kept him ignorant for so long.

Now, if he wants to save his life, in those brief intervals of coherent thought, Michael must think productively, because that's what his tortured mind is telling him: life or death, him or Rose.

He curses his stupidity while understanding well enough why it took him so long to work it out. The irony is hard to define; he ought to feel massive relief that there is nothing medically wrong with him, his system is simply flooded with powerful sedatives, administered day and night by his wife and if only no long-term damage has been done, one day, one bright, brilliant morning, he will recognize his old self again.

He will think straight and walk in a line. He will eat and drink without aid, talk and laugh, and perhaps even love. He will sleep, no more to visit this dark, dreamless pit where he is forced to spend most of his endless hours.

Nights. How he dreads them. How he shrinks from the moment he can feel the side of the bed sink down as somebody – it has to be Rose – sits staring at him, as if she needs to remind herself, to summon the anger that will allow her to inflict the screaming torture she has taken to in such style.

Nights. They are long.

This behaviour is so easy for her. Alone in the house – Michael guesses that much – she has all the time in the world to decide which hour she will come, which night, which method. Methods devised so that it's hard to detect his internal wounds. His festering ear is oozing now, and half the putrid slime passes down his throat. Last night, probably nearer to dawn, she came again and sat beside him; he imagined she was probably speaking before she sat forward and wedged what he thought were two cotton-wool tubes up his nose.

My, what a big nose you have.

All the better to smell you with.

It wasn't until he smelled the blood that his stomach turned over and he tried to vomit.

What kind of perverted hatred would induce anyone to do that? What kind of damaged mind? What twisted motives? What brutal sickness left untreated could cause someone to act out such rage?

The result of this was that his breathing was hampered, and Michael's breathing was just one of his terrors, with his throat so sore and still burning fire, every intake of breath was torture, as if the bar of an electric fire were turned on full in his throat. Now that he knows about Rose he

297

sometimes prays that the night will take him and he'll never have to wake up.

The revelation came when she slapped his face the time he attempted to refuse her filthy cocktail of stupor. That wasn't the behaviour of a wife with her husband's best interests at heart. Even if she had been persuaded by the best medical brains in the land that he had to be forced to take his medication, why would she have slapped him so hard?

The Rose he had known would never have done that. Not even to a dog. His Rose was gentle, loving and kind.

He could only guess that her anger, whatever caused her to turn, was increasing as every week went by. Had some event unknown to Michael triggered off some madness inside her that contented motherhood and marriage had subdued until now? Could the change of life have caused this sickness to raise its poisonous head? Hormones? Boredom? The fear of old age? Her grandmother's madness, the family skeleton? Or an empty nest?

Rose had never wanted the girls to leave home and Michael had struggled as best he could to keep her daughters near by.

In a couple of bored moments in the past, driving in the car, soaking in the bath and walking Baggins, Michael had imagined the kind of effect it would have on Rose if he should ever leave her. Nothing was further from his mind, but that doesn't stop you playing with ideas.

On every occasion he had concluded that such an act would result in her suicide. Even their nightly routine between tooth-brushing, night cream, pillow talk and cuddles frequently included the question, 'You'd never leave me, would you, Michael?' She'd asked him that question so often that it had become almost meaningless; he used to answer without much conviction as he hadn't believed it was necessary.

On the night the truth finally dawned on Michael he dragged at the last vestiges of sensibility when he tried to conjure up Venice. Sleep was claiming him, threatening mental shutdown. Had there been any signs of Rose's impending lunacy that Michael might recognize with hindsight? He took a trip through sleepy lagoons and endless passageways, over bridges and down steps until everything merged into one devilish game of *Tomb Raider*.

It must be dawn, the darkness was lifting and the drug, as usual, was wearing off.

The first question that rushed to mind was had he survived the night without incident? Was some new part of his body aflame? He started at his toes and checked himself through. His ears, nose and throat were as painful as ever, but nothing else grabbed his attention, thank God.

He picked up his thoughts where he'd left them some hazy eight hours before. He had imagined that if he left Rose she would commit suicide. But would she really do that? Wouldn't Rose be more likely to kill him before he could pack his case? An accident with the garden strimmer? An electrical fault in his shaver? Or maybe he'd drop it in the bath while it was still attached to the socket? A tumble over the balcony or a slip on the edge of a cliff?

Perhaps, and Michael wriggled his toes – he could feel them; every one was moving – perhaps she might not want him dead, just captive, helpless and dependent. Terror-crazed.

Oh, dear God. Help me, help me. It was not just his throat but his brain that was on fire.

But how would the notion that Michael was leaving find its way into Rose's head and lodge itself there so securely that time and common sense couldn't shift it?

What reason would Michael have for leaving his wife apart from another woman? There were no money problems, he hadn't got Aids or genital warts and his memory was as sharp as ever. What the hell had persuaded Rose that he was about to desert her, if this suspicion of his was correct? What tremendous discovery would drive her to this sort of mindless depravity?

Belinda's letter! In his jacket pocket. Dear God. She'd sent him so many during those weeks, and he had destroyed them all, except for the one he'd forgotten about.

He struggled to remember the day he found it. He had suggested they go out for lunch. Her response hadn't been enthusiastic, and he had wondered if she had a headache, but her silence hadn't lasted long.

Maybe Belinda had phoned when he was at work, before he could stop her, before he could meet Sheila Gordon and hand the problem over to her. Sheila would have started immediately on an expert investigation, but Michael was in Venice before she could get back to him. Michael groaned out loud; there was no mistaking that sound of despair.

Rose must have picked up the phone and dialled 1471.

She must have listened to Belinda's answerphone message.

Belinda at her most destructive. Jesus Christ, of course; it was all so glaringly simple. The perversity of the situation when Michael remembered his decision to confide in his wife when they came home from Venice slapped him with the ferocity of Rose's hand last night.

She really believed that he and Belinda . . . She didn't question him, ask him to explain. Her worst nightmares had come true and so she'd acted, not to kill him – that might have been far kinder – but to keep him. And so far, dear God, against all the odds she has somehow succeeded.

But so many people know the truth about Belinda. How bizarre that in these last awful weeks the facts about Belinda have not come out. There's Jessie, Daisy, William, Belinda herself and Sheila. Any one of them could save him now. But from what? What petrifies Michael most of all? Death or a permanent vegetative state while Rose, the murderess, makes up her mind?

Michael, in his terror, takes his fears to the ultimate: if he thinks Rose capable of killing, could it be possible, that she, the wife he had loved, was involved in the death of her own father and brother?

No, no. He can't take that further.

Belinda is a family secret based on the assumption, maybe wrong, that Rose would be distraught to discover that her youngest daughter had got mixed up with the girl, and all the unfortunate consequences. How much of this is his own stupid fault, caused by *his* need to protect *her*?

Don't tell Rose. Don't upset Mummy. She's got enough on her plate. Poor Rose.

And because Rose is under such pressure with a cabbage for a husband the thing to be most avoided by her loved ones would be any extra strain. Don't let Mum hear about Belinda. Best to forget it; it's all in the past now anyway.

When he feels the side of the bed go down palpitations pump at his nerves and he knows the meaning of mortal terror.

Once again he is under sentence. Once again there is no shrinking away.

With horror he feels his wife's eyes on him, boring into his soul like a jackhammer at concrete. What can those fiendish eyes look like? What sort of blazing does evil make? Michael would rather not see or know. To be acting out this madness means that Rose is way past compassion or even recognition of the terror of her blinded prey, the man she once claimed to love more strongly than life itself.

He might not be able to see too clearly or hear only muffled sounds, but Michael's nerve endings must be healing, because his sense of feeling is sharp, sharp enough to recognize rough hands at his pyjama strings, impatiently loosening the cords, tugging, pushing him over until it's possible, slowly and awkwardly, to lower the clothing over his buttocks and slide the legs down over his ankles.

Naked from the waist down, legs spread, arms by his sides, he is a pagan sacrifice to the gods of Rose's perverted brain. In frozen horror Michael imagines that he hears the squeak of the bedside drawer on her side. His memory won't tell him what she keeps in it apart from the acid she poured in his eyes what seems like a lifetime ago. Perhaps his memory is trying to deny what it used to know only too well.

Even with his slow responses Michael can pretend to brace himself against pain. Something small and icy rests briefly against the warm inside of his leg. And then a sound he cannot identify, and the pressure of fingers between his legs.

No, no. Not that.

How long can he hold himself ready for agony? Such cold-blooded surgery; the stuff of hell.

The pain in his ear has disappeared.

Nail scissors, that's what Rose keeps in her drawer, nail files, varnish and curved nail scissors with silver handles so delicate they hardly fit a woman's slim fingers. I went to market and I bought a pair of nail scissors, a nail file, nail varnish, nail-varnish remover, night cream, a diary, two pens, cotton buds, a pack of matches from the Hilton Hotel, lip salve, Rennies and cough sweets.

He waits . . .

And waits . . .

Still nothing comes . . . and then she's gone, having caused so much mental suffering that Michael is left half paralysed.

Clever. Clever. The suggestion is almost worse than the pain itself. When, at last, Michael knows he's alone, he feels another sensation. Warm tears roll down his cheeks, consoling him like friends from his childhood, coming from somewhere solid, within which all the blossom and sky memories lie.

TWENTY-FIVE

'ROSE – KILL.'

'My diary,' says Rose, sitting on the bed, exhausted and shattered and utterly bewildered. 'Here, look. The pencil; I keep it in this drawer. What's it doing out on the table?'

'God only knows,' states nurse Susan simply, staring at the long, tall message set amongst the wallpaper roses.

He knows! Michael knows! Dear God.

If only she could have got here first she could have rubbed it off.

Rose turns wearily towards the nurse. She's not dressed. The doorbell woke her and nurse Susan's cheery explanation, 'Sorry for this ungodly hour but I've got a funeral this afternoon – mother-in-law, all pretty awful – and I want to get my priorities done before I go off at lunchtime. I should have warned you, I know. I stupidly mentioned the fact to Michael, chatting on like you do, but on my way out it slipped my mind.'

Oh, she mentioned that fact to Michael, did she? Does that mean that Michael is alert enough to plot against her?

Damn, damn. Michael's medication will have to wait till the nurse has gone.

Rose watches Michael carefully as she sips the hot, sweet liquid.

'We must see this as a positive sign,' nurse Susan explains, seeing Rose's distress and assuming she is in shock. 'The fact that Michael can write is going to mean a complete sea change. From now on, my dear, he can communicate with the world, he's been unlocked from his silent prison. This is a wonderful development. Come on,' she exhorts, 'let's see what happens if we . . .'

And the nurse, stiff in starch, crackles down on the side of the bed and writes in large letters on her medical pad, 'Good morning Michael!'

No response, just a blank stare. He's clever if this façade is fake and Rose imagines those dead eyes following her.

'Never mind,' says the nurse, still flushed with excitement, fixing the tiny pencil between her patient's thumb and first finger. 'If you can hear me, Michael, won't you give me some sign?' While, in an aside to Rose, she mentions, 'It's so interesting how different parts of the brain can repair themselves faster than others.'

Oh dear me, her patient can't hear her, and Rose, holding her breath to staunch the rising nausea, thanks God for her surprising reprieve.

'Look, Michael,' continues nurse Susan, flapping the pad before his eyes and stabbing it with the pencil. 'Look, dear, are you going to show us what you can do this morning?'

Absolutely nothing. Just deadpan.

'Well,' observes the nurse, turning to Rose, ready

305

to comfort her. 'It could be that these odd two words tired him too much last night. But there's no doubt the poor man was trying to give us a sign, and we must be watchful from now on in case he finds the same reserves of energy to make another brave effort.'

'But what was he trying to say?' asks Rose. Is the nurse suspicious? Isn't she disturbed by such a strange choice of words?

'You have to understand that the concentration involved in getting those letters down is what we have to focus on, not what he actually says.' She stares at Rose in her distress and lays a kindly hand on her shoulder. 'Listen to me, my dear, it could be that your husband was making a plea for euthanasia, unaware that his disabilities are only temporary. As far as he knows, this could be a permanent state.'

'He's asking me to kill him?'

Nurse Susan shakes her head. 'That is a possibility, but don't take me literally, it's merely guess-work on my part.'

After the nurse has left, Rose, in a daze, stares first at Michael, who gives nothing away, and then back at the wall, where the dreadful words form a trellis for the roses to wind around.

'Coooeee? Mrs Redfern? Are you ready for me yet?'

Rose hurtles back from her faraway place, and ends up back at the door, knees trembling with shame and fear.

'I'll start down here in the kitchen.'

'*I'm the King of the Castle and you're the dirty rascal . . .*'

306

Yes, she'd been there when Jamie went over the cliff. She'd sat in her arbour of gorse and watched him sail over the edge on his bike, calling out with his best friend, Nicky, 'I can see you, Rosalind Tate. Wanna bun trunky?'

After the metal clunk and the silence, after Nicky went running, face hideous with war paint and Indian feathers flying behind him, Rose knew something so massive had happened that all she could do was run and hide. And she kept on hiding and sobbing and crying for her brother under the canvas hammock cover, where it was dark and green, like being in the woods.

It smelled of mice and mould.

She peed in her pants.

She sang nursery rhymes to pass the endless afternoon until she heard her mother calling in a voice she couldn't recognize.

Comfort, that's what Rose craved. And to feel Jamie's hand tightly wrapped around hers again.

Sudden daylight, a streaming sun blinding her eyes and a vice-like grip around her skinny wrist dragged her into the hell of reality.

'Mummy, Mummy . . .'

No answer.

Dinah dragged her upstairs, tore off her clothes and pushed little Rose into bed.

There were grown-ups in the hall, she could hear them, but she couldn't hear Jamie's voice and his bed was empty beside her, except for his stupid pink rabbit.

The hours went by. It grew dark and then light. No-one came in to draw her curtains or tell her when to go to sleep. Why was she being punished like this?

Why did Dinah come up and bring her scrambled egg on toast, chicken soup, kippers with bread and butter, and glasses of milk and orange squash without speaking? Why couldn't she go downstairs? And where was Daddy? Did he hate her, too? Had Mummy stopped him from loving her?

She read her favourite Enid Blytons all over again, from cover to cover.

'You've got flu,' Mummy kept saying. 'You've got a high temperature. Stay where you are.'

Did Mummy really believe she'd had something to do with Jamie falling?

Pushed him over the edge of the cliff?

Tricked him towards a dangerous track?

The moment she saw Daddy again Rose threw herself into his tweedy arms. It was during the long summer holidays, and she was brown as a nut, with dark curly hair; she clung to his lapels as fiercely as an orphaned baby monkey. He whispered into her ear, 'My dear little girl, my sweetheart, my baby,' he cuddled her and she felt safe, but it took a long time for Mummy to learn to speak to her daughter and touch her again.

The night before Daddy got lost, after they'd eaten a huge, posh dinner and Mother had gone to look around the duty-free shop before she went to bed, Daddy put his arms round Rose again and pulled her close; he smelled just the same as he'd smelled when she was ten and frightened.

'You know how much I love you, Rose. You know that, sweetheart, don't you?'

Rose nodded, half embarrassed.

'I've always been so proud of you. You're such a special child, so very easy to love.'

308

Why was Daddy speaking like this? She grew more and more uncomfortable until she was forced to say, 'I love you very much, Daddy. I love you, too.' But the words sounded stilted because of her embarrassment; she wanted to try and say them again, but that just wouldn't have worked.

'What I want you to understand, Rose, when you're older and you know more about life, the most important thing is, darling, that sometimes love isn't enough. Sometimes,' he stopped and stared sadly out at the sea – it was a brassy silver colour that night – and Rose thought she saw tears behind his eyes, 'people get so wounded that life becomes very hard. I've tried, darling. I've tried . . .'

They all went to bed.

She woke in the night to find his bed empty. She tiptoed out of the cabin to find him, but got lost in the passages.

In the morning Daddy had gone. Radios rattled. They searched the ship and sent aeroplanes out. Mother was hysterical. Rose and her mother came home to absolute silence and the curtains stayed drawn. It was just like after Jamie, but the difference was that Daddy was gone. And it was all her fault.

The months that followed were full of silence, the smell of drink on Mother's breath and the pills she slapped into her mouth with her eyes gimlets of accusing black. Rose lived a solitary existence, waking for school, packing her satchel, preparing her packed lunch, ironing her blouse and tunic and opening tins of beans in the evening.

Daddy, her protector, was gone, so despairing that he had jumped off the ship in search of the kind of peaceful oblivion for which Rose so often yearned during the year Mummy broke down.

Rose was always nice to Mummy; she was so frightened of her she had no option, even when she grew up she was afraid she'd turn.

She used to weep under her sheets, her hands screwed up into little wet balls, 'Daddy, Daddy, I love you. Please, please come back.'

And then, only a few unhappy years later, along came Michael.

There was a time, after Jessie was born, when Rose must have been the victim of some appalling post-natal depression, because her shocking behaviour fills her with shame and horror to this day.

After Michael had left for work she used to come downstairs in her nightie, pick up the phone and tell the Samaritans that she had killed her brother and father.

Angela, the first Samaritan, was not as hysterical as Rose had suspected. Instead, she was patient and understanding. It was Rose, in a state of pure panic, who sobbed distraughtly on the end of the line. 'But what sort of animal am I to be able to do such a thing?' she cried. 'The two people I loved most in the world. I did it. I killed them. I want to kill myself and be with them.'

'Won't you give me a name to call you. It's so much more friendly if you give me a name.'

'No. NO NAME.' Rose was adamant about that.

She phoned the following day, and the next, put out to find Angela gone, but Gregory and Stuart were fine; they listened and sympathized. She was so excited she could hardly sleep at nights, yearning for

310

the morning to come and imagining the next episode. No matter how she embellished the lies they gave her the purest relief. A cleansing.

After all those guilty years, all that blame and nothing said. Sometimes her brain was heaving so much that she worried it might burst.

In the weeks that followed the local Samaritans answered all sorts of calls from nameless women in dangerous places – in phone boxes on bridges, from the top floor of high-rise flats, from grimy tenements beside shunting yards – all threatening suicide and all from the hall phone in Rose's house. All her. Wasn't that dreadful? All Rose in various disguises.

But then the prank backfired. They began suggesting that someone call, confidentially, of course. She imagined them wrapped in brown paper parcels, like the johnnies in Michael's younger days, or in rubbery macs like spies. And the awful thing was she would have liked them to call; she badly wanted that. But she wasn't the woman they thought she was and she didn't dare have her deception exposed. A self-pitying imposter, wasting their precious time. She was only Rose Allison Redfern, lonely and wanting to talk. They would be furious if they suspected.

So she got a tight hold on herself and stopped making any more calls, much to the consternation of Angela, Stuart and Gregory, who knew exactly how it was and didn't care how often she phoned or how much time they gave her.

The voice comes again, shrill with its wash of reality. 'Coooeee, it's me!'

311

Breathing deeply, Rose hurries out onto the landing. 'Good morning, Mrs H. I'm up here, as usual. Give us five minutes, will you?'

'Shall I stick the kettle on? Are you ready?'

'Why not?'

'How's our patient this morning?'

'Oh fine, just fine.'

'Blow me if it's not a miracle.' Mrs H brings happy hands together like a child performer taking a bow.

She throws Michael, now in his chair and established in his place by the fire, a queenly look of motherly pride.

Rose omits the details of the writing on the wall; the way she tells it is as if he's only managed a jumbled scrawl. She tries to enthuse over Michael's improvement and the likelihood that he is mentally more agile than was once believed.

'You don't think he heard me when I said about not wanting to clean his room with him in it?'

'Well, if he did he wouldn't have minded,' says Rose. 'He'd have understood.'

'He's a lovely man,' says Mrs H, welcoming him back from the realms of the dead. 'And I must say he looks so much better. But you say no-one saw him do it?'

'No, I slept in the spare room as usual. I wish I'd heard him get up; I wish I'd been there at that special moment when he must have reached that level of lucidity. I blame myself for sleeping too soundly.'

'Blame, blame, blame,' says Mrs H raising her dramatically arched, pencilled eyebrows. 'That won't do now,' she says, giving her most romantic sigh. 'You'll have to move back in with him tonight. What if he comes round again and you're not there beside him? He can't be left now, night or day. Somebody must watch him. I'll move your pillows and nightie back. That's the first thing I'll do when I get upstairs.'

Mrs H seems nervous around Michael this morning, as if his poor disabled body might suddenly rise from the chair and start chasing her and her bottle of Jif around the house. But what has Mrs H to feel so uncomfortable about? Why would this tortured soul pick on her if he was to rise, berserk, from his torpor and seek out a likely victim?

It wouldn't be the cleaner, and before this whole harrowing episode there would have been no-one he loathed enough to cause him to turn vengeful and vicious. But now . . . Now that he knows. What drove him?

What furious will-power drove this gentle man to override his sluggish brain to get his desperate message across?

How he must despise her.

How he must fear her.

How he must long for revenge.

And the larger question which Rose must face is why she never considered this when she first hatched her plan? How did she ever convince herself that when the time was right she would casually stop his medication and she and Michael would happily resume the relationship they had before?

Incredible as it might seem now, Rose had imagined that guilt over his sleazy affair, combined with his need to make amends, would help him understand her position. But now, after last night's performance, so calculatingly aimed at her, Rose has to think again.

No more lucid moments for him, no more rising at night to scrawl graffiti on the walls. Rose must take complete control. Is this what she's always secretly wanted? Rose must increase the dose, double it if necessary, and begin to take on board the appalling possibility of having to keep Michael beside her, a drooling imbecile, for the rest of his natural life.

Or kill him.

TWENTY-SIX

Mum is out at the theatre tonight, with Jack Bennet of all people, that lecherous old goat. And dinner beforehand.

According to Mum, Jack's wife is off at some overnight conference, so that's why she accepted his invitation, so as not to waste the tickets. But it's so unlike Mum to go out on the spur of the moment like this – and with a man she hardly knows, a partner of Dad's for God's sake – that Jessie and Daisy's suspicions that Mum is about to crack under the strain are gradually and worryingly being confirmed.

Mum's reaction to Dad's muddled scrawl on the wall last night was not surprising, Jessie supposes, although nobody could expect him to write an A'-level essay. 'ROSE – KILL' could mean anything. It could even be a desperate plea for an end to his woes. After all, Dad isn't to know that his mental impairment is temporary; he can't see the daily improvements so obvious to those who love him.

But what if Dad does recover physically but not mentally? Almost the worst scenario.

Jessie had been amazed when yesterday Daisy

came out with the statement, 'Dad's not going to get better, is he? This year, next year or ever?' Jessie stared at her sister quickly; she had sounded almost . . . relieved.

What would Jessie have written, she wonders now, if she wanted to send a message during a brief flash of lucidity when nobody was around to see? Jessie can see why poor Mum is upset, but worried enough to get all dolled up and go out on the town with a man like Jack Bennet?

'I need to be taken out of myself,' Mum said firmly. 'I can't stand much more of this. This house is becoming a prison, and I'm stuck inside, staring out.'

'Is Jasmine with you?' William asks in his cryptic telephone voice.

'No, I'm all alone,' says Jessie. 'Me and this bloody graph, which I have to get done by tomorrow. Jasmine is babysitting back home 'cos Mum's out.'

'How about Daisy?'

'It should be Daisy you're talking to, William, not me. It's she who needs you. Anyway, where are you?'

'You know where I am. I'm in Cardiff, half frozen to death, depressed, hungry and don't ask me about my day. But just wait till I tell you, you're not going to believe me, everything's been turned upside down and I'm on my way back tomorrow.'

This doesn't seem to be the right time to tell William the astonishing news that Dad appears to be making progress, those rather questionable words he had scrawled on the wall last night which sent nurse Susan into vapours of delight but left Mum baffled and nervous. This is the best news they've had since her parents returned from Venice and the whole world seemed to go barmy.

'William, why don't you just try and calm down and start from the beginning.'

'It's not the beginning you'll want to hear, it's what I found out at the end.'

'But you sound so excited, you're muddling me. Tell me what happened today, slowly and sensibly.'

'I found the house; the directory was right. It's called Beachwood and it's on an estate full of Barratt-type homes, with smart gardens, labradors, a sprinkling of Volvos and the odd gnome.'

'And?' The reaction of Belinda's parents, so hostile when Jessie rang them up, should have taken William down a peg or two. Serves the know-all right.

'I introduced myself politely, I said I was carrying out market research and wondered if anyone in their family was aged between eighteen and twenty-five.'

'And?' Had William made any effort to tidy up his image? She doubts it.

'It was odd. Very odd. Old man McNab answered the door, a pretty normal-looking chap, quite smart in a casual way, cords, nice Ralph Lauren shirt in a kind of orange, not short of dosh. He said, "What's this all about," as if I was after ravishing his daughter.'

'He was suspicious?' asks Jessie, smiling. No wonder. William would have done better if he'd come clean and said he was from the press.

'He told me there was nobody living at that

address in that age group and tried to close the door. I made out I was consulting my file and told him I'd got down the name Belinda. He asked me where I'd got that from and I said the electoral register.'

'You're nothing if not determined,' says Jessie. A bloody nuisance more like.

'Yeah, but wait for it, this guy went berserk, asked me where I was from and what I was up to and was I from the local rat pack and how dare I intrude in his private life, digging around asking fucking sick questions.' William sounds quite outraged to have been treated so insultingly.

'Who the hell did they think you were?'

'God knows,' moans William. 'But for some reason that bloke felt threatened, and then his wife called out from the back and he shouted that it was OK, just a salesman trying to flog dusters. Now why would he lie like that?' William asks her.

'You tell me,' says Jessie. 'You're the journalist.'

'I'm stuck in this God-awful pub for the night, like no pub you'd ever want to be found dead in. Lino on the floor and old men with strawberry noses and unzipped paunches sat at the bar, and the stench of disinfectant, no heating and sport on a telly straight out of the ark.'

'No spittoon?' Jessie laughs. 'It was your idea to do this. Don't moan at me, it's not my fault. However miserable you are you don't come near to poor Daisy's suffering.'

'How is she?'

'She's bad. Shall I give her your love?' This is an awkward area. Jessie has always approved of William, the lush, so much more suitable for her sister

318

than the string of guys who have loved her and left her over the years. Why Daisy is so unlucky in love is because she's so unrealistic. Nothing short of perfect will do, and unfortunately her role model is Dad. These days, how can she expect the lads she picks up to reach her high standards? Yet she presses on so determinedly they must feel as if they're being eaten alive.

Jessie's relationship with William is a light-hearted, bantering one, and she doesn't want to spoil it by pushing him too hard. They flirt and spar and avoid awkward topics.

'Where is Daisy?' William asks. He probably feels he has to.

'In your flat, in tears as far as I know, where you should be tonight instead of gallivanting around playing detective. It's a waste of time, William. I don't understand what you're after. Belinda's up here – I've seen her.'

'You're wrong, Jessie. So wrong.'

'Don't be melodramatic, it's off-putting. Tell me slowly what happened next.'

'McNab shut the door in my face so I skipped a couple of houses and knocked up the neighbours. Funny, I felt the NcNabs were watching – the old net-curtain syndrome, except they don't have net curtains in Mulberry Road. Theirs were velvet and beige.'

Jessie feels most uncomfortable sharing William's confidences like this while Daisy, not two miles away, must be praying for a call from her lover.

She can understand why William wants a couple of days away from the pressure, lately their relationship has been far from a bed of roses, but why the secrecy? Why the deception? Why had he insisted on keeping the fire-raising suspicion to himself when lives might depend on the truth?

Now he's home tomorrow and thank God for that.

Jessie's nerves are in shreds. She has even considered persuading Daisy to join her and Jasmine at Mum's house, so she can keep an eye on them all just in case.

All of them, except Mum, have been targets of Belinda's manic revenge. And if William's guess is right, if Belinda caused that fire – Jessie still finds that hard to believe – then the murderous escalation of her sickness rules out nothing, no matter how barbaric.

Jessie tries hard not to focus on this. The motley rabbit is hardly proof. It wouldn't stand up in a court of law.

'They were all sniffy types, typical of the area, not willing to talk,' says William, and she knows he's rolling a cigarette by the way his voice comes and goes and the rattling of his battered tin in the background. 'I popped into the newsagents/deli for a paper, and this gothic kid with purple hair and a nose ring started eyeing me up.'

'You wish,' sneers Jessie.

'I gave her a fag outside the shop and said who I was looking for. She knew Belinda. She called her Belle. Some luck; she was at the same school. God, she reeked of dope. The last she'd heard was that when Belinda came back from college they sent her to Bullwood Hospital.'

'So is that where she's supposed to be? Has she escaped? Is the place still standing or have they chucked the sickos out to freeze to death under bridges?'

'I went straight there,' says William. 'It's twenty miles out of town. Safer, I suppose, when you think. I even bought some shortbread and a *Cosmopolitan* magazine, making out I was a visitor.'

Hospitals, urgh, they terrify Jessie, who has never been inside one except to visit. If Jessie was Dad she would be terrified of being incarcerated one day in one of those sterile mausoleums to disease and death. Good for Mum; she defended him and kept him home, and with luck it looks like it's paid off.

'I tried to slip in without being noticed.'

'Some chance.'

'It worked. Or it would have worked if I hadn't got lost. I felt like a patient, wandering around with a quizzical look on my face through lots of brightly coloured areas that would drive you mental if you weren't already, and rigid seating in squares so you have to be sociable at the coffee machines. I took hours following signs for the WRVS canteen; I fancied a sandwich but it was closed. There was nowhere to smoke except outside, where they'd put two massive great ashtrays; the paving round the rickety seats was one thick carpet of dog-ends. I sat there coughing with everyone else. Shit, I thought, a TB clinic would be more like it.'

'Why didn't you ask, for goodness' sake? Why didn't you use reception?'

Why must William be so dramatic? Jessie has this graph to do and no matter which way she turns the paper it doesn't make sense. She's going to have to go down the corridor and knock up Sally or Kate for help, but if William drags on like this they're likely to be in bed.

Jessie swaps hands, her right one is cramped and sweaty, the phone is sticky, while William drones on. 'Some wards were locked and some looked like playrooms, full of primary colours and round, comforting furniture. Actually, I felt quite at home; I wouldn't have minded a stay – a short one.'

He's loving every minute of this, Jessie thinks. He's the nosiest person she's ever known save for Mum. 'You're lucky they didn't keep you in.'

Will she tell Daisy he's phoned or not? Jessie hates to deceive her sister.

'I was searching for the kind of ward that might specialize in Belinda's age group.'

'Some chance, you nerd. It's the NHS,' says Jessie, marvelling at William's ignorance.

'Well, how was I to know?' he snaps back. 'But you're right; they've got even numbers of men and women together, just like Bedlam, so I gave that up and went to reception, exactly as you would have done in your superior wisdom, and said I was visiting Belinda NcNab. They shoved me in a waiting room with a wilting palm and some goldfish till a nurse came in to ask if I was a member of the family.'

'So you said yes.' Maybe he does have something to tell her. Is this why William is drawing this out to give himself a dramatic finale? 'But William, where's this leading? Did you find Belinda? I am quite busy—'

'Hang on! Hang on! There's not much more. Just be patient. I said I was her brother. I said I'd been in Bosnia and hadn't seen her for months. So this

322

nurse flicked open a file, gave me a look and asked if I'd been home yet. I told her I didn't live at home, but the cow had already made up her mind and told me I should write in and make an appointment to see the nursing supervisor. There was no point in arguing; she was a jumped-up piece of work and she must have guessed I was faking it. I started to wonder if Belinda had jumped over the wall and they were protecting themselves, worried about the publicity damaging their reputation.'

'They thought you might be a reporter?'

'I did wonder about that, yes.'

'You're lucky you weren't escorted out. They must have bouncers in those sorts of places.'

'I wasn't going to get anywhere by going through official channels so I drifted round to the front again and joined a group of serious smokers rolling up round the main entrance. I thought, this lot must be trusted or they wouldn't let them have matches.'

'And then you felt you were among friends.'

'Yes, I did, funnily enough. They were charming people, no madder than me, so we got talking and got quite chummy, and when I started talking about Belinda McNab I drew quite a fascinated crowd around me and, hold your breath – I'm warning you, Jessie, wait for it . . .'

Jessie imagines the scene.

She would smile at all this if it wasn't so sinister and personal. William wouldn't be down there now if it hadn't been for her and her stubborn stupidity. She had slept with Belinda, shared her bed and her body with her. And if she hadn't, if only she hadn't, maybe Granny would still be alive.

'Belinda's dead,' William drops the bombshell.

Jessie feels she's been kicked in the stomach. All the breath has left her body and she folds herself round the phone. '*What?*'

'Belinda died months ago, soon after she was admitted to Bullwood. She hanged herself from a curtain rail. They tried to revive her – no chance.'

'Jesus, no!' Jessie's brain reels. This can't be right. 'But I told you. I saw her. I'm sure I saw her.'

'You thought you saw her; you expected to see her because she'd been back in touch. You were a nervous wreck at the time, if I remember rightly; anyone in a fringed curtain with coloured hair and boots and Belinda would have sprung to your mind.'

Jessie is only able to stutter, 'Who told you she was dead?' She vaguely remembers her futile search for Belinda's address at St Marks and the secretary's confusion when she found the file was missing. Had the college been officially informed? Had the secretary not been told? Was it college policy to endeavour to keep tragedies like this covered up?

'I don't believe you,' Jessie says shakily, trying for a firm response.

'It's true. Fellow patients tend to remember calamities like this – well, they would, wouldn't they. Are you surprised? The hospital was in turmoil, obviously. There were internal inquiries, statements were taken, new rules applied and, according to one extremely nice woman who slept in a bed near Belinda – Hilda, I gave her my grapes and the magazine – your old buddy was a troublemaker and caused no end of mischief. You could say that in her short time at Bullwood Belinda had been quite memorable.'

'So you're taking the word of an inmate?'

'Mainly Hilda, and several other inmates. But don't call them that; they're patients actually. Typically, all the smokers were sane.'

'Does that explain why Belinda's parents were so iffy about being approached?' Jessie tries to recall her phone call to them. And if what William is saying is true, her name alone, coming so unexpectedly, must have chilled them. They probably blame Jessie for their daughter's pitiful death. Jessie Redfern was certainly part of the whole bleak picture of Belinda's last unfortunate year: her expulsion from college, Dad's involvement. And then . . . The tragic subject of their daughter must have been too sore for them to touch, and to be asked where she was living, Christ Almighty, how bloody insensitive they must have thought her.

'That would make sense,' says William, 'people turning up on their doorstep asking painful questions when all they're doing is trying to forget, or come to terms with their distress.'

'But she can't be dead. There's the notes, my tyres, the coat, that disgusting hot dog – she'd been in my room – and hell, what about the fire? You must have been wrong about the fire?'

'Whoever's doing this isn't Belinda, but it's someone who knows all about her, and you and what went on, and they must know that she's dead.'

This is too much. 'Why? *Who on earth?*' Jessie stops in her tracks. 'I still can't believe it, William.'

'I thought you'd say that, so I went to the cemetery, back at Mulberry Road in Cardiff, to St Mary's Church, the nearest C of E, and the new cemetery plot across the road – the main one's crammed, there's no room any more.'

Jessie asks quietly, knowing the answer but not wanting to hear it. 'You found her grave?'

'Belinda McNab, aged nineteen years, beloved daughter of . . .'

'Stop it! Stop it!' This is all Jessie's fault.

. 'May she rest in peace.'

Amen.

'William, where are you now?'

'I'm about to leave the hospital. Just got to bid farewell to my new friend Hilda.'

'Who?'

'My informant. Hilda. You must meet her one day. You'd get on. She's lovely.'

TWENTY-SEVEN

Just as outside his windows the last of the damp autumn leaves scatter and disappear, so Michael's hopes are blown aside, swept away to rot into nothing.

How Michael would have loved to see his grandchildren before he died. Their first birthdays; those wonderful family Christmases. How proud he would have been to see Jessie qualified, to see Daisy married as she so longs to be. How he was looking forward to his retirement, and more time spent at home with Rose and his garden. The holidays they might have had, the places he will never now see, the books he always meant to read and the experiences he had promised himself. Like learning to fly, swimming with dolphins and canoeing through the rain forest.

And tiny things, which are just as important, such as exploring the local lanes and byways on horseback, building a sauna and re-weatherproofing his fence.

His cry for help went unanswered. It had taken all he had.

It had taken a grinding effort to scratch out those

eight letters, and if he ever manages to find that kind of energy again, the likelihood is that Rose will be first on the scene to carry out more punishments.

Strangely he still can't hate Rose.

He can fear her, feel anger and fierce repulsion, but knowing and understanding her as well as he does, he realizes she isn't responsible for her psychopathic condition. She loves him – or she used to love him – and he's spent the majority of his life secure and happy in that knowledge.

Someone, and he suspects he knows who, has terrified and undermined Rose to such an extent that, vulnerable as she always was, she has been tipped off the edge of sanity.

Belinda? Who else.

And for all Michael knows Belinda is still goading his wife, threatening her and manipulating her in the same scheming ways she once used on him. Happily, the second time around, he had Sheila Gordon to go to, but because he and Rose went off to Venice so soon after that meeting, he never got to hear the result of Sheila's inquiries.

He'd assumed that Sheila, reliable and efficient, would deal with this distressing matter quickly. But what if she hadn't succeeded in putting a stop to Belinda's recurring mania, presumably by contacting Belinda's parents, who can't have known what she was up to. And, at the last resort, he had guessed that Sheila might contact the police.

As Michael sits, so powerless and bloody speechless, beside the fire, dreading the next calculated attack, which he fears could well be his last, he curses the high-minded reasons that made him hide so much from his wife. Why did he feel such a need to protect her that he kept the Belinda business from her? Why was he so afraid of her reaction to Jessie's embarrassing difficulties? His behaviour, born from habit, is the direct cause of his present plight.

Quite apart from the magnitude of Rose's certifiable delusions in turning him into a helpless cripple, quite apart from the malicious nature of her vindictive punishments which, so far, he has survived, how the hell does she imagine this nightmare is going to end? And what does she think will happen to her if this diabolical behaviour comes out? Michael is no solicitor, but it's not hard to imagine the sort of penalties a court would dole out to someone found guilty of such callous, cold-blooded cruelty.

And if she kills him? What then? A life sentence for murder and, perhaps, the opening of two yellowing files kept in some coroner's office because . . . maybe her father? Maybe her own brother?

His daughters turned into freaky exhibits, exposed to the worst kind of publicity, shamed, shunned and shattered, the rest of their young lives warped by events in which they were merely two innocents? These black thoughts of Michael's pain him far more than the idea of his own demise.

Christ God Almighty – so near and yet so far – if only he could tell Rose the truth about Belinda, and promise that if she stops this madness, and he recovers completely, he will take no action against her.

But would that be enough? She would lose him, and that's the bottom line, that's the monstrous fear that drives her.

No matter how much he understands her, Michael cannot imagine living one night in the same house as the sick woman who has done him such harm. He would continue to support her – naturally he would – and he would do his best to ensure her happiness – that she received the right psychiatric care in a suitable secure environment – he would probably continue to love her in his own protective way, but he could never for one second trust her again.

Interestingly, today, the presence he imagines is Rose has had little to do with him, and last night, throughout his tortured, wakeful anticipation, she gave him his medicine later than usual and slept in the chair by the door.

Someone was there. The night light was on, and he imagined he could hear pages turning. It could, of course, merely have been a night nurse coming on duty, a new care routine to give Rose some relief.

In spite of himself his sleep was deathlike. No dreams, no images.

This morning Rose dosed him again and so far, to his great despair, he feels fuzzier than usual. A natural reaction to his failed cry for help.

He hopes suffocation is how she will end it. In his weak state, maybe that process wouldn't take too long. As weak and confused as Michael is there is no way he could put up a fight, so it would leave no bruising, but if they did a post mortem they might discover blood in his lungs.

But would they bother with a post mortem on somebody already half dead? And isn't Rose, so steeped in her psychopathic rage, well past caring about consequences?

It isn't the end which bothers him now, it's what Rose might decide to do as her last and most barbaric punishment. If Belinda has convinced her that Michael has been led astray, if there's a sexual connection, then Rose might go straight for the jugular – and Michael isn't thinking about his throat. The memory of that moment two nights ago, when he felt that nudge of cold steel between his legs, haunts him relentlessly.

Whenever he spirals up from the depths Michael's thoughts spin more and more towards the horror of that most agonizing possibility. He has heard that the pain comes later in cases of a quick amputation by machinery or shark attack, but he doubts it applies to the slow and deliberate cutting of exposed flesh, sinew and muscle. He remembers a visit to a farm as a child, when the farmer, a friend of his father's, was busy in a barn and they went to find him on his wife's instructions.

The calf was roped, its back legs yanked apart, to a partition in the shippen, and the knife the farmer used to slice the poor creature's testicles was small but lethal. Michael looked away too late, at first not able to comprehend such a grotesque procedure without anaesthetic. He saw the quick cut, the blood, the dark purple squirt of disinfectant and the rolling white eyes of the victim. He heard the sharp bleat of pain and the farmer saying matter-of-factly, 'It doan hurt 'em. Right as rain in a minute, old son. You see.'

Rose would be in no mood to effect such an action speedily and with mercy. That farmer had a lifetime's experience of nipping off animals' balls, whereas Rose's agenda would be quite different. His balls would make a secondary target. She would be after inflicting the maximum damage before she attempted either to staunch the bleeding and hide the deed under layers of bandage or despatch her husband for good.

And won't that make good reading? It wasn't hard to imagine the headlines and the distressing effect this would have on his daughters. Bad enough when a man is found dead, hanging with a tangerine in his mouth. How much juicier this story would read.

The climax to this macabre business is looming closer every day. If there was any way, anything on earth he could do to halt this doomed race towards mayhem, he would have thought of it by now; he would have already done it. The only option he has left now, and he has no alternative no matter what the repercussions, is to hold his medicine in his throat and attempt to regurgitate it when Rose leaves.

Look how pathetic he has become, reduced to the memories of an old man with a limited time to live.

His pride when he set off for his first short journey pushing Daisy in her pram. His need to shout his joy to the world and his indignant amazement at the discovery that not everyone was as thrilled as he.

The shock when Jessie came along three years later and proved to be such a different temperament to her contented older sister. The nights without sleep, the tantrums, the tears. 'Night terrors,' said the health visitor. 'Nothing we can give you, I'm afraid. It's just a matter of time. Normally it's the first child that's the problem, but then, all children are different.'

All those bloody platitudes while Rose was going round worn to a frazzle from sheer exhaustion and self-doubt. Where was she going wrong? Was there something the matter with this toddler? Should she be insisting that they see a behaviour specialist? She used to ring him at work, crying, incoherent, which made him feel selfish because secretly he was relieved to leave the madhouse every morning.

Every single outing ended in tantrums. Every meal time turned into a nightmare. Every bedtime a horror story while poor little Daisy sat watching nervously, frightened by her baby sister, on whom she had piled her three-year-old hopes of companionship and fun.

But the experts had been right. Apart from a few small difficulties expected during adolescence, and discounting the unfortunate Belinda fiasco, Jessie has turned out happy and bright and she and Daisy have been especially close since way back in early childhood.

Great kids. Gentle kids. He is a lucky man.

He remembers them crying on their first and only visit to the zoo, where Michael had taken them, quite unthinking about how caged animals might appear in the honest eyes of a child. They wept through *Dumbo*, too, and clutched each other for comfort. How carefully Rose had to check the TV so neither of them were exposed to the worst scenes of hunger and death. How caring they were, how like Rose in their concern for the underdog, the small and the helpless.

What hilarious times they had had, such laughter, such sweet innocence. And yet, at the same time, how easily they could twist him round their little fingers. Picnics, buckets and spades, fairgrounds, parties. 'Don't let them go so near the edge, Michael.' 'Get Jessie down from that tree right now!' 'Take those scissors away from that child.' 'She's far too small to cross that road on her own.'

All those echoes from the past, with Rose, like a mother hen, so afraid for their safety. Knowing how much she had suffered, and why, Michael humoured Rose. He always went along with her wishes, often to his children's fury.

No, Michael couldn't have hoped for a happier, more adorable family, and he wonders now, if they had been boys, would he have felt less protective?

Is it healthy that even now, plunged into the helpless degradation of a drooling imbecile, his mind should be more concerned with their fate than his own? Is it normal that he should have concerned himself over their various relationships – more, in truth, to satisfy Rose – after they grew up and left home? Shouldn't they have learned, by now, to stand on their own two feet, and prefer their independence to running straight home whenever there was a problem?

Some kids do. But these are his kids; these are different. He would have given his life for them, and so, back then, would Rose.

At least his affairs are in order. Michael has been lucky to earn enough in his life to put aside a fair proportion for insurance purposes. And, as an accountant, his know-how has helped him make wise investments. Naturally, on his death, all his worldly goods go to Rose and, he supposes, should she be convicted and imprisoned, they will be held in trust for his children.

Jesus. Can he be sure about this?

When Michael made his last will Rose was sane, but she is no longer the woman he knew. What if there's no post mortem and Rose gets away with her crime, just as she may have done twice before, and in her unstable state of mind gives no thought to Daisy and Jessie? He imagines them sleeping under boxes . . .

Why is Michael assuming that Belinda's latest twisted endeavours are directed solely at him? She might well be targeting Daisy and Jessie, turning Rose against them, trying to split the entire family in her deranged bid for vengeance. What the hell has been going on in that vast world that is closed to him now? Are his daughters safe? Is Rose safe?

Michael must keep a hold on his thoughts. He is building Belinda up out of all proportion, from a devious child with behavioural problems, into a schemer as reckless and disturbed as poor Rose. When Belinda wrote that childish notelet she could have had no inkling that Rose's reaction would be so extreme should she happen to find it. Belinda was only trying to cause trouble in her own fevered, attention-seeking fashion. So it's not Belinda's fault that her actions triggered such an explosion of misunderstanding and mental malfunction.

No Rose this evening? Rose is certainly not one of those who help him to stumble upstairs.

And it's no good Michael trying to guess whether one, or both of these are his daughters. His hands are unreliable sensors, his brain cannot measure size or shape, his ears send echoes that cannot be defined and his eyes monitor a series of diluted shapes which it cannot yet decipher.

335

These two struggling people – female – could be nurses or neighbours or even his sisters come back from California for all Michael can tell. But he doubts this last guess as they were never very close, the youngest, Gale, being eight years older than him. They have their own lives and families, who he has never met. He assumes they have been told about their brother's wretched condition, but a sympathetic letter would be more likely than a visit.

The fact that they undress and wash him means, Michael hopes, that these are helpers of some kind. He can't imagine the neighbours round here popping over on any regular basis. Such intimacy is discouraged, limited to occasional shopping, redirecting letters, taking in a parcel, or, at a push, allowing overflow parking when there's a party, so long as they're invited of course.

They lie him on the bed, whoever they are, and gently remove his clothes.

They won't dress the sore on his back, that is Rose's job and no wonder. It wouldn't do for anyone else to see the livid inflammation of that pusy, infected place.

They won't sponge him down, that is part of the morning routine, just a wet flannel round his face and a quick going over with the toothbrush is all he can expect at night, thank Christ. The less Rose has to do the better as far as Michael is concerned.

Then, last thing at night, she gives him a jab. Tonight could be Michael's last chance to fight it.

What lies in store for him in the next intolerable eight hours of darkness? Will he see morning? Will the pain be endurable or will he, please God, pass out?

336

TWENTY-EIGHT

'Hubble bubble toil and trouble, and they say disasters come in threes,' observes Mrs H, intrigued to know the reason why the young Redferns are coming over for 'brunch', and on a working day, too.

If only it was just threes, thinks Rose, still trying to recover from her excruciating embarrassment of last night.

When Jack Bennet's invitation had arrived all Rose could see was a flash of blue sky, a doorway of hope in the gathering darkness.

She wanted out. She wanted protection, a man to lean on and love her and take her away from the horrors of her life.

Now that Michael had worked things out, how was it going to end? This question haunted her days and nights. Would it truthfully be so terrible to allow Michael to recover and go off with his tart Belinda rather than endure weeks, maybe months of watching him suffer. She finds it hard to look at him now, just an empty dummy, living proof of her relentless cruelty, let alone touch him.

But the likelihood of a reasonable ending was

always a sick fantasy. Why oh why had it taken her so long to figure this out? Michael isn't going to wake up, stand up unaided, get himself dressed and disappear into some happy-ever-after sunset. He knows what she is doing and has made one hostile protest already, and to make sure of his future silence his dosages must be increased and Rose must stay with him all night, every night.

When Michael wakes up her world will end. And how is Rose going to stand up to the consequences of her abominable actions? The disgust of her children? The chattering of the neighbours? A court case, perhaps resulting in years in gaol?

Why oh why, and what sort of state was she in when she made her wretched plans – it all seemed so simple then, almost natural. The fear of losing him had affected her reason. How had she ever sincerely believed that, given time and space, Michael's affair would splutter out, leaving him and Rose to carry on as normal?

Whatever happens now Rose has lost Michael. The rest of her life will be spent in chains, a hellish legend like Myra Hindley, or Rose West . . . her namesake? Peeped at and prodded by medical experts, the ogress of the tabloid press and a target for disturbed inmates.

Why the hell hadn't she bowed to the inevitable, like thousands of other women do, and let Michael just leave her?

Last night Rose took the bull by the horns and threw herself shamelessly at Jack Bennet. It was interesting to watch his change of expression. Firstly, when she started to flirt, he grew flushed and pleased and responded with gusto. That was the pleasant part of the evening.

She started to make enquiries about his apartment in the Algarve and boastfully he went into glowing detail. The facilities were unbeatable – pool, golf, restaurants, beach, sauna, tennis and all the rest. When Jack retires in five years' time, he and Barbara plan to spend most winters there.

'But it's empty at the moment? You don't let it out?'

'Barbara doesn't like the thought of strangers using the bathroom.'

Rose described the misery of living life with Michael. She missed the companionship, the laughs, the outings and the sex.

Jack understood. He called her a brick.

His hand covered hers and she let it rest there and met his eyes.

He went on to explain, in a gravelly voice, how unhappy his own marriage was and how easy it is to get trapped, to take a partner for granted, to be stuck in an emotional rut and feel an overwhelming need for new sensations and excitements.

'I know what you mean, Jack,' said Rose, determined.

'You're a beautiful woman, Rose,' said Jack.

Rose smiled. 'You haven't worn so badly yourself.'

Then he rose from his chair and kissed her over the primrose table arrangement.

He must have kicked off a shoe because his socked foot started slithering about between Rose's legs.

'What will you do', Jack asked her with a glitter in his eye, 'if Michael never recovers?'

She sent him a meaningful look. 'That depends, Jack, doesn't it?'

'Why don't we skip the theatre, have a few more drinks, stay here and just talk?'

By the time they were playing with their puddings Rose had moved the agenda on to the unsatisfactory and sad effect of fleeting, meaningless affairs. Opposite, Jack sat rather oddly; his foot had almost reached her crotch.

Jack looked surprised. 'You mean, if you did take a lover you would expect a long-term relationship with him?'

'Oh yes. I'm not that shallow,' said Rose. 'And I doubt you are either, Jack.'

'A commitment?'

'Definitely. Ideally, more than that.'

It seemed that Jack could not conceive what she meant by that remark.

She sipped delicately at her Van Der Hum while Jack swirled round his brandy, trying to work out what she was getting at.

'How idyllic it would be to start out completely over again,' said Rose mysteriously.

'With a new person?'

'A new person, a new home, a new country, a whole new life.'

Jack's foot retreated and his eyes left hers to watch the liquid lick at the bulbous sides of his glass. 'And you would be prepared to do that?'

'I think I might,' said Rose in sheer desperation. 'If I found a man who was big enough to dare to join me.'

As the truth dawned Jack sat back in his chair. 'And I believed you and Michael had such a marvellous relationship. Barbara and I both imagined you would stick with him through thick and thin, no matter how long it took.'

'So you thought I was seriously unavailable?'

'Well, yes . . .'

'You were surprised when I accepted this invitation from you tonight?'

'I was surprised,' Jack admitted, 'but fascinated, and you know I've always admired you, Rose, and been attracted to you sexually.'

Rose tipped her face to its most attractive angle. She caught her bottom lip with her teeth. 'And now I'm responding.'

'Barbara and I . . .' Jack started slowly.

'Don't tell me you need to work,' Rose burst out. 'If you're anything like Michael you could live off your investments for the rest of your life. You've got a second home in Portugal. You could provide very well for Barbara, and she's got her own career anyway. You've no kids to worry about, you say you've always been interested in me, so what's holding you back?'

'This is very sudden, Rose,' said Jack Bennet, paling. 'This is not the kind of decision one should make on the spur of the—'

'And I thought you were such a bold man!'

'What you're talking about, it's unreal, it's a dream.'

'But it needn't be, if we just grab the moment.'

'You're not yourself,' Jack tried to console her. Her voice was rising. Other diners were turning their heads. 'And no wonder, with all that you've

341

been through these past weeks. I can understand where you're coming from.'

Rose gasped. 'Jack, my life is a mess, a bloody mess.' She turned her voice into a whisper. This had to work, it just had to. 'Help me out of it. Help me!'

Jack, unprepared for an evening of counselling and trying to conceal an enormous erection, which admittedly was shrivelling fast, said gently, 'It's not me you want, is it, Rose? It's a way out. And I'm sorry, but I can't take advantage of you in this frame of mind.'

'You coward!' Rose stared hard at the cloth.

'You want me to leave my wife, give up my work and come with you to live in the Algarve on a permanent basis? That's what *you* are suggesting, correct me if I'm wrong. And I have to tell you, Rose, whatever you think of me, I could never leave Barbara. We love each other. Now that might sound odd; I know you think I'm a randy cad, screwing around but . . .'

She had to have one last try. Very controlled now, and aware of her surroundings again, she spoke in lowered tones. 'Don't let me down, Jack. Please don't. Do you think this was easy for me, to come here tonight and offer myself? At least allow me to use your apartment. If you feel anything at all for me I beg you . . .'

'I'll have to ask Barbara.'

'Balls,' said Rose quietly.

'She will suspect there's something—'

'Balls, balls, balls.'

How she hates to plead with a man like this. She has no pride left, just desolation.

Jack lifted his hands like a pair of buffers. 'OK,

OK, cool down. If you want our apartment you can have it. I'll tell Barbara you want to spend some time there looking for a holiday home for yourself and Michael. But I don't want this backfiring on me, Rose. And I do have to ask you, if you feel such an urgent need to leave home, who's going to take care of Michael?'

Michael? Must she keep up this farce? 'If necessary he will have to go into a nursing home. That's what everyone's pushing for anyway. But', and the tears started in her eyes, 'I have to think about me, now, Jack. It's my sanity that I'm afraid of losing. And I'd be quite grateful if you kept my behaviour tonight between you and me. I'm not proud of it.'

He saw her home.

He didn't come in.

She sat beside Michael all night, watching.

So Rose, a member of the criminal classes, has her retreat.

She can be in Portugal within hours if she needs to be, rubbing shoulders with the English elderly, stateless people, runaways and fugitives, with their golf clubs, whist drives and leathery tans, and that is some consolation. But alone, frightened, unprotected – all the same reasons that made her commit her dreadful crime in the first place. To Rose, who lost her daddy, a life without a protector is a life full of fear, madness and menace.

Daisy wouldn't say why they needed to speak to her. She merely told Rose to prepare herself; they had something important to say.

Rose sits, stunned, beside Michael as William

343

takes the role of spokesperson and describes the long history of Belinda McNab, the creature of Rose's nightmares.

The faint hum in Rose's head becomes a rhythmic drumming. This can't be true. There is some mistake. She hangs on to the fireplace to stop herself from falling. 'Steady on, Mum. Cool it,' says Jessie, who seems to feel she's disgraced the family with her little same-sex flirtation.

Rose listens, transfixed, as William relates as briefly as possible the consequences of Jessie's affair: the stalking and the threats that led to Michael becoming involved and everybody believing that the worst was all over. And throughout all this family disruption Rose had been left in the dark.

'But then she came back,' Jessie interrupted.

'We thought she'd come back,' William corrected. 'Jessie even imagined she'd seen her; she was so wound up she saw danger behind every shadow. But by then Belinda was dead; she'd hanged herself at Bullwood Hospital.'

Rose chews on her fingers. Are they honestly telling her that Belinda was no more of a threat to her marriage than a splinter in a thumb? Who was it, if not Belinda?

'Somebody else was warning Jasmine, leaving vile signs in Jessie's room, following her round, slashing her tyres, cutting Daisy's coat and even' – William breaks off and looks at Jessie; now he lowers his voice – 'even starting Dinah's fire.'

'Somebody else?' Rose's voice is hoarse, breaking.

'And we don't know who,' says William.

* * *

In the cold light of this sad afternoon Rose starts on a letter. She tried to make her goodbyes to the girls sound as normal as possible. Half an hour ago they hurried off with William to find Jasmine and warn her. Rose has two hours to go before she leaves for the airport to make her escape, before someone unearths the knowledge that will destroy her.

She puts her Christmas list to one side – oh yes, she'd started on it vaguely before they went to Venice, just a few ideas, nothing inspirational. She was going to buy Michael a digital camera. He would have loved fiddling around and experimenting with it. Now she won't need to do that any more.

Poor bewildered Mrs H is breaking her back to find out what's going on, so far to no avail, but Rose can't risk hanging around.

Two hours to go. If she misses that plane she's finished. Years of imprisonment would kill her.

Rose locks herself in the bedroom and lugs down two cases from the top shelf of the cupboard. In the mirror she sees herself, silent, frightened and staring. One handle still bears the Venice label; tells of a happier time, before the world turned upside down and tipped her off the edge into this dark abyss.

She lights a cigarette nervously. If Belinda is dead, then, dear God, who?

Does this mean that after everything she's done to him Michael is truly innocent? That none of this was necessary? How can she think on that and stay sane?

She doesn't care what she packs. What she looks like no longer matters. Nevertheless, out of habit, she sweeps her favourite Clinique from the dressing

345

table into a padded bag. She's in two minds over swimmers; T-shirts, sweaters, jeans and a couple of dresses are all she will need. To Rose the kind of life that awaits her is almost worse than death; she's tempted to end it all with a razor blade, at least she would die in her own bath, in her own home and country and be buried in an English churchyard, suicides and murderers now being welcome. But not beside Michael, not any more.

But what if she fails and they find her and drag her off to some asylum?

She shoves her cases under the bed in case Mrs H comes upstairs and spots them. She dislodges her wedding dress in its plastic cover. Tears start in Rose's eyes, but there's no time for that nonsense now. There are hundreds of ampoules and little black bottles still in there amongst the frills, and these, dress and all, will go in the bin bag the dustman collects the next day.

Time is passing. Soon Mrs H will look at her watch and say, 'Well, if you're sure, I'll be off.' Then Rose can make a dash for freedom.

To write her last letter to Michael, Rose goes downstairs and sits beside her husband. A recumbent, opaque-eyed figure, does he know she's here?

She writes down her feelings with an unsteady hand. Where to start? What to say when you're writing about thirty years of love? She feels no anger, just sick despair. None of this need have happened. A tender melancholy replaces the torment. Her eyes rest on familiar objects without seeing them before drifting back to Michael, always Michael; it has always been Michael.

He loved me. If Rose has known any certainty in her life it is that fact.

The joy she used to feel coming home, knowing that Michael would be there waiting. The fun of putting on a dress she knew he would admire; the happiness of cooking a meal and watching him tuck into it; the absurd sound of him opening the wine and cursing while he searched for clean glasses; the safety she had found in his arms.

But what does Rose think she's doing? Only indulging in a dream, trying to replace the heart-break. All gone. All gone.

Probably everyone in the world has toyed with wicked ideas which never must be told. Why did she have to follow that one particular thought? Why would the ache of it not be stilled until she had carried it out? What despair made her act upon it?

Rose writes on.

The clock on the mantelpiece strikes two.

Both strokes go unnoticed.

'Right oh,' says Mrs H. 'If you're sure I'll be off.'

Rose looks up from her letter. 'Yes, you go, Mrs H. I know you've got shopping to do.'

Rose seals the envelope and writes Michael's name on the front. She places it on the table, rushes upstairs to retrieve her luggage and struggles back down with it, puffing hard. She leaves it beside the front door with her car keys while she goes to say goodbye.

She takes his weary face in her hands and raises it towards her. She blinks away the tears; they mustn't spoil this last sight of the man who for so long was her life. Perhaps happiness is not meant to last.

Maybe they're right, it's only meant to exist for the moment. But you have made me happier than I ever imagined possible. 'I'm sorry, Michael. I am so, so sorry.'

She looks into his eyes for an answer, but there is nothing there.

In the midst of this the doorbell sounds, loud and shrill it grates on the moment, sounding as obscene as a small child cursing. Rose jumps. Don't say they are back already. She has missed her moment; they'll see her suitcases. What excuse can she give? Do they know already? Is this Daisy and Jessie, or the police?

'Hi,' says Jasmine, her large face beaming roundly.

God help me. Rose's heart leaps, then sinks like a stone. Jasmine is in the house before Rose can splutter a reason not to admit her.

'I thought I'd pop round as usual,' says Jasmine, removing her navy fleece to reveal freckled arms muscling out from the sleeves of a white Aertex blouse. Her watch strap is a sportily striped blue-and-white stretch nylon. Under her arms are two crescent-shaped sweat stains. She rasps her large hands together, hands worn smooth by wooden bats, and goes to stand by the fireplace, so the stiff blond hairs on her chin catch the light. One flame reflects off her crucifix like a signal. 'How's he doing? Any more writing?'

Rose sits down gingerly; her legs are too weak to allow her to stand. She can't miss her plane. She can't.

'I've been out all day,' says Jasmine. 'Great fun.

We took Class Five to the matinée of *Peter Pan on Ice* at the Palace, and you should have seen their little faces.'

Rose shivers. The magical words 'Peter Pan' sound wrong in these fraught circumstances. Jasmine has brought in the winter with her.

Should Rose warn Jasmine about Belinda's impersonator? William must have missed her because she obviously doesn't know. But explaining all that, and the emotion that goes with it, would slow down Rose's dash for freedom.

If she doesn't leave soon she will miss her plane, and she has to call at the bank before she heads to the airport. She has told them to empty the deposit account into the current account. It's only a couple of thousand pounds, but she's going to need that and more. It's a pity Mother's insurance won't get paid out for another six months.

'Did I see cases when I came in?' Jasmine asks matter-of-factly, her small red eyes missing nothing. She can't know anything; she'd be full of it.

'Just some clothes I've grown out of,' Rose quickly replies. 'I've been sorting them out for the nearly-new shop.'

'Jolly good,' says Jasmine gamely. 'D'you want a hand out to the car with that? It looks heavy.'

Rose nods feebly. Why bother to protest? With the cases stashed in the boot of the Saab it would take only a second to be behind the steering wheel and on her way to the airport. She has booked her flight by credit card and her passport is safe in her bag. The keys to the Bennets' apartment in Portugal are with the agent on site, and Jack has assured her the man's been informed of her imminent arrival.

Everything is in place.

My God! The way Jasmine lifts those cases. She has the strength of a man; she could be a Russian runner. Is she on steroids? Or is that build normal?

'What have you got in there?' says Jasmine, coming back indoors as if the house belongs to her. 'The kitchen sink?' Rose watches carefully to make sure she has replaced the car keys.

This tension, this zigzag of lightning in the air, is going to give Rose away in a minute, and there seems to be no way round it. Try as she might Rose cannot disguise her guilty urge to be gone.

'Is everything all right, Rose? You seem more strained than usual?'

'No, no, I'm fine. Really.' But while Jasmine is standing here Rose is embedded here, like an anchor.

'Is there anything you'd like me to do? How about peeling the spuds?'

This fiasco cannot go on. The strain is becoming enormous. Rose has to speak. She finds, with surprise, that she can stand up if she leans against the fireplace. She fights to keep her voice steady. Her fists are two tight balls of fear. 'Excuse me, Jasmine, but I have to leave now. You'll stay with Michael for me, won't you. Just for a little while.'

Jasmine holds her eyes. Hers are startlingly bright. There is something in that stare that penetrates deep into untouchable places. What is Jasmine trying to say? Why is she here? Rose, on the verge of collapse, suddenly knows what those eyes are asking. They accuse; they demand an answer. Rose, dizzying, gives it in a voice that's tired with the fighting. 'You know, don't you? You know what I've done?'

'Yes, Rose. Everything. All of it.'

Rose's voice trembles. There is no way she can alter it. So this is the sender of the sympathy card and the message, 'I know'. But why would Jasmine use the letter B? Why not sign her name? Rose is too shattered to concentrate on puzzles. 'H-how did you find out?' she asks, dazed. 'How long have you known?'

'From the beginning.'

When was the beginning? Try as she might, Rose can no longer remember.

TWENTY-NINE

It was a moment of sheer, still horror.

'God, I'm so thick. It's her; it's Jasmine.' William slapped his forehead as some buried truth began to dawn while they sped towards Kingsmead School. 'Yesterday morning, when my friend Hilda told me to give her regards to the nurse, the psychiatric nurse who befriended Belinda, I wondered who the hell she meant. What nurse? I didn't know any nurses. Why didn't it register? Why the hell has it taken this long?'

'Are we supposed to know automatically what you're talking about?' asked a baffled Jessie beside him.

'It's Jasmine,' William repeated like a robot. 'Bloody hell. All along. Jasmine was Belinda.'

'You're mad,' said Daisy from the back. She'd refused to sit in the seat beside William, still sulking, still hurt and determined to show it.

'The psychiatric nurse. Who else? It has to be Jasmine, friend of Jesus and befriender of Belinda.' William swerves in his excitement, brakes screech and Jessie gasps, 'Jesus! You jerk, watch out!'

'According to my friend Hilda, the talkative

patient at Bullwood Hospital, when Belinda went and topped herself one nurse was badly cut up. They'd formed quite a bond, Hilda told me after I gave her a packet of fags. The nurse was into cricket and she tried to get Belinda interested; she'd formed a team at the hospital. Now who else but Jasmine would do something as freaky as that? And what's more, according to Hilda, Belinda's parents went into denial after she hanged herself and refused any kind of counselling.'

'So Hilda was right about one thing,' said Jessie. 'She knows what she's talking about.'

'Oh, Hilda's not mad,' William assured them, 'just frightened of the world.'

'It can't be true. Why would Jasmine . . . ? Such extremes? Why would she, unless Belinda and her had something going?' Daisy sounded as shocked as the others. 'Revenge? She was only her nurse, after all. You can't be right, William. You're guessing.'

'Perhaps they were lovers; it's possible when you think about it, although Jasmine's never come on to me. And if that's true,' Jessie took up the thought with a hand to her mouth, as if to deny to herself what she said, 'what if Jasmine blamed me for her patient's suicide? Lover or not, Belinda would have confided in Jasmine. She would have known about our relationship and how Belinda reacted afterwards. She would know about the part Dad played. She could have come here intent on vengeance.'

'It's too far-fetched.'

'Real life often is,' said William, cutting his speed, white-knuckled.

'For God's sake, don't slow down. We've got to get there. We've got to find Jasmine. But hang on, let's think about this, let's try and stay calm,' shouted Jessie, unable to swallow. Her mouth was dry, like she'd had an extraction with cocaine. 'Is what William says so unlikely? Jasmine pounced on me that first day at Kingsmead, but I didn't mind, I needed a friend.' Jessie paused, remembering. 'She was open and genuine. And when she told me about Belinda's phone call, supposedly warning Jasmine off, she never criticized me or made a fuss. Well of course she wouldn't, would she, if what we're thinking is true? And look how helpful she was? Nothing was too much for her.'

'Kingsmead School and St Marks have close links,' William pointed out, swerving to avoid a cyclist. 'So if Jasmine was out to get Jessie, a job there was a guarantee that they'd meet at some point.'

Jessie was quick to confirm, 'Every one of our year spent a day there.'

'And wasn't it Jasmine who encouraged you to make that call to Belinda's parents?'

'She did, and she must have known what their reaction was likely to be.'

'But to set fire to Granny's house? Christ! When she knew Granny was in there?'

'And the rabbit with the chain round its neck? What did that mean? What sense does that make?'

Daisy suddenly blurted, 'I remember now, she called on Granny for a silly church jumble. Granny told her to search the attic; I was there when she came down carting a black bin bag full of stuff. Granny wanted to see what she'd got, so she started showing her, piece by piece, but she never reached the bottom of the bag because Granny got too impatient. She must have found the rabbit then; she must have found it in some manky corner and thought she'd use it to add to the horror.'

William stopped the car and asked them outright, 'So do we go to the law right now?'

'I'd rather have it out with her first,' said Jessie. 'Give her a chance to explain. It could be that we're way out of line, but I don't want to miss the chance of hearing her admit what she's done.'

'And what if we don't find her straight away?' They were driving up the school drive now. 'Can we afford to take the risk that she's not about to cause more violence?'

But there was a major problem with this. They had no facts to prove their case. Would the police believe that Jasmine deliberately applied for a job near her old patient's college? Would they accept William's assumption that Belinda and Jasmine were close for a time, maybe too close, at Bullwood Hospital? Would they swallow the improbable story that Jasmine, intent on revenge, posed as Belinda, hassled Jessie and Daisy and started the fire that killed their grandmother? Or would they find this too far-fetched, a drama invented by the press?

Unless Jasmine admitted to what she'd done under pressure, the whole thing would be treated as pure fiction. 'Let's see if she's here first,' said William. 'Let's see what she says and then we can make the decision.'

THIRTY

That's it, Rose can stand no more. At the sight of her daughters led by William she dashes past them towards the car. She must go before Jasmine tells them; there's no time for goodbyes. But will Jasmine try to stop her?

'Mum?'

Rose twists the car keys in sweating fingers. Thank Christ the engine leaps into life.

'But Mum . . . where . . .?'

'Look after Daddy. Take care of him for me.'

They were sure they would find Jasmine here.

After the chaos dies down, after the last spit of gravel has settled and the puffs of exhaust fumes are just white veils of mist, Jasmine, calm and plausible, takes Rose's vacant seat at the fireplace, oddly still, hands pressed together, with a pink sheen of righteousness on her face.

This is the room where, in years gone by, they roasted chestnuts on that fire, played Pictionary on that rug with best friends Angela and Bryony, crayoned on that small side table. The Christmas tree always stands in that corner. A tiny piece of paper chain is still stuck by Blu-tack to the picture rail.

Calmly Jasmine defends herself against this gruelling interrogation.

'I can't tell you *where* Rose has gone, but I do know *why* she has gone.'

Jasmine's indignation is as great as her astonishment. She demonstrates her outrage at the accusation that she deliberately caused Dinah's death with a pursed mouth, a set expression of saintliness and a head held high as a martyr tied to a burning pyre. Let the flames lick round her as they will, Jasmine Smith has personally been promised eternal salvation.

'Jesus sent me here, not Belinda, God rest her soul.'

Jessie wants to slap her face. Jasmine's high moral tone is out of place here. Jessie's sane and sensible mother has fled hysterically into an early dusk with no explanation whatever. Jessie has spent the last two frenzied hours with a man who can hardly abide to be in his lover's company and a tearful, lovelorn sister who appears to be numb with shock.

In that time, while they searched in vain, Jasmine's image has metamorphosed from sick psychopath to devilish monster who must be stopped at all costs. In their mad scramble to find Jasmine, both she and William shared the burden of knowing what this sadist was capable of while they wasted time seeking her out.

They should have gone straight to the law. Once

again this was poor Jessie's fault. Selfish, selfish, selfish. She wanted a face-to-face confrontation with her own personal devils. And now here Jasmine is, in her home-made pulpit, glowing with self-righteous indignation.

In this room where they learned to roller skate over the smooth wooden floor. The same room which cools them in summer and warms the family in winter. The room where children in party dresses played musical bumps and spilled their jelly.

'I came here to help,' pronounces Jasmine sanctimoniously. 'To give back something to the family who had made such an impression on poor Belinda. Especially your father, who was kind and patient and understanding. He gave her hours of his time. His support was unfailing, and in her own sad way Belinda loved him. I knew finding Jessie would be easy, but I was shocked when I realized you all believed that Belinda was still alive.'

'So why the hell didn't you tell us?' asks William in astonishment.

'Because poor Belinda's identity was being abused by somebody else,' says Jasmine, as if her reasoning ought to be obvious. 'Some other tortured soul. The important thing was to find out who, and being the outsider I felt I was best equipped to deal with the mystery. There were lessons to be learned.'

'Which you were going to teach us, for God's sake?' Jessie fights to keep control. 'William, stop this, we should ring the police right now.'

'Wait,' he says, 'this could be interesting.'

358

There are no doubts in Jasmine's mind. 'For poor Jessie, who imagined she saw Belinda, the shock of all this must have been traumatic. She had failed to deal with her guilt, thus blocking the chance of salvation, although they had once been so close, I noticed that she never mentioned Belinda.'

'Shit. I never spoke about her because I couldn't bloody well stand her and the menace she turned into.'

'And then,' continues Jasmine, ignoring the interruption, 'I got that extraordinary telephone call when you and Daisy were at Dinah's house, purporting to be from Belinda. Of course I knew it wasn't Belinda. But after that I was deeply involved. After that Jessie was forced to explain. Remember?'

'So you are saying,' says Daisy, still pale but restive with indignation, who has held back her emotions until now, 'that it wasn't you who slashed my coat, who left that obscenity in Jessie's room, ruined her tyres, stalked her and, eventually, driven to it by serious insanity, set fire to Granny's house?'

'I did not,' states Jasmine, formal as an accused in court. 'It wasn't vengeance that brought me here, I came to repay you for your kindness. I am a Christian – I love peace and I love God. To do what you are accusing me of would be to turn my back on the merciful Lord.'

'But you can't deny that, at Bullwood, you were Belinda's friend.'

'I did befriend Belinda,' says Jasmine, a pious smile lighting her face. 'Belinda needed befriending. All the nurses had one special patient as part of the healing process.'

'Too sodding right,' mutters Jessie. 'But your precious friendship didn't do her much good.'

'Sadly no,' says Jasmine. 'But her soul is now dancing amongst the clouds in heaven.'

That was Baggins' favourite rug. He used to pee on the door post when he got overexcited, when they'd left him for too long and they came back inside calling his name. When they made their special camps, Jessie and Daisy would bundle up the sofa cushions and chuck the throw over the top.

Jasmine's fanatical stance is not going to be weakened by further hostility, so William asks her gently, 'You say you came here to help us. How did you hope to achieve that, Jasmine? So far I see no sign of success.'

Jasmine tells it like a fireside story. 'It wasn't just Jessie who needed my help. A far larger picture was revealed to me – an invalid father, a mother in turmoil and two young women being threatened by some tormented soul. Some devil was using Belinda's name to plague and torture you all, and it was up to me to use all my strength to support and offer guidance and comfort.'

'Bollocks,' says Jessie. 'Get real.'

Jasmine, briefly unnerved, bursts out, 'I did encourage you to come to my church. I wanted you to help with the children, to be shown the spirit of true mercy. I tried to involve you in the nativity play, I thought that might be a way in. But all the time, and you can't deny this, I tried to lead the way by giving comfort and succour to you and your family.'

'And that lucky chance, that job at Kingsmead?'

360

'There's a desperate shortage of properly trained nurses, particularly psychiatric ones. Schools like Kingsmead advertise regularly, it's not just hospitals.'

Is it remotely possible that this bizarre story is true? There's certainly no trace of hesitation.

'What were you doing to Mum when we got here?' asks Daisy. 'What made her run out in a panic like that? Don't deny she was upset and don't deny that you caused it. You must know where she's gone. You must know more than you're saying.'

'You are still closing your eyes to the truth,' says Jasmine with a despairing sigh. 'Open your eyes and your hearts. If only you possessed my strength, given to me with the knowledge that Jesus sees and knows all things.'

Dad sits slumped in his chair, happily unaware of the battle around him. Not one of them is concerned that Rose might never return, not with Michael so needy, she has to be back to give him his dinner, and his bath.

'Your mother is the poor sinner who has been using Belinda's name,' says Jasmine boldly, larger than life in her tracksuit bottoms and her stained Aertex shirt. 'Somehow she found out about Jessie's affair – I suspect that Michael told her – and she was determined to punish her daughter.' Like a crusader she goes on bravely into the dumbfounded silence that greets her monstrous announcement. 'And tonight I told her I knew. She asked me outright, and I spoke the truth.'

Jessie laughs, a cold, tight sound, and glares, hard-eyed, at Jasmine. 'You're evil, Jasmine, that's all. Pure evil. The missionary from hell.'

'No, stop. Let's hear what she has to say. Let's hear just how twisted she really is. Tell us why, Jasmine, why would Rose act like that? Rose knew nothing about Belinda; she'd never heard of her till this morning.'

'What makes you say that?' asks Jasmine.

'Because Dad never told her.'

'You don't know that.'

Jessie looks quickly at William; she sends Daisy a frown of unease.

'You're wrong,' Jasmine continues with her preaching. 'Rose knew all about Belinda, and my guess is that Michael told her when they were on holiday in Venice. She was shocked. She was nauseated by the very idea of her daughter having such a godless relationship. Then he fell ill, a double blow to a woman already undergoing difficult changes in her life.'

'This is just sick.'

'Jessie, just listen.'

'No, I won't listen. I can't listen to this shit. Is Jasmine seriously suggesting that Mum, at her age, with all her problems, went creeping round to my room with an old jam rag wrapped round a turd and deposited it on my carpet? Can she honestly see Mum in her camel coat, loitering in the library with a pair of garden shears in her pocket, dashing into the staff lav and savaging Daisy's coat all in the name of punishment? Because of one lesbian affair? Is she trying to tell us that Mum would torch her own mother's house, the mother she loved so dearly and went out of her way to look after?'

'Is that what you expect us to believe?' William asks Jasmine. 'And if so, why didn't you tell us before?'

362

'Only the Lord sees people's souls. Only he understands what drives them. I don't know what caused Rose to behave in the way she did. She was in turmoil. I know that; I've spent more time with Rose lately than any of you.' Jasmine shrugs and lifts her eyes. 'As far as the fire is concerned, I'm certain Rose wouldn't have done that. I believe the fire was an accident.'

'But you have no proof of what you are saying?'

'Only that the last words Rose spoke to me were, "You know, don't you? You know what I've done?" And then she left. You saw her.' Jasmine's eyes shine brightly with fervour. 'And I doubt you'll see your mother again.'

William breaks the silence. 'Does anyone here agree with me that there is a very remote possibility that Rose did cause that fire?'

'No!' cries Daisy. 'How could you? I refuse to listen to this despicable—'

William carries on quietly, 'Think about it, be calm for a moment. There's a mass of buried conflicts here. Rose had an odd relationship with her mother. She was too forgiving, too kind and unnaturally patient, as if she was afraid of something. Now I don't know why this should be and I'm not saying I'm right, all I'm saying is that I think it's possible, and if Rose has left home, that would be the reason.'

'What the hell do you mean? You're taking Jasmine's ravings as fact,' shouts Jessie in exasperation, unable to take any more of this. 'She's lying, can't you see that? You're bloody forgetting her links with Belinda, and the odds are she came up here to avenge Belinda's death, purely and simply.'

'Why would I want to avenge her death?' Jasmine's astonishment must be genuine. 'Belinda was an unhappy person, she is safe and contented now with Jesus.'

This is getting right out of hand. William will put a stop to it. 'Surely it's up to the law to decide. They can break Jasmine's story or support it. We can't afford to leave her at large just in case.'

'Wait, William,' groans Daisy. 'You don't think that by some awful irony they might believe Jasmine's story and start thinking that Mum might have—'

'That's hardly likely,' snaps Jessie.

'But where is Mum? Why doesn't she phone? Why didn't she leave a note?'

'She did,' says Jasmine self-righteously. 'It's there, behind you on the table.'

William picks it up and passes it to Daisy. 'It's addressed to your dad,' he says.

It's very grey in this room, as if the first real dark of winter joins the group of people inside. A heavy blanket comes in from the west. 'I think we have to read it,' says Jessie, taking it reluctantly and slitting open the envelope.

My darling,
    I love you.
    I have done such things I never thought possible. I have harmed those I care about most in this world. I am in such pain now I can hardly write, and I know I can never be forgiven.
    I love you. I'm not asking for forgiveness. After a lifetime of love, all I have done is

betray you. There are no excuses save the old fears, which you know have followed me throughout my life and made me so hard to live with. Fear of loss, fear of myself, fear of the cruelties of the world. Perhaps that's what turned me so cruel. That old habit women have of hurting those they love the most.

I love you.

Thank you for finding something in me that you could love, too.

I had to go. I could never face your waking eyes. I could never face Daisy and Jessie when they find out what sort of person I am, and what monstrosities I am capable of.

Fondest love for ever, Rose.

The damning pause that follows lasts an uncomfortable time, until Jessie puts the letter down and folds her hands in her lap.

Jasmine still stands by the fireplace, that daft look of bliss on her face. What is she thinking? That they need her now? That they want her blessing? This little family so cruelly bereft.

'Get out of here,' says Jessie quietly.

'I don't think you quite—'

'Get out,' says Daisy, feeling sick.

'I think it best if you leave,' says William, standing up to see Jasmine out.

'But Michael; he needs me, I can help!'

'Just go – please, for God's sake,' says Jessie, in a broken voice that can hardly be heard above the homely crackling of logs.

THIRTY-ONE

Night approaches all too swiftly.

Michael's sensations are muddled; there are more aches in his arms and legs, unused for so many weeks, than he has felt before.

Dizziness nauseates him. Even the texture of sound is changing. The shadows over his eyes are lifting, and although sleep still claims him, much against his will, his moments of wakefulness are more real and less like a racing ride through a tunnel.

The nightly uncomfortable journey upstairs seems to him to take place later than usual, but his sense of time is still weak. Then there's the same old routine – up the stairs and into bed, the removal of his outer clothing, the demeaning cleaning, the changing of his incontinence pads – but this night the hands that wash, dry and pat his body with powder are gentle and caring.

He imagines he can hear soft voices, but that could be part of a dream, a wishing.

He knows that Rose will come later. Rose always comes, if not to inflict some form of torment then just to give him his medication, which he will, once again, attempt to refuse because defiance is his only salvation.

Soft fingers seem to stroke his forehead, and this time they don't cause the grating sounds he had become used to when touch alone could cause explosive echoes in his ears. Perhaps he is becoming immune. He imagines a kiss on his right cheek.

Pins and needles, a new sensation, and one which fills Michael with fearful dread. No matter how small, any unrecognized symptom can mean the infliction of some new torture, the intended result not yet fully known. The headache that has been part of him for as long as he can remember is gradually becoming more comparable to the kind of headache he used to have, before Rose's infernal treatment began, the kind of headache that responds to an aspirin. If Michael ever does recover from this backwater of hell he will never again complain of such a minor inconvenience.

Alone now to face the long night, Michael is awake long enough to experiment with his old successes.

He attempts to roll his head smoothly without that awkward, jerky manner he has accomplished with enormous will-power on a couple of previous occasions. This time he succeeds, but without the exhaustion and hours of sleep which invariably follow. He sees that the telephone has been moved from his bedside to the dressing table. But even if it was right beside him, would he be able to reach it, lift the receiver and dial?

Starting with his little finger he marvels at the strength of movement and, ever wary of the cramps which might follow, he concentrates on the rest of his hand. He lifts it from the top of the duvet, no dithering. He directs it straight to his eyes. It feels heavy and dead, a thing quite separate from him, and he remembers the same sensations after sleeping on an arm sometime in his bewildering past.

What is happening to him? His heartbeats resound and shake through him like a piledriver going into wet sand. He fights off sleep like a man clinging to the edge of a cliff.

Rose must come in a minute. The seconds pass and his fear escalates. She must be late tonight, he has never been allowed to reach this heady level of consciousness before. Any movements he can make while he's competent must be a bonus for his unhealthy, crippled body. No matter how pathetic they might seem to the able-bodied, to Michael these small successes feel like the greatest athletic feats.

After furious instructions to a brain still confused, he manages to bend his knees so that his feet are flat on the mattress. He brings both arms up over his head in triumph, and imagines himself on some podium, being garlanded with flowers. The crowds cheer, his anthem is played, but he has no wife in the audience to rush towards him and embrace him. No. Jesus no. He won't let his heart sink, not now. He can't afford to, not when he is reaching such dizzy pinnacles of physical achievement.

Michael rests, flattens himself and conducts some preliminary tests on his face. He thinks he is raising his eyebrows. Incredible. The brain's instruction immediately obeyed. He discovers that frowning pulls on his head and causes some unpleasant sensations, while a small smile appears to relax those wasted facial muscles.

He practises the opening and closing of his eyes, quite recovered now, thank God, from that unforgettable acid bath. His ear, nose and throat still pain him constantly and he fears there is something septic inside, some permanent damage, but up until this marvellous moment he had believed that such an impairment would never seriously concern him. What need does a vegetable deep in the soil have for perfect senses?

Still he fights off that yearning for sleep, so afraid that these might be his last conscious moments.

Where is Rose? Hysteria threatens.

Could he get out of bed unaided? Is he strong enough to meet such a challenge?

He moves his head so that he has a full-length view of his body, neatly encased, like a shrouded corpse in a coffin. Does he dare to dwell on the hope that he might be able to fend her off when she comes with his medicine tonight? He knows how weak he is compared to the strength of an angry, determined and maybe mad woman, but his own desperation is terribly real. If it came to the test, could he muster all the power he has left in one last struggle for life?

Gingerly Michael attempts to move to the edge of the mattress and sit unaided. If he could get himself upright he might be able to hobble to the telephone or, if there is a nurse somewhere in the house, maybe open the door and call? But can he speak? His last puny efforts were disastrous.

Michael edges himself across the bed crablike, and clears his throat as best he can, ignoring the flaming pain this causes. What words is he going to need? He knows the number – 999 – easy enough to press with one finger, then he must give his name and address. He has heard that's sufficient for the emergency services, and even if the phone goes dead they are bound to follow up the call.

A cry from the grave. A voice from the dead. But at least a recognizable sound, even if from a soul in torture. Sleep demands his presence more forcefully as every second passes. These urgent demands being made on his unpractised body and mind are taking their toll in the recognized manner.

Rest. Rest. There's a clamour for rest.

'M–M–M' How he hates to have his name shortened to Mike. Hah, that's funny. If he could only form that abbreviated word how happy he would be to be addressed that way for ever. 'Mike. Mike R–R–Red.'

But will they hold on that long in a busy emergency department?

Maybe he should concentrate on his address. For God's sake, a name doesn't matter. Just as long as they know where to come. Just as long as they don't hang about and recognize this as a real emergency.

Damn damn damn! His right leg is just about over the edge, but his left refuses to follow; it jerks from some invisible string. Calm down, Michael. Calm down, give it time. But I don't have time, he sobs self-pityingly.

When the door opens Michael freezes. Too late. His last chance. Too late.

He braces himself for the attack he knows is bound to follow. When Rose sees the progress he has made she will take immediate action, and that

370

action could take many forms, he knows that only too well, but first the drugs, the gagging and choking as the bitterest gall blocks his swollen throat.

Nothing happens. She is taking time to witness his helplessness. How pathetic his efforts seem now. He is back in the centre of the bed in a fraction of the time it took him to ease himself over to the edge. Just a few pulls and pushes are all that's required to wipe out half an hour's solid, painful labour.

Michael's relief is enormous, doublefold, when he recognizes that the sudden presence is not his wife, and that he can make sense of the sounds.

He can hear. OK, his reception isn't in stereo, the sounds only reach his good ear, but this vivid experience is exactly the same as coming up from submersion in water.

'Daddy, it's me.'

Daisy? Three magic words. He will never forget them.

Oh, thank God. Thank God.

Gone are all scheming plans, apart from the one about lifting himself off his bed and throwing his arms round his beautiful daughter. How can he communicate fast enough before Rose follows Daisy into the room and dismisses her – medicine time!

But Daisy appears unaware of the turmoil her father is going through. This is only to be expected, Michael supposes, with huge disappointment. This poor child must have visited his room so many times without a response, why would she suddenly look for one now? No, Daisy has a job to do, part of the routine, he guesses, and one of the many tasks he

371

would normally be unaware of because of sleep, damned sleep.

Another, more anxious thought strikes him as he lies back in the centre of the bed, where he has been so expertly positioned. His mind is fuming over ways and means of communicating with his daughter, he mustn't underestimate the shock he could cause her by making too many co-ordinated movements. Somehow he will do this, but he must take it slowly, for Daisy's sake.

Why is she fiddling around with his mouth? For what reason is she pushing on his teeth?

Now he can actually feel Daisy's long sleek hair sweeping his face as she stares into his mouth. She feels his tongue. She pulls it. It hurts. Once again the nail scissors come out of the drawer; he can hear the chink as they drop on the wood. Perhaps there's a sore place here which, with his greater pain, has gone unnoticed and needs treating before Rose gets home?

But this is a matter of life and death, and Michael is about to make his first, desperate bid for attention when Daisy says quietly, 'My, what big teeth you have. All the better for eating you.'

With a sound like a laugh, but nothing human, she slips her slim, dainty fingers through the scissors' silver handles. While Michael digests the meaning of this in a mind battered numb by shock, Daisy lowers the sharp, curved scissors towards the root of his tongue.

'And now, because of you, even William has gone.'

She directs the curve of the sharp little blade so they half circle the large pink muscle that is the focus of her anger. She raises it between the finger and thumb of her spare hand and brings the scissor blades together with all the force at her command.

As the first snip of the scissors slices his tongue, Michael rips up from his bed and, with one swipe of his hand, knocks his daughter sideways.

He reels back, gagging from the searing pain, and clamps his hand to his mouth, only to see with horror that Daisy, crouched beside the bed like a lynx, is preparing for a second attack. She flings her body over him, with the scissors raised in her right hand, blades together and flashing in the dark like a tiny dagger. She brings down her weapon again and again, aiming at his mouth. Her pretty face between her sheets of black hair is unrecognizable, ferretlike in its sharpness; her small white teeth are bared for attack, her flaming black eyes dilated with hatred.

'STOP!' Michael's first word, and it's perfect.

Where has this new power come from? He is upright now, not standing yet, but the strength in his arms is sufficient to hold this hell-cat at bay. But her uncontrolled thrashing at him continues, 'I lost them all. I lost them, you bastard. I lost them, Daddy, because of you . . .'

'Daisy?'

'You never wanted me to be happy. You wanted me home. You wanted me to be yours.'

Where the hell is this shit coming from?

Daisy shrieks convulsively as she smashes, tears and rends asunder in her desperate struggle for freedom. Now she is aiming straight at his throat. 'You and Mum, you were in it together. She told you and you bloody did it.'

Hell. He's losing his grip. Her wrists are too soaked in slippery sweat to give him a hold.

Blood from his wounded mouth floods the mattress. He feels as if his knees are swimming in it. Pain maddens him. He tries to force open her hand so that she drops the scissors. Again and again he bends it to breaking point, but Daisy's strength is formidable.

Michael is hardly aware of the moment William rushes into the room, followed by a screaming Jessie. All he knows is that some furious weight suddenly falls off him and he can slump, groaning, gripping his torn and wounded flesh.

Hospitals. How blissful. Never again will Michael describe them as the last trolley ride to the crem.

At least they've stuck him in a medical ward, although everyone keeps telling him that his mental scars are the ones that will take longest to heal.

Jessie, still trying to be brave after losing half her family in one tragic stroke, reassures him that Daisy is well and being looked after. 'She didn't know Belinda was dead, that didn't matter to Daisy, she just saw it as a way of punishing us for working together against her.'

Michael is still as baffled as he was when it was first put to him. His hands push into his untidy hair. 'But Rose and I never held her back.'

'Mum was too overprotective and you always took Mum's side against her. And the experts think that, to start with, all she wanted was to spoil your Venice holiday. She made that first phone call to Mum, and you did the rest by forgetting about that notelet in your pocket.'

374

'But Christ, Daisy didn't stop there. And I believed it was your mother – those nightly visits through the French windows. I could have lost my sight, my hearing, and eventually it would have been my life.'

'Dad, Daisy worshipped you, and until I came along she was the apple of your eye. I was trouble. I wouldn't sleep, I had tantrums and all your attention turned to me; she even remembers a time when you were reading her a story and I came in and pushed her off your knee.'

'It happened all the time. You were vile. *Little Red Riding Hood*, her favourite . . .'

'After that she refused to believe that the woodcutter came and saved the child. She cut the last page out – I remember that; she scribbled all over it.'

'I let her down.'

'She thought you were perfect.' Jessie lowers her eyes. 'So did Mum.'

Michael is near to tears. 'But that baby stuff, so long ago.'

'She never stopped trying to find you again in some other human being. But no man came anywhere near you. In her eyes you had doomed her to failure.'

Even with the best treatment available Daisy is unlikely to be seen in the library in time to read the next Christmas bestseller.

Michael's anaesthetized tongue, with its deep cut down the centre line, is less painful than his throat, which they say will soon mend with antibiotics. He needs surgery on his ear, but as that's not urgent there's no point in traumatizing his body further.

Relentless and heartless physiotherapy is forced upon him twice every day, but the upside is that his guilt-ridden doctor, Neil Jarvis, who has a fully stocked cellar, is in the habit of bringing gifts in atonement.

William brings in the answerphone tape he has found in Daisy's earring box. They play it beside Michael's bed. Together they listen to the false Welsh accent, the harsh tones mixed with the barely disguised hostility. 'She used her fax line,' William says. 'And every time I went out, which became more frequent as time went on, she switched tapes. She used an old, damaged tape to disguise her answerphone voice.'

'I never recognized the number,' says Michael.

'I don't think anyone did,' says William. 'Daisy hardly used it and nor did I. We mostly used e-mail.'

Daisy believed that drama and tragedy were the keys to William's heart, after all, her own baby sister had ensnared her father that way.

But Daisy knew nothing of the part Rose had played in the drugging of Michael, and neither, of course, did Jasmine. Nobody knew about that till now.

'But to scare you in the way she did. Why, Jessie?'

'Attention seeking. Just another way to trap William. Like the fire. Poor Daisy. Another trage-dy. But she couldn't have got it more wrong. William just couldn't handle the pressure.'

'Poor Dinah.'

'Poor Dinah. Daisy loathed her. If William failed to respond to Daisy after the shock of the fire, if he didn't give up everything and devote

376

himself to Daisy's distress, when the hell would he?' Jessie picks at a seedless grape. It's good. It's sweet. She plucks a few and, blinking back tears, looks sadly at her mutilated father. 'I ought to have worked it out when Daisy told us that Jasmine had gone up to Granny's attic to search for church jumble. She tried to make out that was the moment Jasmine had found the pink rabbit, but Granny would never have allowed some stranger to poke about up there, her grand-daughters, yes, but not Jasmine. I just didn't think. I was hardly listening.'

There's so much Michael fails to grasp. It might become clearer, he supposes, when he gets to meet and talk to Daisy, as Jessie has already done.

There is a suggestion by some police shrink that Daisy's sickness might be inherited, passed down through the genes. After all, Dinah's mother had spent the last ten years of her life incarcerated in an asylum. Michael has his doubts. He said to Jessic, 'That's unlikely as Rose wasn't affected. Some people might call Rose's behaviour insane, but there was a desperate logic behind it, and apart from her possessive streak she's never behaved cruelly before. Rose would never deliberately hurt anyone. No, Rose wasn't mad like her grandmother, neither was Dinah, so why would Daisy be blighted? This is nothing to do with genes.'

Daisy has been charged with the murder of her grandmother, but is being held in remand in the hospital wing. There's no doubt her behaviour will be put down to temporary insanity. 'But why bother with that grotesque rabbit? Her grandmother was dead, what more sympathy did she crave?' questions Michael.

'Maybe it was the intrigue,' says Jessie, guessing. 'The whole Belinda thing, I reckon. To Daisy's distorted mind it made the whole drama more engrossing. And it worked, in a way. It certainly got William's attention, but not in the way Daisy wanted. All William was interested in was getting to the bottom of it. I thought he was just after a story. I was so horrible to him.'

'You always are,' says Michael, smacking her hand off the fruit bowl.

'I don't understand, Dad,' starts Jessie, 'how you can still feel anything for Daisy after the things she did to you.'

'You don't stop loving your kids,' says Michael. 'Whatever they do, you still care.'

'And Mum?'

Michael looks away. He isn't able to answer.

Eyes turn in her direction as she walks through the ward towards Michael's bed. Her black velvet coat swings behind her. Her high-heeled boots are made of soft leather and click as they strike the polished lino. A haze of designer perfume touches the air behind her with sensual fingers.

Love is in her large green eyes. She's been waiting for him for so long – so many secret assignations, so many lonely hours.

'They told me to bring you this,' says Sheila Gordon, opening her bag and producing Rose's letter. 'They say you can probably cope with it now.'

But Michael crumples it in his hand as she leans over and kisses him softly.

'I said I would wait for you, no matter how long it took, and I did,' says Sheila. 'I'm here, as promised, if you still want me.'

'There's only ever been one answer to that,' Michael replies. 'And I don't need to tell you what that is.'

Sheila smiles at him lovingly. She brings two long-stemmed glasses out of an ice-blue cool bag. Expertly she pours the champagne. She hands one glass to Michael and touches it with her own. 'Sooner than later, that's all. Cheers.'

'Sooner than later,' he says. 'To us.'

And wet wine on smiling lips tells the rest of the story . . .

. . . Well almost.

EPILOGUE

The following year. Random extracts from Rose's diary:

June 14th.

Mother's insurance came through today via M's solicitors, thank God. At last I'm able to search for an apartment of my own and get free from Barbara's interference. One bedroom, I think, with a garage. One of the newer additions to the complex. Less pretentious, more homely?

Went for coffee this a.m. with Sylvia and Adelle, followed by lunch with Glo at club. Aerobics p.m., as usual, and karaoke at Reid's bar. Sang 'My way'. Felt sick.

Rather less formal letter from Jessie. Still happy with William. Quite a U-turn there. Daisy coming on well, but hasn't asked about me yet.

No word from M.

July 1st.

Deposit down on bijou apartment. Calling it Baggins' abode. Vernon came to check it out for me after nine holes this a.m. with him, Julia and

Brett. Bought a new four iron at pro shop. Must put in more practice.

Lunch at golf club.

Quiz night at Reid's bar. For a joke they stuck my name on the bar stool in the corner.

Letter from Jessie. Great relief all round. Daisy cleared of murder charge. M is seeing somebody else.

No word from M.

August 30th.

Crowds in pool appalling. Such terrible types of people. Mostly time share. Drove to mountains with Vernon. Nice lunch at Villa D'Or, but can't stand Vernon's driving and he drinks far too much.

No sleep. Too hot. Awful nightmares. Terribly depressed.

No word from M.

September 10th.

Jessie and William planning globe-trotting next year. No mention of calling here.

Hair at Wendy's this a.m. Gone very blond.

Tennis Club Summer Ball at Hotel Miranda. Vernon particularly irritating tonight.

No word from M.

October 19th.

Vernon's wedding to Patsy Taggert. Boozy reception at Reid's bar. Midnight swim. Didn't get to bed till 4 a.m. Tried to write *that* letter. Still unable to sleep. Prozac not helping much.

No word from M.

November 24th.

Won ladies' handicap competition. Silver cup and set of glasses. Danced with George, the pro, all night.

Stayed night here.

Awful.

Don't know when brave enough to face golf club again.

No word from M.

December 24th.

Nice card, glass vase and letter from Jessie and William.

Extraordinary – Jasmine given permanent post at Kingsmead School.

Hair at Wendy's this a.m. Streaks, silver and platinum.

Shopping brunch with Sylvia. She says smart, clingy, black dress with daring neckline suits. Will wear it at Reid's tomorrow. No doubt Vernon will oggle.

Card from M. Says he and Sheila are coming over in January to 'discuss certain matters'.

No more entries from now on – too dangerous. *The place*, beside the loose balcony rail where the fall goes sheer to the cliffs below. *The time*, when I bring out the drinks as the sun sinks over the yardarm. No problem envisaged. Mother would know. Mother always suspected, and Mother, as usual, was right. It only took the suggestion of taking that eroded path. Jamie was easy peasy. Daddy, being heavy, was naturally far more difficult.

THE END

THE WITCH'S CRADLE
by Gillian White

Barry and Cheryl had become famous. Desperately poor, living in a tower block with their two small children, they were possibly the most famous family in the country after the Royals. Their fame had come, not from wealth or success or glamour, but from the attentions of a television company, who had made them the subject of a fly-on-the-wall documentary.

Cheryl was prepared to do anything – *anything* – to be a media star. She thought that the public loved her – and, indeed, for a while it seemed that the nation had taken this simple, gutsy, poverty-stricken couple to its heart. But then it all starts to go horribly wrong. Cheryl has a third baby – and is transformed in the public's eyes from a plucky but unlucky trier to a profligate sponger on the state. She desperately wants to be loved – and then, mysteriously, all her three children go missing. Have they been abducted? Murdered? Or is there some even more sinister explanation for their disappearance?

'This fast-paced tale explores the ruthlessness of the media when transforming real life into drama'
Good Housekeeping

0 552 14756 6

A SELECTED LIST OF CRIME NOVELS
AVAILABLE FROM CORGI BOOKS

14221 2	WYCLIFFE AND THE DUNES MYSTERY		
		W. J. Burley	£4.99
14117 8	WYCLIFFE AND HOW TO KILL A CAT		
		W. J. Burley	£4.99
14115 1	WYCLIFFE AND THE GUILT EDGED ALIBI		
		W. J. Burley	£4.99
14661 7	WYCLIFFE AND THE REDHEAD	W. J. Burley	£4.99
14043 0	SHADOW PLAY	Frances Fyfield	£5.99
14174 7	PERFECTLY PURE AND GOOD	Frances Fyfield	£5.99
14295 6	A CLEAR CONSCIENCE	Frances Fyfield	£5.99
14512 2	WITHOUT CONSENT	Frances Fyfield	£5.99
14525 4	BLIND DATE	Frances Fyfield	£5.99
14526 2	STARING AT THE LIGHT	Frances Fyfield	£5.99
14223 9	BORROWED TIME	Robert Goddard	£6.99
13840 1	CLOSED CIRCLE	Robert Goddard	£6.99
13839 8	HAND IN GLOVE	Robert Goddard	£5.99
13281 0	IN PALE BATTALIONS	Robert Goddard	£6.99
13282 9	PAINTING THE DARKNESS	Robert Goddard	£5.99
13144 X	PAST CARING	Robert Goddard	£5.99
13562 3	TAKE NO FAREWELL	Robert Goddard	£5.99
14224 7	OUT OF THE SUN	Robert Goddard	£5.99
14225 5	BEYOND RECALL	Robert Goddard	£5.99
14597 1	CAUGHT IN THE LIGHT	Robert Goddard	£5.99
14603 2	SET IN STONE	Robert Goddard	£5.99
14602 1	SEA CHANGE	Robert Goddard	£5.99
14623 4	THE RETURN	Andrea Hart	£5.99
14584 X	THE COLD CALLING	Will Kingdom	£5.99
14561 0	THE SLEEPER	Gillian White	£5.99
14563 7	UNHALLOWED GROUND	Gillian White	£5.99
14564 5	VEIL OF DARKNESS	Gillian White	£5.99
14765 6	THE WITCH'S CRADLE	Gillian White	£5.99
14555 6	A TOUCH OF FROST	R. D. Wingfield	£5.99
13981 5	FROST AT CHRISTMAS	R. D. Wingfield	£5.99
14558 0	NIGHT FROST	R. D. Wingfield	£5.99
14409 6	HARD FROST	R. D. Wingfield	£5.99
14778 8	WINTER FROST	R. D. Wingfield	£5.99
14047 3	UNHOLY ALLIANCE	David Yallop	£5.99